THE
MISSING
SIXTH

Also by Mark Graham:

THE HARBINGER (1988)

THE

A Novel

MISSING

by

SIXTH

Mark Graham

Harcourt Brace Jovanovich, Publishers

New York   San Diego   London

Requests for permission to make copies of any part of
the work should be mailed to:
Permissions, Harcourt Brace Jovanovich, Publishers,
8th Floor, Orlando, Florida 32887.

Library of Congress Cataloging-in-Publication Data
Graham, Mark, 1950–
    The missing sixth/Mark Graham.
        p.   cm.
    ISBN 0-15-160576-9
    I. Title.
PS3557.R2158M57   1992
813'.54—dc20   91-4023

Printed in the United States of America

First edition

A B C D E

For Erin and Colin

My thanks to the following for information and inspiration freely given: Susan Manchester, Bill Taylor, Judy Shafran, Arnold Goodman, Alane Mason, John Graham, Hank Wierman, Fred Spinney, Tom Cella, Anne Peterson, and those friends and family who have stayed by me all along.

"It has come to the attention of trusted friends that the receptacle within which the Missing Sixth is contained has been reported found. . . . All pains must be taken in seeing to its possession or destruction. . . . Though the receptacle's presence on foreign soil will make its procurement through any but proper channels hazardous, its procurement is essential."

Circular #2452, Executive Council, *Afrikaner Broederbond.*

JUNE, 1988

THE THIEVES were four in number. They were experienced and patient men. But for the piercing of clay-hardened soil by shovel and pickax, an asthmatic cough, and an urgent whisper, they worked in near silence.

In contrast, other night sounds played havoc with the imagination. The passage of a semitrailer. The hoot of a great horned owl. The wind strumming the branches of ancient oaks. Each sound played upon the one before.

Ironically, the silence more than the sounds reminded Ari Paros of the last time he had violated an employer's "directive." A violation he had paid for with a bullet in the back.

Yet he was an hour away from a similar indiscretion. Why? They had been hired to steal a single painting and were being paid an exorbitant amount to do so. Still, walking away with but a single painting from a gallery filled with virtual masterpieces had never made sense to Paros. Then they had devised a plan; or, more accurately, one had been devised for them.

Paros disliked the idea of tunneling. Unfortunately, the entire estate, eight thousand acres, was surrounded by a stone wall ten feet and nearly six inches high. A million granite slabs, nine years, sixteen hundred men: Paros had read the history. But the problem was not the height. The problem was an intricate web of magnetic detectors and vibration contacts that coursed over and around the entire wall. Paros had never encountered anything like it.

The dry creek bed in which he now crouched exited the estate beneath a two-lane highway. Their tunnel ran beneath the concrete and steel wall that sealed the wash at the property line. It had taken two nights and nearly eleven hours of digging, but now Castille had broken through at last; Paros could see him at the mouth of the tunnel. A man of titanic stature, his beard a flaming red, his eyes as bright as a cat's, Castille was more than a friend; he was the one man in the world Ari Paros could truly say he trusted with his life.

Not so the others. Renucci, on the one hand, was a local recruit from back home. He was a loner and a cheat, and was thus controllable. Hulster, on the other hand, Paros didn't know from Adam, and that scared him. Hulster was a last-minute replacement. Their original fourth, another local, had taken ill two days before departure. Hulster was the *principal's* choice. Paros hadn't objected. His reasoning then was that you don't make waves with the guy who's handed you a once-in-a-lifetime job like this one. Now he regretted it.

Paros shimmied through the tunnel, crawled into the wash on the other side of the wall, and scrambled up the bank. The others followed.

They used binoculars in search of mounted horsemen and spotted two Land Rovers instead. They saw ostriches, as slender and elegant as dancers, shuffling among dozing cattle. A half mile to the east, the outline of a guard tower lurked on the horizon. To the west, a beam of white light played over the ground, projected from a helicopter as yet too far away to be worrisome. Overhead,

2

a moon the shape and hue of an ivory tusk emerged from behind a wall of menacing storm clouds.

They hoisted backpacks. Castille shouldered two coils of nylon rope. As they followed the creek bed into the heart of the estate, they felt the first drops of the rain Paros had been dreading.

They paused every hundred yards, burrowed into the overgrowth of willows and cattails, and listened. Twice they heard the rumbling of a Land Rover. Once the random sweep of its floodlight filled the wash at their feet.

After a half mile Paros spotted on the north bank what remained of a yellowwood tree struck down by lightning three years before. The blackened stump was their first marker.

Alone, he scrambled on hands and knees up the side of the bank and glimpsed the Land Rover's fading red taillights as they disappeared into a grove of trees. The helicopter was by now far to the west; its white light scored the horizon. Paros could see horsemen, two of them, following the course of a man-made aqueduct a half mile away.

Once they were out of sight, Paros focused on the mansion and the grounds surrounding it. An open pasture ran from the wash fifty yards over to a split rail fence. Beyond the fence, a stand of oaks shadowed the estate's famous protea garden. A pond separated the garden from the horse stables to the west. A mile to the east a macadam road led from the estate entrance to a circular drive at the front of the house. The house, Paros knew, was built around a central courtyard. The gallery was on the second floor facing the courtyard.

He turned to the others and nodded.

In single file they shimmied up the bank and a moment later were on their feet and running flat out through the pasture, to the fence, and over. They fell in among the trees and froze.

Beyond the trees, on the far side of the garden, stood the timbered gazebo that was their second marker. Again they ran, in pairs this time.

One last burst took them from the gazebo, along a footpath of slate and flagstone, across a manicured esplanade to the house. They crowded together in a small, narrow postern that had once served as an entryway for a previous owner's help, but hadn't been used in two decades.

Marker number three was a turret twenty yards to the south.

Paros slung the first block and tackle over his shoulder. He slid along the wall to the turret and the sprawling vine that grew upon its face. The vine was supported by a heavy trellis. The trellis provided a ladder past three floors of darkened rooms to a wide, half-timbered gable where Paros attached the first pulley. From there, he hoisted himself onto a stone-tiled roof. Castille and Renucci followed. Hulster huddled at the rear of the postern and waited. He took the paper off a stick of chewing gum and tossed it purposefully on the ground.

Alone, Paros scrambled along a narrow roof ramp up the valley to the peak. He secured a length of rope to the base of an octagonal chimney, curled the other end around his waist, and eased himself down the far side of the roof. A fountain lit by blue and red spotlights dominated the courtyard below. Paros anchored the second block and tackle to a beam member the size of a railroad tie. He slid down the rope to a third-story balcony and flattened himself against the wall. Castille, with Renucci stationed now on the roof, was less than a minute behind.

The gallery was a story below.

As planned, the French doors off this balcony were unlocked. Beyond was a bedroom, stuffy and stale from disuse.

Castille tossed aside a Persian rug and together they

4

moved an empty dresser. Paros knelt down on a floor made of hardwood strips and, with the aid of a small flashlight, made his calculations. The gallery's alarm system was based on the uninterrupted flow of microwaves. The system's transmitter and receiver, according to the diagram they had been supplied with, were attached to the wall directly below. From his backpack, Castille drew a small nail pull, a tube of lubricant, and a razor-sharp carving knife.

He used the knife to expose the heads of nails holding down three of the floorboards. Paros used the nail pull and lubricant to coax out each nail, eighteen in all.

Beneath the floorboards was a thin layer of insulation. Beneath the insulation was a sheet of foil necessary to deflect the microwaves back into the gallery. The insulation Castille tossed aside. The foil he carefully stapled to the ceiling below. To the foil's surface he secured two rubberized suction cups. Around the cups Paros cut a circle fifteen inches in diameter.

Their diagram indicated that the bullhorn-shaped transmitter was attached to the wall twenty-six inches below the ceiling. An intrusion of any kind, they knew, would upset the standing waves of the system and thus trigger the alarm.

There were, however, two possible exits built into such a system: a dead spot directly above the transmitting antenna—doubtful in this instance—or a time-delay relay that allowed the intrusion signal to persist for three to four seconds before activating the alarm.

Paros readied the wire cutters. At his signal, Castille raised the suction cups, the foil, and the circular section of ceiling. Below, the coaxial cable connecting the transmitter to the receiver was clearly in view. The cutters broke through the plane of the ceiling. Three seconds in which to have the cable severed; Paros counted them off in his head.

It took less than two.

Outside once more, they scrambled down the rope to the second-floor balcony and another set of French doors. These too swung open at the touch of a hand.

The gallery beyond was cut into fourths by crossing photoelectric light beams, knee high and extremely sensitive. Yet only direct contact with either beam would initiate the alarm. Therefore, the likelihood of floor detectors presented a more immediate concern. For this, Castille took a mat knife from his pack and exposed the blade. Working from the doors inward, he began slicing through the carpet. A pattern became clear: the detectors were spaced diagonally along the floor at half-yard intervals. Disconnecting them all would not only be time-consuming but risky; instead, Castille simply relaid the carpet, section by section, and marked the location of each detector with a blue felt pen.

Paros followed. From the sitting area at the near end of the gallery he collected a leather-covered footstool and an inlaid cherrywood end table. These he placed on either side of the first light beam, forming a bridge of sorts, which Castille used to cross into the second quadrant. Castille continued: dissect, detect, mark. While Paros waited, he took in the gallery piece by piece. A Chagall, a Picasso, a Matisse. He knew the names, but matching them to the works was beyond him. In Paros's eyes, art was a well-tuned Ferrari, a perfectly balanced Webley-Scott, a shapely woman.

He took the colored photograph from his shirt pocket and studied it. Four red circles and a black star marked their targets. When the paintings were firmly fixed in his mind, Paros struck a match to the photo, watched it erode into a crust of ash, and used his heel to crush the remains into the carpet. Then he followed Castille's grid over the bridge into the second quadrant.

He stopped in front of the first work, a pastel rendition of a ballerina. Patiently he explored the painting, the

6

frame, and the mounting, front to back, top to bottom. The tilt switch was located beneath the frame's lower right corner. Paros used a magnetic file to deactivate the connection.

He lifted the painting off the wall. Castille was waiting beside him with a black nylon bag. An adhesive strip sealed the painting and its frame neatly inside.

Paros moved on. From the depths of a dark and haunting oil, the forlorn face of a young peasant woman sought his gaze. Paros ignored her. He concentrated instead on the tilt, this time finding it in the upper right-hand corner. When this painting too was free and sealed inside its own bag, Castille took both parcels back out to the balcony. There he slipped the eyelet at the top of each bag onto the S hook dangling from the end of the rope and gave a slight tug. Renucci was on the roof waiting. He hauled the paintings up, used the walk rope to work his way to the other side, and carefully lowered the parcels into Hulster's eager hands. When he returned, two more bags were awaiting him.

The fifth painting Paros carried out himself. Castille followed him up to the roof. They climbed the roof ramp to the crest and back down the other side, then carefully eased down the trellis to the ground and slipped along the wall back to the postern.

Ten seconds later, they heard the horseman. The staccato clap of hooves on stone, a snort—then dead silence. A shaft of high-intensity light spilled from the end of a flash; it panned the flower beds and walkways of the garden, reflected on the lattice frame of the gazebo, and followed the footpath across the esplanade. Just then, the storm broke. Overhead, lightning cut a jagged gash across the face of the clouds. The horse shied at the bellow of thunder that followed, and deep within the postern Paros saw the rider extinguish his light. At last, he loosened the reins and the horse moved on.

Two minutes later the four thieves parted. Castille

and Hulster took possession of the fifth painting, that destined for their employer, and set out for the creek bed. Paros and Renucci gathered up the other four, a parcel in each hand, and followed a cobblestone path west beyond the esplanade, around the silvery pond and a fenced training ring to the stables. They were soaked to the bone by the time they reached the tack room.

Beyond the tack room lay the grooming area, which adjoined the stalls themselves. Wood floors creaked, and a pure white Arabian stirred.

The last six stalls were vacant, separated by head-high panels of thick plywood mounted on either side of four-by-four posts. Exactly as they had been described to Paros. The effect of the construction was to create narrow air spaces between the panels. They used two of these spaces to hide their parcels.

Empty-handed, they retraced their steps and rejoined Castille and Hulster in the trees beyond the garden. The rain was slowing; it had quit altogether by the time they were through the tunnel. They made their way quickly up the bank to the road and then across into the sparse woods adjacent to the estate. Their van was parked a quarter of a mile from the road under a tall pine.

Hulster climbed behind the wheel and started the engine. Paros opened the rear doors of the van and carefully laid the painting inside. Renucci and Castille lit cigarettes and breathed a joint sigh of relief. It was premature.

Over the hum of the engine they never heard the footsteps. Nor the raising of the pistol, nor the cocking of its hammer.

It took two bullets to take down Castille. A single head shot felled Renucci. Paros bounded from the van with a sawed-off shotgun in his hands and was dead before his feet hit the ground. Hulster stepped slowly down from the front seat.

"It's me, Hulster," he said with an air of confidence. "Everything's fine."

"The painting," was all the killer said in reply, still clutching the pistol.

"In the van," Hulster said, staring now at the barrel of the gun and trying to usher it away with a toss of his head. "In the back. We took care of the other four just like you said. Everything's fine."

"Excellent. You've done well. I wish it made more sense, but it doesn't, does it?"

"What doesn't?" Hulster took a step to his right. The barrel of the gun stalked him. He backpedaled. Hysteria crept into his words. "What doesn't make sense?"

"The sacrifices." The killer's voice had an indifferent ring to it. "The sacrifices we make."

2

TO A COUNTRY that drank itself to sleep every night, Michael Meade had come to resurrect himself.

Meade had drunk himself out of an editorial position with the *Los Angeles Times*. He had missed one too many deadlines with the *Washington Post* and walked away from the *Tribune* job in San Francisco because eight hours behind a desk had served only as an excuse for more drinking. The Cape Town assignment with the Bay City's other paper, the *Chronicle*, was, in effect, his last chance. By then, the many awards that had over the years been bestowed on him in honor of his investigative prowess—a National Journalism Award and a Pulitzer among them—were no longer opening the doors they once had. Still, Meade realized he could have done worse, much worse.

In fact, it was a homecoming, of sorts. Meade had been born in Pretoria forty-two years earlier, though his first memory was of being tossed around in the surf at Old Orchard Beach in Maine by his paternal grandfather.

Thus, there was history here. Personal history. A sister lost in childbirth. A father buried beneath a simple headstone in a military cemetery near Johannesburg, six months before his only son was born.

So Meade—lean, pale, and dour-eyed like the father he had never known—had returned, and his own son, Sean, had accompanied him. Meade was still of two minds about that arrangement. The father in him was thrilled; the pragmatist argued that it was time his son got out on his own. The father saw the scars on his son's wrists; the pragmatist told him the wounds inside had healed.

It was a forty-minute drive from the city to the estate called De Greyling, and no one had called to cancel his interview with Sir Cas Greyling. Meade's recent exposés on the local prison system had become a rallying point for several activist groups, and the retired Minister was evidently determined to see that the conservative viewpoint received equal time. Meade wondered now if the collection of police cars and vans patrolling the perimeter of the estate weren't the makings of something better.

Neither, as it happened, had anyone told the guards at the entrance whether the interview had been canceled. They placed a call to the house, and Meade found the response surprising. He was prepared for an apology, yes, but not, as the guard put it, Sir Greyling's insistence that he accept the apology in person.

The road to the house, lined with slender oaks, led to a circular drive and a marble wishing well. The house filled Meade's windshield, an enormous jumble of half-timbered gables, stone-tiled roof, jutting octagonal chimneys, and crenellated turrets. The brick was a subtle, mottled raspberry—not a trick of sunlight, but a color contained in the brick itself.

The effect absorbed Meade even as he climbed out of the battered Land Rover he had bought off a used-car lot the day he'd arrived in Cape Town. Car and owner, he had decided then, were of a similar mold: ragged around the edges but not quite ready for the junk heap.

On his way to the house, he stopped at the wishing

well at the head of the walk, fished in the pockets of a charcoal-gray sport coat, came up with an American penny, and tossed it in. The wish, he told himself confidently, was right on the tip of his tongue.

He was met at the door by a butler in tails, who escorted him directly to the gallery. The policeman guarding the door had a ruddy face and a fleshy nose.

"This the one?" the policeman said to the butler. He gestured indifferently with a cigarette, but his voice rang with animosity. "Our forgotten American?"

"Yes, sir."

"The victim of some unfortunate miscommunication, that right?" He said this to Meade and anchored the cigarette in the corner of his mouth. "Well, does our victim have some papers he'd like to share, or would that be too much to ask?"

Meade produced a press card and passport, and the policeman bent over them for a full minute.

Meade used the time to his advantage, standing in the doorway of the gallery and filling his mental notebook with details. He noticed the blank spaces between paintings that looked familiar even to him.

The center of attention in the room, Meade observed, was not, however, the empty spaces on the wall; it was an elderly man in wrinkled slacks and a mohair sweater. His face was long and equine with wild, unruly eyebrows. Long silver hair was parted high on his head and cascaded over the tops of his ears. He was surrounded by a striking young woman in blue jeans, a thirtyish-looking man in a bathrobe with pajamas underneath, a maid, and two detectives taking notes.

The policeman eased off his stool now and pushed his hat off his forehead. He passed back Meade's passport and press credentials. Though he hadn't smoked in three months and couldn't explain the sudden urge, Meade borrowed a cigarette.

"Who discovered it?" he asked. "Greyling?"

In reply, the policeman offered a match and a lengthy stare which informed Meade that he was acting the impertinent American.

"My instructions said this. They said to allow the reporter access to the gallery. Fine," the policeman said. "My instructions didn't say a thing about questions. I suggest you save those for your host."

"You're very kind," Meade replied. He stepped inside now. A couch and love seat covered in Haitian cotton, Regency armchairs, and a coffee table of pale walnut stood between the entrance and the rear of the gallery. There was also an open bar. A wineglass stood half empty next to an ashtray and a half-smoked cigarette. Both, Meade noticed, were stained with lipstick.

The end table and footstool still straddled a now inactive photoelectric beam. A bespectacled youth in a white smock brushed fingerprint powder onto the surface of the table. Meade walked over. "Good morning. Forensic?"

"Yes, sir." The young man looked up; his tone had a respectful quality to it. "I'm Hawthorne. Peter Hawthorne."

"Michael Meade. How does it look?"

Hawthorne returned to his work. "All and all, I'd say not too good. What with five original masterpieces gone without a trace and four men—" The face came up again, the expression one of embarrassment. "Look at me. I'm talking to a bloody reporter, aren't I? Don't tell me. Don't tell me—from the States."

"San Francisco."

Hawthorne took a deep breath. "You sound like a cop," he said. "Look like one, too."

Meade looked down at his coat and tie. "That's no compliment."

Hawthorne grunted. He took his brush and powder and left Meade alone with the empty spaces on the wall.

13

The brass nameplates under them sent a flutter through Meade's stomach. Then he heard his own name, like a resounding trumpet call.

"Meade, is it?" Sir Cas Greyling thrust out a bony hand. His grip was firm, almost aggressive. "I'm Cas Greyling. Lousy bastards made a dent, didn't they?"

The word *dent* struck Meade as a trifle patronizing. "Some dent," he said.

"One hell of a thing to wake up to, that much I can tell you. A Degas, a Vermeer, a Matisse, a Modigliani, and a Rothko." If there was any hint of the pain Greyling must have been feeling, Meade couldn't detect it in his voice. "One hell of a thing."

"I can imagine. I'm sorry."

"And I'm sorry about the foul-up. My office damn well should have called."

"No apology necessary," Meade said.

"I appreciate that. Coffee? Or tea? It's a little early for a drink, I suppose."

Now what Meade caught in Greyling's voice was a measure of watchfulness, of one man feeling out another. "No, thank you," he said, then glanced back at the wall again, nodding. "Not the easiest pieces in the world to sell, I don't imagine. Once the word gets out—"

"The word, as you put it, won't get out, Mr. Meade. Despite the similarities, this isn't sunny California. We've got four dead men lying out there under a tree." Greyling noted the effect this pronouncement had on Meade. "That's right. Our thieves. Or at least four of our thieves. A falling out in the ranks, I suppose. Or a sellout. All well and good, except the four are as white as you and I. And in this part of the world, that's like setting off an air raid siren. The catchall phrase is 'internal security'—not a matter given over to public scrutiny, if I'm making any sense. The theft of art antiquities?" Greyling shook his head, and his silver hair shook with it. "Until the smoke

14

clears, it won't even make the papers. Not here, and not in San Francisco either, Mr. Meade. Don't get any ideas. You'd be expelled the next day. And that rather bombastic newspaper you work for would be barred from the country, straight-out. Forget it. It's not worth it."

The words and their vigor seemed to seed an another thought. Sir Greyling's eyes pinched together and he held up a crooked finger. "Do this instead, why don't you?" he said. "Take a look into my paintings. See what you can uncover. Hell's bells, the police won't be doing me much good there. Maybe you can."

"Unlikely."

"I know your reputation."

"A reputation built a long time ago."

"You've been off the bottle for what—ten months? So you're a little rusty. From what I hear, that still makes you the best investigative reporter in the country. And you're here, right? I'm willing to call it *fate*, if you are." Meade took note of another subtle change in Greyling's voice, something more calculating. "We'll call it a business proposition, of course. Naturally, one with suitable rewards."

"I'm flattered. I suppose. Unfortunately, I'm onto something else at the moment."

"Ah. The prison thing, sure. I can see that. Good stuff, too. This thing—well, hell, I can see about a dozen dead ends myself, and I'm about halfway to senility as it is. I understand your position. I tell you there's no story, and then ask you to waste your time anyway."

Meade held the elder statesman's gaze a moment longer. Out of the corner of his eye he noticed the abrupt departure of the young, fair-haired man in the robe. In time, he said, "I didn't build my reputation chasing stolen art, Sir Greyling."

"No, you went after bigger fish, didn't you? Politics and big business, mostly. And then drank yourself out of a job. What? Dig up one too many politicians with dirt under their fingernails?"

Meade didn't answer.

"I've read more than a few of your stories, Mr. Meade. I've even read your book. You're an idealist. Or *were*," Greyling scoffed. "So you found out that even the good guys wear tainted hats. Always have, always will. Now the *Chronicle* sends you over here to cleanse yourself and rekindle your political outrage. You think this part of the world is where idealists get well? You're a dreamer."

Actually, Meade thought, the dreamer in this case sat behind an editorial desk in San Francisco. His name was Art Carpenter. He and Meade had formed their friendship in the late sixties at the University of Colorado. They protested the same issues, did the same drugs, read the same literature, and idolized Kerouac and Kesey. Carp was still a believer. And while he had faithfully carried the torch, he had watched Meade being eaten up by his own cynicism. When the drinking got the better of Meade, Carp didn't know what to do. At first he trivialized, then scolded, then let the friendship run cold. The Cape Town assignment was Carp's idea, partly to assuage his own guilt, partly to satisfy the everlasting dreamer who had never completely given up on an old friend.

As a means of avoiding the subject of his background, Meade glanced overhead at the transmitting antenna and severed coaxial cable. He examined the opening in the ceiling.

"Microwave," Greyling said. "Very sophisticated, under normal circumstances."

"Then your intruders were either incredibly lucky or extremely well prepared."

"Suggesting . . . ?"

"Nothing." Meade buried his hands in his pockets. "Is it new?"

"The alarm system?" Greyling shrugged. "Two years, give or take."

"I assume the police have already asked you about the system's designer?"

"The police—"

"Is this our reporter, Cas?" The woman who took her place at Sir Greyling's side at that moment wore bleached jeans and a sleeveless jersey. Thick black hair had been tied haphazardly off a high forehead. Dark eyes, eyes almost oriental in shape, were bloodshot, traced with red lines and captured in circles of fatigue, yet they were still playful and mocking. She was, Meade guessed, in her mid to late twenties.

"Ah, Mr. Meade. May I present my houseguest, Miss Rita Hess."

Rita shook Meade's hand with the firmness of a business competitor. Then she took hold of Sir Greyling's arm, and did so, Meade saw, with exceeding gentleness. "This ordeal has taken its toll on you, Cas," she whispered. Her accent was thick, yet her voice had a breathy quality to it. "You look exhausted. I daresay Mr. Meade wouldn't mind a bit if you were to take a short rest."

"Mr. Meade and I were just discussing the procedural problems facing our paintings." The response had a paternal ring to it. "He was asking about the alarm system. About its designer."

Rita seemed to view this as an opportunity to affirm her place as Sir Greyling's confidante. "The system was designed by the curator of the Stellenbosch Museum of Fine Arts, Mr. Meade." Now she eyed him with aloofness. "Her name is Farrell DeBruin. I would suggest you talk to her if you're looking for information on that subject."

For the longest time, Meade didn't respond to this. His vision blurred momentarily. DeBruin. But, of course, it was impossible.

Sir Greyling took a step forward. "Mr. Meade, are you—?"

"The name DeBruin. Is it a common one?"

17

"I wouldn't use the word *common*, no," Sir Greyling answered carefully. "Certainly not Van der Merwe or Botha."

"The name Gideon DeBruin?"

"Farrell's father." Greyling studied Meade's reaction, and then added, "Gideon's expected here at the house tomorrow night, in fact. Why?"

"Nothing, nothing really." Meade shook himself. "A name from the past."

"I can tell you, Farrell was damn confident about her system. That much I know," Greyling said. "I recall her once saying it would take a mind as devious as her own to bust it."

"I hope she laughed when she said that," Meade replied. He watched Hawthorne, the forensic scientist, lifting filaments of some black substance from the carpet. Then he crouched in front of the balcony doors and ran a finger along the unbroken panes of glass, taking note of the undisturbed foil alarms. Rising again, he said, "May I ask who discovered the theft, Sir Greyling?"

"Rita, in fact."

"I don't envy you that," Meade told her. "When was it?"

"A little before eight, actually. I often take tea in the gallery." She followed Meade's eyes to the wineglass and ashtray on the bar, then cleared her throat and chuckled. "I was hung over. I thought some wine might help."

"A fallacy I once subscribed to myself." A pencil had somehow found its way into Meade's hand. "I assume the inner door to the gallery is locked at night?" he asked.

"It's locked every hour of the day and night," Rita Hess answered, "to be more accurate."

"Then you would have your own key."

"Of course she has her own key," Sir Greyling replied. "Rita is a guest of the house. The gallery is hers to enjoy."

"I'm sorry," Meade said, shaking his head. "A minute ago I was accused of sounding like a policeman. My accuser may have had a point. I must have taken you seriously, Sir Greyling."

"Ask your questions," Greyling insisted. "I started this thing."

"The young man in the robe. The one who just left—"

"My son, Terrence. And yes, he also has his own gallery key." Greyling threw out a hearty laugh. "Though his ignorance of art stacks right up there alongside his lack of interest."

"Does it?" Meade said. He was staring at the ravaged south wall again. He told himself he didn't want anything to do with Sir Cas Greyling's paintings. This talk of his reputation. Of fate. This wasn't about his reputation, and it had nothing to do with fate. It was about a sticky problem someone hoped would be solved before the police got around to making a mess of it.

So why was he being sucked in? Why hadn't he walked out that door? Oddly, Meade wasn't surprised when he heard himself say, "You're a persuasive man, Sir Greyling. With your permission, I'll have a look around."

In return, a hint of satisfaction slipped into Greyling's voice. "Do that, Mr. Meade. Do that. Any problems, you know whose name to drop."

3

MEADE EXITED to the balcony. The ropes and pulleys that led to the roof had been tagged and dusted. He took the stairs to the third-floor bedroom. Fingerprint powder formed a glaze on the balcony doors. A detective collected tools and examined a square of tan stationery.

Along the outside of the house the turret, vine, and postern had been roped off, but were unguarded. Meade heard voices on the roof above. He stepped past the barricade. Inside the postern's narrow corridor a blue chalk mark encircled a red-handled pocketknife and what looked like a gum wrapper.

Beyond the barricade, he followed four sets of footprints across the esplanade, through the formal garden, and into the oak trees where Ari Paros and his three companions had briefly paused. Meade climbed the split-rail fence. He watched a springbok prance heedlessly through the pasture.

The footprints led to the creek bed and more barricades. A man in a white smock huddled over an empty backpack in a thicket of willows. A scaffold had been erected on either side of the wall. Meade climbed over. He was accosted by two policemen and promptly rescued by a third. The third was Captain Jacob Bartleman, a slight, rakish man with a trimmed mustache. During Meade's seven-month tenure here—against all odds, given their respective professions and nationalities—he and Bartleman had developed an arm's-length friendship.

Even from where he stood, Meade could see the bodies. Four of them. He begged a cigarette. "We're out of it," Bartleman told him. "Fogwell's in charge now."

Meade recognized the changing of the guard: the process by which the Security arm of the police relieved the Criminal Investigation arm of its duties. Bartleman, a member of the latter, and obviously incensed over the disregard of his authority, had the look of a man spoiling for a fight.

"And the paintings?" Meade asked.

"What about the paintings?" Bartleman replied. "Larceny. Simple larceny."

"The theft of a Matisse? I don't know much about art, but the theft of a Matisse sounds grander than simple larceny."

"That's right, you don't know much about it," Bartleman agreed. "Stay out of it."

"Would any collector or museum curator with any kind of reputation touch paintings that important knowing they'd been stolen, Jacob?"

"They've already got a buyer."

"What?"

"The bastard who wasted the four bastards who stole the Matisse in the first place," Bartleman replied. "Figure it out."

"Too easy."

"Stay away from it, Michael. I like you. You do good work. We need prickheads like you here. Stay away from it."

"Greyling asked me to look into it."

"Fuck. 'Greyling asked me,' he says. Fuck." Bartleman peered through narrow slits at the American and picked ruminatively at his mustache. "Greyling wants a hero, Michael. Someone to stick his nose into business not his own just out of the pure goodness of his heart. You Americans love that bullshit. You walked into Greyling's life at the exact right moment. You not only gratify the hell out of his enormous ego, but also serve as a subtle reminder to Security that they'd better not rest on their laurels too long."

Meade didn't answer, and Bartleman blew out a stream of smoke. "All right. Out of respect for Sir Greyling's enormous ego, I'll give you the tour. Keep your notebook in your pocket."

The tour, Meade imagined, was more out of spite for Security than respect for Greyling, but he didn't argue.

The scene looked like a movie set. Lit by a ring of purple spotlights, the four bodies lay exactly where they had fallen. Attendants with body bags awaited their cue. Cameras flashed. Fingerprint powder covered the van, inside and out. The director, whose nightstick danced from the end of a leather thong, was a stout man of military bearing in the blue and gray of Security. His name was Colonel Blair Fogwell. He stood over a portable table absorbed in the examination of a handgun and three bullet casings.

"A 9-mm Walther," Meade said as they strolled by.

"Very good." Bartleman was obviously surprised. "Got some years on it. Seven bullets, all from the one gun, it looks like. Fogwell's talking pro."

"Five miles from the nearest town and half as many from the nearest neighbor?" Meade shook his head.

"Don't tell me. You would have chosen something with a little more firepower. Like an Uzi, maybe? Or an AK-47?" Bartleman caught the spark in Meade's eyes. "Don't forget the paintings, wise guy. One stray bullet might puncture a canvas without much damage, but a stray burst from one of your ghetto cannons? I can just see one of Sir's beloved masterpieces looking like Swiss cheese after a hailstorm."

"Which doesn't mean you don't agree with me."

"It means it's not my problem," Bartleman said. "I wish to hell you wouldn't make it yours."

A roped corridor led away from the van and the bodies, protecting a single set of footprints. The prints approaching the van were shallow and weathered. Those retreating had taken form in the wet ground after the rain. Samples of both were being filled with plaster casting. But there was something else as well. With each alternate step there was a curious impression, a circular companion a half-inch in diameter within which concentric circles were inlaid.

"A cane," Meade said. "Or walking stick of some kind."

"Michael, God Almighty, you're a genius. A fucking genius. I swear to God, you Americans never cease to amaze me." Bartleman slapped his side. "Yeah, a cane's a good guess. A cane or a pogo stick."

"A cane makes only slightly more sense," Meade replied. He looked again. "Would Forensic normally take a cast of something like that?"

"That's what they're here for, pal," Bartleman replied.

The tracks led through a trampled thicket of scrub oak, down a rocky grade, and onto a flat meadow cordoned off on three sides by rope and flashing standards, and guarded by Security policemen wearing both side arms and whips.

Bartleman pointed to the tire tracks, evidence of a careful arrival but a departure in considerable haste. "Our getaway car. Get a load of the footprints."

"He stopped at the trunk."

"But no cane print. Not a trace."

"A single track to the van and back," Meade said. "One trip. One man. Are there others?"

Bartleman didn't answer. He was on his way back. When he reached his unmarked Toyota, he offered a last word of advice. "Watch yourself on this one, friend. It's got trouble written all over it. Security doesn't like it much when outsiders start dabbling in their affairs. I thought you'd learned that by now."

Meade hitched a ride back to the estate in a police van. He got out at the front gate and spent five minutes talking to the guards there.

Then he walked the quarter mile back to the house. A father, a son, one houseguest, and an army of hired hands under an acre of roof and twenty-five octagonal chimneys. Meade put himself in Cas Greyling's shoes and found life pleasantly complicated.

The butler told Meade he could find Rita Hess in the garden off the solarium. The solarium smelled of sulfur from the spring that fed the whirlpool. The garden was recessed and hidden by an ivy-covered brick wall. Eucalyptus trees formed an arch at the entrance, and four slate steps carried Meade into the garden. A mosaic of square tiles brought him to a lily pond. Rita sat in a wicker chair beside the pond. She still wore the same faded blue jeans but had traded her sleeveless top for a turtleneck. Jet black hair fell in waves halfway down her back. She held a cup and saucer of fine china, and steam rose above the cup. She tipped her head.

"May I ring for tea?" she asked.

"Fine." Meade took the chair opposite her.

Watching, she graced him with an amused smile. "Cas told me to be particularly—accommodating. He says you're committed to helping us find our paintings."

"An interesting choice of word."

"What, *committed?*"

24

"No, *our*."

"Well, paintings like those—" she said, her rising shoulders emphasizing her sincerity, her laugh fluid and low in tone, "—one becomes attached."

"I can imagine."

She looked into his eyes and seemed satisfied, saying, "Let me see. Your first question has to be: Where, pray tell, was this wanton woman during those most critical hours last night? She must be a devilish thing."

"The guards at the entrance noted your departure at 9:56 P.M."

"Very precise."

"You drove a white BMW convertible."

"What else? My God, it was a beautiful night when I left."

"You didn't offer your destination, and the guards would never ask. You returned, a little groggy-eyed, but no worse for wear—an assessment of the morning shift— at 3:45 A.M., leaving your car in the drive and entering with your own key by the conservatory door."

"That has a ring of accuracy to it." Rita toyed with a silver lighter inlaid with abalone shell. Three half-smoked cigarettes lay in an ashtray on the arm of her chair. "You know how it is."

"Suggesting the company of an attractive member of the opposite sex."

"Yes, you're right as rain. The company was both male and, I would like to think, reasonably attractive."

Tea was served, along with a platter of cheese croissants. Rita poured for them both. She watched Meade douse his tea with two teaspoons of sugar and most of the cream. An amused grin ripened into a throaty laugh. "You would have preferred coffee, obviously."

"Tea is fine," Meade answered without looking up. "And the gentleman?"

Rita paused a moment, then sighed. "The gentleman's

name was Vincente. We didn't bother with last names. Or maybe that was his last name. We met at a reception for the Italian foreign minister at the Concordia Hotel in Green Point. They served the most outlandish Cornish pasties. I drank a Riesling from the L'Ormarim winery, if that helps. My friend drank some disgusting brandy from Paarl. We left the party around midnight, I imagine. It was probably 3:00 or 3:15 when I left the hotel, replete and satiated, if that's what you're wondering."

"The reception, at the Concordia: I assume it was an invitation-only affair?"

"If you only knew the number of invitations Sir Greyling throws in the trash every week. Sometimes I need a night on the town."

"Your Mr. Vincente—he was staying at the hotel?"

Rita lifted her shoulders again, this time in ignorance; her eyes widened. "He had a key to a room, anyway."

"And you didn't notice anything unusual on the road back home? Or when you parked your car?"

Rita shook her head. "I've thought about it all morning, but there's nothing to remember."

Meade watched every gesture. The balancing of cup and saucer, the crossing of her legs, a strand of hair pushed carefully off the face. He wasn't thinking about Rita's journey home; he was thinking about the lock on the inside of the balcony doors off the gallery, and that on the bedroom doors a floor above. He was thinking that, despite her feigned grace and poise, Rita Hess was not totally at ease with the opulence of De Greyling.

In the interlude of silence that followed, Rita took a moment to freshen their tea, and still Meade watched her, by now absorbed in the magnetism of her face. The high forehead. The pronounced widow's peak. Dark, arching eyebrows. Her skin the color of walnut, her complexion smooth as high-fired porcelain.

And yet there was an earthiness to her gestures. Sally, though blonde and rangy, had also had such an earthiness about her, whether working in the garden, scrubbing down their boat, or making love. Her mother had been a schoolteacher and her father a crane operator, a background Sally longed to escape but never could.

Now Meade wondered about Rita's own background and speculated aloud: "Germany."

Rita returned his smile. "My home's Hamburg," she said easily. "You've been there?"

Meade shook his head. "Sir Greyling called you his houseguest. For much longer?"

"My visa expires next month."

"Unfortunate."

"Oh, I might argue that. I've been on holiday too long."

"You arrived home at four last night. You entered the gallery at about eight. Four hours. Did you sleep?"

"I read. Alcohol—" Rita shrugged, tilted her head back, and laughed. "My God, not only does it give me a hangover; it won't let me sleep. *Tried* to read, would be more accurate. Dozed some, I think. Finally I gave up."

"I'm sure it doesn't matter. It's almost certain the theft took place before that." Meade drained his tea and grimaced. "Sir Greyling mentioned that you have your own gallery key. Would the same key operate the lock on the French doors?"

Rita peeked at Meade over the rim of her cup. Then she uncrossed her legs and deposited the cup on the table. "Now that you mention it, I really can't say. You see, Cas insists the doors remain closed. The temperature and humidity controls—that sort of thing."

"I understand." Meade came to his feet. "The tea was—better than I anticipated."

Rita forced a smile. "Brazilian."

"By any chance, did you notice the doors when you entered the gallery this morning? Whether they were unlocked or ajar? A natural impulse might have been to look outside."

Rita expelled a rush of air and arched her back. She rose. "My natural impulse was to trade my tea for booze, Mr. Meade. What I felt was panic, not curiosity."

"Panic? Really? I'm surprised. You don't seem like the type," Meade replied. He bent down to admire a tiny purple bloom, then started across the garden, and caught himself in midstride. "You entered the house by the conservatory door last night. Which is—"

"Which is next to that hole in the wall used by those men. Yes, yes, and yes again. You see, the late Mrs. Greyling had a chime fetish, and there are, hanging from the inside of the front door, three lovely Swiss bells. Three very noisy Swiss bells."

Meade smiled, almost sheepishly. He thanked Rita for her time, bowed his head, and made a humble exit.

Terrence Greyling was standing at the end of the front walk staring down into the wishing well. He wore a long terry-cloth robe over pajamas. His thick mass of blond hair looked as if he hadn't yet combed it that day. His face had a particularly youthful look, but Meade guessed he had to be around 35.

Meade started with an introduction and then fashioned a consolatory comment about the theft. Neither elicited a response; the younger Greyling continued to stare, eyes glazed, a hand gripping the old-fashioned iron crank.

Meade tried again. "The Chinese have a proverb," he said. "A wishing well is only a mirror, a reflection of the wisher and his belief. The well has depth only insofar as the wisher's vision of his own soul, his own unconscious. Something like that. You know the Chinese."

"*The Ballerina* was his treasure," the son said, and Meade assumed he was referring to his father. "Did he tell you? Edgar Degas. He always regurgitates the drivel you find in those overwritten art history books. Like the lighting, or the delicate draftsmanship, or the subtle use of color. Forget that. It was the girl: he couldn't take his eyes off her. Anyone could see her beauty; even I could see her beauty. But he could *feel* her presence." Terrence blinked, as if surprised by the thought materializing in his head. "I think she was the daughter he could never have."

"Really?"

"*The Ballerina* was his first buy after the doctors told my mother another pregnancy would kill her. He'd spend hours with that god-awful pastel. Have you ever been jealous of an inanimate object?" He didn't wait for an answer, but his boyish face came up to meet Meade's with muted anticipation, and a belated grimace captured his entire face. Just as quickly, however, the well reclaimed his attention, and he said, "I suppose I felt it even more so when I saw his face this morning. I mean, there was *hurt* in all its glory. Real pain."

With a brittle and piercing screech, the crank yielded grudgingly under the pressure of Terrence Greyling's hand. His voice took energy from the sound: anger, Meade thought, that could easily have been mistaken for petulance. "He buys his art and then keeps it. I've never understood that mentality. Buy it, hang it on the wall for a year, and then sell it off, I say. Put some profit in your pocket, and move the hell on. He should have sold the Degas aeons ago. Pleasure fades in time, just like a new suit of clothes; that's what I keep telling him."

"And what does he say?"

"He puts his arm around my shoulders and tells me what a great kid I am. He means it, too. I'm convinced I'm a worthless geek, and he thinks I'm the ace of spades." He turned the crank again and looked Meade straight in the eye. "Haven't you ever, just once, looked out there and wished it were you who'd pulled the trigger? You who'd set the record straight?"

Meade fumbled for a response, but Terrence Greyling was quicker. His smile had returned and he added, "You won't tell the police I said that?"

4

FIRST AND FOREMOST, there was Table Mountain. All that was Cape Town lay humbly at its feet.

The ramparts and cliffs that formed the sides of Table Mountain had been cut flat for many miles—thus the name—and waterfalls of white tumbled in silent cataracts down its cliffs. The city itself coiled in and around the mountain's vast skirt on three sides, and at its feet two oceans collided.

Meade parked his Land Rover in a visitor's space across from the Cape Argus Building; the *Argus* was an English-language newspaper considered liberal in its stance against everything Afrikaner. A pair of armored personnel carriers rumbled past. The mammoth carriers were called Hippos. They were escorting government trucks filled with black deportees. At a stop sign Meade heard a low chanting coming from inside the trucks.

Soldiers patrolled a street corner where colored fishermen sold snoek, a coveted pike-like fish, from the tailgate of a battered pickup. He went inside. The newsroom was on the third floor.

Meade's presence in Cape Town hadn't warranted the cost of an office. Instead, the *Chronicle* had "rented" a space for him here. His rented space consisted of a metal desk, two swivel chairs, and a computer terminal.

The novelty of his presence, however, was not that he was an American from San Francisco; the novelty was the twenty-three-year-old Smith-Corona typewriter he'd plunked down in the middle of his desk. Someone had taken to leaving him short typed notes whenever he was out. "The Stone Age Man Returneth." "Welcome to the 20th Century, Yank." "Two Fingers Are Better Than Ten." This last one, a blatant reference to his typing style, hurt.

Still, Meade knew enough about the computer to access his messages. There was one from Sean. "Dad, Sorry I've been out of touch. School and such. What about breakfast? How does Saturday morning look? Nine o'clock at the Shack?"

Though Sean had, in fact, enrolled in graduate school at the University of Cape Town, Meade suspected that his real education was being gleaned outside the classroom. At Berkeley, Sean had barely scraped by with a degree in telecommunications. His academic problems had nothing to do with lack of intelligence; there were many reasons, his mother's death first among them.

Like his mother, Sean was essentially an introvert. Berkeley, however, had brought out the extrovert in him. He would listen to speeches denouncing the U.S. presence in Central America or praising student revolts in China like an objective reporter; then he would debate the issues with his father as if fathers were the enemy. For the extroverted side of Sean, Cape Town had been irresistible. He had created a series of convenient rationales for making the trip with Meade. Their father-son relationship, Sean had decided, was in need of work. Which was true. Furthermore, the graduate program here was considered the equal of any he could find back home. Which was not true; it was only easier to get into.

Either way, Meade looked forward to breakfast and

he put it on his calendar. Then he called up his current story on the local prison system; the article was due in San Francisco in three days. He contacted the Office of Bantu Affairs and the Minister of Police. For the second time in as many days, both refused comment. Uninspired, Meade switched off the computer.

Instead, he opened the book on modern electronic security systems he had checked out from the paper's library. He was perusing the section on microwave devices when an uninvited black man threw himself into the chair beside his desk. Meade extracted a pencil from between his teeth. The man set a cup of hot coffee and an opened can of Diet Coke on the desk. He chewed on the end of a cigarette, smoke rising past squinted eyes.

His first words were, "Welcome to the twentieth century, Yank."

"You!"

He reached out a hand, a broad grin exposing the gap between his teeth. "Cam Fazzie," he said, the *a* in his last name rolling off his tongue as if it were a well-rounded *ah*.

"I was expecting Oscar Wilde or Jack Benny," Meade said.

"You got lucky." Fazzie gestured with his cigarette. "The coffee's for you."

"I take cream and sugar."

"Oh, right." Fazzie dug through the many pockets of his safari jacket until he discovered the packets of cream and sugar. He directed a thumb toward a corner of the newsroom inhabited by a half-dozen black reporters and three photographers. "We call it the Ghetto."

"The *African Edition*," Meade said, nodding. Every white-oriented newspaper competed for black readers by offering a black edition as often as four times a week. Though strong on sports and crime, advice columns and gossip, the *African Edition* sought out its hard news in the townships and homelands. "I've seen your byline. You do good work."

"Some days are better than others. Last month we lost Lucas Ranosi. Banned for three years. In March, Maud Botbyl was arrested over some matter of a source she wouldn't reveal. She still hasn't been charged." Fazzie shrugged. "Down in the townships the comrades are necklacing everyone with a suspicious wrinkle in their brow, and the vigilantes are playing baseball with petrol bombs. News, right? Restricted. Me? I'm working on a piece about contaminated dolphin fish. You?"

"Restricted," Meade replied.

Fazzie nodded. He hesitated a moment and then said, "Your son's a hell of a handball player."

"Then that's what this is all about," Meade said, gesturing at the coffee. "How do you know Sean?"

"From the university. About four months ago. I gave one of those incendiary speeches that get too close to the truth. Funny, though, it didn't scare Sean off."

"Naturally not."

Fazzie threw out a wary smile, but his voice was pleasant when he said, "He and I had coffee afterward. We worked out together a couple of times. One thing led to another. You know how it goes."

"I'm not sure I do."

"I made the mistake of introducing him to one of our photographers. I think they're in love."

"Terrific."

"Her name's Mieta. Obviously you two haven't met."

"Not yet," Meade said.

"No, Sean would be a bit gun-shy about that. Anyway, very easy to fall in love with, Mieta is. Very easy."

Fazzie reached out for his Coke. He drank, belched, and drank again. When the can was empty, he glanced down at the opened pages of the security alarm book. "We heard something about De Greyling."

34

"Did you? That's fast."

"The police station is like a sieve, Yank."

Meade tipped his head. "I'll remember that."

He pushed a two-page summary across the table. Reading, Fazzie dug into his jacket and came away with a slim yellow box. At the top it said, "Mills—England's Luxury Cigarette." He offered the pack. "What about the tools?"

"They left everything."

"Suggesting that the tools came from somewhere in the area. Which suggests the thieves didn't."

"I didn't know the *African Edition* had a crime beat."

"We don't. But I haven't always been in such an honorable profession," Fazzie admitted. He moved from his chair to a vacant desk across the aisle, and back again. He prowled, catlike, head thrust forward, shoulders acutely uneven. "And the egg suckers at police headquarters aren't talking, of course."

"Not to anybody, the way I understand it. Not to art dealers, not to collectors, not to museums, not to anyone who might be in the market. It's a confusing approach," Meade said with a straight face.

Fazzie chuckled. "Not as confusing as it seems, Yank. The police here consider it a show of weakness to bring unsympathetic neighbors in on their problems. Which means they won't be using outside sources, either. Scotland Yard, the Carabinieri, the FBI? Not on your life."

"Any theories?" Meade asked.

"More than likely you had five thieves, and one of them decided he wasn't in a sharing mood." Fazzie sounded indifferent, but he orchestrated with his finger. "I'd bet on an inside job though, given the likes of that alarm system."

"At least an inside contact."

"Or, try this. Four creeps. They're brought on board by a wealthy collector. Someone who knows the gallery, or who's bought off one of the maids, maybe. And in the end this wealthy collector figures, Why have witnesses?'

"I'm told Forensic found only four sets of footprints inside the estate. Not the killer's. The killer had his or her own car parked a quarter of a mile away." Meade tried the coffee and grimaced; he added another sugar and the rest of the cream. Then he said, "The alarm system bothers me. They knew the layout better than they should have. The system's designer is a woman named Farrell DeBruin. She's curator of a museum in Stellenbosch."

"You're staying with this thing."

Meade sighed. "Greyling's too eager that I should, and the police are too eager that I shouldn't. Any ideas?"

"At a place like De Greyling, the help outnumbers the residing tenants seven to one. The help tend to blend into the background, you know, like tree stumps. It gets to where no one notices them."

Meade finished the thought, saying, "So if the bad guys did have an inside contact, then the help might be a place to start—"

"Hey, I just dropped by to introduce myself, Yank. I thought you should be aware of the high quality of Sean's friends."

"—and the help would talk to you before they would talk to me."

Fazzie laughed and shook his head at the same time. "Oh, yeah, that they would. If I could get past the front gate."

"Try."

Now he laid two cigarettes on Meade's desk. "I might just do that, Yank. I might just do that."

Thirty kilometers outside Cape Town, basking at the foot of the sheer stone cliffs of the Papegaaiberge, lay triangular fields of grapevines in colors as distinct as the changing leaves of fall: the origin of wines three hundred years rich in tradition. The fields, dotted with stooped and bent workers, were interspersed with whitewashed, elegantly Dutch farmhouses and barns.

Stellenbosch itself stood poised on the banks of the tumbling Eerste River. One look, and Meade felt his mood tumbling right along with the river. It wasn't that the ancient oaks along Dorp Street were too perfect, which they were. Or that the blushing pink bougainvillea were too idyllic. Or that the spotless white veneer of the university was too contrived. And it wasn't that, while the Afrikaners claimed a political revolt had seized *their* school, the only disturbance Meade could detect was a halfhearted rugby match on the intramural field.

And it wasn't the alarm system either, though Meade realized under normal circumstances that would have been a logical place to begin.

It was the unforeseen revival of a lifelong obsession. The offhand mention of a name. DeBruin. Gideon De-Bruin. As a child, Meade had heard the name enough times to have it firmly implanted in his brain, along with the story of its bearer, the man responsible for his father's death. In repetition his mother had meant only to honor his father and keep his memory alive. Meade understood that now. His grandfather had told the story with more venom, but the same intent. Yet, with each retelling the child had dreamed of revenge and, in his wildest fantasies, plotted a death as heinous as the one the man named DeBruin had condemned his father to.

But that, Meade reminded himself, was a long time ago. And what if there was a connection between the DeBruin in his past and this museum curator named DeBruin? What could he possibly say to her? Would she have even the vaguest idea what her father had done during the war? Would a father share those kinds of memories with an adoring daughter?

An overwhelming impulse to flee back to the city

was laid to rest by the appearance of a thatched and gabled homestead with a carved sign out front that read Stellenbosch Museum of Fine Art. A Dutch facade, including a carved fanlight, rose above mahogany doors. Louvered shutters and latticed windows reminded the visitor that the whitewashed museum had been someone's house a century ago. The sward of grass out front had probably been littered with toys once, Meade thought.

Inside it was cool, and a self-portrait of Rembrandt hung in the vestibule. Tourists strolled through intertwining rooms with lofty ceilings.

A black woman passed from room to room serving wine in stemmed goblets. Meade declined, asking instead for the curator's office; the woman in reply gave a demure nod toward an opened door beyond the information counter.

The counter was deserted, so Meade slipped around it to the door. He stopped at the threshold. A woman in the room beyond stood in repose before a painting—a cubist depiction of what could have been the Rocky Mountains. Meade's eyes abandoned the work totally in favor of its viewer. She was slender and pale, and from this distance, her face looked almost like porcelain. Her hair was carelessly arranged, the color of straw. Her long arms were thoughtfully crossed, and she held a frosted cocktail glass close to her cheek.

Alone, she appeared relaxed, absorbed. She *radiated*, Meade thought. The instant he knocked, however, she straightened. Each movement became an exercise in control.

"Yes?"

"I startled you. I'm sorry." Meade didn't move; he felt like an intruder on a scene of intimacy. He introduced himself.

"An American in Stellenbosch," she said in reply. "Sounds like a B-movie."

"Not a very complimentary thought."

"We get our share, I suppose. Tourists, mostly."

"Hoping to see the perverse flaunting of white rule, I imagine," Meade said.

"No doubt. We also get the occasional reporter, hoping to spot a thread of dissension in the ranks."

"And do they?"

"I tell them they're looking under the wrong stones. Stellenbosch is seamless, you see, and therefore boring and hopeless."

Her voice had an old-world flavor. She studied him with busy eyes, dissecting and dismissing. Then she returned to the painting, touched its surface, and jotted a note on a sketch pad attached to the easel. When she looked back, she seemed genuinely surprised that he was still there. "Meade, did you say?"

"Michael Meade."

She pulled generously on her drink and found refuge on the edge of a solid wood desk. Meade could see in her face and eyes that she was well into her second drink. Third, he thought, if she holds it well.

She said, "I'll assume you know who I am, since you're here; I'll also assume it's business, since you don't look like most tourists we get."

"Then you haven't heard? The police haven't been here?" Meade cast a thoughtful glance at the painting. "I'm one of your occasional reporters. From the *San Francisco Chronicle*. I'm here at the request of Sir Cas Greyling. I'm told you were responsible for the microwave alarm system in his gallery."

"A great and terrible secret, out of the bag."

Meade focused momentarily on Farrell's hands, then on her rich brown eyes and the lines of her face. The former conveyed impatience; the latter, indifference.

"Last night," he said, "your system failed."

Farrell slipped off the desk, and circled it. She held the drink in her hand, Meade noticed, like a shield.

"And?"

"Four men dead. Five paintings gone," Meade said. Her face tightened as Meade recited the artists and the paintings involved. "According to the omnipotent Sir himself, you boasted of your singular ability to break the system you claimed impenetrable."

"Since when, I wonder, has the omnipotent Sir started taking members of the media into his confidence?"

"He appears to have more faith in me than in your own police department."

"Yankee ingenuity, I suppose." She looked at him with equal measures of understanding and contempt. "They must have beaten the time-delay. Three and a half seconds. They must have been tipped."

"By someone who knew the system as well as you, then."

"No one knows that system as well as I do. I designed it. I employed three different firms during the installation." Farrell drained her glass. "They came through the ceiling."

"Which firms?"

Farrell was on the verge of protesting but evidently decided against it. Instead, she took a notepad from her desk and scribbled three names.

"You think Cas suspects me?"

"He didn't use those words, if that's what you mean." Meade glanced at the names. Only one of the three firms had a local address. When he looked up again he asked, "Five paintings like that—how much would they be worth?"

"Plenty," Farrell answered. "On the legitimate market, thirty million pounds."

"Then it's a profitable business, art banditry?"

"It's a profitable business, Meade, because there's no risk. The bastards are never caught. When they are, they spend about five minutes in jail anyway, so the police figure, why bother."

"On the illegitimate market, who's buying paintings like those?"

"That's the problem. The paintings they chose to steal." Farrell ran a finger thoughtfully around the rim of her glass. "If an art thief knows exactly what he's stealing, the value of the work and the status of the artist, for example, and if he knows exactly how to get at what he's stealing—and these gentlemen obviously did—then he more than likely knows who's buying, too. But a thief with those qualifications doesn't steal a Matisse, or a Vermeer, or a Degas. He steals a Dufy, or a Vlaminck. A painting that can slip through the cracks."

"Then the four from De Greyling were hired by a private buyer with no intention of showing his collection in public or ever putting the works on the market. At least not in the near future."

"It's possible."

Meade took a step toward the desk. "What if they're not in it for profit? At least, not in the conventional sense?"

"Ransom, you mean. Personal or political ransom."

"Here, in this country. For the exchange of one of your better-known political prisoners? Or the release of ten or fifteen thousand uncharged detainees?"

"It's possible," Farrell said again. This time she turned away.

An uncomfortable silence ensued, and Meade searched for a way to bridge it. He said, "Tell me about Greyling."

"Tell you what about Greyling?"

"Your relationship."

"Relationship? I'm a consultant. In the business of art. Nothing more."

"The business of art. I've never thought of it that way."

"Welcome to the real world."

41

"Consulted how? Like, what paintings to buy? Where to buy them? For how much?"

"It's a fine line between consulting and competing, Meade. You saw the man's gallery."

"Has he—cost you, then? As a competitor? You and the museum?"

"He's managed to acquire a few pieces at our expense, yes." She shrugged. "But outbidding the competition is part of the business."

"Any of the five?"

Farrell stared. "The Modigliani, for one. Two years ago. And I remember going to London—this was in the early eighties—with an eye on the Matisse, *Plum Tree at Noon.* I also remember the bidding starting out ten thousand pounds above my limit. It was always my intention to steal those two back. I threw in a couple of others just out of—"

She broke off suddenly.

"What is it?" Meade said. "You remembered something."

Farrell shook her head. She peered down into an empty glass. When her head came up, she was smiling. "No, I was just thinking how tasteless my joke sounded. Forgive me."

Meade placed himself in front of the painting: not looking, however, but puzzling. Finally he said, "Farrell. That's an unusual name. Elegant."

"Elegant?" Her voice spilled over with scorn. Meade detected a crack in the veneer of her confidence, and it opened directly into her past. Her next words confirmed it. "I can imagine my father's response. You see, he was frustrated over the thought of having a girl in the house. He'd planned on naming his third son after a great-uncle named Anton Farrell, a renowned German shipbuilder. True story."

"So he dropped the Anton and got his way anyway."

"Always."

"And does your father still have the scar on his right cheek? From the war?"

"God, yes. It's as ugly as—" Farrell hesitated. "You know my father?"

"The Anvil of the *Ossewabrandwag*."

The glass in Farrell's hand suddenly slipped to the floor, and the sound of it breaking wrenched Meade out of his memory.

"Is that what this is all about? A bunch of pitiless old Afrikaners and their obsession with Nazi Germany?" Farrell's voice shook. "How could you know about that? Why in the name of God would you bring it up?"

While Farrell backpedaled to her desk, Meade bent down and began collecting shards of glass in his hand. He dropped them gingerly into a nearby wastebasket.

"Leave it," she commanded. "Just leave it."

He arose, drawing his eyes reluctantly away from the glass, and said, "On February 16, 1945, an intelligence officer in the South African Defense Force uncovered a German safe house in a Johannesburg warehouse district. Military intelligence had been searching for it for months. South Africa was, of course, still officially a member of the British Commonwealth at the time. But that night the safe house was manned by a group of Afrikaners. Afrikaners waging their own personal battle—"

"In the name of Adolf Hitler and his Third Reich. I know the story, thank you."

"They were called the *Ossewabrandwag*. The Ox-wagon Sentinel. A name you're obviously familiar with. What this officer discovered was a mobile radio operation sophisticated enough to have been filling the airways of southern Africa with four years of pro-Nazi propaganda. Printing presses worn from endless replication of Hitler's speeches. Three men ran the presses that night."

"One of them being the notorious Anvil of the *Ossewabrandwag.*"

"Your father had a reputation, Farrell."

"He could pick up a radio dispatch with a toothpick, isn't that how the story goes? He could rig a bomb from a cigarette lighter."

"The officer made it back to his car and was halfway through his report when a bomb exploded in the back-seat. He died on the operating table. He was twenty-six years old. My mother was three months pregnant at the time."

A recessed bar was built into the office wall. Farrell poured gin into a new glass and drank without turning. She said, "I'm sorry."

"No," Meade replied. "That was uncalled for. Totally uncalled for. And not the reason for my coming here, believe me."

"But I don't believe you."

Meade couldn't face her. He found refuge in the broken glass again. Embarrassed and unnerved, Farrell joined him, saying, "Clumsy and stupid."

With an outstretched hand she followed the stream of glass under the desk and when she withdrew the hand, blood oozed from her finger and thumb. "Clumsy, stupid, and careless."

She was near tears. For a brief moment their eyes locked, while Meade held fragments of glass in his hand and Farrell pressed a bloody finger to her lips. It was an exchange fraught with emotions Meade would have gladly paid money to understand. Farrell's perfume added an accent as delicate and powerful as the final stroke on a painting.

"I thought I was over it." Meade tossed the glass in the basket and came to his feet. "I guess yesterday that might not have sounded so trite."

"Don't say that." Farrell hastened back to her drink.

"An ugly man who happens to be my father killed your father. Don't try to make me feel better."

Meade crossed the room to the bar. He stared hard at the vodka bottle, and actually reached out for it. But when he found himself pouring, it was tonic water over ice.

"Do you dream?" he asked, for no apparent reason.

"Not if I can help it," Farrell replied. "You?"

"With unflagging regularity." Meade laid a business card on the corner of Farrell's desk. "And I'm expecting a masterpiece tonight."

One of the alarm companies Farrell DeBruin had employed during the installation of the security system in Sir Cas Greyling's gallery was located on the outskirts of Stellenbosch. It was called Precision Alarm and Electronics, Inc.

Meade was searching for a reason to go on with this. An art theft was a three-inch, page ten story in San Francisco; in Cape Town it was an unprintable story. Meade had been sent here to find cracks in the armor of the ruling National party, not to cater to the whims of ex-Ministers. So? So Greyling had pushed harder than he should have and, in doing so, touched a personal nerve. Farrell DeBruin had touched something deeper.

The man in the pin-striped suit identified himself as a systems architect. The one in the wool shirt and corduroys was the chief installer.

"Farrell? The woman can be a certified, grade A tyrant," the architect said. He shook his head and snorted. "Never in my life have I seen anyone so compulsive. You would've thought the Greyling thing was the first blessed job we'd ever worked on with her. Checked every circuit, every line, every connection. Not once—you might expect that. I'm talking about every time she walked through the door. Drove us all half up the wall. Thank God she's something worth looking at."

"She knew her business, though," the installer said. "You can't deny that. The lady knew what she wanted."

"What she wanted was to make bloody well sure we didn't know what she wanted." The architect ran a hand through his hair. "We never did find out if the thing really worked. Obviously it didn't."

"And Greyling?" Meade asked.

"We saw more of the Minister's son than we did the Minister," the installer announced. "He had a habit of strolling around in his robe all day long with a wineglass in his hand."

"A regular gadfly with all the questions," the architect agreed. He caught the installer's eye. "And that nonsense over the dancer! Remember that?"

"The dancer?" Meade asked.

"A girl in one of his daddy's paintings." The architect started to laugh.

"Maybe that explains the robe."

"A ballerina," Meade said.

"That's the one," the architect answered.

"Smart, though," the installer was saying. "Kid was smart. Could fool you. Lull you to sleep one minute and then, *wham*, ask something like, 'What's the difference between a proprietary alarm system and a central station system?' Or, 'Couldn't you neutralize the photoelectric light beams by shining a flashlight into the photo detector?' Stuff like that."

Meade chewed on the end of a pencil. "What about Greyling's houseguest? Her name is Rita Hess. Dark, attractive, long black hair?"

The architect shrugged.

"Sure," the installer said slowly. "Oh, yeah. We came back from a lunch break one day, and there she was. Must've made an impression, I guess. I can even remember what she was wearing. Blue jeans and this silk thing. Bare feet. Just roaming. She had a pencil in her mouth just like you. We surprised her, I think. I felt bad about that. We never saw her again after that. But I knew when she'd been there. Usually in the morning before we'd show up. You'd catch a hint of perfume. Sometimes a coffee cup with lipstick on the rim. That kind of thing. Yeah, I remember Rita, all right."

5

THE EXECUTIVE COUNCIL of the Afrikaner *Broederbond* convened in the basement chapel of St. Stephen's Dutch Reformed Church on Shortmarket Street. The Council represented at the highest level the organization's thirteen thousand members and its 820 cell groups.

At age forty-nine Paul Kilian, president of the country's largest industry bank, the Central Bank of Cape Town, was the youngest member the Council had ever enlisted. He was also, arguably, the most ambitious. Kilian had graduated with honors from the University in Stellenbosch in three years, and from law school in Pretoria in two. He'd earned his captain's bars after three years with the Reconnaissance Commandos in Namibia. By the time he was thirty-four, he had wrestled control of the bank away from an ailing father.

As he made his way down the dimly lit stairway to the chapel, Kilian heard conversation, heated conversation. He wasn't surprised.

"You're late, Broeder Kilian." The Council chairman's voice exuded impatience. Unusual, Kilian thought. An air of composure was, after all, a prerequisite for the chairmanship. The man's name was Dr. Harrison Venter.

He was thin-lipped and balding, his face pinched. In his life away from the Bond—if there was such a thing—Venter served as the chancellor of Rand Afrikaans University in Johannesburg. He was approaching the end of his second, and last, term as chairman. This meeting was to have been one of celebration, but the turn of events at De Greyling twenty-four hours before had changed all that.

Kilian took his seat opposite Gideon DeBruin. He could feel the inquisition of those bulging eyes, but could muster in return only a curt nod. More than the eyes, DeBruin's scar—a purple river running parallel to his jawbone—unnerved Kilian. He avoided DeBruin's gaze and peered momentarily down the length of the table. The chairman, too, was glaring at him. Finally he focused on the chapel wall.

Kilian was an avid reader of history, and the evolution of St. Stephen's Church fascinated him. In the eighteenth century, an English fort had stood on the site of the church. In the early nineteenth century, the fort became a prison, its lower levels a dungeon. Fifty years later, when the Dutch community banned the use of the guillotine, they introduced, instead, a crude but effective version of the gas chamber. They used sulfuric acid and coal gas and the mixture was piped through vents in the walls. Eighty-two years ago, when the prison became a church, the underground chambers were converted into wine cellars, or storage rooms, or private chapels exactly like the one in which the Council now gathered. The gas vents were still there, covered by the same corroded iron shutters that had controlled the flow of gas a hundred fifty years ago. And they were still functional; Kilian had discovered the cable-operated controls in a small room down the hall, now a janitor's closet.

"You've seen this, I imagine," DeBruin said. He used the tip of his cane to propel an opened newspaper across the table.

Kilian suppressed a weary sigh. "More good news?"

"I suggest you read it," DeBruin replied.

Kilian raised an eyebrow, taking in the rest of the table: Johannes Van Rooy, the Reverend Pieter Crous, Jan Hugo. Then he scooped up the paper. The page one story in the late edition of yesterday's *London Times* was titled, "U.N. Applauds Formation of Adlai Commission."

Kilian didn't need to read more than the first paragraph. The Adlai Commission was the latest in the never-ending parade of Jewish movements bent on tracking down and purging from the face of the earth the last Nazi war criminals—several of whom, Kilian knew, were seated around him at this very moment.

He scanned the article for an accounting of the vote. "Unanimous."

"But then, we're not foolish enough to think that's our only problem, are we, gentlemen? The Adlai Commission?" said Jan Hugo, his voice raw from the relentless advance of emphysema. He was a dreary man with a pencil-thin mustache and mottled skin. In conjunction with his position on the Council, Hugo was also chairman of the South African Broadcasting Company. "The Adlai Commission hardly changes the fact that the four men we hired are now slab ornaments in the city morgue. Nor does it change the fact that the painting they were hired to steal is now further from our grasp than ever."

"There's another thing this Commission doesn't change, Jan Hugo. It doesn't change the fact that someone's declared war on us, and done so with a damn lethal blow. We spent four months putting together that plan," Gideon DeBruin said, forming into words the very thought that played on each of their minds. "It was simple and it was good, and it was about two minutes away from succeeding. It didn't because someone got inside our heads."

"A stolen painting is worth about 7 percent of its market value," they heard Paul Kilian say. "Our thieves were contracted at a price of 10 percent. A third down, the rest on delivery. At that price we received a guarantee of silence. With that much money held out until delivery, it would have been in their best interest to observe that guarantee, not to mention exercising a certain diligence in seeing the delivery made."

"You're suggesting the problem goes beyond our thieves, Broeder Kilian," DeBruin said. "I concur."

"I'm suggesting," Kilian corrected, "that our problem goes beyond the *painting*. And what remains, beyond the painting, is the Missing Sixth. And no one has yet dared put a value on that, have they? Now far be it from me to point a finger, but our four slab ornaments were your province, Gideon. According to you, they could have had no knowledge of the Sixth."

"The finest art historians in the world don't know what's hidden in that painting. We're only guessing ourselves, are we not? One, whether the bloody document even exists, and two, whose names appear on it even if it does exist."

"We know whose names goddamn well might appear on it though, don't we?" the chairman burst out. "Well?"

There was fear in his voice; as much out of character there as impatience. But in another lifetime, in a war the chairman would just as soon have blotted from his memory, he had been filled with fear, and he had suppressed that fear with cruelty and prejudice. In those days he had dreamed of hearing his name on Hitler's lips. The honor of it. Unearthing the overseas Jewish pipeline from Lisbon to Cape Town had fulfilled that dream. But there would have been no glory in just closing down the escape route; they had shot the Jews one by one as they made their way ashore. In those days, he hadn't worried about witnesses; he was young, and the thought that they might lose the war never occurred to him.

Jan Hugo, wheezing and coughing, understood the look

on his friend's face. For him it evoked the memory of a valley outside Pretoria, the unmarked grave of 123 Jewish nationals whose remains, upon close examination, would surely confirm death by execution.

"My point, Mr. Chairman," DeBruin said, "is that the odds against our thieves having any knowledge of the Missing Sixth are extraordinary."

"Our thieves are dead," Kilian said. "It's a moot point. The question is whether the person *now* in possession of our painting has that knowledge."

Gideon DeBruin pushed away from the table and stood. He was, even at the approach of his seventieth year, a robust man. His flat nose and full lips gave his scarred face a brooding air. "I think it would be foolish to assume otherwise, Broeder Kilian. Don't you?"

"Then how?" At Kilian's question, DeBruin sank back into his seat. A web of near silence spread over the room. A sugar spoon tinkled the sides of an empty teacup. A pencil pecked relentlessly at a notepad. A foot tapped unconsciously at a table leg.

It was the chairman who succumbed to the pressure first. Rising, he stepped in front of a portable serving stand and poured hot water over a fresh tea bag.

One by one, the others followed his lead, until only DeBruin and Kilian remained locked in the tension. The elder statesman, the confident upstart. And now, rivals. DeBruin the party man, Kilian the independent. It was no secret that DeBruin was next in line for the chairmanship. Recently there had been rumors of Kilian mustering a challenge.

"I'm wondering, Gideon, if dismissing our thieves so readily is wise?" Kilian asked. Heads turned. "Our European contact—?"

"Kanellos. Yeorgi Kanellos."

"Yes. Tell us, how much information was Mr. Kanellos given about his team's—" A soft tapping, emanating from the chapel door, brought Kilian up short.

"Ah, our policeman," DeBruin said.

Paul Kilian had never met *their* policeman. Policemen were new to the Bond. There were now only seven in the entire organization. No brigadiers or general-majors, deadwood waiting out their pensions. No English speakers, no divorcés, no halfhearted Dutch Reformers, no members of the wrong political party. This particular policeman had been sponsored by Gideon DeBruin. He had almost been disqualified because of his penchant for flying on the Lord's day, a grossly unacceptable activity.

"So?" the chairman said to the newcomer; the presence of an outside participant in a closed council meeting invoked an old rule: no names.

"C.I.B. has been taken off the case" was the answer.

DeBruin studied his protégé. Feet spread, hat in hand, hands locked behind his back. Calm. DeBruin liked that.

"That was our decision," Venter replied.

"Except the idiots in charge couldn't find a clothes hanger in a full closet," the policeman replied.

"Have you anything positive to report, good Broeder?"

"I know Pathology and Forensic are having a field day. How much of it's relevant, I can't say yet. The murder weapon is a 9-mm Walther. A P38 class. Old. A collector's model by now, but very effective. The problem's that all the markings have been filed. That's not promising."

Gideon DeBruin listened to this with special interest. The Walther P38 was, indeed, a collector's model. He knew that because one hung in his gun rack back home, an acquisition from a gun show twenty-some years ago. But it was queer; was that something that was done with Walthers back then, filing the markings? His gun, and now the one used at De Greyling. He wondered if there were many others.

"Final reports won't be in from either Forensic or Pathology until this afternoon, but the minute they are, I'll know. And the minute I know, you will."

"And?" Paul Kilian sensed there was something else; he saw a shifting of the policeman's eyes.

"Sir Greyling. He's—evidently got his own man turning over stones."

"A private investigator?" The chairman sounded incredulous.

"Journalist."

"Have you a name?" Kilian asked.

"Meade. Michael Meade. An American."

"Meade?" Now the chairman laughed. "The guy's a lush."

"He's clean," was the answer. "And when he's clean, he's nobody's fool."

"Then he'll warrant watching, won't he?" Kilian replied.

"Why stop there?" Gideon DeBruin interjected. "Why suggest a liability when we may have stumbled upon an asset? Why just watch him, when we may be able to use him?"

6

THREE HUNDRED years ago, a beautiful people with slanted
eyes and chocolate skin were abducted from their homes
in Java and Malaysia by Dutch traders. They were herded
into the dank, rat-infested holds of tall clippers. The few
who survived the six-thousand-mile trek across the waters
of the Indian Ocean to a burgeoning colony known in those
days as *De Kaap* were sold at auction. Slavery and forced
interbreeding slashed away at their history. But unlike the
cultures of the Hottentots and the Bushman, which passed
into oblivion, remnants of the Malay tradition endured.
Stories and songs. Paintings and carvings. Music and architecture. And religion.

Three hundred years ago those same Malay slaves were
granted living space at the foot of Signal Hill, in what is
now part of downtown Cape Town. They called it the
Malay Quarter. Flat-roofed houses with narrow doors and
carved fanlights stood in the shadows of the mosques and
minarets that celebrated their Islamic faith. Cafés reeked
of the spicy, aromatic smells of *samoosas* and *tameletjie*,
curry and cinnamon. The men often wore the traditional
fez. The women tied scarves in such a fashion as to suggest the yashmak. The Malays were allowed to work and

worship in the Quarter, but they were still classified as colored. So at night, the mosques became silent as tombs and the minarets mute while the Malays took their places in the townships out on the Cape Flats.

Nevertheless, by day, they had turned the Quarter into a flourishing marketplace. Sidewalk stands sold hand-tooled jewelry and beaded wear, handwoven baskets and carved statues, dried fruit and fresh vegetables. Shops sold antiques and alabaster, shells and rocks, mandolins and dulcimers.

Meade parked his Land Rover in an alley off Short-market and Wale. The streets of the Quarter were cobble-stone, the sidewalks built of slate. And like San Francisco, both rose in grades that were at once breathtaking and eerie. On the corner, two men strummed mandolins and stared into the empty hats at their feet. Meade gave them each a rand note but didn't stop to listen.

In the liquor store across the street he bought whis-key in half-liters. Six bottles. A prime for every pump, his grandfather would say. By now Meade knew about the Malay underground, a network of pot and cocaine dealers, numbers runners, pimps, fences, and thieves. And he knew that if the Greyling theft had local roots, then the Malays would almost certainly have wind of it. Meade's grandfa-ther, a career beat reporter, would also say, if you don't know whom to ask, start at the bottom.

With that bit of advice ringing in his ears, Meade talked to a pimp and two of his ladies on Church Street; a fence in the lobby of the Rua Hotel on Burg; and a dealer in the park next to the open market. Without luck.

He cornered a meth-drinker in the alley behind a boarded-up movie theater, a rusted coffee can filled with wood alcohol clamped between two shivering hands. On good days, this one supported his habit informing for the police, but today his lips were purple and his tongue was too swollen to talk.

Finally, Meade acquainted himself with a taxi driver whose only passengers were thieves and fences, buyers and prospective buyers. Only the big stuff, he told Meade in confidence. Electronic gadgets, mostly, jewels and, yeah, the occasional art piece. Anything lately? *Nada,* he said. Zilch. Not even a rumor.

A name, then. One name.

Meade found the restaurant the taxi driver had told him about in a basement below a butcher's shop. The Jambi. He entered through the back door and paused long enough to stick a finger in a huge vat of steaming curry.

"It's close," he said to the chef. "Ten more minutes."

"Fifteen," the chef snapped. "Are you eating?"

"Looking, actually. For a Mr. Nelson December."

Something else had happened when the Malayan slave dragged his half-starved body out of the hold of his Dutch death ship three hundred years ago. He was robbed of his identity. Names were erased and replaced. When he emerged from the bonds of that slavery in the late nineteenth century, the Malay set about reestablishing the identity he had been cheated out of. New and unusual names emerged. Like *Thursday* or *September* or *Easter,* after a child's time of birth; *Adonis* or *Caesar* or *Napoleon,* from the heroes of mythology or history; *Patience* or *Courage* or *Joy,* from the virtues a parent hoped to bestow upon a newborn.

The man in the corner booth had been born on Christmas Day four decades past. His mother had once shaken Nelson Mandela's hand. He was alone. Except for the many petitioners who passed before him every day, he was always alone. Nelson December suffered the pox of interbreeding. His broad African face was cream-colored. He had a flat, bulbous nose, pockmarked skin, an Afro of red hair, and eyes bluer by far than any sky Meade had ever seen.

"We have nothing to talk about, Mr. Michael Meade."

Nelson December didn't bother to look up. Before him sat a plate of *samoosas*. He used his fingers to pick at the fish, bread to soak up the oil. "I know why you've come. I knew two hours ago."

Meade sat down anyway. He put his last bottle of whiskey on the table. From the cab driver's cryptic tip, Meade had deduced that Nelson December was both fence and front man. He considered approaches. Jousting. Confidential. Straight business. No, Meade thought, flattery.

"Five of the most expensive paintings in Africa. A gallery built like a jail. A deal like that, you'd know about."

"That's true," was all December said.

"I'm not working with the police. If I were, you'd know that, too."

"You're working a side of the street you're not too familiar with, is what I've heard." When his head came up, December probed Meade's face, sucked each feature in through his hypnotic blue eyes, and yawned. Then he observed the whiskey. He snatched it up. The laugh that rang from his throat was rusty with disuse. "You don't think much of my asking price, do you?"

"I couldn't afford your asking price. The whiskey's a gesture of goodwill."

His eyes zeroed in on Meade again. Cigarette-stained fingers cracked the seal on the bottle. He waved it under his nose. Then he drank, grimaced, and drank again.

"Cheap," he said, when the whiskey was gone. Meade waited, and eventually Nelson December offered, "You're looking in the wrong place. It was an outside job. I can't even offer you gossip."

"Who can?"

So one name led to another, but they all led, in the end, to Nico Mustapha. In Nelson December's opinion there were only two art restorers worth considering. Miles Roundtree, an English speaker of aristocratic roots, was *the* restorer in Cape Town, *the* restorer in all Africa. Nico Mustapha, a colored of Malayan descent, was only the *best* restorer in all Africa. Seven months in the country and Meade was beginning to understand the difference.

In Nelson December's opinion, no one could match a restorer as a source of hearsay and gossip in the world of art. He heard from the street and he heard from the galleries. The restorer was the indispensable link. He made the old look new again, the broken, whole.

Nelson December had mentioned the studio's back entrance. It opened, Meade found, onto a narrow, half-lit alley.

The studio was a flight up, squashed between an ancient mosque and a low meeting hall. The door was propped open by a bronze casting of an elephant. A screen was heavily barred and locked. A red light blinked, hinting at an alarm system. Meade knocked, waited, and then knocked again. He pressed his face against the screen.

Beyond the door a man sat, not ten steps away, at the head of a potter's wheel. He was portly, his hunched shoulders rounding him out even further. His arms were fleshy and his fingers pudgy. He held a magnifying glass in one hand and a sable brush in another. Before him, on the wheel, sat a double-headed anthropomorphic vase with inlaid obsidian eyes. Meade heard a low drone of tuneless humming. He knocked again, harder.

The restorer started, looked about until the source of the disturbance had been identified, and then grunted. He set his tools aside and unhooked his wire-rimmed glasses from his ears. He adjusted hearing aids in both ears and hopped to his feet.

"Ah, yes, the young man who tried to buy off Nelson December with a half-liter of whiskey." He used two keys on two locks. The blinking red light paused. "Cheap whiskey, as the rumor goes. I admire that."

"Word travels," Meade said.

Nico raised his shoulders. "In this neighborhood, good sir, words have wings." The restorer's face was the color of butterscotch and pudding-smooth. Slanted eyes gave him an appearance far more Oriental than African. His hair was a thin stubble of gray and black, and he wore a small red skullcap on the back of his head. A mixture of contentment and irony laced each word as it left his mouth. "And you think I can help you. I can't."

"I remember reading an article once, about a Goya slashed in a half-dozen places by a madman with a razor blade. This was in the National Gallery in London, I think. Scotland Yard placed it in the care of an Italian restorer, and by the time he was finished—well, evidently it was remarkable." Everywhere wooden shelves were crowded with paints and varnishes, sponges and polishing cloths, brushes and picks. Candles flickered on the face of a spectrometer, while fluorescent tubes glowed overhead. The Koran lay open next to an X-ray machine. Meade stopped in front of a silver serving set nearly black with corrosion. "His name was—"

"His name was Luciano," the restorer said, relocking his door and perching before the wheel again. "Restoration, you know, is a delicate balance between art and science. The skilled artist with no knowledge of pigments and their history defeats his purpose. The restorer who has mastered the idiosyncracies of aging and the trickery of microchemistry without a feel for an artist's brushwork or his method of sketching is destined to botch a damaged work beyond repair. The painting you're referring to was Goya's portrait of Charles IV. Unfortunately, Luciano used a lacquered filament tape to bind the razor cuts on the back. Within a year the tape had stretched a half centimeter and another restorer was called in."

Meade shrugged. He moved from the serving set to the potter's wheel, deftly raising the vase and running his hand over the surface.

"From a recently excavated site in Turkey, of all

places," Nico announced. "A fake. They'll use some ridiculous technique called thermoluminescence to date the clay. The surface texture tells me all I need to know."

"Poorly fired," Meade agreed, recalling his pottery phase in college. "Imagine. All that work, and they couldn't even bring the kiln to temperature."

"Imagine," Nico mimicked. He slid away from the wheel. He gathered up a tack hammer and a handful of stretcher keys. Then he stepped behind an oil painting held upright by vise grips. "Your thief will have no luck unloading the Matisse, you know. Not to a legitimate buyer, anyway. People like to steal the poor man's work as much as they like to copy it. Therefore, any dealer or collector with any sense at all treads lightly around a Matisse. And the Vermeer. Can you imagine? The man only produced forty paintings. Other than the one Sir Greyling snatched up six months ago, there hasn't been one on the market in years. Nelson December knows that. He wouldn't touch it even if he could."

"And the Malay underground?"

"The underground prefers drugs to old masters." Nico graced the American with a thin smile. He turned back to the painting, then back to Meade again and abruptly laid his hammer aside. "There was a rumor. A year ago, maybe eighteen months. Word had it that some group, foreigners, with influence and money, of course, were planning a raid on one of the country's national museums. I heard it was the Jo'Burg Gallery in Joubert Park; that's how ripe the rumor was. According to the grapevine, their plan was to use the take for some political purpose." Nico retrieved his hammer. "Word had it the Soviets were behind it."

"And?"

"It was a rumor, my naive American. A rumor in the world of art is a deal that falls apart because too many people know about it."

Meade took a pencil from his pocket, as prop, not

tool. He circled the painting on which the restorer now concentrated. "Another impostor?"

It was an abstract with cartoon caricatures floating across the canvas. The artist's name was Stern.

"Hailed by the critics for her vigorous brushwork and 'fast' colors," Nico said. "It's only ridiculous, good sir, not phony." Nico rolled his eyes toward the far corner of the studio. "Give that one a look, if you're interested in the romance of criminal art."

The painting rested on an easel, set in a small alcove. A camera stood on a tripod before it. The only light was a tangential beam from an arc lamp positioned at the extreme left side of the work. The effect was surrealistic: a blur of raised brush strokes, palette knife incrustations, and flaking paint. A close-up of the moon's surface on a bad day, Meade thought. He punched a switch on the alcove's inner wall. Light flooded the space, and the portrait of a handsomely dressed woman jumped from the canvas.

The restorer was at his side suddenly, chuckling. "It's a Boucher. Portrait of Madame Isabella."

"Yes," Meade said, though neither the name nor the painting was known to him.

"No." Nico gestured at the woman's gown. "He used a wonderful shade of cobalt blue. Here, here, and here."

"Impeccable taste."

"Except for one minor oversight. You see, cobalt blue wasn't developed until 1804. François Boucher, poor fellow, died in 1770." Nico wiped his eyes and replaced his glasses. "In fact, before you leave, Mr. Meade, why don't you do this decrepit old restorer a monstrous favor and carry our masterpiece into the other room for me."

It struck Meade the moment the framed painting was in his hands. He saw in his mind the murder scene and the cordoned-off lane that led from the thieves' van to the clearing where the killer's car must surely have been parked—and the single set of footprints to and from the car.

Meade transferred the painting to the workbench. "Could a single man carry five framed paintings, much the same size as this one, on foot, for a distance of six hundred yards?" He pictured the incline that led to the clearing, the loose dirt, and the impression that appeared alongside the footprints. "A man with a cane? Or a staff?"

"Perhaps. If the paintings were somehow bound—"

Meade hoisted the Boucher a second time. He was dubious; it was the bulk, as much as the weight. So he tried to imagine some logical reason for the killer's leaving behind one or more of the paintings. Had he been interrupted? Or frightened? Yet the police had found no evidence of any of the five paintings.

Had he cut the canvases from their frames and stretchers? If so, what had he done with the frames and stretchers? Buried them? Burned them? Yet there would have been little time, and no reason not to just drop them there. The only other alternative was that there had only been one, or two, or three paintings for the killer to take after all.

MEADE ORDERED griddled scones and coffee from a walk-up diner on Church Street.

He walked and ate. The city brimmed with people. Blacks wore coats and ties, much the same as in Atlanta or Chicago. There were differences, however. A sign read, No Dogs and No Blacks. Another said, White Race Group Only. A soldier tacked a revised curfew sign on the wall. Tension was an undercurrent here, a riptide.

At Caledon Square he stopped at the police station and entered by the front door. Today he didn't check in at the front desk. Forensic was on the second floor. Off-white was the color of choice here: walls, floor tiles, even the attendants' uniforms. The air hummed.

Peter Hawthorne's jaw dropped when he saw the American.

"I can't talk to you," he said when Meade mentioned the theft.

"Can't, or won't?" Meade replied.

"Take your choice."

"Has anyone from Larceny contacted you?"

"The thinking hereabouts, mate, is that when they have the killer, they'll have their paintings."

"You haven't been contacted."

"I can't talk to you. Nothing personal, believe me. It's just the way it is. Rules."

"And you don't flout the rules."

"Flouting them might get *you* a ticket back to the States. Flouting them lands *me* behind bars without a key or a prayer." Hawthorne took off his glasses and sighed. "Hey, listen, mate. Believe it or not, I'm in your corner. But having coffee with the press is like taunting a bull with a red flag. You just don't do it."

Meade backed off. "Is Captain Bartleman privy to your information?"

Their eyes locked. "If he asks, I'll tell him. Fair enough?"

Back at his own desk in the newsroom, Meade telephoned the station. Bartleman, he was told, wasn't available. Meade left a message. Two minutes later, a reporter from Sports came by and told Meade there was a call for him on a direct dial line in their department.

It was Bartleman.

"Your phone's hot, wise guy. Wise up," he said. Meade cursed himself; he was still a half step behind the reporter he once was.

"Standard procedure, pal. Know why? Because you're sticking your nose in Security's honey jar, that's why."

A twinge of excitement, like the batting of a butterfly's wings, stirred in Meade's stomach. He took this as a sign of encouragement and ventured, "I talked to Mr. Hawthorne in your Forensic Department this morning. I did all the talking, like I had some kind of disease."

"It's called impertinence," Bartleman said. "It's called sticking your nose where it doesn't belong."

"It's not that he's averse to conversation."

"It's the relative health of the guy on the other end of the line. I got you."

Bartleman shared what little he knew already and said, "You'll hear from me. Same number. Don't move."

Meade checked his watch. He turned in his chair, gazing down one length of the U-shaped newsroom toward the Ghetto. Fazzie wasn't there, but a lone female photographer was. She was tall and statuesque. Even with cameras draped over both shoulders, she moved like a dancer. She wore a beret over closely cropped hair, and even from this distance her face held Meade's attention. This, surely, was Mieta, the photographer Fazzie had introduced Sean to.

Meade was tempted to walk over, but didn't. The introduction would happen, he told himself, if and when Sean wanted it.

Five minutes later, Fazzie caught Meade with his feet propped up on the desk and an empty notepad in his hand.

"You look comfortable, Yank." Fazzie dropped a box of cigarettes on the desk. "The story coming up through the seat of your pants, is it?"

"I discovered something wonderful about your country."

"I know. It's just like California except the lady who does the laundry carries it on her head."

"I discovered that if you're here, then the police know you're here. If the police don't know you're here, then there are about a half-dozen laws with a claim on your head."

Fazzie shook his head. "I give up."

"De Greyling's four thieves. Foreigners. Illegal entrants," Meade said. "They were killed between 2:00 and 2:30 yesterday morning."

Worry lines formed at the corners of Fazzie's mouth. His voice was thick with distrust. "That's the kind of information that comes from the egg suckers down at police headquarters in Caledon Square, Yank. True?"

Meade held the black reporter's gaze. He had asked

around about Fazzie and learned that his commitment to the *cause* had been costly. Fazzie was deaf in one ear from a police beating administered five years ago during a raid in Langa. His uneven shoulders were the result of a pickax handle used on his back during an interrogation. He had also spent twenty-two months in jail—most of the *African Edition* staff had been imprisoned at one time or another—ostensibly for refusing to name a source. Fazzie was a stickler for the rules—a well-worn volume of *The Newspaperman's Guide to the Law* sat on his desk next to the computer—but revealing one's sources in the townships meant certain death to a journalist's career. You took the ax handle instead, every time.

"I'm expecting a call back," was all Meade said. "He'll use a pay phone."

"Egg sucker."

Fazzie finished one Coke and cracked another. He paced, and when the pacing got old, threw himself back into the chair. He lit one smoke from the last. Meade could see him searching for something to say; he tried anticipating it, just for practice. He couldn't have been more wrong.

"You a married man, Yank? Sean never mentions his mom."

It was probably the one question Meade wasn't prepared to field. He said, "I was. She died. Four years ago."

A rush of air escaped Fazzie's lungs. "Sorry."

Meade was on the verge of confiding the whole story when the phone in Sports rang.

Fazzie picked up the extension. Meade chewed on the end of a pencil.

They heard Bartleman say, "Forensic tells me they won't know about the castings for the tires or footprints until this afternoon. Same goes for the companion print, the cane. On top of that, our lab man voiced some concern about the chances of a quality cast for the companion print. Says the impressions are unusually shallow for a walking aid, in some cases almost indiscernible. Figure it." Bartleman snickered. "You'll like this better. They found a gum wrapper outside the house, in the entryway our recently departed crooks used."

"I saw it," Meade said.

"Comes to pass that it's the product of someone or something called Gourmet Travel, Inc., a German firm. They're a catering company for European air and train lines. They service four airlines that fly into Africa. Alitalia in Rome, Lufthansa in Frankfurt, Luxavia in Luxembourg, and Olympia in Athens.

"And the cigarette butts found at the site of the killings? Turkish tobacco. But the filters were imprinted with the word *Britz*, from an East German city of the same name. For what it's worth, marketed mostly there and in Czechoslovakia."

Meade listened. His grandfather would have called this "cut-and-paste" investigating, he thought. Then he said, "Anything else?"

"They found a diagram of the gallery in a bedroom on the third floor. Done with a hard edge of some kind, the lettering included. Drawn to scale. Very precise."

She was chewing on a pencil, the installer at the alarm company in Stellenbosch had said about his one encounter with Rita Hess.

"Pen or pencil?" Meade asked.

"A number two pencil. The paper was a heavyweight bonded type, hard surface, with an embossed border. A tawny color, almost tan. Good quality. Expensive. Forensic also found traces of a gray powder on the gallery carpet. Ash. From photographic paper. I think I'm supposed to be bursting with pride when I tell you it was a color print."

"Is it standard procedure in a case like this for the victims' fingerprints to be forwarded to Interpol in Paris?"

Meade asked. "Or does that come under Colonel Fog-well's definition of global prostration?"

"Even a hard-boiled Afrikaner has to prostrate himself once in a while, wise guy."

The conversation ended. Fazzie replaced the extension. "You're supposed to think you've just been handed the bloody Holy Grail, right?"

"He may have been more generous than we think," Meade said. He told Fazzie about his visit to Nico Mustapha and the rumor of a Soviet-sponsored art heist in Johannesburg. He also described his visit to the Stellenbosch alarm company and the installer's comments about Terrence Greyling and Rita Hess, and about Rita's pencil, in particular. "And the cigarettes, from Britz, in East Germany—"

"Could be had on the black market in like, what, a half-dozen countries, maybe?"

"In the Balkans. Or the Mediterranean. Put that together with the gum wrapper and the airlines he mentioned."

"Alitalia in Rome, or Olympia in Athens. Except if you're a creep with a record, you avoid Rome like the plague."

"Exactly."

"Well, hallelujah, Yank. Four Greek thugs—"

"*Hired* thugs." Meade raised his shoulder. "The photo was their final instruction, telling them which paintings. It had to be."

"All right then, the question is, Who had that kind of access to the gallery beforehand?"

They stood at the window, smoking. Behind them phones jangled and the day's news trickled in. Fazzie was talking about the Concordia, the hotel where the party for the Italian foreign minister had been held two nights ago— the party attended by Rita Hess. "The Concordia's what's known as an international hotel, Yank. There are no color restrictions in the international hotels anymore. Same goes for their restaurants and nightclubs. Can you imagine? And the most wonderful part is, you actually find blacks there once in a while. Of course, they're not from the Cape or the Transvaal, mind you. More like Miami or Rio.

"Anyway, I talked to the concierge at the reservation desk. She was magnificent, Yank. Hips! I asked her if the police had been around. No, the police had not been around. So I asked about the reception. Two hundred seventy people. Maybe half from out of town. I told her about Rita's friend, Vincente.

"I told her Vincente's money belt had been left by a unanimous benefactor at the paper. I even produced a note. I told her if I couldn't locate Mr. Vincente I'd have to leave the belt with the police. I'd rather leave it with her, I said, if only I knew for sure he was at the hotel."

"Very good. And?"

"And she had a ream of computer paper in front of her within about sixty seconds. And guess what?"

"No Vincente."

"*Three* Vincentes. One a lower-level diplomat from the Italian consulate in Pretoria, married, six kids. I got hold of him by phone. You can imagine his reaction. The reception? Strictly business. The wife? No, she wasn't along. Rita Hess? Never heard of her. But he did admit to some female company, 'man to man,' as he put it. Described her as a string-bean blonde, bought and paid for." Fazzie crushed out a cigarette. "The other two were both visiting dignitaries, one from Caracas, the other from Milan. Both checked out the next morning. I haven't tried following up. I don't see a visiting dignitary bragging to the media about his out-of-town conquests.

"After the Concordia, I went out to De Greyling. I hitched a ride in with a bus load of migrants. One of the estate's security guards happens to speak my language. He says Rita's activity that night isn't unusual. Says she's out three, sometimes four nights a week. A busy lady."

"With or without Greyling?"

"Friday night's their night. Like clockwork. Dinner and a drive, something like that. The rest of the time young Rita's on her own."

"And Terrence?"

"Jekyll and Hyde. It depends on who you talk to. The devoted son. The wayward son. The flirtatious son. The hateful son. That one came from a gardener who claims to have witnessed, from afar, I should tell you, a shouting match between father and son in which Terrence ostensibly cursed the old man's name and threatened to burn the place right to the ground. It turns out the fight was over Rita Hess. Terrence wanted her visit cut short. Greyling kept calling 'it' an accident. What *it* was, the gardener never figured out, except—and he was reasonably certain of this—it had something to do with the gallery."

"When did this take place?"

"March, the gardener said. He remembered because the oaks were just beginning to change and the ostriches were getting frisky. I love that. Anyway, for what it's worth, there was a general consensus among the four or five people I talked to that things have gotten progressively worse between Rita and Terrence since then."

Fazzie threw on his jacket. Then he laid two cigarettes and a pack of matches on Meade's desk. He was halfway to the elevators when he pulled up again. "Sean doing all right? I haven't seen him in a while."

"Neither have I. We're having breakfast Saturday, assuming he doesn't cancel."

Fazzie's eyes widened, and then he was gone. Meade watched his departure almost ruefully, remembering other collaborators, other friends, and other relationships that never had a chance or disintegrated from misuse or disregard or simple lack of substance. But that was history, he told himself, gazing down at the cigarettes. A chance is something you make for yourself. Substance is a pearl hidden on a path of stones. He spent three matches lighting one of the smokes. The other he slipped into his breast pocket.

On his way out of the city Meade stopped at the local offices of Lloyd's of London, the insurer of Sir Cas Greyling's art collection. Inside, columns of pink marble rose to a vaulted ceiling, with maroon carpet at their feet. Smoked-glass windows obscured a rain-drenched street. Urns arranged with tall stalks of pampas grass were placed strategically about an empty waiting room lit by a crystal chandelier. A bored receptionist summoned a bald, pompous Englishman with the perfect splash of color in a perfectly fixed bow tie. His name was Plumb.

He responded to Meade's question as to whether Lloyd's was the Greyling insurer by dabbing at his upper lip with a handkerchief and snorting, "By and large."

The Englishman's unease was well disguised. Meade assumed he must have known about the stolen paintings; but then again, he had yet to run into a Lloyd's investigator at the scene. Only now did the realization strike him as both odd and disturbing.

He also realized the ethics involved in broaching the subject on his own. So he began, "I understand there's a problem."

A sigh accompanied a well-rounded shrug. "You've talked to Sir Greyling, then."

"Several times," Meade replied seriously.

"It's been six months now since he denied us access to his gallery. The biennial appraisal is a requirement of his policy. It's for his benefit as well as ours. His refusal leaves his policy completely up in the air. The policy is being reviewed at this very minute at our home office in London. I'm walking on pins and needles."

Not the theft at all, Meade thought. Remarkable.

"He told me that at the rates he's paying, the appraisal shouldn't be necessary." Meade improvised. "Sir's words weren't quite so mildly put, but I'm sure you can imagine."

"Huh." Mr. Plumb paced, stiffly, a scowl stretching his face. "Our rates can't be matched in the whole bloody industry, if the truth be known. Excuse me, but it's true."

"Then why?"

"He calls it a bloody intrusion. Two days? And no one is as unassuming and discreet as this office, I assure you." He used his handkerchief again. "I've tried to explain to him that without the biennial appraisal, Lloyd's has a legal right to deny coverage."

"A legal right to deny coverage in what event?"

"Fire. Theft. Water damage. Earthquake. The Last Coming." He tucked the handkerchief back into his pocket and hid his hands behind his back. "To deny coverage is to deny coverage under any circumstance."

8

ACCORDING TO FARRELL DEBRUIN, the alarm system at De
Greyling was monitored by two sources—the district police station in Caledon Square forty-five minutes to the
south, and the station house link in Malmesbury, thirty-
five minutes closer to the north. Meade decided on a visit
to the latter after Farrell said, "You won't get anything
from the Boers out in Malmesbury, but that's more than
you'll get from the Boers downtown."

He used R302, the two-lane highway that paralleled
the Greyling estate and passed within sight of the murder
scene. The paintings filled his head. He had lived for two
days now with their names—*The Ballerina; Plum Tree
at Noon; Two Women and Their Music; Young Woman
in Red; Wind, Rain, and Isle*—and had painted them with
images uniquely his own. Odd, that to this point he had
failed to request photographic copies from either Sir
Greyling or the police. An oversight in the beginning, it
was now intentional. Why? Was it the child in him sa-
voring the mystery?

Yet as a child Meade had been raised primarily by his
grandfather; his mother worked days and some nights as
a bank teller. His grandfather championed a life of self-

reliance. He considered treasure hunts a silly waste of time and, if not a bad influence, then certainly an afterthought to school and chores and part-time jobs.

The rain subsided. A rainbow arched above the horizon directly ahead. A scent that could only be described with inadequate adjectives—clean, fresh, pure—filtered through the open window of the car.

Meade imagined himself in Kansas. The road swept through endless acres of winter wheat. A tractor inched along on the shoulder. A fruit stand at the edge of town sold oranges and apples. The tallest buildings in town were the grain elevator and the church steeple. The women wore white ankle socks and flower-print sundresses. The men wore dungarees and flannel shirts and spit brown froth from chewing tobacco at the foot of every landmark.

There were differences. For one, the wheat here grew a rich shade of green—in June—and the trees along the riverbank were called yellowwoods. For another, the people in the farmhouses spoke a language that sounded like a sputtering machine gun, and the people in the beehive huts spoke with a *click-click-click* poetically inserted between every other word.

Meade had to contend with the farmhouse variety. The police chief and his deputy were brothers. Their cousin sat behind a metal desk tinkering with the insides of a radio, a cigarette dangling from his lower lip.

The chief was a stubby man with a large waistline. He wore oil in his hair and long gun-nut sideburns. His brother was a head taller and, despite a thin mustache, seemed more an unhappy boy than a man. He stood in front of a television set, sulking. The cousin, on the other hand, had a tendency to chuckle at everything the chief said.

"We're about sixty seconds away from a lunch break," the chief said to Meade. "I don't guess you'd be particularly interested in lamb chops and gravy."

"They'd better do something with that gravy, is all I can say," the cousin said and blew smoke in Meade's direction.

The brother watched Meade from behind the desk. The show on television was American. A "Family Ties" rerun. "We get 'The Cosby Show' too, you know," he told Meade.

"It's one of my favorites."

"Your Mr. Cosby makes about thirty million dollars a year and everyone here thinks he's your average American Kaffir." (Kaffir was the Afrikaner equivalent of "nigger.") Now the chief was intent on watching his brother. Their cousin had set aside his screwdriver. "The White Right hereabouts calls your Mr. Cosby *daardie lelike ding met die vitpeul oe*—"

"Take it easy, bro. Take it easy," the chief said. "Something tells me that's not why our journalist friend came."

The brother didn't blink. "Know what that means? It means 'that ugly creature with those popping-out eyes.' "

The cousin chortled. "We get 'Hill Street Blues,' too. All of 'em. 'Dallas.' 'Falcon Crest.' All of 'em."

"The White Right thinks your Mr. Cosby is a propaganda tool of the fat man in Pretoria. Our beloved prime minister."

"Is that so?" Meade said.

"That the fat man in Pretoria is trying to brainwash us all into believing that all blacks are just like the Huxtables," said the brother.

"He means regular human beings," the cousin interpreted.

"What do you think?" the brother asked Meade.

"I think—" Meade allowed his gaze to absorb the ramshackle office. "I think Sir Cas Greyling was right. He speaks highly of your operation here, Chief."

The chief tugged at the brim of his hat. "Just doing the job we get paid to do."

"He said you'd be modest about it. He said his alarm system is tied into your office. That's a serious responsibility."

The chief stole a drag from his cousin's cigarette. "I wouldn't necessarily call us the old goat's first line of defense."

"That's wise," the brother snorted.

"Well, maybe his second line," the cousin suggested. "That's if you don't count that horseback brigade he's got tromping around in the cow shit out there."

"Has it ever happened?" Meade asked. "The alarm?"

The cousin bellowed. "It happened, all right. The chief was sitting right here in my chair when that crazy thing went off. I swear to God, I've never seen a human being jump so high."

The brother took off his hat and walked to the window. The cousin slapped his leg. The chief tossed him a daggered look and said, "Yeah, it happened. About three months back. March, sometime. I had both our cars out there faster than a case of premature ejaculation. False alarm. Here's the old goat's live-in standin' there with a sheep-sheared grin on her face."

"The Hess woman?" Meade interjected.

"Yeah, yeah, the Hess woman. Sweeta Rita, we call her. The old goat tells us it was all a mistake. Tells us the lady happened to pick up one of them bronze statues he has sittin' round the gallery there, not knowing it was wired like the paintings and the rest of it. No problem. No harm. Our counterparts in the city didn't have any objection, so we bent the rules a hair or two and didn't say nothin'. Case closed."

"You were satisfied, then?" Meade asked.

"Except for the fact that only a blind person couldn't see that every statue in the place is tied into the system, sure, I was satisfied."

———

"If I don't get out of here for a while," Rita Hess told the stone-faced Colonel Blair Fogwell, her fingers toying conspicuously with the gold locket hanging between her breasts, "you're going to find me swinging in the trees with a glazed look in my eyes, and probably as naked as the day I was born, too."

"Not a very pleasant thought," Fogwell agreed, looking down his nose. "What did you have in mind?"

"My dear Colonel, how does a woman usually free her mind of the turmoil invading her house? Shopping! The surest cure for depression. Hasn't your wife ever told you that, you poor man?" Rita arched her back and smiled, thinking: *If* any desperate woman would ever have such a wretched thing as you. "Be truthful. An hour or two can hardly have an effect on your investigation, now can it?"

"It's your safety we're concerned with, Miss Hess," Fogwell said, now slapping his nightstick against his palm. "You'll be back before dark, of course."

"You have my word," Rita said magnanimously.

Fogwell was still watching her as she climbed behind the wheel of the silver Mercedes. Rita thrust a bare arm out of the window and waved. A tantalizing smile creased her lips, a smile that died the instant Fogwell turned away.

Rita took the R45 access road to the N7 freeway. A two-car team began following her three miles from the estate as she passed through Abbot, a village which consisted of a gas station and grocery store. A white Ford and the patented blue Toyota: Security wasn't even being subtle, she thought. They would never have been so careless with a man.

It was the colonel who brought back memories of the baron, and the baron who reminded her of home—Elze, a village of poverty-stricken farmers outside of Parchim on East Germany's northern plain. Her father grew potatoes for fall harvest and raised sheep for spring shearing. He rented nine acres from the baron. The baron, who bore a whip at his side and a withered scar on his forehead.

Life was a brutal clockwork. Every Wednesday, without fail, Rita's father drank vodka in the village until he could hardly stand up. Afterwards, he would stumble home through fields battered by merciless winters and bleak summers.

On these same Wednesdays, Rita's tubercular mother quilted with her neighbors, and while she laughed and sewed, her drunken husband would spend himself between the legs of their only daughter. Like a madman. On Thursdays, it was the baron's turn. Mostly, Rita was embarrassed by the welts he would leave with his whip; she didn't know any better. Of course, her mother knew, but when the rent came due the second Tuesday of each month she pretended she didn't. She mollified her conscience by taking her daughter on occasional visits to her sister's in East Berlin.

It was on one of those visits, when Rita was nineteen and an empty-eyed but not so empty-headed beauty, that she met a man called Arman, the Saxon. Arman bought Rita sauerbraten and wine in a café on Landshut Street. He enchanted her with stories of ancient Saxony and enticed her with his illegal forays across the border, with adventures in Bavaria, in Hamburg, in Bonn. Rita noticed that, like most men, Arman made certain she knew not only of his exploits, but of his money.

Arman called himself a middleman. *Conversion* and *control* were his two favorite words. He liked to talk about the changing world, the quiet revolutions. He talked about the new enemy in the East and the old in the West. Rita listened. She understood from the beginning that Arman was a practitioner of his own philosophy and that he would use her if he could, and she allowed him to set his bait before her. Rita also grasped Arman's foolish habit of showing his hand before the game was played out. He was a man; that, Rita thought, was explanation enough for his weakness.

And, as with the colonel, and the baron, and her

father, she could see the effect she had on him. A carelessly buttoned blouse, a skirt unconsciously hitched above the knee, a tongue drawn across ruby lips.

Arman followed her back to Elze. And though he was subtle with his offer, Rita understood it, comprehended that Arman was, as he had said, simply a middleman. She toyed with him. She exploited her few weapons. Her body, her sultry voice, her relentlessness. Arman lowered his guard. He revealed to her the essence of his game. Names, places, key words.

Then Rita set her own trap. It was a full moon the night she seduced him. Her screams of rape raised a panic in the town, and Arman found himself at the mercy of Elze's people's court. By morning, Rita was aboard a train bound for East Berlin. Of Arman's fate she never learned, nor cared.

When Arman's superior in Berlin heard Rita's story and correctly judged her mettle, Rita was dressed and fed and coached. For two years she was coached. She came to judge the sophistication of her new associates by the suits they wore, the cars they drove, and the number of gray-headed men they entertained. They referred to themselves as the Red Wheel. And though she didn't fully understand industrial espionage and technological sabotage, she quickly learned the meaning of Arman's reference to the *new* enemy in the East. Taking down the *dreamer* in Moscow might have been a frightening proposition for an uneducated twenty-year-old, but Rita would have paid any price, to any suitor, to escape her bleak provincial existence. Politics, she quickly learned, was a suitor of endless potential.

Twenty-two months later, she was smuggled west. Successful assignments in Spain and Morocco convinced her associates that Rita was the correct choice for Cape Town.

A year of patient introductions in West German social circles led in time to the Greyling family in Munich. Her escort that first evening was no less than Finance Minister Peter Roethke. Once seen, Rita was impossible to forget. She stayed on in Munich. She took up tennis at the urging of Anna Marie Greyling, niece of Sir Cas Greyling, and gardening under the tutelage of Aunt Germaine, his sister.

A visit to the Greyling estate in South Africa was arranged. After three years of mourning his wife's passing, Sir Greyling welcomed the newcomer with open arms. After six weeks Rita graciously accepted Greyling's personal invitation for an extended stay at the estate. And then she was given her assignment: infiltration of the Afrikaner *Broederbond*'s Executive Council.

In the beginning, her associates had called it a minor assignment. Among the Brothers, she was told, there were surely allies to the Red Wheel cause. Allies with money and influence. Rita's job was simply to identify them.

Then came the unforeseen revelation of the Missing Sixth, and her assignment took on increased significance, as they put it. She was ordered to find it without being told what "it" was. Find it, and they wouldn't have to cultivate allies at all; the allies would quickly present themselves.

When she got to the city, Rita slowed. She peeked into the rearview mirror and caught sight of the white Ford. On Strand Avenue, in the city center, Rita pulled into the underground parking lot beneath Happenstance, a department store renowned for its European fashions. She took the elevator to the main entrance.

An escalator transported her to the second floor and the fashion show in progress there; models sashayed in Issey Miyake's dyed cotton and Geoffrey Beene's tailored night wear. Rita took a seat along the runway and kept an eye on the escalator. The two men arrived sixty seconds apart. One wore sunglasses. Sweat tinseled his forehead. The other's suit coat bore the brunt of many hours behind the wheel. He loosened his tie.

Rita allowed herself to be noticed. She tried on three outfits and toyed with an armload of accessories. Her Security escorts toured the lingerie department, looking distinctly uncomfortable. Each trip Rita took to the dressing rooms lasted a few minutes longer than the last. She couldn't decide.

The salesclerk suggested a pantsuit by Lagerfeld and a blouse by Yves Saint Laurent. To these, Rita added a sweater, two belts, and a handbag. As she entered the dressing room area, she glanced back. The escorts had moved into the accessory department. Rita left the clothes in the furthermost stall and slipped through an unlocked door into a corridor leading from the dressing rooms to a back room where the tall, lank models were pouring themselves into new gowns and rushing back onstage. Under different circumstances, Rita could easily have been one of them.

A freight elevator took her back to the first floor. She used a side exit. She hailed a cab on Georges Avenue and, ten minutes later, entered Sea Point. East of the city center, this wealthy suburb lapped at the foot of Signal Hill like stagnant water. Palm trees and bougainvillea had once flourished in the wild here. Now cubicle high rises and stubby offices grew beside cubicle apartment houses and stubby condominiums.

Rita ordered the cab to a halt in the alley behind the Humboldt Building. The BMW was there, in the by-the-month parking space she had rented eight days ago. She paid for the cab and waited two minutes before starting out.

Beyond Sea Point, sandy beaches gave way to cliffs and rocks and restless surf.

Clifton, further along the coast, was a different kind

of suburb, quaint and weather-beaten. Solitary strips of narrow beach were protected by granite promontories. Rita kept a cottage here, under a name she had chosen with care from an American phone book: Lisa Henderson.

The cottage rested in a nook created by four ancient pines. It was quiet. The neighbors were older. They didn't mind a renter who kept to herself. A BMW in the drive wasn't out of place. Rita let herself in the back door. Moisture collected along her spine. Her hands were clammy with anticipation.

The cottage smelled of mildew. The shades were drawn tight. A bedroom, bathroom, and kitchen alcove were devoid of furniture. The previous tenant had left an overstuffed chair in the living room. Rita's one contribution had been the installation of a telephone.

The painting was propped against the hearth of a stone fireplace.

Rita laid it facedown on the cottage's hardwood floor. She knew the original work had been relined with a second, unground canvas many years ago. Untouched, the second canvas stared back at her.

From the bottom of her purse Rita dug out a gray mat knife. She knelt down. Calmly, she exposed the blade. Near the center of the relining canvas, she cut a thin, shallow line. The canvas frayed at the edges as she separated it gently from the original. Then she inserted the blade tip and carefully slit the relining canvas. Moisture gathered in the furrowed lines of her forehead. Her heart worked furiously in her chest even as she held her breath. Now she peeled the newer canvas away from the old. Panic welling up inside her, she leaned closer, searching frantically between the layers.

"This can't be." Rita was startled by the sound of her own voice, the guttural pitch. The words seemed to come from a different body than her own.

Futilely, she ran her fingers beneath the stretchers.

She took a long screwdriver from her purse and pried the painting from its frame. Breathless, she rocked back on her haunches, hands childlike in her lap. It was not there.

The telephone rang. Rita answered it on the twelfth ring.

A voice said, "Well?"

"It isn't here." Rita felt the weight of the phone, a weight that grew even as the silence grew. "There is no document. No envelope, no document, no nothing. Do you hear?"

"I heard. You're absolutely certain?"

"We've been duped. Or misled." Her voice was cold. "I don't know which."

"Then we'd better find out."

Rita struggled to her feet. She carried the phone in one hand and reached for the mat knife with the other. She faced the cottage window, drawing the shades apart. The euphonious coo of a turtledove cast a momentary spell over her.

"Start at the beginning," she heard the voice say. "Greyling bought the painting six months ago, in January. We know that. It was shipped from Europe in a sealed crate, under guard. Greyling told you that himself. He and the people from Lloyd's met the painting at the harbor and escorted it back to the estate. As far as we know, it's never left the gallery. Are we in agreement?"

"But it did. One time. Yes. My God, yes! To be cleaned and retouched." The words spilled out of Rita's mouth, her breath fogging the window. She heard thunder. The sea beyond was pale under a dome of gray-black clouds. She dug the blade of the mat knife into the wall.

9

IN CONJUNCTION WITH the prison exposé Meade was working on, he spent thirty minutes with the warden of Pollsmoor Prison, an institution described by former inmates as a combat zone.

It was dark by the time he reached the perimeter of the Greyling estate. The bodies of the dead had long since been metamorphosed beneath the various cutting tools of Pathology, and the van was now parked in a police garage, undergoing its own dissection. Security was still on the scene, however, with floodlights, foot patrols, and a lone detective.

When the detective asked him what he was doing there, Meade said, "Putting myself in the shoes of the killer."

The detective shook his head and wished him luck, and with a high-beam flashlight in hand, Meade began a tour through the surrounding stands of yellowwoods and pines. He guided the flash under low-lying branches, behind the occasional outcropping of rock, and over the wild grass. The terrain was hard and rocky and unforgiving. He counted up his rewards: a turned ankle, soiled cuffs, and enough footprints to convince him he wasn't the first to scour the area. Still, as the moon rose above the horizon, Meade could understand the killer's resorting to a cane or staff. In the pitch black, without the overflow of flood-lights, each step posed hazards; and the killer would not have risked the aid of a flashlight. The cane provided support, but not the kind of support that would have allowed him, or her, to transport five framed paintings over this terrain.

With this in mind, Meade worked his way back toward the clearing where the killer's vehicle had been parked. A fallen tree bridged a dry gulch. Meade perched on top of a rounded boulder and slipped his hand into a breast coat pocket in search of a cigarette he knew had already been smoked. A truck rumbled past on the road below; its headlights threw a yellow glow on the wall surrounding the estate. The Greyling mansion was a black stain in the night haze.

Meade tried freeing himself from the bonds of his previous thinking. He stepped from the shoes of the killer into the shoes of the thieves. What if the paintings, he considered, never left the estate at all?

The stables of De Greyling were deserted at this hour. The stable hands, like the rest of the estate's hired help, took Friday night dinner together in the clubhouse.

Alone, Rita Hess stroked the thick black mane of the horse called Topaz, the Gallant One. The thoroughbred responded by dropping his vast head and nuzzling her. His eyes were flecked with yellow, hence his name; and they flared with anticipation.

Rita had often ridden Topaz, in the early morning, when the spill of endless nightmares drove her from her bed. In recent years Topaz had grown too unpredictable for the master of the house, and for now, Sir Greyling had taken a fancy to the sleek, snow-white Arabian two stalls down, named Sasha. For months now, Topaz had refused to carry anyone but Rita. His long stride delivering her like a shadow across the estate's wild grass was the closest thing to heaven Rita had ever experienced. No man, she thought, could ever provide such purity of spirit.

Rita doubted the horse would survive the fire, but she slid the bolt away from his stall gate with that hope, nonetheless. Then she climbed down.

Outside, a breeze arose. It tiptoed through the cracks in the stable walls and carried with it air heavily scented with rain. A driving rain was the worst possible scenario. Rita put the thought out of her mind. She hoisted the five-liter plastic jug of gasoline with both hands and pushed through the gate of the next stall. A chestnut hackney pawed the ground. He shook his slender head.

The bedding in the stall was sawdust, a foot thick. Salt blocks and a half-filled water trough flanked a wooden rack heavy with loose hay. An opened manger cradled a grain mixture of oats and bran. Each of these Rita doused with gasoline. And when the odor set the horse stirring, Rita soothed him, her strokes firm, her words mocking only in that they were so genuine.

Mechanically, she moved from stall to stall—in turn she visited Sasha, who hardly moved a muscle. Then another hackney, his coat a mottled gray. A young orange gelding retreated to the back wall and ducked its head. And finally, another thoroughbred, sixteen hands tall and stately in his fifteenth year. In each stall Rita poured the poisonous nectar of their demise, and upon leaving slipped the bolt from each gate, oddly hopeful.

There were seven vacant stalls. In each of these Rita poured gasoline over the dry bedding. She splashed it on walls and flooring and, finally, poured what remained over the stall walls where the paintings had been hidden. *It had to be done:* those were his words, not hers, but Rita understood. Encouraging the theft of the other four had been her idea in the first place.

When the jug was empty, Rita headed back to the grooming area that separated the riding horses from the tack room and, further on, the stables of twenty-three workhorses. On a shelf next to a jar of dried jerky and a hot plate was a kerosene lamp. It belonged to a stable hand named Ama Siluma. Beneath the shelf was an unmade cot and a photograph of the stable hand's family. Rita shoved the empty jug under the cot. She took the lamp from the shelf and quickly retraced her steps.

She set the lamp on the edge of a hayrack in the fifth stall. The base of the lamp was stoneware, half filled with fuel. The chimney was glass, two hands high. Rita lit the cotton wick and turned the flame low. From the pocket of her jacket she took a small wooden box. From the box she removed a circular wax mold. The mold was three and a half inches in diameter and less than two inches deep, with a series of air holes punched along its upper edge. The mold fit perfectly over the upper rim of the lamp's chimney. Then, from the box, she extracted a small bottle containing two ounces of liquid benzol. This she poured with great care into the mold.

The flash point of benzol was forty degrees Fahrenheit. Contact with the flame below, once the wax melted, would result in a small explosion sufficient to ignite hay, sawdust, and gasoline instantly.

Five minutes later, Rita was in her bedroom dressing for dinner. The guests were already arriving. This was to be not a social occasion but rather a philanthropic gathering, and Terrence had been on the verge of convincing his father to cancel the affair. He had cited the turmoil of the last two days, the dismay over their loss, that kind of nonsense. Rita's argument had been more pragmatic.

"Why not get the damn thing over with," she said, which was more Sir Greyling's style and thus carried the day.

———

While the heat of the kerosene lamp's flame ate away at the wax mold attached to the rim of its chimney, Meade searched a narrow gully with a trickle of water running through it, the hollow in the trunk of a dead willow, and a scree of moss-covered boulders on the side of a steep hill. Finally, he made for the clearing where the killer's car had been parked. Barricades and rope still cordoned off the area. In the purple haze of the floodlights, a man in a blue suit coat toyed with a tape measure and took notes. A policeman in uniform paced and smoked and studied the approaching figure.

When Meade was a dozen paces away, the policeman took a last drag on his cigarette and flicked it into the night, orange embers falling in a languid arc. A hand came to rest on the butt of a pistol.

"This is a restricted area, sir."

Meade nodded but didn't stop. "I'm one of the good guys."

The plainclothesman, suddenly alert, was on his feet and taking long strides in Meade's direction. "Something wrong with your hearing, friend? The man said you can't come in here."

"I'm here as a favor to Sir Greyling," Meade said. From his coat pocket he produced a press card and passport. "I'm not here to step on any toes."

The detective studied Meade's papers, then showed his displeasure by slapping them against a closed fist. Finally, he thrust them out. "Look, but don't touch" were his parting words.

Meade stepped between barricades. He craned his neck toward the sky and sniffed the air. The scent of the trees smelled so much like home that it hurt.

"Any visitors tonight?" he said, trying to draw the policeman out with a casual tone.

"Greyling's son made an appearance. Out of the blue. An hour, maybe ninety minutes ago."

"Did he?"

"I gave him a short tour to satisfy what he called his curiosity. I think he'd been drinking." Meade stopped and faced the policeman, who corrected himself. "Rather, I *know* he'd been drinking. He said he was intrigued by the prospect of one man knocking off four armed crooks with a handgun and a single clip."

"He said that?"

"Like I said, he'd been drinking," the policeman answered. Footprints partitioned by chalk lines led them into the heart of the clearing. "The kid seemed to know a thing or two about firearms, anyway."

"Any in particular?"

"You mean the Walther? Yeah, he mentioned the Walther, all right. He also mentioned a Browning, a Beretta, a Mauser, and about a half-dozen others. The kid was enjoying himself; I let him talk. In the end, I kinda hated to tell him that only one of the four was actually armed."

"Any reaction?"

"He laughed."

Meade stepped between a set of tire tracks and used the flashlight to cut down on the shadows. The tracks led him to the edge of the clearing. He manufactured a mental image of the car as he circled the space. It was apparent where the car had been parked, and obvious by the footprints that the driver had spent time at the trunk or tailgate.

He simulated the driver's movements. In the instant before he stepped away, an object on the ground reflected the beam of his flashlight. It was something embedded in one of the shoe prints and hidden by a layer of dirt; a slice of metal or a piece of plastic, perhaps. Meade bent down, and realized at once that it was only the intensity of the flash and the coincidence of the angle that had caused the object to be visible.

Then the detective was standing over him. "Whaddya got?"

Meade tipped his head.

The detective cleared away the dirt. It was neither metal nor plastic, but a long, narrow piece of gold-tinted cellophane. The detective held it by the edge. A red and blue band, like a strand of tinsel, dangled from its side.

"A cigar wrapper." He shook his head and chortled. "A goddamn cigar wrapper. Our killer, he was celebrating. The asshole was celebrating."

The detective was right, Meade was sure of it. A cigar wrapper. Was that conclusive evidence that the killer was a man? Meade couldn't immediately identify the reason for his reaction, but, oddly, he felt deflated. Why? Any threads of speculation were quickly severed. As Meade righted himself, he was drawn to a geyser of orange flame spouting from the heart of De Greyling.

At that very moment, he knew.

"The paintings," he muttered under his breath.

By the time Meade arrived, Topaz, the tall thoroughbred, and Sasha, the white Arabian, were circling the blaze like mad specters. Pearls of sweat poured from their coats.

Fourteen casually attired diners stood in the light of the flames, watching as the panicked horses bounded into a corral ringed by burning fence posts. Behind them a black man, dressed only in shorts and bearing a small rectangular object, escaped just as the roof of the stables collapsed. He raced between the animals and threw his weight against a wooden gate that led to the safety of an open pasture.

The fire roared. Timbers cracked and popped and tumbled. Smoke billowed into the night, burning the onlookers' eyes and invading their lungs.

Meade was certain it was arson, and if he was right about the paintings having been hidden somewhere on the estate, then there were only two possible reasons for the fire: as a diversion while the paintings were removed from the premises, or as a means of destroying them.

Fourteen diners—Meade studied them as he approached, and he did so from an angle that allowed him to observe their fire-lit faces while his own remained shrouded in darkness. Rita Hess, he saw, stood taut and unmoving. Cas Greyling's hands rested on her shoulders. Terrence Greyling pounded the sides of his legs with clenched fists, his chin thrust forward.

Next to him, a woman was sobbing. A man tossed his dinner jacket on the ground and dashed toward a barn imperiled by encroaching flames. Two others followed. Another man supported his wife, and she clutched his arm. A second couple was holding hands. A third pair dared not move, the fingertips of each somehow glued to the other's sleeve. A bent man leaned heavily on his cane.

Sirens split the night as three patrol cars converged. A fire truck from Malmesbury swept through the front gate.

The man with the cane straightened to his full height. He struck a match to the ash of a long cigar. When he turned his head, the fire lit the thick features of his face, and the scar across his cheek flashed a dull purple. Meade came to a sudden halt, a hollow ache in his stomach.

"DeBruin," Meade whispered to himself. "Gideon DeBruin."

The face turned away, and the scar and thick features were hidden again. With his cane and his cigar, the man shuffled back toward the house. He stopped beneath a columned portico and turned. A casual gaze took in the sky, the other guests, and the fire, and then came to rest on the stranger peering across the esplanade. For an instant, their eyes locked. Then the man disappeared inside the house. Meade was still staring at the closed door when the hook and ladder and its escorts from Cape Town arrived.

Moments later, he found himself peering down at the spot where the old man had been standing minutes before. He crouched down, touched the soil with his fingertips, and saw where the tip of the cane had made at least a half-dozen distinct impressions. Five minutes later, Meade was cloistered in a vacant room on the second floor of the estate with a telephone in his hand.

His first call was to Cam Fazzie. Meade told him about the fire, and asked him what he knew about Gideon DeBruin.

His second call was to Peter Hawthorne. The grogginess in the forensic scientist's voice told Meade he had roused the man from a deep sleep. Hawthorne listened, but didn't reply to Meade's request. When the connection went dead, Meade realized he might have made a grave mistake. Would a twenty-five-year-old forensic scientist's phone be tapped, simply as a matter of course? Were there any phones in the country that weren't?

Still-hot coals cracked and popped in the charred remains of the stables. Steam rose from the ruins.

The mottled hackney, the burnt-orange gelding, and the aristocratic thoroughbred of fifteen years had all perished, but all twenty-three workhorses had been spared. Topaz, the Gallant One, and Sasha, the master's Arabian, had been driven to pastures out of sight of their ravaged home.

To the east, a soothing dawn was rapidly breaking. The arson inspector, dressed from head to foot in fire-resistant nylon, surveyed the ruins at De Greyling with tempered delight. He plucked a seared trophy from the ashes.

"Strictly speaking, Mr. Meade, only gases burn. A fact you may not have been aware of." His name was Fick, and he was enjoying the singular attention of the American reporter. Arsons weren't printable material at home, because arson-related fires implied some act of terrorism.

The local media didn't waste their time. "Now obviously, to have yourself a fire like this one, you need combustible material. Then again, you could say that about a camp fire, couldn't you? And there are only three combustible materials that I personally can think of: you got solids, you got liquids, and you got gases. Easy enough, except that any solid or liquid with what I call *burning properties* still has got to be heated sufficiently to liberate what I call *flammable gases*. You with me? All right, then, these same gases will in turn have to be raised to the proper ignition temperature. Fine, and—"

"Thus, there must be present a burnable material and a suitable heat source to raise this fuel to a kindling point. Very instructive," Meade said. He felt dazed with fatigue, and soot clung to his face, hair, and every inch of his clothes; he was not in any mood for a lecture. Nonetheless, he tempered his voice. "However, along with your meticulous probe into the cause of the fire, Mr. Fick, I'd be grateful if you'd keep your eyes open for the remains of as many as five very expensive paintings . . ."

10

SEAN MEADE LIVED in the university district of Ronde-bosch. The University of Cape Town campus, a sprawling complex of brick and ivy, occupied the wooded slopes on the east face of Table Mountain. The neighborhoods of Rondebosch huddled at the base of the mountain in their own unworldly cocoon of oak and maple trees. The university was English-speaking and remarkably liberal, radical even by South African standards.

Sean occupied the second floor of an ancient manor house adjacent to the railway line. Over the years, the estate grounds had been given over to three apartment houses, two-story structures of colonial design carefully arranged around a courtyard laden with daylilies, white roses, and palms. Sean had found something of home in the old place and had balanced that with the area's astronomical rents by taking on a part-time job in the university's reference library.

Meade met him in a café called the Shack. A White Race Group Only sign was posted near the entrance, but the mixed crowd inside indicated the rule wasn't enforced.

"You're becoming something of a mystery man,"

Meade said when they were seated. A grin brought life to his haggard face; he'd managed a shower and two hours of sleep. "Tracking you down is like working overtime at the job I already have."

"That bad?"

"Even your friends are starting to inquire."

Sean's eyes narrowed now. "Really? What friends?"

Meade lit the crumpled cigarette he had been hoarding for the last eight hours. He said, "Does the name Fazzie ring a bell?"

Sean sat back in his chair. "It should."

A waitress stepped silently to the table. Meade ordered espresso and a plate of scones. Sean ordered sausage, eggs, potato cakes, a side of waffles, coffee, and juice.

Meade raised an eyebrow and said, "You're dieting."

"Guilt," Sean replied facetiously.

His long hands, hands he had gotten from his mother, were wrapped around a porcelain coffee mug. Meade refused to fight the urge to peer down at the scars on his son's wrists. The two-inch purple tracks seemed blessed with a life of their own: three on the left wrist, two on the right, an oddity Meade had often pondered, often dreamed about. Five scars and one life jacket, the numerical assemblage of a hundred dreams.

"Is he trouble?" Meade asked.

"Fazzie? He's a good reporter. A good writer."

"I know that much. I'm concerned about his extracurricular activities."

"Like trying to make some changes in the rat-hole system he lives under? That sounds like an extracurricular activity more people should look into, don't you think?"

"Is he trouble?" Meade asked again.

"Dad, every time someone here stands up and says 'This is no way to live,' it's trouble. You used to believe in that kind of trouble."

"That kind of trouble has landed your friend behind bars and done some serious damage to his health."

"And he's still at it," Sean replied. "Doesn't that say something for the kind of trouble he's causing?"

"The speeches and rallies and the controversial literature are one thing, Sean. Something tells me he's in deeper than that. Is he?"

"Dad—"

"Are you?"

"No."

Sean didn't elaborate, and Meade didn't press the issue. Instead he said, "Are you still seeing the photographer? Mieta?"

Sean's eyes widened with surprise. Then he looked down at his coffee. "Fazzie talks too much," he said.

"She's attractive," Meade replied. "Very. And I like the way she carries herself."

"You'd get along well with Mieta," Sean answered. "She still thinks that peace has a chance."

Meade tipped his head. "You like her."

"When we're not screaming at one another, it's great," Sean said. "What about you, old man? You look like shit. You're smoking again, and you call what you just ordered breakfast?"

"Work."

"Work?" Sean laughed, with vigor, another gift from his mother. "You're supposed to say a *woman*, not goddamn work. Wild, outrageous sex. You're supposed to say, 'I'm being ravaged to death, kid.' Not, 'work.' "

Meade couldn't help but laugh himself. "All right. The next time I get ravaged to death, I'll order sausage, eggs, *and* scones."

"So?" Michael held both hands out, expectantly.

"So?"

"There are women by the thousands in this city, old man. That's what. Available women. Look around. The question is, have you done anything about it?"

Meade actually thought about it. Would it be fair to count Farrell DeBruin and Rita Hess? What about Rita? If things were different? One night at the Concordia? But Meade knew it would never happen. Too cold, too dangerous, too self-assured. And Farrell? Sure. In another lifetime. Meade shook his head.

"It's gonna fall off it you don't use it, Dad."

"Could we change the subject?"

"What's it been? Three dates in four years? That's not giving yourself much of a chance."

"Has it ever occurred to you that I'm too old for this thing you call dating?"

"Absolutely," Sean agreed. "Forty-two. God, ancient."

"It's the word, I think," Meade said. *"Date.* It sounds so—insignificant, so trite."

"It sounds like too much work, you mean." Sean's smile was broad and contagious. "Take a look in the mirror sometime, will you? You think I came upon this gorgeous mug of mine just by chance?"

Over breakfast, they talked about school and work. Meade told Sean about De Greyling and the paintings. Eventually he broached the topic he had been leading up to all along: Gideon DeBruin. For some reason, Meade had never mentioned the name to Sean before. True, they had talked often about the war, about Sean's grandfather and his death, but never about the Anvil of the *Ossewabrandwag.* Why? Was it to spare Sean the burden that came with knowing? Or the hate? Meade couldn't say. And why bring it up now? He didn't know that either. Still, when he saw the empathy and resolve that etched its way across Sean's face, Meade knew the decision was the right one.

On returning to the newsroom, Meade found Cam Fazzie lounging in his chair. His feet were propped up on the desk, a cigarette dangled from his lips, and dark glasses rested on the tip of his nose. A telephone was wedged between his shoulder and ear, a computer keyboard lay on his lap, and in his hands he held two black-and-white photographs. On the desk were two cans of Diet Coke and a half-eaten sandwich.

Meade's appearance led to a sudden dispensing of phone, keyboard, and cigarette, unraveling of feet, clearing of desk, and finally, presentation of photos.

"This is Ama Siluma," Fazzie said. "A stable hand at De Greyling. The dregs from the arson squad are convinced the fire began in an area where Siluma's kerosene lamp was discovered, a long way from the grooming room where it was supposed to be. The egg suckers from Security have, in turn, latched onto the idea that not only might they have an arsonist on their hands, but maybe, just maybe, there's a connection between Siluma and our four dead heroes."

Fazzie threw up his hands; he gestured toward the coffee machine at the end of the hall, and was gone. Meade studied the photos. He identified the one as a duplicate from the once infamous, though now defunct, passbook. The other was from the files of current identity cards issued to all South Africans. The card stated Ama Siluma's age as twenty-six. He looked like a teenager.

When Fazzie returned, Meade held the photos up. "Guess who Security's pyromaniac is? The same kid who risked his neck last night saving twenty-three of Sir Greyling's workhorses."

"Lost everything he owned, which isn't to say he lost much," Fazzie said. "Well, all except a photograph of the family he hasn't seen in eight months. He risked his neck for that, too."

"I'm curious. Does the person who starts the fire do that?"

Fazzie set a cup of coffee on Meade's desk and tossed cream and sugar packets next to it. Then he fished a brown paper bag from one of the pockets of his jacket. He laid it next to the yellow cigarette box at the center of Meade's desk. "I found this last night after you called. I have a hunch it'll tell you more than you want to know." Fazzie tapped the bag with his finger. "A little reading material. But not for here. And don't ask me where it came from. It's about as banned as they get, Yank, so tread very, very lightly. Deal?"

Meade drew the bag closer. Inside was a thin paperback. The cover was missing and the pages had been ripped halfway through. The title on the spine read, *The Ossewabrandwag and the Grey Shirts: South Africa and the Third Reich.*

"This thing with DeBruin," Fazzie said. "I have a feeling there's more to it than you're telling me."

"You must be a reporter," Meade answered. Then he told Fazzie the story of his father's death, and felt relieved for having done so.

In time, Fazzie said, "A hellish way to go. I guess it's a little late to say I'm sorry, but I am." Fazzie pulled up a chair. He glanced at the book. "I went through most of it this morning, and a certain G. DeBruin, no first name and no middle initial, was definitely a steamroller in the *Ossewabrandwag.* There were over three hundred thousand members in that upstanding group, Yank. Twice the number enlisted in the entire South African army during the same period."

"Remarkable."

"Ironically, G. DeBruin's nom de plume, 'Anvil of the *Ossewabrandwag,*' didn't come from the English, or the Jews. It came from a group of fellow Afrikaners. Afrikaners who evidently didn't see eye to eye with the local Hitler brigade. They called themselves the West Alliance. And according to this wee book here, confrontations between the two groups tended to be on the brutal side."

Meade shook his head. "I've never heard of the West Alliance."

"Probably not. It was Jewish supported. From Europe and the States. Small but well funded, the book says. Ready for the curiosity? One of *their* more prominent members just happens to have the same name as a certain art collector with a rather large estate just north of town."

"Greyling."

Meade tapped a cigarette from Fazzie's box, came to his feet, and crossed to the window. The obtuse reference to G. DeBruin did not surprise him; the use of initials was typically Afrikaner. Picturing Sir Cas Greyling in a Jewish-backed resistance movement proved more difficult, however. But what if it were true? The two had broken bread at the same dinner table last night. Could two men of such radically different backgrounds rectify those differences to the point of scooping meat and potatoes from the same platter?

"You could ask him, you know," Fazzie said, as if the question were written all over Meade's face.

Meade came away from the window. "What about the stable hand, Siluma?"

"No charges, no lawyer, no visitors." Fazzie shrugged. "I could talk to the stable boss. Probably the closest thing the kid has to a dad."

"Will he talk to you?"

"Hey, Yank, didn't I tell you? I speak six languages. For your benefit, English. For mine, South Sotho. For others', Zulu, Xhosa, Tsongo, and, of course, our beloved Afrikaans. Six."

"That's half the problem with this country of yours," Meade called out as Fazzie stepped into the elevator. "Nobody knows what anybody else is saying."

"It's the stew, Yank," Fazzie shouted back as the doors closed before him, "not the ingredients."

11

THE TWISTING MACADAM ROAD came to a halt a third of the way up the east face of Table Mountain. Bartleman's Ford was the only other car in the lot.

Here, the forest was thick with stinkwood and yellowwood, ferns and assegai. A hummingbird skittered from heath to orchid. Meade heard the barking of baboons the moment he climbed out of the Land Rover. Then he heard his name.

He looked in the direction of the Ford and saw Bartleman climbing out, walking toward him. Was there someone else in the car with him? Someone hunched down in the passenger side of the front seat? The shadows made it difficult to tell, and a moment later Bartleman was taking him by the arm.

"Fogwell's clamped the lid down," he said, guiding Meade to a wooden picnic table. "And in this case, the lid covers a very large pot."

"You're jeopardizing yourself." Meade wanted to ask why, but didn't.

"When Security fumbles the ball, Michael, they cover their asses by eliminating the competition."

"Is that how it works? Fumble the ball and then arrest the first thing that crosses your path?"

"You heard about the stable hand." Bartleman tugged at his mustache. "Arrest is a little on the strong side. There's been no arrest."

"Detention, then." Meade's eyes widened. He didn't welcome these tentacles of suspicion; he and Bartleman had laid the foundation of a friendship over the last six months, but Meade also recognized that policemen didn't share information purely as a gesture of goodwill. It was a question now of testing the waters without giving away too much of what he himself knew. Which, he admitted, wasn't much.

He said, "Jacob. The fire at De Greyling last night was no accident. The paintings were there, at least some of them." And for effect he added, "I'd bet on it."

"Speculation is an editorial luxury, pal. That's not what I get paid for. It's not what you get paid for either, last time I checked." Bartleman sat at the table, forming a steeple with his hands. "Why? In the mood to speculate? OK, tell me. Why, if the theft is a money deal, and I can't think of anything else to call it, why trash the take?"

"Diversion."

"That's one hell of a diversion, all right."

Meade took a pencil from his pocket. He circled the table. When he rounded Bartleman's back, he glanced across the lot at the Ford. The sun had emerged from behind the clouds now, eliminating the shadows—but there was nothing to see. Either he was a victim of his own imagination, or Bartleman's passenger had sensed his own carelessness and hunched further down in the seat. Meade finished his tour. He took the bench opposite Bartleman.

In a casual, almost flippant tone, he said, "Then maybe our thieves were doing some business on the side."

"Right. And they were counting on someone on the inside to get the other paintings out later. Is that what you're saying?"

"If they knew the theft wouldn't be publicized. And if they knew their employer wouldn't find out."

"Good business, bad plan."

Meade changed directions. "What did Forensic have?"

"Not much that seemed worth much," Bartleman replied. He gave a dispassionate accounting. "Our hit man wore size 11½ shoes, very worn. According to the casts, he walks with a heavy instep, right foot in particular. Explanations? One, his shoes are a poor fit, or two, he favors his right leg for some reason. Which would explain the cane, wouldn't it?"

"Size 11½ shoes." Meade thought of Rita Hess and Terrence Greyling. Did a size 11½ shoe exonerate them? When Forensic explained the heavy instep as a sign of a poor fit, did that include the possibility of shoes two or three sizes too large? If either Rita or Terrence were involved, did the shoes imply an accomplice? Did Gideon DeBruin favor his left or right leg?

"And the murder weapon? The Walther?"

"A gun with no markings and no prints—I wouldn't hold my breath." Bartleman shook his head but didn't elaborate. "We're not particularly hopeful about the thieves' van, either. It looks like a township heap. In which case, we'll never know." There were as many cars in the townships of the Cape Flats as there were people. Half had been stolen twice over, and half were either permanent lawn ornaments or someone's living quarters. When Bartleman said, "In which case, we'll never know," he meant, "In which case, they wouldn't bother looking."

"The killer's car, on the other hand, was a full-size rig. The good news is that only two cars manufactured around here fit the wheelbase measurements Forensic came up with. A Ford Taurus and a Mercedes station wagon."

"And the bad?"

"Is that Cape Town is crawling with both. This one was practically new, though. Tires had less than a thousand kilometers' wear on them. A steel-belted radial manufactured in Port Elizabeth. Standard equipment on both." Bartleman's face twisted with indifference. His eyes wandered. "That's it, pal. Like I said, it's not much to go on."

Meade stood up and faced the mountain. He watched an eagle with something dangling from its claws disappear behind the cliffs. Bread crumbs, he thought. They were feeding him day-old bread crumbs and in the process confirming his suspicions. Meade was disappointed.

He said, "It'll take twenty-five men a week to track down that car, Jacob. So that's obviously not why you dragged me up here."

"Last night you called forensic specialist Peter Hawthorne at his home. You made an unauthorized request for his services, and he complied. Unfortunately, Mr. Hawthorne is no longer working for the South African Police Force—"

Meade turned. A spasm of anger gave way to self-recrimination. "No."

Bartleman sighed. "He was a hell of a good kid, Michael. One of the best. All you had to do was call me. I would have given the goddamn OK, made it part of the bloody arson investigation or some such shit. Now the kid's got no job and not much of a future."

"Where is he?"

"Having a cast made of Gideon fucking DeBruin's cane. Brilliant. Just fucking brilliant, pal."

"And was it a match?"

"Are you crazy?" Bartleman reined in his rising temper. "No. After all that, no."

"Then it was close."

"Similar, yeah. Similar. Like almost every bloody cane or walking stick ever made. Listen. The man was five hundred kilometers away from Cape Town that night. Some twopenny town called Klipplaat. I know; we fly out of the same airport."

"You checked?"

"Yeah, yeah, I checked. I respect your opinion that much, at least." Bartleman slapped the bench top and rose to his feet. "I like you, man. You're a wise guy and a troublemaker, and I like you. But you're halfway out the door. One more screwup and I won't be able to help you, and neither will Cas Greyling or St. Peter or the bloody man on the moon. Am I getting through to you?"

"I'm sorry about Hawthorne. Can you do anything?"

"I don't know. I don't know. I'll try." Bartleman met Meade's gaze and held it. "Listen to me, will you? Forget San Francisco, pal. Forget Washington and forget Los Angeles. Their rules don't apply here."

How to beat the system?

Last night Meade had asked himself if a twenty-five-year-old forensic scientist's telephone might be tapped just as a matter of course. Now he had his answer, and a case of paranoia too. His office phone was also being monitored, he knew that; his whereabouts might be, as well.

Meade parked the Land Rover in the dank caverns of the paper's underground parking lot. He hailed one of the company drivers, a Mike Tyson look-alike, and jumped into the backseat of a company Toyota.

"You're alone," Meade said, crouching down on the floor.

The driver understood; this was a game played daily by the *African Edition* staff, and on occasion even by white reporters. What didn't make sense to him was Meade's desire to be taken to the police station on Caledon Square. He took him there anyway, or, more accurately, to an alley a half block away. "Meet me here in ten minutes," Meade told him.

Five minutes later Meade was making his way up the police station stairs to the Forensic Department. He introduced himself to a plump, dark-haired secretary as Peter Hawthorne's uncle. He'd heard about Peter's dismissal and was worried. There was no answer at his home and no car in the garage. Had anyone heard anything? The secretary directed Meade to a friend in Fingerprints.

The friend turned out to be a lively young technician with a blond ponytail. Sharing Meade's distress, the girl suggested he try the university, where Hawthorne taught a twelve o'clock law enforcement class three days a week.

Out on the street again, Meade had the driver find a pay phone on Harrington, and called Sean's apartment. Sean was halfway out the door and late for an astronomy class. Meade explained about Hawthorne. Could Sean pass on a message?

At 2:45, Meade was back in the underground parking lot again. When he reached the Land Rover, Peter Hawthorne was sitting in the backseat.

"Cat and mouse, it seems," he said as Meade piled in.

"I cost you your job."

Hawthorne shook his head. "I could've told you to bugger off."

"You didn't—why?"

The forensic scientist shrugged. "I like my work, you know. Good at it, too. There's no glory or glitter. Just this magic we do. These minor discoveries that with a little luck might just set the investigator on the right track. The colder the trail, the more he leans on us. Forensic evidence is hard to refute in court, mate, unless it never makes it to court. The investigator is not supposed to decide which evidence the court should see. But it happens, and when it does, it rather makes a mockery of my work. Make any sense?"

"It makes sense."

Hawthorne chain-smoked. The scent permeated the interior of the truck, but Meade didn't have the nerve to ask for one.

"It's about the cane impression, of course," Hawthorne said. "The one by the house. What did they tell you?"

"Close," Meade answered.

Hawthorne emptied his lungs of smoke. He coughed and shook his head at the same time. "It's not that simple. Not that simple at all. You see, the ground outside the estate, at the murder scene, is a hard clay. A fact I wasn't aware of when you called last night. They used a dental plaster for the cast there; I might have done the same, though plaster of paris sets up a bit better outdoors. But the problem was more the depth of the impressions. Or *lack* of depth, to be more accurate."

"I heard that," Meade said.

"The ground is different around the house. Sandy. Who knows why? Mother Nature. So I used a paraffin and water mix. It's an old trick. Also, the impressions by the house were more pronounced than at the murder scene. According to South African law, the two factors together produce a margin of error unacceptable in court. Fine, I can buy that."

"But—"

"But in a case that's not exactly raining down with results, dismissing the possibility of a match, a reasonably high probability, in my opinion, makes no sense."

Meade was already climbing out of the truck. He leaned back inside. "I can have a job for you back in the States in five minutes. I guarantee it."

Hawthorne's eyes widened. He smiled meekly, hoisting his shoulders. "This is home, mate. Home. For better or worse."

There were two municipal airports within reasonable driving distance of Cape Town. The English used Claymore South; the Afrikaners, *Kaap Provinsie*. Meade placed his call to the latter from a phone in the Argus cafeteria.

He fell back on an old ploy. He used the name Sergeant Drew Ackerman, calling, he told the control tower, from Colonel Blair Fogwell's office in Caledon Square. "Can you tell me if Gideon DeBruin's flight from Klipplaat has touched down yet? It's urgent. Mister—?"

Always take names, his grandfather had taught him. People jump that extra inch when they know their name's being tossed around.

"Steyn."

"Mr. Steyn."

"Sorry, not exactly sure what you're driving at, Officer. Mr. DeBruin returned from Klipplaat yesterday morning. He hasn't come or gone anywhere today."

"That doesn't coincide with the flight plan Mr. DeBruin left with us Monday, Mr. Steyn."

"Departed Klipplaat from his private strip at 6:40 A.M. yesterday. Arrived back here at Cape Town 9:55, twenty minutes behind schedule. No stops. It's right here in front of me, Officer. I'd be glad to send it over."

"His private strip." Meade laughed, one working stiff to another. "I love that."

"It's called money."

"You got it. Any passengers?"

"Nah. Solo."

Three hours' flight time, Meade thought. The thieves were killed between 2:00 and 2:30. Which would have required DeBruin to make an unscheduled flight earlier in the night, as early as midnight, to a private strip near De Greyling. Immediately after killing the thieves, he would have returned to Klipplaat in time to satisfy the demands of his scheduled flight home.

Meade didn't stop at his own desk. He went straight to the Ghetto. Except for Mieta, the room was deserted. Mieta was tall. She could look Meade straight in the eye, and did so.

There was an initial moment of discomfort, and then

Meade held out his hand. Mieta's grip was strong and sure; he liked that.

"So?" she said. "Does this mean you approve?"

"I would have preferred a personal introduction."

"Sean was sure you wouldn't. He says you've gotten cautious in your old age."

"I'm disappointed," Meade told her.

"Maybe you and your son should get to know one another better."

There was neither malice nor condescension in Mieta's tone, merely observation, and Meade had no reply. What he said was, "I need a favor. And Sean probably wouldn't approve of my asking."

"Do we need his approval?" Mieta said. "I assume it's business."

"Fazzie and I are working on a story—"

"A story without much of a future, the way I hear it."

"I have reason to believe that a businessman named Gideon DeBruin may be involved. He needs watching."

"And you're looking for somebody with extraordinary cunning for the job," Mieta said. The comment produced a nod Mieta didn't return. Instead, she said, "Well, if I'm thinking of the same Gideon DeBruin you are, then it occurs to me you're also talking about somebody without an ounce of brains or the good sense to know a viper when she sees one."

"I'm talking about somebody with plenty of both," Meade replied.

Mieta's eyes never left him as she draped a camera over each shoulder, wrapped a scarf around her neck, and fixed a beret on close-cropped hair. "So I'm interested. So point me in the right direction."

12

THE SECURITY POLICE had paid two separate visits to Farrell DeBruin in Stellenbosch, but the visits were not what she had expected. Their questions had focused almost exclusively on the design and function of the security system in the gallery at De Greyling and on the contractors used in its installation. Information they could just as easily have obtained from Greyling himself. The possibility of her involvement had never been broached. The only one who ventured such a hypothesis was that half-starved American, the journalist. No, the police had come to give Farrell the message that she was not to comment on the matter of the theft or the gallery to anyone, the media above all.

Following their second visit, Farrell determined that a trip to her father's house in Sea Point was unavoidable. She had been assured, by her father's personal maid, that the master of the house was not expected until later that evening.

Buoyed by a Bloody Mary and two glasses of champagne, she left the museum in the hands of her assistant.

Two years ago Farrell had purchased a navy blue BMW in what she called "a moment of self-indulgence." Now she rarely drove it. The rusted-out Honda hatchback, she insisted, served her better anyway. Not that it *fit* her better. Farrell wasn't quite sure what, if anything, truly fit her.

There was only one road from Stellenbosch to the city, and that was a two-lane highway that wove between the bracing peaks of the Papegaaiberge. Farrell had never been able to figure out how she could blithely ignore these snow-dusted wonders but could never manage to block out the monotonous rows of tiny, neat houses that stretched beyond view once she reached the N2 freeway. It was called Mitchell's Plain, a modern-day township. Prefabricated cracker boxes. Four walls, four rooms.

Thoroughfares of unnatural width cut through each of Mitchell's Plain's sprawling neighborhoods. The anomaly was that only two of these corridors gave access to the freeway.

Farrell's father had explained it as a practical matter of security. In case of trouble, the wide roads gave Security Branch and the army easy access. Helicopter transports could land at any intersection, planes could taxi down the concourses, armored personnel carriers could roam with easy maneuverability and clear vision, and storm troopers could form impenetrable gauntlets between neighborhoods. In a nutshell.

Farrell took a fatalistic approach to her father's lessons. Life was short. You could run from the pain but you couldn't escape it, and it didn't make much difference whether you shared a single outhouse with ten other families or listened to the beating of your own heart, half-drunk and alone, in a house with five bedrooms. In a nutshell.

For the next ten miles, Farrell drove with her eyes locked on the painted lines of the freeway. Then she crossed the tracks into the city and exited the freeway at Canterbury Avenue.

It was Saturday; the streets swelled with life. Vendors sold dried fruit, handwoven baskets, African beads, and dyed cloth. A flea market sold Boer War relics and Mexican art, reconditioned furniture and used auto parts.

Servants and maids haggled in their employers' names over a colored fisherman's catch of snoek, crayfish, and oysters. A band played. Policemen peered from beneath stiff-brimmed hats.

From the top of Signal Hill, the Noon Gun sounded. A puff of smoke drifted skyward, and startled pigeons skittered from the cobbled walks to Victorian rooftops.

Western Boulevard led Farrell seaside around the Hill and skirted the Green Point Golf Course. Farrell had used the clubhouse there for a bracer more than once, and she debated the idea now. But she knew better. One always led to another, which always led to well-rationalized excuses for inaction.

The DeBruin house, a rambling half-timbered affair, was the oldest structure in Sea Point. Perched on a rocky promontory, it gazed out over the green waters of Three Anchor Bay. Farrell parked out back in the guest house drive, out of view of both the main house and the street. A garden vibrant with bougainvillea led to the side porch of the main house. She used her own key.

In the kitchen, the maids were busy polishing silver and laughing. A radio in the background played gospel music. Farrell walked into the glass-enclosed conservatory. She made straight for the portable bar and poured gin over ice.

Until yesterday, Farrell had forgotten the fuss her father had made when she mentioned that a lost work by the seventeenth-century Dutch master Jan Vermeer had been rumored found somewhere on the European continent last year. The painting was called *Two Women and Their Music*. It had been looted by the Germans during the Second World War from a Jewish financier named

Joseph Shapiro and was presumed destroyed during the Allied bombing of Munich.

Now she remembered. The occasion had been one of those rare dinners where family matters had forced a meeting. She remembered the date, mid-December, because she had spent the morning decorating her Christmas tree.

When she had told her father that Christie's in London would list the work in its "Important Old Masters" auction the following month, a seeming obsession was seeded. Oddly, though, it wasn't his fervor over the Vermeer that had taken Farrell by surprise then; it was his unlikely fervor over something that was also significant to her. The son of a bitch had always viewed his daughter's success with disdain, believing the art world full of petty nonsense, the perfect place for a woman. A painting, in his view, was a vehicle for profit—nothing more.

Never before had he cared about the painting itself, Farrell reminded herself now. Never. Still, she hadn't been so self-assured then. She had made it clear to her father that no museum in Africa could compete in the derby for this painting. It was one of only forty ever created by Vermeer, one of only two left in the private sector; it might go as high as twelve to fifteen million pounds. Her father had responded by telling her to reserve her seat at the auction immediately. Within two days he had produced bidding capital of twenty-five million pounds. A private donation for the benefit of the museum. Period. No questions asked. Meaning, Farrell had known then, the *Broederbond*.

It hadn't mattered; a Vermeer was a curator's dream, and with twenty-five million pounds it would be hers. Two weeks before the auction she traveled to London to inspect the work.

Eight days before the auction the painting was scratched from the program. The following day, a three-paragraph article appeared in the *London Times* announcing that Jan Vermeer's *Two Women and Their Music* had been sold to Sir Cas Greyling, of Cape Town, South Africa, for an undisclosed amount. The seller's name was not revealed.

Over time, Farrell had managed to forget her feeling of defeat—only to have it resurrected two days ago by the appearance in Stellenbosch of an American whose father may have perished at the hands of the Anvil of the *Ossewabrandwag.*

Farrell drained her glass. Her father's private study was on the second floor. The key was hidden in the base of a porcelain statue. The instant Farrell stepped into the tiny room she felt a moment of actual paralysis. This room—all oak and mahogany, leather and chintz—had been off-limits when she was a child. A musk of age and decay hung in the air. Her mother's portrait gazed down from above a rolltop desk, happier than Farrell ever remembered her in real life. The video camera in the upper corner of the room was a new addition, one Farrell had no knowledge of and never stopped to consider.

She closed the door.

A framed mirror hung on the wall opposite the desk. Farrell had discovered the *Broederbond* documents three years ago in the safe behind this mirror. Father and daughter had been arguing. Both had been drinking: standard fare in the DeBruin home.

Her father had taken an urgent phone call in the library. Left alone, Farrell had noticed the safe door, ajar. She had never forgotten the rubrics at the tops of those files. CELL 108—Members Only. A.B. CIRCULARS—Absolute Security. BANTU AFFAIRS—Classified. ANC DIVERSIONS—Immediate. ELECTION STRATEGY—Conservatives vs. Progressives. At least a dozen others. Sheer terror had kept her from opening any of the files then, but the safe's combination had been taped to the inside of the door. She'd never forgotten it.

The mirror was hinged on one side and held close to

the wall on the other by a magnetic catch. The safe behind was rectangular. Farrell whispered the combination as she maneuvered the dial. The wheel turned. With a sharp click, the safe opened.

Thick folders, some yellow with age, filled the silver interior. Four stacks. She took each of these and placed it on her father's desk. The file headings were familiar, but there were also two newly minted additions. POWER SHARING – Partial. EX. COUNCIL, A.B. – Absolute Security. The Brotherhood's Executive Council. Was it possible he had risen that high? Shouldn't she feel pride? Instead there was a very different emotion, and she suddenly became aware of a hollowness in her stomach, the dehydration in her mouth.

Farrell spread this last file out before her. The first rumors of the Vermeer's existence, she recalled, had been whispered in her ear by the curator of Cape Town's National Gallery last November. The occasion was the opening of the National Contemporaries exhibit in Johannesburg.

Farrell began with circulars dated the following January. She tried skimming, but found that impossible; the contents were far too compelling.

"Covert dialogue with the African National Congress must continue, while acts of terrorism, whatever the source, must be attributed to them without exception . . ." Circular #2331

"English speakers must be drawn back into the National party fold. In this regard, fear is our best ally. Selected acts of violence or destruction . . . in the heart of English-speaking communities, should facilitate this matter. . . ." Circular #2378

"New political strategies must be explored. . . . Publicly, we must begin a course of compromise, of negotiation. Privately, we must utilize this new flexibility to exploit our position both here and abroad . . ." Circular #2401

"The release of long-standing black prisoners must surely be considered. Age is our enemy in many of these cases, and the positive ramifications of Mandela's release, in particular, cannot be overlooked . . ." Circular #2421

By now, Farrell was feeling the effects of a morning's worth of alcohol, and a second gin from the liquor cabinet hadn't helped. The circulars were too numerous.

She forced herself to skim, and, in doing so, nearly overlooked Circular #2452, which read, in part, ". . . the receptacle within which the Missing Sixth is contained has been reported found. . . . We are informed that it will be sold at auction at Christie's of London on January 21st . . ."

Farrell read the words a second time, and a third. Her eyes drifted; on the desk was a photograph of her father. He was shaking hands with the prime minister and smiling with an unabashed delight Farrell couldn't recall seeing before.

She opened her purse. A gold pen lay on top of her datebook. A business card with Michael Meade's name on it lay beneath the book.

Now she was being watched.

Five minutes before, her father's limousine had dropped him, quite uncharacteristically, at the walk in front of the house. Now he stood in a tiny control booth in the basement, the monitoring station for the house and grounds. Gideon DeBruin stared unemotionally at his daughter's image and the curious expression on her face. And the other details: the opened safe, the familiar files, the circular she held in her hand, the stationery she scribbled on.

Then it came, the only emotion he had ever been able to identify. He called it emptiness and dread and frustration, but it always felt the same. Like a dead weight around his neck.

He watched his oldest daughter, now his only daughter, replace the file, watched her fastidiousness with the safe door, the mirror, the arrangement of his desk, the brandy snifter. When the study door closed behind her, DeBruin stared for many minutes into the deserted room.

Reluctantly then, he left the control room. But the dread had a cancerous element to it; it spread indiscriminately. He paused at the head of the stairs. A dull pain festered in his leg. He couldn't face the outside world, not yet. Instead, he stole away into the game room down the hall.

This was his room more than any other in the house; the only one he had furnished without some insipid decorator's advice. Ivory festooned the liquor cabinet. A brass lamp hung over the pool table. The trophies of a yearly safari filled three walls. He tarried, stroked the vast head of a sable antelope, brushed the fur of a black leopard, and with his cane touched the nose of a cheetah. Simple acts that buoyed him.

He strolled the length of the room. The back wall enshrined a fifty-year-old gun collection. So many he had lost count. The dueling pistols, the derringer, and the muzzle-loader were still favorites. The .22 long shot was his first, a gift from his father. The Vickers-Maxim revolver, his most recent. He took it from the rack. Flipped off the safety, checked the chamber, and peered with one eye down the length of his outstretched arm. Set his feet. Panned the room. Paused long enough to put an imaginary bullet between the eyes of a startled gazelle, zeroed in on the cue ball at the center of the pool table, and drew a bead on a brandy bottle at the bar. He turned on the gun-filled wall again; took out a phantom guerrilla with an automatic rifle in his hands, a pirate with the flintlock raised—and then froze.

The revolver dropped involuntarily to his side. He stared at the empty space in a case meant for four handguns. The 9-mm Browning, the 1930 Webley-Scott, the

World War II Mauser, the Walther P38. The Walther was gone.

"God in heaven." His fascination over the similarity between *his* Walther and the one used in the Greyling killings had been pushed aside by the more pressing matter of the painting. An underworld favorite neatly pared of its markings; that there would be two such guns didn't seem the most unlikely thing in the world; it was a killer's gun, after all. Now he stared at the empty hook and felt an overwhelming weakness in his knees.

13

MEADE WALKED THROUGH the news department to Sports. A stairwell took him down to the second floor and the advertising department. He rode an escalator to the clamorous room of computerized printing presses. Finally, he left the building via an underground delivery portal.

A delivery truck dropped him at a parking lot on Adderley Street, where a company car had been left for him. He ducked behind the wheel. Driving out to De Greyling, he kept a constant vigil on the rearview mirror while chastising himself for focusing too much attention on Gideon DeBruin.

Bartleman had stated that the killer wore size 11½ shoes, the shoes of a good-sized man. And that the killer walked with a heavy instep. Hawthorne, the forensic scientist, had questioned, if not refuted, his own department's assessment of the two cane impressions. If you worked hard, he thought, you could read a complete work of fiction into those lines. But the same magic could also be worked on the holes in Rita Hess's story and the idiosyncrasies of Terrence Greyling.

Meade turned on the radio, but he was in no mood

for music and immediately switched it off again. Yesterday, his own son had accused him of abandoning the values that had driven him all these years, and Meade had no legitimate retort. Today a bereted photographer suggests that he and his son are like strangers, and he changes the subject. Where had these twenty-two-year-olds learned to pack so much truth into such concise statements?

Meade rolled down a window. An ostrich, its slender neck pitched forward, raced through a herd of indifferent cattle. The estate loomed on the left.

When he arrived at the house it became clear that arson, or suspected arson, was serious business in this remote corner of civilization. Meade counted seven men in nylon coveralls, boots, and gloves still scrounging through the debris of the stables. One carried a portable air tank on his back. Another probed gridded sections with a hydrocarbon detector. Two others huddled under the rays of an ultraviolet lamp. As Meade stepped over a roped barricade he saw Fick, the team leader, poring over the dials and meters of a gas chromatograph. Meade peered over his shoulder.

"Most useful," Fick said, as eager for Meade's attention as he had been before. "This thing actually separates the different elements of almost any damn thing you can think of and then tells you exactly what it is."

"Impressive. And?"

"Suffice it to say that it was a proper good night for a fire. A breeze that would have brought a young maiden's hair to life without creating a fuss, and, for just that essential dose of intrigue, a threat of rain."

"And the building?"

"Open to the air. Excellent ventilation. No glass, no aluminum. Seasoned wood, sawdust, hay. A veritable field day." A note of approbation infected Fick's voice. He removed a glove and scratched an ear. "Oh, did I mention the bromine and lead compound we discovered?"

121

Fick gestured like a proud father at another toy of the trade. He called it an electron spectrometer. Meade sighed.

"Leaded gasoline," Fick said. "The lead and bromine aren't susceptible to evaporation."

"No, you didn't mention that."

Fick was delighted. "Then I don't suppose I mentioned the kerosene either, did I?"

"I'm aware of certain deductions being drawn from a certain kerosene lamp—"

"Security's deductions, Mr. Meade, not mine." Fick was not to be deterred. He used his fingers to count. "Gasoline, kerosene, and, momentarily baffling, a trace of something else."

"Another accelerant?"

Fick answered by saying, "Come, Mr. Meade. We have something for you." They stepped back over the barricade again and stopped at the opened doors of a small panel truck. From inside, the arson inspector retrieved two rectangular tin boxes, both closed and sealed with plastic. "What these contain, sir, is the closest we could come to anything resembling your framed canvases. We've taken samples for our own collection. As far as I'm concerned, what's left is yours to have and hold."

"Where?"

"We were lucky." Fick gestured with a gloved hand toward the charred stubble of two stall walls. "The soil between the panels was soft enough to absorb a centimeter or two of whatever it is you have there."

"Then it was arson."

"Much too early to tell," Fick replied firmly. "So sorry."

"Off the record, Mr. Fick. An educated guess from a man of expertise."

Fick surveyed the grounds. "Arson. Yes. And a thorough job of it, too."

122

Meade noticed the motorcycle as he entered the city on the N7 freeway. It was a touring bike; the rider wore a gold helmet. Meade went straight to the Argus Building. Twenty minutes later, a company car filled with night reporters dropped him in the Malay Quarter. It was nearly dark. The muezzin sounded from the tower of a stone minaret, calling the faithful to prayer.

Meade peered through the barred doors of Nico Mustapha's studio and caught sight of the restorer in an alcove reciting *Salat*. He waited. It was only a moment before Nico pattered to the door.

"Come in. Welcome," he said.

"I disturbed you," Meade said. "My apologies."

Nico's smile was genuine. "Evening prayer becomes a habit. Habits become acts without meaning. A disturbance adds appreciation." He smiled again, this time turning an eye to the rectangular tins in Meade's hands. "My day has been terribly uneventful up to now; are you about to do something about that?"

Meade deposited the tin boxes on the corner of a crowded workbench. He broke the seal on the first, and a musty ash scent leaked out; inside it looked as if someone had shoveled the remains of a fireplace into the box. "I have a theory—" Meade began.

"You seem to be a man of many theories."

"Theories more like hunches," Meade admitted. Pacing, he absorbed the pungent smell of mineral spirits, stared into the eyes of a Chardin portrait, and stroked the handle of a salt-fired wine carafe. "Which is to say, these boxes may contain the remains of Sir Cas Greyling's stolen paintings. Or of some of them, at least."

Nico's eyes fluttered. Meade told him about the fire the night before.

"And you, trusting soul, would like me to give credence to your theory," Nico suggested.

"Yes."

"These—" Nico hoisted each container in turn "—should, I suspect, be in the hands of the police and their Forensic Department. Proper channels, you Americans call it."

"I was assured by a certain arson inspector that the police have what they need. As for the quality of their forensic lab—it's more personal prejudice than a lack of faith." Meade shrugged. "I prefer dealing with the best, is all."

When Meade got back to the newsroom, there were two messages on his computer. The first was from the *Chronicle's* foreign editor in San Francisco, Art Carpenter. It was a pleasantly worded reminder that his prison exposé was due for this week's Sunday edition, and a follow-up was expected for the next Sunday, as well. Meade may have disdained the computer, but he had fallen in love with the fax machine, and both his article and research notes were on the wire ten minutes later.

The second message read, "The Circle Club. 6:00–6:30. Meet me. Fazzie."

The Circle Club was located in Wynberg. Wynberg was a "schizoid suburb," so called because it straddled the *line*. White Wynberg, west of the line, was a nervous, spooky community of working-class Afrikaners. Meat and potato folks who didn't need a holiday for an excuse to hang out the flag. Identical row houses, boring in their loyalty to the color white, neat in their dedication to well-tended yards, were sequestered from the "other side" by a vast shopping center, which in turn was sequestered from the "other side" by fence-enclosed railroad tracks.

Black Wynberg, east of the line, was livelier: crumbling neighborhoods with broken sidewalks, postage-stamp-sized yards, wildflowers and weeds, bungalows melded of concrete and clapboard with corrugated metal roofs and miniature verandas. The denizens this side of the tracks were colored. *Colored* was a variable term, Meade realized, for some amalgam of white and black blood. The amount wasn't significant; it was a matter of the authorities knowing about the black blood.

The Circle Club was housed in a converted taxi depot. Inside, a gutted black and orange taxi was suspended from exposed rafters. Cigarette smoke mingled with subtle whiffs of hashish. A saxophonist improvised a sultry ballad.

Meade wove his way between vinyl-covered tables. Cam Fazzie was propped up against the back wall with a Coke in his hand. He looked relaxed, something Meade hadn't seen before.

Meade took a chair and raised an eyebrow at the surroundings. "You've decided my cultural repertoire needs expanding."

"Fazzie was hungry. He also felt like sitting down. You tell Fazzie where he can do both at the same time in your part of town."

What do you say to that? Meade thought. There were three half-empty plates on the table, a Coke, a coffee cup with traces of lipstick on the rim, and a water glass with slices of lime and lemon at the bottom.

"You had company," Meade said.

"You just missed them."

Meade gestured at the water glass; the lemon and lime combination was distinctively Sean. "Anyone I know?"

"I didn't mention that you were coming," Fazzie said. He was embarrassed. "I guess I didn't think you would."

Meade stared at the plates, sighing. "How's the food?"

Fazzie pushed his plate across the table. A portion of yellow rice was seasoned with cinnamon and raisins, and Meade found it disappointing. "It's missing something. Chicken, or crayfish?"

"I was hungry, remember?"

Fazzie tossed a pack of cigarettes in Meade's direc-

125

tion. A waitress hurried over. Meade glanced at the table next to theirs. A goblet of red wine, two empty shot glasses, and a mug of beer. It was that time of night; clammy hands, a thick tongue, and a dampness beneath his clothes that wasn't the heat: the diabolical registering of an old feeling. The *need* for a drink. Not the urge, for the urge was a constant. The need. It happened every night; some nights were worse than others, and this was one of those. The simplest question—why?—produced the simplest of lies: the events of the day, a lack of sleep, dead ends. Lies. Still, he hung on to the lies even as the need festered. He ordered coffee and grimaced.

Fazzie drew a piece of paper from his shirt pocket. "This was on your desk. Feedback from the arson inspector. Fick. I took the liberty."

Meade nodded. "The other accelerant."

"Liquid benzol. It's an industrial chemical. Used in making varnishes and lacquers and dyes. Stuff like that. Very flammable, very poisonous. According to your Mr. Fick, not an over-the-counter item. Rather, a licensed purchase through a licensed wholesaler."

"Where does that leave the stable hand, Ama Siluma?"

"Siluma doesn't have a driver's license, much less a manufacturer's license. Understand. Siluma is Shangaan. They're a docile people, Yank. Your salt-of-the-earth type. I got some history from the stable boss. Siluma was born on a farm. He knows animals, not chemicals. He can't read, so even if there was a bottle of benzol under his cot, he wouldn't know what to do with it."

"He's still being held, though."

"No charges, no visitors, no lawyer." Fazzie toyed with a straw. "Oh, yeah. There's another thing about the Shangaan, Yank. They don't fare so good behind bars."

"Who does?" Meade said.

Fazzie quickly changed the subject. "So what other

126

news?" Meade filled him in on what he had learned from Bartleman and Hawthorne.

"This egg suck drags you halfway up the mountain and tells you nothing." Fazzie rocked in his chair. "Then he hedges about the cane print. There's a message there, Yank. They're telling you that circumstantial evidence doesn't cut it with someone like Gideon DeBruin. And the police? They'll bend over backwards to make sure it never has a chance."

"Naturally we're supposed to take the hint."

"Naturally." Fazzie fished a piece of ice from Sean's water glass and held it to his bad ear.

"You all right?" Meade asked.

"I traded my hearing in for a lifelong headache. The doctors say there's nothing they can do. I'm used to it." Fazzie dropped the bloodstained ice cube back into the glass. "Every so often it ruptures. It's ugly, I know. Sorry.

"Anyway," he said hurriedly, "I spent some time this afternoon looking for a connection between DeBruin and Greyling. Some source of friction beyond their wartime differences."

Meade was still looking at the water glass; the ice had tinged it pink. "And?"

"DeBruin's fortune is in textiles. He owns forty-two knitting mills, sixteen cotton mills, two blanket factories, and a couple hundred thousand Angora goats. Greyling is a land man. He owns acreage and mining interests in all four provinces." Fazzie jabbed a cigarette at the pages in his notebook. "Both their families back in the old country, in Germany, have money coming out their ears."

"Politics?"

"Both National party. Nats, we call them. Greyling served in the House of Assembly for six terms. Liked to rock the boat. Try as they might, the Nats were powerless to unseat him; they used him as an example of their open-mindedness instead. DeBruin's sat on a handful of government commissions, but always by appointment." Fazzie rocked forward. "That's their pattern. Greyling the public servant, DeBruin the private entrepreneur. They're both on the board of an organization called the Heart League, a philanthropic group of some type, and reputedly as clean as a whistle."

"So they have money, power, and egos the size of San Francisco Bay. What about their spiritual lives? Dutch Reformed?"

Fazzie used a finger for emphasis. "DeBruin wears it on his sleeve. He's an elder in the *Nederduitse Gereformeerde Kerk*: the NGK, to us heathens. Big, nearly a million members. DeBruin's on their Finance and Appropriations Committee."

"Greyling?"

Fazzie shrugged. "His family is German, his roots are Afrikaner, and his party line is the Nats. Therefore, his church should be Dutch Reformed, but it isn't. Being as Sir is such a liberal, I checked the Church of England, the Anglicans, and the Presbyterians. Nothing. So I reached back into the past and found a mother with the maiden name of Kramer—"

"Kramer's a German name."

"And sometimes Jewish. Remember the West Alliance—"

"From the war. I remember. Jewish-backed. And?"

"Synagogues don't keep public records of their members. But a friend ran a computer check on Greyling's income tax records. The month after he resigned from the House of Assembly, he wrote a check for two hundred thousand pounds to the Essenes Society. Know it?"

Meade nodded; a crooked smile played on his lips. "The Essenes Society. Very good."

14

THEY WERE CARELESS. Meade didn't see the motorcycle until the last second.

It was parked at the corner on the sidewalk. Meade recognized the gold helmet perched on top of the back-rest. The rider came out of the alley. He was dressed in blue jeans and a glossy black jacket. He raised the auto-matic rifle at the exact moment Fazzie and Meade reached the company Honda.

They were careless, but also the beneficiaries of good fortune. As Meade spun around, the headlights of an on-coming car threw a reflection off the barrel of the gun.

He grabbed Fazzie by the coat and yanked him to the ground. He saw an orange flash; the first burst caromed off the cement and sent a spray of broken concrete into the air. The second burst tore into the Honda's front bumper and shredded its front tires.

"Move!" Meade shouted and threw himself across the car's trunk, over, and onto the street. An onslaught of bullets followed. The Honda's windows exploded and glass rained down on the street. Meade dug the keys from his coat pocket and crawled along the side of the car to the front door. He reached up for the door handle, pulled it open, and scrambled inside. He glanced over his shoulder just in time to see Fazzie diving into a stairwell beneath the restaurant. A tracery of bullets followed him; sparks jumped off the guardrail protecting the stairs, and a pall of red dust rose from the brick wall behind.

Meade turned the key, and by some miracle the engine started. The motorcyclist returned his attention to the Honda now. He was thirty yards ahead, legs spread, the rifle held shoulder high.

Meade slipped as far down in the seat as possible and stepped on the accelerator. The two flat tires flapped loudly, but he aimed the car at his assailant. The last burst was short and ineffective; it tore into the headrest above Meade and destroyed the matting of the backseat.

The Honda jumped the curb onto the sidewalk and picked up speed. Meade peeked over the dashboard and caught a brief glimpse of the cyclist diving to his right. He heard a groan as the front bumper grazed the cyclist. He spun the steering wheel, slammed on the brakes, and the car slid to a stop. Out his side window, Meade saw the gunman limping toward his motorcycle. He threw the Honda into reverse and cut a half circle into the mouth of the alley. The car stalled. By the time Meade had it started again, the motorcycle was near the end of the block and accelerating.

Meade pulled up to the stairwell. He threw open the door as Fazzie clambered up the stairs, then bounded into the front seat. "I think we've caught someone's attention, Yank."

Meade was staring down the street. "We should be dead."

Fazzie's hands shook as he lit a cigarette. "Yeah, not much of a shot, was he?"

It took the police thirty-five minutes to respond to the disturbance call in black Wynberg. Meade didn't wait. He hailed a cab and gave the driver directions to the Malay Quarter. He got out two blocks from Nico Mustapha's studio. It was 9:30 when he knocked on the door.

A sheen of sweat coated his face as he replayed the shooting incident for Nico. "You're involved," Meade said. "I'm sorry. But you need to know."

"I've lived a long life, Mr. Meade." Nico gestured toward the workbench, and when Meade spied the contents of the two rectangular tin boxes his spirits tumbled even further. The debris he had seen before was now separated into charred particles of wood and blackened threads of cloth scattered over four sheets of sterilized paper. On the other hand, the slide samples and numbered strips of photographic film that surrounded a pair of high-powered microscopes offered a measure of hope.

"Your hunch is now a theory of some substance, Mr. Meade," the restorer said. "But as with most theories, we start with an assumption. We assume those in charge of the stable fire investigation to be both professional and thorough. If so, and the contents of the containers you delivered to me represent all that was lost in the fire, then we can consider ourselves fortunate. Take a look."

Nico gestured at the sooty material on the first paper, labeled "Box One, Painting One." He used stainless steel tongs to sift through it, and came away with a minute corner section of wood. "Canvas stretchers," Nico said, but in truth, all that remained were fragments of the tongue-and-groove joints that once held the stretchers at precise right angles.

"Fate presented us with a gift, and so it is only right to begin there. Please take note of the mitered tongues. There is no genius involved here, only a matter of history. You will see the tongues are three in number. Which might prove meaningless were it not for the fact that the three-pronged method of building canvas stretchers was unheard of prior to the late 1940s, and for some years

131

thereafter was purely an American practice. Does that tell you anything?"

"The Rothko?" Meade guessed.

"Ah, bright boy. *Wind, Rain, and Isle.* The only painting of the five done after 1940. The only one done by an American. Now observe. From the same box, but alas, not the same work."

Nico took a hypodermic needle in one hand and gestured toward one of the microscopes. Meade leaned over the eyepiece. A moment later he saw the tip of the needle expel a minute droplet onto a glass slide. He rotated the objective lens, and veins of red spread over a sea of milky white.

"Cadmium red," Nico announced. He held up a tiny swatch of blackened cloth. "And this is canvas. I used a vibrating needle to probe its surface for microsamplings of pigment. What you're looking at is the result. You see, it seems that in the late 1800s, artists and color merchants became obsessed with an idea prosaically dubbed 'a permanence against aging.' They were referring to their paints, by the way, not themselves. Everyone thought the problem was solved with the synthesis of the dyestuff *mauve.* Not so. The new synthetics were as unstable as they were unpredictable. Poor chaps never knew what they would get from one batch to the next. Cadmium reds changed all that; they were really the first synthetic dyes with both lasting color and uniform consistency. The year was 1909.

"Of the five paintings lost at De Greyling, only two were done after 1909. We know there were no cadmium reds in Mark Rothko's work. However, ten years after the dye's introduction, an Italian named Amedeo Modigliani, living out the last year of his wretchedly unhappy life, created one of his finest works. He called it *Young Woman in Red.*" Gingerly, Nico set the canvas scrap back on the paper. He said, "It's unfortunate, after all that, that no one will ever look upon that masterpiece again."

Then, with considerably less care, he removed the slides from the microscope and replaced them with two others. Onto each of these he discharged tiny amounts of fluid.

"We are into the second box now," he said. "Look for yourself."

Meade toyed with the eyepiece and adjusted the objective lens, and in the end could decipher only pools of clear solution. "Nothing," he said.

"For the moment," Nico replied. He used his tongs again, this time displaying, for Meade's benefit, a badly charred hunk of stretcher, a right angle three and a half centimeters across, and the precious morsel of canvas that dangled from it. "Oddly, the painted surface of this work revealed a distinct lack of pigment. Devoured, I feared at first, by the heat. I was perplexed—it shouldn't have been so—until I considered the works involved. Look again." To the pool beneath the left eyepiece Nico added a minute drop of chlorine. The transformation was immediate: particles of yellow and blue almost magically rose to the surface. To the second pool he added a tincture of mercury. Over a period of seconds, the solution began to coagulate, to separate and crawl. "Without boring you with the details, Mr. Meade, proof positive of the presence of some type of pulverized coloring matter mixed with gum. In a word, pastels."

"*The Ballerina!*" Meade exclaimed.

"1877. Edgar Degas."

The Ballerina was his treasure, Terrence Greyling had said.

In silence, Nico arranged a last series of photos, busied himself with another set of slides, and eventually said, "I'm sure you know, Mr. Meade, that for centuries now, artists have been treating their canvases with what we call *grounds*. A ground protects the canvas and gives it surface. Nothing more. The Italians preferred a mixture of gypsum and glue; we call it gesso. In northern Europe they mixed chalk with an animal glue or, in some cases, resin oil. Others advocated the use of lead white. But remember that prior to 1850, only natural sources of chalk were used, from Troyes or Rouen or Orléans. Yes? And then, along came the stodgy old English. What did they do? They proceeded to develop an artificial substitute, made from calcium carbonate. Artists liked it because it gave a whiter, more homogeneous finish. But the scientists found something more subtle . . ."

Nico invited inspection. Under the left eyepiece Meade saw a uniform surface, like the desert floor. Under the right, an eerie crystal-like formation, very much alive.

"Natural chalk comes from marine ooze," Nico told him. "It's littered with the fossil remains of a million unicellular algae. Thus, the busy little colony under the right eyepiece. It's an old sample, from a Van Dyck I once worked on. The other, on the left, is from our fourth painting."

"Fossil-free," Meade exclaimed. He looked up from the microscope and pinned his eyes to Nico's somber face. "Post-1850, then."

"The Matisse. *Plum Tree at Noon*. Painted in 1899."

"Nico—"

"Yes, Mr. Meade. Five paintings. One survivor, at least presumably. Jan Vermeer's *Two Women and Their Music*." Nico removed his glasses. "The oldest of the five. Perhaps the most revered. Some would say the most mysterious."

The University of Cape Town's vast library facility showed its enthusiasm for learning by keeping its doors open until midnight on Friday and Saturday nights. Which meant extra hours for the staff: Sean worked the night shift every other Saturday. Meade's call found him doing double duty in both Humanities and Science. Meade spiced his request for more reading material on Jan Vermeer with enough intrigue to whet Sean's interest.

"Here's what I remember from the encyclopedia: he's from Delft, in the Netherlands," Meade told him. "He was born in the seventeenth century. He was a contemporary of Rembrandt and de Hooch and the like, which puts him in some good company. And some historians evidently consider Vermeer to be the best of them all."

"You're making me feel stupid."

"His output was limited. Which makes him very collectible, also very valuable."

"A natural for the De Greyling collection."

"Pull a couple of books off the shelves for me, will you?"

"Be careful," Sean said. "I might become unbored."

Unlike Nico Mustapha, his fellow restorer Miles Roundtree was a bit of a celebrity in Cape Town.

His gallery, across from the Cultural History Museum on Adderley Street, was both swank and austere. Nederburg wines were served by black men in tuxedos from 10:00 in the morning until 5:00 in the evening, whiskey and champagne until closing at 9:00. A Paris-trained luncheon chef created tantalizing delicacies five days a week. A trip to the Roundtree Gallery was an event.

His daughter, a failed artist, had taken over the gallery fifteen years before and discovered, in the process, her true gifts: salesmanship and theater. Miles still recommended the art; Allison, in turn, had a relentless flare for procurement and marketing.

At the Roundtree Gallery, an Alexander Calder mobile, reasonable at fifteen thousand rand, wouldn't last a week. A Japanese scroll from the Kamakura period commanded a price of twenty-one thousand rand. A stoneware jar by Bernard Leach could be purchased for a mere five hundred. A surrealistic fantasy by Max Ernst, on the other hand, would cost its buyer eighty thousand in pounds. The find of the season was a previously unknown Chagall, *Village Within a Village*. Allison had yet to set a price. She would, instead, field private bids before its unveiling next week and make a killing in the process.

It was all well and good. Miles Roundtree, now sixty-three, had taken it all in stride. The Afrikaners adored him. He was quaint, quick-witted, articulate. His name was on every social register in the province though he never attended any of the many parties to which he was invited. Allison, robust and undaunted, was his surrogate, and she loved every minute of it. On the other hand, the English-speaking community took a reserved pride in their countryman's success. Their quiet dinner parties were more to Miles's liking, and it was considered a major coup when he accepted.

Reputation, however, had not diminished Miles Roundtree's first love, restoration. Opening the gallery twenty-seven years ago had really only been an excuse for setting up his studio in the heart of the city. In those days the gallery was stuffed with consignment art from any painter or sculptor with a hint of talent. As he serviced customers Miles would be covered from head to foot with paint, the scent of varnish following him like a shadow.

These days, Allison insisted his visits to the gallery floor be rendered in a coat and tie, with his hair combed, and his hands scrubbed. A silly nuisance, the restorer called it. He would complain about the lack of atmosphere and excessive pomp, the muted colors and the coy lighting; but in the end, of course, he always did his daughter's bidding. He didn't mind. On the contrary, he was damned proud of her. The way she ran the place, her dedication, her enthusiasm; she always seemed to be having fun. They were a pair, father and daughter. Partners, and more than that—in her words—good buddies.

Still, his studio, now located above the gallery, was house and home. And as it did at Nico Mustapha's studio, a light burned late along the narrow stairs that led from the alley out back up to the Englishman's inner sanctum of restoration.

The beehive beneath him was quiet now, while "his" music played in the background. Rossini, Handel, Vivaldi. Allison called "her" music spirited, alive, a pulse that opened a customer's wallet. But Miles Roundtree had no use for the likes of U2, or Paul Simon, or Juluka. They all sound the bloody same to my ears, he thought, standing now with a palette knife in his hand, carefully mixing lead white with an antiquated blue called smalt. When the mixture was deemed a match for the palette of the eighteenth-century Venetian painter Francesco Guardi, Miles faced the painting. It was a badly scarred depiction of the Lagoon of Venice.

He dabbed a sable-haired brush into the paint, leaned close to the watery blue of the lagoon, and was a brush length from the canvas when a gentle tapping came from the back door.

Momentarily ruffled, Miles consigned his brush to the paint tray again and stood up. He was wearing a denim apron over a white shirt and bow tie. He hadn't heard the footsteps on the stairs and wondered why.

At the door, he peered through latticed windows and a steel-barred security door. The last thing he would have expected at this time of night was a woman, much less a woman dressed as this woman was. Her gown was long, midcalf, and hugged her body with a sensuousness even a man of Miles's age could not overlook. She wore pale gloves, a fur wrap, and heels. A lustrous string of pearls glowed at her throat. She smiled and nodded, gestures of recognition that only perplexed the restorer. Dark eyes widened, conveying need if not urgency.

The intercom had been Allison's idea, and it was at times like this that Miles gave thanks for her paranoia. He leaned toward the speaker and pressed the *talk* button. "Yes?"

"This is terrible timing, Mr. Roundtree. I'm sorry. I know it's late, sir." The speaker was well aware that the gallery downstairs would be closed the following day,

Sunday. She had waited, quite intentionally, until the restorer's daughter had departed an hour ago. Then she had followed her. Only when she was certain of the daughter's destination, the Roundtree weekend retreat in the Strand, had she returned. "Mr. Roundtree, I'm Rita Hess. I'm a houseguest of Sir Cas Greyling. Out at his estate near Malmesbury? I'd like to talk to you about a painting you restored for Sir Greyling. It was some time earlier in the year, I believe."

"I've only done the one."

"Yes, sir. The Vermeer. The painting was stolen two nights ago. Did you know? May I come in, please? It's a bit chilly this evening."

Miles Roundtree hesitated. The circumstances, he told himself, were worthy of suspicion. What was she doing here? And at this time of the night? Then he shook his head, chastising himself. She's a woman, for goodness' sake. And look at her, you old fool. He switched off the alarm and unlocked the dead bolt. A secondary lock released the security screen.

"Come in, come in." The restorer chuckled. "Excuse the precautions, won't you? I must be getting old, and there is no excuse for that, I don't suppose."

"Quite the contrary. You can't be too careful in this day and age." Rita flashed an ingratiating smile. "I'm the one who should be apologizing."

"A terrible shame about the—incident at De Greyling."

"Then you are aware of the theft."

"Not that it's a public matter, mind you. It's the trade, you see."

"Yes. And yes, it is absolutely devastating. You can imagine what Cas is going through." Rita removed her fur and laid it casually across her arms. She didn't remove her gloves. She surveyed the studio for cameras and found none. "I'm hoping it would be possible to see the photographs and X-rays of the restoration, Mr. Roundtree. Review your notes, perhaps? I know it seems like a strange request."

"For what purpose, Miss Hess?"

"Because it is quite necessary, believe me."

Miles returned to his palette. He was aware, at once, of a subtle hardening in his visitor's voice. "And *you* must believe *me* when I say it is quite imposs—"

"Your daughter. Allison, I believe, is her name." The blunt interruption stole the restorer's breath away. "She has a house on the Strand. A manor house on Percy Avenue, overlooking the bay. Correct me if I'm wrong."

Miles Roundtree stared with blurring vision at the Guardi, panic nibbling at his stomach. "You're quite correct. But I'm more than a bit confused. Is there a connection between Allison and Sir Greyling's painting?"

"Yes. Oh yes, there most certainly is. You see, I must tell you, Mr. Roundtree, that I am prepared to use your daughter as leverage in order to obtain what I have come for." This first statement rang with truth; that which followed, however, was a complete fabrication, though Rita's voice never varied. She said, "At this very minute, a man of very few scruples is with your daughter, at her house, no doubt sitting across the kitchen table from her. Should you cooperate in a manner that strikes me as anything less than satisfactory, my associate will remove Allison's left ear. Continued resistance on your part will result—"

The restorer held up a hand. His forehead and upper lip beaded with perspiration, and all color drained from his face. To hear such a thing about one's own daughter; he nearly lost control.

"Yes, I thought you would see it my way," Rita whispered.

She followed the restorer from the studio into his office: a cluttered desk, a swivel chair, bookshelves, and against the back wall a bank of wide filing cabinets. The

139

cabinets were organized by date only, each year carefully printed on a strip of masking tape and pasted across each sliding door.

Miles Roundtree needed both hands to open the drawer labeled "Current." Inside, the files were listed alphabetically by artist. It was the second-to-last file. "Jan Vermeer of Delft, The Netherlands. 1632–1675. *Two Women and Their Music.* Greyling, Cas T. Received Feb. 2. Delivered Feb. 18, 1988." The file contained a batch of meticulous notes, a series of colored photos, two pen-and-ink sketches, and a ring of color samples. Inside a separate manila envelope were the X-rays. This envelope was sealed with a simple string tie.

Defeated, the restorer passed Rita Hess the file and withdrew. On the wall next to his desk were two X-ray lamps. He switched one on.

"Is there more?" Rita asked, clipping an X-ray negative to the face of the lamp and spreading the photos over the desk.

"This is everything," Miles replied. He hadn't foreseen this lie, nor could he have explained the motive behind it. Yet he continued, "The painting was in remarkable condition for something of that vintage. All that was required was a simple surface cleaning and touch-up."

Rita scanned the restorer's notes, which, in fact, supported this diagnosis. The notes talked of test results, paint formulas, and procedural steps. She pressed the X-rays one by one to the lamp. Each took her, layer by layer, into the painting. The surface, the pigments, the ground, the canvas, the unground reinforcing canvas, even the stretchers.

"Where is it, Mr. Roundtree?"

Miles was momentarily nonplussed. The panic in his stomach crept now along his spine. "I'm sorry. Where is what? You, you can't possibly mean the painting. You don't think that I—"

He was silenced by the shattering of glass as Rita Hess slammed the butt end of a pistol, exposed for the first time, into the X-ray lamp. Glass exploded and rained down on the desk top.

"A man of very few scruples—" She used the phrase for the second time, "awaits my call. The time is 10:22. In eight minutes, should he not hear from me, he will act. And believe me, your daughter will experience a terror she could never have imagined. Neither of us wants that."

Miles Roundtree recognized a new emotion. Helplessness. "I must sit down," he said meekly.

"The Vermeer was fitted with a secondary canvas. A reinforcing canvas."

Miles leaned heavily on his desk. His lungs fought for air. "That is not an uncommon practice. The secondary canvas on Cas Greyling's painting was in acceptable condition. I never considered replacing it. Do you—?"

"There was," Rita broke in, "pressed between the original canvas and the relining canvas, a sealed envelope. Much like this one." She held up the manila envelope in which the X-ray negatives had been stored. "Inside was a document written in 1944. The seal on both the document and the envelope belonged to—" Rita caught herself in midsentence. "Where is it, Mr. Roundtree?"

"On my word of—"

"Don't for a minute think your daughter's life will be the first sacrificed in this pursuit. And your intransigence—"

Miles Roundtree pushed away from the desk. He struggled to his feet. "This—document, this incredible document that has caused you to violate my privacy and strike fear into the heart of my daughter, was not contained in the painting I restored five months ago for Cas Greyling. The X-rays you have just looked at were taken the day I received the painting, nearly a week before I laid a hand on it." Miles seized the negative which looked beyond the original canvas to the relining canvas. "Do you think an envelope containing one, or ten, or a hundred pages could hide from the eye of the X-ray? You could have seen the wrinkles on the paper. Do you understand?"

"You are a liar."

In despair, Miles Roundtree clenched his fists. "Think, Miss Hess. You have my daughter. Could any mere piece of paper compare to her life? There must be something you've missed, some alternative, some other painting. *Something*."

A sharp breath caught in Rita's throat. *Something you've missed, some alternative, some other painting.* The revelation nearly brought her to her knees. For a split second, a tremor shook her from head to foot. Was it possible? She scooped up the X-rays.

While she peered incredulously at each, Miles Roundtree stared bleakly at the hands of a nearby wall clock. It was 10:29.

"My daughter—"

"Is in no danger, Mr. Roundtree." Rita returned the notes, the photos, the sketches, and the color samples to the file. The X-rays she slipped into the envelope. She fastened the tie. The file she returned to the cabinet; the envelope she tucked into her purse. Then, to the barrel end of her pistol, she attached a five-centimeter-long cylinder. When the silencer was in place, she turned back to the restorer. She saw the horror on his face and felt the tingling of her own body.

"You've given me hope, Mr. Roundtree. In return, I'll make certain there is no pain."

15

IN THE DARK of night, the Honda felt like a cocoon to Farrell DeBruin. She was aware only of the road, the pitch black, the card in her hand. He lived in Muizenburg, off the southern flank of the mountain. It was late. This, she told herself, was crazy. She had been driving for hours, as far as Stellenbosch and then back again. She had stopped in Rosebank for a martini; it hadn't helped. Was it he, or was it her father who drove her on? She repeated the question and then answered with another. Did it always have to be her father? Did the son of a bitch have to touch everything in her life? Was she that bloody spineless?

The question was overwhelmed by a flood of anxiety. Would he have anything to drink? Would he offer? The thought made her sick. And scared her. My God, was she that far gone?

The village lights of Muizenburg brought a measure of relief but no answers. Muizenburg was a beach town of cobblestone streets and Victorian mansions, surf shops and antique stores.

As it was, she stumbled upon Lambert Street only because the turnoff basked in the yellow glow of an old-fashioned street lamp. The house was a wood-framed three-story that clung precariously to the hillside. It was dark inside. There was no car in the drive.

Farrell turned off the engine but didn't move. For the hundredth time, she asked herself why she had come. The answer, a voice of encouragement told her, was so close she could almost taste it. Something righteous, a new beginning. Something like taking a stand, for once in her life. But it was more embarrassment than rectitude that propelled her out of the car; if he was home, he had certainly heard the engine.

Slate steps led her past a waist-high fence and a lawn desperately in need of mowing, up to a boxed veranda. Even in the dead of night, the house had a neglected air about it. Vines impatient for spring covered the porch, where a broken swing dangled in a corner.

The front door was open, and Meade was standing in the doorway, a shadow in the darkened hall. Farrell gasped. "My God, I didn't see you."

"What are you doing here?" Meade asked in a low voice.

Farrell was a moment answering. "Your dream," she said eventually. "I was wondering if it was the masterpiece you thought it would be."

He held open the screen. "You remembered."

Farrell stepped in. "Remembered? I've been overwrought with curiosity."

"I was here, in this room," he said. "I heard a voice, in the kitchen, pleading for help. There was a terrible scratching on the walls, but the entryway was blocked. I started tearing the wall down, brick by brick. When I broke through, the kitchen was completely bare. All except for a magnificent yellow bird. I could see it was desperate to escape. And I could see that it was a simple matter of opening the back door. But what I saw most clearly was that the bird needed me to open the door. And when I did, it soared—like it was the first time."

Farrell studied him. Then she looked at the dark room, at walls void of decor, except for a solitary painting above an empty mantel. At the suitcase on the floor. At empty bookshelves flanking an unused fireplace. At a couch and chair and coffee table that didn't match and surely came with the rental. At a turntable and speakers and a half-dozen albums. "What does a man like you do for fun, Meade?"

"Fun? That's a seductive question."

"A journalist with empty walls dreaming of a magnificent yellow bird desperate for flight." She walked to the mantel. The painting above it was a watercolor of an ostrich herd in the last rays of a golden sun. "Almost empty walls, I should say."

Suddenly Meade was beside her, and he saw Farrell's shoulders tense. He tipped his head toward the painting. "My son, Sean. A good start, don't you think?"

"He has talent."

"He's lazy." Meade faced her. She crossed her arms. "You smell good."

"Are you going to offer a lady a drink?"

"We can't stay here." Meade walked quickly into the kitchen. From an otherwise empty cupboard above the sink, he took an unopened bottle of Russian vodka. This was his reminder, his temptress, his admonishment. He threw the bottle into the suitcase and closed it. He took Sean's picture off the wall.

"You're leaving—why?"

"You've put yourself in jeopardy coming here, Farrell." Meade handed her the watercolor. He hoisted the suitcase and a plastic bag filled with books and photographs. "We'll take your car."

As they drove down the hill into Muizenburg, Meade told her about the shooting. At the entrance to the local croquet club, he got out and opened a long chain-link gate. Beyond the club grounds, a dirt road descended into a copse of tall pines; the air was scented with them. The land here, Meade explained, was owned by the same woman from whom Meade rented his house; it was the off-season on the Cape, and she had offered him the use of her private beach. Meade often ran there. The sod house hidden among the dunes had once been the dwelling place of a former caretaker and the woman's lover. It had a bed, a couch, a gas stove, a stone fireplace, and windows open to the air. A tiny refrigerator occupied one corner.

Meade stacked the books and photos on the floor. He laid the suitcase on the bed and reclaimed the vodka. He filled a copper teapot with bottled water from the refrigerator and lit a burner on the stove. There was a single tray of frosted ice cubes in the freezer compartment, and he filled a glass with them. He poured two ounces of vodka over the ice.

"You've been here before," Farrell said, taking the glass.

"Let's put it this way, I prefer the floor to the couch." Meade watched as Farrell stood Sean's watercolor on the mantel. When the water started boiling, he made instant coffee. Then he sat on the floor and sorted through the stack of photographs, catalog reproductions of the Greyling theft. Finally, he laid them aside and turned his eyes on Farrell instead.

She joined him cross-legged on the floor. She held the glass to her cheek and said, "You're asking yourself why I came tonight?"

"I assumed you'd get around to it."

"You don't know me very well." Farrell drank and then drank again; then she hid behind a question. "So, have you always searched for stolen art, Meade, or is this a recent avocation?"

"Never." Meade shrugged. "Yours was the first museum I've walked through in—in years."

"Then why?"

"Insatiable curiosity."

146

Farrell peeked over the rim of her glass. "No, I don't think so," she said. "I think there's a yellow bird trapped inside you somewhere and you're trying to find the door. So why Cape Town?"

"It wasn't by choice," Meade said. He hadn't scrutinized a woman so closely in years; it was like free-falling. "My latest employers deemed it necessary. It wasn't exactly a demotion, they tell me. More of a reprieve. See, I used to drink on the job. Like you."

"Sorry it was a problem for you," Farrell said evenly. She focused on the books stacked on the floor at Meade's feet. Five biographies and one reference. Farrell was drawn first by the "Restricted" stamp on the latter, and then the title. *The Pillage of Europe's Great Art Treasures.* The author's name, Dr. Emery Shapiro, struck a chord, but Farrell couldn't place it. She searched for biographical notes but found none. There was no sleeve photo. Shapiro? When it didn't come, she traded the book for the photographs, arranging the five side by side on the floor.

Meade shook his head. "Forgive me. I shouldn't have said that. I'm not in a very good position to be judging anyone. And even if I were."

She looked up. She appeared ready to reply, eager to; when something—not control, Meade thought, more like a coiled spring that time refused to unleash—sapped her of the energy.

He told her about the fire. He mentioned four paintings, vaguely, and not by name. Arson, he told her, without mentioning his visit with the restorer, Nico Mustapha.

Farrell stared. "Are you certain?"

"I'm afraid so."

When she was able at last to shake herself free, Farrell gave her attention to the reproduction of Henri Matisse's *Plum Tree at Noon.* It was a mooring, and she clung to it. She said, "Matisse didn't give much thought to his palette, did he?"

Plum Tree at Noon focused on a solitary tree set along a grassy esplanade in Paris. The esplanade was surrounded by well-tended gardens and topped by a slash of purple sky. A clutter of bright, pure colors, seemingly indiscriminate in their selection, left the contents vague and illusive.

"Such is Matisse," Meade replied convincingly. "Color for its own sake. Like a spontaneous dip in a cold lake. Like running naked on the beach."

Farrell bit back a smile. "Meaning he was lazy, like your son." She tossed the photo aside. "Next."

The proletarian mother in Modigliani's *Young Woman in Red* was seated on a straight-back chair in the corner of a bare room. She wore a simple red dress. Her hands were folded in her lap. Her face and torso were intentionally elongated and narrow, her expression yearning.

"An amazing blend of tenderness and sensuality," Meade said. He saw Farrell's raised eyebrows. "The suffering of the world is reflected in those eyes. Like a Picasso, in his Blue Period."

"Like a Picasso when Picasso was eight, not blue," Farrell replied. She turned to Mark Rothko's abstract, *Wind, Rain, and Isle.* It was very simple, an overlapping of unequal rectangles in various shades of greens, yellows, and blues, all superimposed over a field of light gray.

"Mr. Rothko had an image of himself," she said. "Something about one man's attempt at changing the viewer's consciousness through color transformation."

"I can see it on your wall now."

"Of course. Right next to the Modigliani."

They both laughed. Meade poured another vodka for her and more coffee for himself. When he returned, Farrell was still shuffling through the photos, glancing at one, disregarding another, poring over a third. Was she avoiding the Vermeer? He wondered. Was it possible she knew? Was it possible she didn't?

Finally, she settled upon Edgar Degas's pastel *The Ballerina*. In it a solo ballerina, her arms outstretched, danced on a bare stage. Her white lace dress, rising like the wings of a butterfly, was captured at the height of a graceful leap.

Farrell said, "There's such movement in his work, such passion. It draws you in, doesn't it? 'Here, I'm an open book. Read me.'"

"Really?"

"Treat yourself, Meade. Look at the way he uses the light. Pure genius. It's as if a veil has been lifted from your eyes."

"Child's play."

"On the contrary." Farrell smiled, this time without restraint. "Bordering on child's play."

"I'll accept that. For the sake of our relationship," Meade said. He argued internally against the ongoing progression of a feeling. A feeling, he told himself, unappropriately tantalizing given the situation, one he hadn't experienced in a long time. If he were a surgeon, he would remove it. Meade focused on the timbre of a foghorn far out across the bay. History, he thought, looking back at Farrell, wouldn't allow it. Even if she could.

He said, "We haven't talked about the Vermeer yet."

Was the hesitation he sensed in her of his own making? Meade didn't think so. In time, Farrell took the reproduction of *Two Women and Their Music* in her hand. She drank and studied it at the same time.

Two women. The first was standing before an instrument called the virginal, a forebear of the harpsichord. Her back was to the viewer. The other was seated with a mandolin in her lap, an impenetrable gaze turned upward to her companion. In the foreground was a table, draped with a pleated cloth and adorned with a brass fruit platter and porcelain vase. A broad shaft of light filtered through a leaded window. A black and white tiled floor, a timbered ceiling, and a framed painting against the back wall formed a backdrop for the rounded women and their rich, flowing gowns. The I. V. Meer signature, with the initials in monogram, stood out in the top left corner.

The absorption Meade saw in her eyes said what a thousand words never could. She returned the photo to the stack, saying, "I think it speaks for itself."

She tugged at a loose strand of hair and rattled spent ice cubes, betraying her anxiety. Had she come, as Meade suspected, to talk about her father? If so, she seemed now to be slipping away. He tried to draw her back.

"Does this audaciousness about art run in the family?"

"Audaciousness?" The description surprised her. "Audaciousness *is* a family flaw, Meade. Trivializing art is what runs in the family—what's left of it. My father denounces art as a safe haven for homosexuals, Kaffirs, and the weak-minded. A good place for women, given the competition. Like using makeup. Unnecessary but tolerable."

"Speaking of weak-minded."

"Encouraging his daughters in art was one of Daddy's insidious ways of reminding us both how worthless we were in comparison to his sons. This was between drinks, you understand." Farrell hoisted her glass mockingly, but Meade could see that she hurt. "My sister, Shar, took the son of a bitch seriously. Five years ago, she chased down a bottle of Valium with a liter of vodka."

"Farrell, I'm sorry," Meade said.

Farrell was on her feet now, touring the room and touching the walls with an outstretched hand. "Do you believe in past lives, Meade?"

"I'm confused enough with this one."

"Something tells me I was once a knight in King Arthur's Court or a centurion in Caesar's army. Something noble." She stopped in front of Sean's painting again, and gently touched its surface. "Something tells me I must have screwed up pretty bad to have come back in this body."

Was she fishing for a compliment? Meade doubted it. It didn't fit. "I rather like that body," he said.

"What do you know?"

In response, Meade held up the reproductions. "I know you know more about these than you're saying. And I know you didn't come tonight to socialize. Even if I have enjoyed it. Every time you turned over one of these photos I could see it in your eyes. Unfortunately, with every airy comment, we made it that much easier for you to walk out the door without telling me."

Farrell drew a deep breath. She set the glass on the arm of the couch and started for the door. "Which doesn't sound like a bad idea."

"It won't go away."

She stopped at the door, eyes fixed on the beach and sea beyond. "You said four paintings. They found the remains of only four, you said. And the other? Which was it?"

"You know that already," Meade replied. He watched Farrell's shoulders sag, her head bow.

"You have a reference book there called *The Pillage of Europe's Great Art Treasures*. Have you read it?"

"No. Not yet." Meade thought of Sean's cautionary note, of the "Restricted" stamp. "Why?"

"Then you don't know about the author, Dr. Shapiro." It had come to Farrell only moments before. "Very much an authority on Hitler's art plundering. Very much an authority. You see, the Shapiro family were among Hitler's victims. Their art collection was worth millions. Jan Vermeer's *Two Women and Their Music* was part of that collection. But the painting was lost sometime after Hitler got hold of it. Eaten up by the war, most people thought. Its reappearance last year created quite a stir in the art world. I can't help but wonder if Dr. Shapiro ever even knew."

The screen door closed behind her. Meade listened to the report of her footsteps, the whir of the Honda's engine, and the ensuing silence. Then he walked back up the hill to the croquet club and the telephone.

16

THE GHETTO WAS MORE communal than the rest of the newsroom. Everyone used everyone else's desk. Computers, research guides, paper clips, aspirin, laughter, even sympathetic shoulders were all common property. When the reporters weren't in the field, which was rare, the room seethed with activity: ringing telephones, flashing terminals, chattering keyboards, voices raised in four, five, or six different languages, photographers and reporters endlessly on the move. It was the first place Meade had felt safe in the last fifteen hours.

"Have the police paid you a visit yet?" Fazzie asked him.

"I'm not expecting it."

"Good. You're learning. Want to speculate with me as to exactly who it is that's got it in for us?" Fazzie raised a hand. "Never mind. The list is probably too long. But we're close to something."

"Then we know more than I think," Meade said.

Mieta set a tray of donuts on Fazzie's desk. She dropped into an empty chair and swung her legs up next to the computer.

"Rumor has it that someone's playing rough." Mieta's

dark eyes studied them each in turn from beneath the edge of her beret. Then she drew a stack of black-and-white photos from her bag. She tossed them, like playing cards, one at a time across the desk. "Well, I'll tell you about my day. Take your minds off it.

"DeBruin's textile business is headquartered in the Malan Building on Foreshore. I picked him up there. He lunched at the Nashua Café a block from the office. His companion there was the Reverend Pieter Crous."

"Crous is the Moderator of the *Nederduitse Gereformeerde Kerk*," Fazzie interjected. He flipped the top on a Diet Coke. "Not to be undersold, Yank. Very, very powerful."

Meade studied the photo. "After lunch?"

"A straight shot back to the office, a briefcase in both hands." Mieta snatched a donut from the tray. "The only curiosity in his day was a hurried departure at about 4:15. A chauffeur, no attendants. He goes straight for Sea Point. They stop in front of a very simple manor house with about twenty-seven rooms overlooking the beach."

Mieta dealt Meade two photos, the house and De-Bruin, excellent clarity. "All right. By now I'm riding in the back of one of our delivery trucks trying to make my camera look like a Sunday paper. DeBruin gets out at the curb. Opens the car door himself, just like any stiff anywhere. Then the chauffeur pulls the car down the block and parks around the corner. Figure that. The stiff, he doesn't use the front door to the house. He goes through the garage. Twenty minutes later, a woman comes out." Another photo slid into Meade's hands. "She uses a side door, like the one at the front has some kind of disease."

"Farrell," Meade whispered.

Fazzie glanced at Mieta. "That's the stiff's kid. I think our American friend here thinks she's cute."

"Does he? Well, for some reason, Farrell's car is parked out behind the servants' quarters. She acts nervous. Uptight for some reason."

"The woman was born uptight, Mieta," Meade said.

"Anyway, she doesn't waste any time getting the hell out of there. DeBruin, on the other hand, doesn't make an appearance again for a good hour. When he does, he seems preoccupied. He dawdles on his way back to the car. Which, from my meager observance, is not his style." Mieta swung her legs off the desk, brushed crumbs from her blouse, and circled. She stopped behind Fazzie and leaned on his shoulders. "So I expect him to shake it straight back to the office; the man has workaholic written all over him. Not so. A couple of minutes later he's walking back to the house; less dawdle though, more purpose. The chauffeur puts the limo in the garage. The stiff, meantime, jumps behind the wheel of this shiny little Mercedes coupe. My heart's *bleeding*. And then he just drives, aimlessly, like it's a Sunday afternoon in November."

"That's springtime in this part of world, Yank."

Mieta ruffled Fazzie's hair and started throwing her camera gear together. "He uses the car phone three times. Short calls. The minute it's dark, he makes a beeline for Kenilworth. Guess where? The racetrack."

"The only people around that place after dark in the winter are queers and meth-drinkers," Fazzie told Meade.

"By now the camera's not doing me much good, but my eyes tell me the car he's pulling up next to looks very much like one of the blue bombers driven by our local police."

"Shit," Fazzie said.

"The stiff jumps into the front seat. They talk for maybe ten minutes. That's it. Is that the man's normal Saturday night? Who knows. You guys are the scribes; I'll let you figure it. Me, I gotta run. I imagine Mr. DeBruin makes an appearance at six o'clock Mass, and I'm not about to miss that."

Meade held up the photos. "How careful were you?"

"I used three different cars, the delivery truck, and a

155

lot of help from the boys in the motor pool." Mieta
shrugged. "The same game you're playing, Meade. Isn't
it fun?"

When Mieta was gone, and the Ghetto was quiet, Meade
tossed four thin files on Fazzie's desk. "Interpol's response to Security's information request about the four
thieves."

"How?" Fazzie asked, spreading the contents on his
desk.

"Bartleman."

Fazzie lit a cigarette. He scratched intently at the back
of his neck. "These people are feeding you information
about a case that's quarantined under the Police Act. I'm
telling you, Michael, they don't do that."

"Of course they don't. But it's their game. Their rules.
If I don't bend the rules, then I concede the game. And
I'm not ready to do that yet."

"OK. Fine. Just try to remember, will you, that this
isn't New York on a bad day. Or San Francisco during the
sixties. This place is a goddamn police state, Yank. They
not only open your mail here, they take pleasure in reading it. Taps on half the phones in the country. Files on
every English-speaker, black, Indian, and colored with more
than a fourth-grade education. And probably half the Afrikaners, too. You think it's just us poor black folk that's
been getting the shaft all these years? Well, think again.
It's every half-wit who sneezes out of the wrong side of
his nose."

Meade reached for the files. "I can understand it if
you're in over your head, Cam."

"We're both in over our heads, Yank." Fazzie was on
his feet. Meade could see the turmoil. The fumbling for a
cigarette, the broken match, the stick-man pace. In time
Fazzie said, "I only see three responses."

Meade opened the top file. He paraphrased. "Ari Paros.

Age 31. Born in Athens, Greece. A suspected member of the underworld there. Arrested twice, once in connection with an armored-car heist in Piraiévs, and once for political extortion. No convictions.

"These other two—Kyriako Castille and Nicholas Renucci—look like smaller fish from the same pond. Similar underworld connections. Burglaries, petty thefts, and three convictions for larceny. No indication, however, that any of the three have been involved in any kind of art deal before."

"So obviously your friend wasn't giving away as much as I thought," Fazzie said. He punched orange cigarette embers at the fourth file. The photo and prints of the quartet's last member had been returned labeled "Not Listed." The fourth man, in other words, had no record of any kind with any of Interpol's participating members. Meade stared at the face. The years—by Meade's estimate thirty-five or forty of them—had not been kind. But it was time enough, in any case, to have gained some experience, and without experience he would never have been hired for a job as big as De Greyling.

Meade stood up. He journeyed to the window. Outside it was a morning more like spring than winter. In San Francisco, he thought, they would pay a king's ransom for a day like this. For the first time in years he felt compelled to act; getting up in the morning had ceased to be a battle. He felt pushed. And he felt something else, as well. The urge to push back.

Rita Hess roamed the motel room with only a towel wrapped around her, her feet bare, her legs unblemished and muscular, her hair undone and wild from his busy hands. She pushed an empty ashtray across the dresser top, ran her fingers over the back of an overstuffed chair, and toyed absently with the dial on the television. The sound of his electric razor filled the air. Water splashed against the porcelain of the bathroom sink. She stopped at the window, drew apart the curtains, and stared out into a U-shaped parking lot. A car churned away at loose gravel. A Vacancy sign flashed orange and yellow below the motel marquee.

She turned, pressed her shoulders against the cracked plaster, and drank in the cool of it. His suit coat was hung in the room's only closet. The hand-held tape recorder, she knew by now, was in the left outside pocket. She had discovered it during their second night together. Mostly he recorded the less formal of his business encounters; she wondered if the other members of the *Broederbond*'s Executive Council knew he also recorded their meetings. She doubted it.

The problem had been devising a means of copying the tapes in the very few minutes when they were not in bed together. The motel rooms they used, at Rita's request, were always bed-and-bathroom affairs like this one—except for one time at the house in Sea Point—and it wasn't as if they hung around together once he had spent himself. Rita insisted they keep it brief.

The problem had taken less than twenty-four hours to solve. The day after she had made her discovery and passed the news on to her "associate," Rita had been presented with a microcassette recorder of her own. To the untrained eye, the modifications appeared almost childlike. Tiny jacks, connected to one end of a simple conduit, had been fused to the machine's microphone and earplug outlets. A razor-thin magnetic disk at the other end of the conduit attached to the head of the machine from which the recording was to be taken. This allowed the information to pass from one machine to the other in the time it took to fast forward both cassettes. Rita didn't know how or why, and she didn't care.

She heard the shower. She waited for the shower door to close and then scurried across the room to the closet.

She took the recorder from the suit coat pocket, removed it from its case, and laid it next to her own on the closet floor. Step one: check the counter on his machine: without fail the tape had to be returned to its original setting. Step two: check the tape speed. Step three: rewind the tape. Step four: attach the disk to the head. Begin. Rita counted off the seconds in her head, in tune to the running water beyond the bathroom door.

The second side was twenty seconds from completion when the water went off. She heard her name. *Don't panic.* The machines clicked off simultaneously. It took another fifteen seconds to return his tape to side one and run it back to its original setting. She heard her name again, louder this time. Detach the disk, close the machine, slip it back into its case, return it to the left pocket. The bathroom door opened just as Rita was burying her own recorder in the bottom of her purse.

She came off the bed. She walked with long strides toward him, her look savage and taunting, hands holding black hair at the back of her head. She stopped an arm's length away, lips parted.

"Do you want me? Right now? Here, on the floor." She let the towel drop, making no attempt to conceal herself. As always, she could see that the very sight of her left Gideon DeBruin light-headed. "Well? Do you?"

17

ON HIS WAY OUT of the building, Meade stopped at the international wire-service desk. He gave the woman at the desk the addresses of seven fellow journalists, all trusted colleagues, all currently stationed at various locales in the Middle East and Mediterranean. She promised him that a photocopy of the fourth, unidentified thief's face and Meade's request for assistance would be sent out to each of the seven within the hour.

He was stepping into the elevator when the woman flagged him down. "A message just came through the switchboard," she said, handing him a yellow piece of paper. *I'm at 771-0980. Use a public phone. Mieta.*

Meade took the elevator to the second floor and the "Emergency Only" stairs to the motor pool. Three company vehicles emerged on the street minutes later. Meade was in the last of these, on the floor in the backseat. Another car, a Toyota, had been arranged for him at a parking meter in front of the public library on Queen Victoria. Meade used a pay phone in the delicatessen next door to call Mieta.

After they hung up, he pondered the news of Gideon DeBruin and Rita and then placed a second call, to the local Lloyd's of London office. He was directed again to the Englishman, Mr. Plumb. Meade asked about the Vermeer.

"I'm sorry, but that type of information—"

"Strictly confidential, Mr. Plumb. You have my word."

"We examined the painting in London, naturally," Plumb told him after a moment's consideration. "The day before the sale."

"Then the painting was automatically attached to his policy."

Plumb cleared his throat. "No, actually. Sir Greyling allowed our sixty-day grace period to expire."

"Grace period?"

"Naturally, with a client of Sir Greyling's stature we don't press the formalities. The paperwork, and so forth. We allow sixty days during which the new purchase is attached retroactively to the policy currently in effect. The formalities are thus handled through less obtrusive channels, if you get my meaning. Neither Sir Greyling nor any of his representatives responded to our correspondences during that period. We assumed he had chosen a secondary insurer."

"The Vermeer is not currently insured by your firm?"

"No. No, it's not."

Meade pointed the silver Toyota north toward De Greyling. His resolve was to think the affair through from the beginning, but a woman changing a flat tire on the shoulder of the road made him think of his grandfather. "A woman who can't change her own flat tire deserves it," he once said. Meade stopped anyway. Grandfather also used to say, "A man without compassion is doomed to die in a desert of his own making."

Forty minutes later, Meade was standing in a glass-enclosed conservatory accepting a cup of English tea from Greyling's personal maid. Sir, she informed him, would be down in no time at all.

Ten minutes passed. Meade hadn't touched his tea.

He was leaning over an exotic orange blossom with silky-haired leaves when he saw on the shelf below a thick, worn volume with the words *The Mishnah* stamped across its cover. The Mishnah, he recalled, was the part of the Jewish Talmud that dealt with the ancient laws of Judaism. He flipped open the cover. On the title page was an inscription: *Dad, To the appreciation of our heritage. With love. Your son, Terrence.*

"It's called mimetes, Mr. Meade." The words came from behind and had the effect of rousing Meade from a shallow slumber. He closed the book. "Mimetes slendidus."

Meade turned. Sir Cas Greyling used an open hand to indicate the silky-leaved protea. "Indigenous to the Cape, I've been told. There's an old Khoisan folktale of one fateful spring long ago when all the plants of the Cape came to life. And in that one grand moment of glory, the protea were deemed king of them all and granted life eternal."

"That was before the Khoisans were so ungraciously wiped out, of course."

Greyling raised a bushy eyebrow and smiled dryly. "Unfortunately eliminating the Khoisans as possible suspects in the invasion of my gallery. Too bad."

"And the destruction of your paintings."

Sir Greyling looked genuinely startled. "The destruction of my paintings? If I may ask, what the hell are you driving at?"

Meade ran a hand over his chin. "Four of your paintings have been found, Sir Greyling. They were destroyed in the stable fire. The remains were discovered yesterday by Security's arson investigators."

Obviously dazed, Sir Greyling sought out the nearest chair. "How do you know all this?"

Meade described the samples he had received from Fick, the arson inspector, and his visit with Nico Mustapha.

"And this restorer, you say he's a Cape Malay?" The words were steeped in irony: a defense mechanism, Meade thought, that didn't suit the retired Minister very well. "And you consider his abilities superior to those of a major metropolitan forensic department?"

"At least more diligent."

"And you trust him."

"Our problem is not Mr. Mustapha's honesty."

It was curious to Meade how long it took Greyling to ask which of the five paintings had survived. And when he finally did so, it came across almost as an afterthought. His reaction to the news of the Vermeer was unreadable, certainly unremarkable.

"I'm curious about your dinner party the night of the fire," Meade said. "About your guests."

"It was a business affair and boring, Mr. Meade. Believe me."

"Indulge me," Meade answered.

"Twenty-one years ago my wife, Janis, started an organization called the Heart League. She had a partner, Lucy DeBruin."

"Gideon DeBruin's wife."

Greyling nodded. "Both deceased now. But the foundation goes on. We're funding a hospital in the bushland. And that's what dinner was about. Satisfied?"

"And your guests?"

The guest list included Johan Pelzer, president of the Carling National Bank in Cape Town, and the advocate Sterling Theron, both accompanied by their wives; the Heart League's cochairs, the Willem Muellers; a current Member of Parliament from Natal named Erasmus and his female companion; Gideon DeBruin and Paul Kilian, both unaccompanied; plus Rita Hess and Terrence Greyling.

"There are no suspicious characters in that lot, Mr. Meade. Rest assured."

This disclaimer struck Meade as curious, but he thought better of commenting.

"Tell me about the Vermeer," he said instead. "Your gallery doesn't reflect an affinity for the Dutch masters. Or, in truth, much of anything painted before the mid-eighteenth century."

Greyling responded to this by rising to his feet. He crossed to a portable bar near the door and splashed brandy into the bottom of a crystal snifter.

From the bar, he said, "No, you're quite right, Mr. Meade. I don't have much good to say about the early masters. Too damn theatrical, it seems to me. The Vermeer? I knew practically nothing of the man and little enough of his work until eight or nine months ago. A friend in the art world back home informed me of the availability of *Two Women and Their Music.*"

"A friend in the art world back in Germany? The Vermeer was an investment, then?"

"It's amusing, actually. I've been applauded by half the Afrikaner community for bringing a piece of their heritage home to them. A reminder of their roots. All that crap. Amusing." Greyling tugged on his brandy. He seemed to drift, to withdraw into a memory; the emotion of it was clearly evident on his face. "No, the Vermeer was not an investment, Mr. Meade. It was a power struggle."

And then he caught himself. He fashioned a droll grin and then an ineffectual laugh. "After all, Vermeer managed what? Forty works in his short life? Every curator and collector from Japan to America and back had their eye on that canvas. And would gladly have sold their firstborn to get their hands on it, too. It got the blood pumping in an old man again. And good Lord, why not? The man's considered a genius."

Meade didn't respond. Facing the windows, he held onto the earlier phrase. *It was a power struggle.* Yes, but not with any other collector, or any other museum. That,

164

Meade reminded himself, was only a competition bred of money.

He watched Greyling's reflection in the glass. The old man stood with his brandy in hand and a look of distraction on his face. Meade followed the look beyond the window to the formal garden. Rita Hess was there. Clearly, Meade thought, she had come straight from the motel. In her hand, Rita held pruning shears. The winter roses she attended to were ivory in color.

"A lovely lady, your houseguest," Meade said.

"Oh, she's a lovely one all right. Lovely indeed."

"I take it Miss Hess has great appreciation for your art collection."

"What? Oh, yes. Yes. She'll be pleased to hear the Vermeer is still with us in one form or another," Greyling said absently.

Rita and DeBruin. If one or the other had the painting, Meade thought, why was she still here? And where did that leave Terrence? Meade couldn't help but recall the falling-out father and son had suffered over the matter of extending Rita's visitation rights. Without preamble he said, "Is Terrence your sole heir, Sir Greyling?"

"I knew you'd get around to that question sooner or later, Mr. Meade." Greyling made a lengthy study of his drink. "There are family considerations, certainly, but yes, Terrence is my principal heir."

"He and Rita, I gather, are not close." Meade waited as Greyling studied him with new respect. Then he said, "Four months ago you refused Lloyd's of London's request for a biennial appraisal of your gallery. Your policy is in limbo. And you haven't reported the theft yet. Why?"

"Mr. Meade, I'm not certain what you're driving at. Insurance companies have a way of making mountains out of molehills where their own benefit is concerned. If my policy is in limbo, as you say, I haven't been informed of the fact. And it occurs to me—" Greyling set his brandy snifter aside and took Meade by the elbow, "that the matter of my insurance can hardly play a part in the pursuit of my paintings . . . painting."

"Do you now intend to report the loss of the four due to the fire?"

"Of course." A smile of paternal exasperation touched Greyling's lips. He was overtly leading Meade toward the door and into the hall. "Obviously I'm just not in as big a hurry as you are."

"Since the Vermeer isn't insured, to whom exactly will you report *its* loss?"

Greyling stopped suddenly, and then continued. "Lloyd's isn't the only insurance company in the world."

"I'll find the reason, you know."

"Which suggests that you'll continue looking into the Vermeer. Be it my desire or not."

Meade didn't offer a reply. At the head of the stairs, they faced off. He said, "Would you consider yourself a Zionist, Sir Greyling?"

Now there was no smile, and exasperation turned to indignation. "Your questions, I think, have gotten out of hand, Mr.—"

"In some circles of the world a two-hundred-thousand-pound contribution to an organization as radical, or at least as controversial, as the Essenes Society would be sufficient grounds for labeling one a Zionist."

The answer was indelibly etched on Greyling's face. "You are a resourceful man, Mr. Meade."

"One last thing," Meade said. "For curiosity's sake. Does your friendship with Gideon DeBruin go beyond the scope of your . . . philanthropic interests?"

"Why do you ask?"

Meade mentioned the cane prints at the murder scene and those in front of the house. "The police, for their part, insist there was no match."

"Then you have a suspect and they don't."

"You and DeBruin opposed one another in the war. Vehemently, from what I've discovered about the *Ossewabrandwag* and the West Alliance. An impressive hurdle for two people to surmount."

"I'll say it again, you're a resourceful man. What's your point?"

"I'm not sure."

Sir Greyling descended the stairs. At the front door he turned, eyes burning. "Hurdles of that magnitude are not surmounted, Mr. Meade, they're disguised. As fate would have it, our wives met. Long ago. For them, there were no hurdles. They became friends. Good friends who didn't need their husbands' approval. Leaving Gideon and I to tiptoe over the coals of a fire that time might choke off but will certainly never extinguish. Can you understand?"

"As I said," Meade held his gaze, "I was only curious."

18

THE SMELL OF INCENSE tainted the air in the stone chamber beneath St. Stephen's Church. Gold candelabras flanked an otherwise bare altar at the rear. The six men of the Executive Council of the *Broederbond* were all somberly dressed in dark blue or black. It was an apt look for a Sunday. Paul Kilian called it "the attire of presumed guilt."

But guilt was not the reason for their meeting here today, Kilian knew that. It was fear. Fear manifested in these men only by slight tics in behavior otherwise well-honed by years of having things exactly their own way. From behind the pages of his newspaper Kilian studied these tics. Harrison Venter, the chairman, was only half-absorbed in the task of preparing tea, and burned a finger in the process. Reverend Pieter Crous cocked an ear toward the stairs and the rectory above, despite the two armed men standing watch there. Johannes Van Rooy was scanning a three-line circular the Council had rejected a month before. Jan Hugo was staring back at John Calvin's portrait. And Gideon DeBruin, chewing thoughtfully on an unlit cigar, seemed focused on the iron shutters and ancient gas vents which, a century ago, caused many a condemned man to confront fear at another level.

Kilian stared at DeBruin's cigar. It was a Diego Royale. The cigar wrapper found two nights ago in the clearing near De Greyling, at the spot where the killer's car had been parked, had come from a Diego Royale. There was a partial print, the Forensic chief had told Kilian in private, but not large enough for identification purposes. Likewise, the comparison of the cane impressions was less than definitive. The police called the similarity refutable. They called the cigar wrapper unsubstantiated. But Kilian was not the police. As for the Council, he had not as yet discussed these matters: there would be, he thought, a more appropriate moment—a moment of greater weakness.

Now there was another matter. DeBruin's daughter had paid a visit to the house on Sea Point yesterday, and DeBruin had departed his office in an uncharacteristic flurry. Kilian knew this because it was only prudent, as he put it, to have eyes in high places. And he knew enough about this particular father-daughter relationship to be sure it wasn't an impromptu rendezvous.

Kilian set aside his newspaper. The chairman took his place at the head of the table. He said, "I talked to our people at Security. They're making about as much progress as we expected."

"In other words, they're making no progress whatsoever," Kilian intoned. "And our own investigation? Gideon?"

DeBruin lifted himself from his chair. He used his cane to guide him in a tight circle around the room. With his free hand he probed his jacket pocket and touched the *record* button on his tape recorder. "There was a problem," he answered.

"A problem?"

"With our team. A late replacement."

The Reverend Crous groaned. "Good Lord. What happened?"

"Did our people talk to the contractor?" Kilian asked. "Kanellos?"

"Our contractor knew nothing of the fiasco that followed the robbery. However, he did admit that one of the team was taken ill some thirty-six hours before departure. Sick enough to get himself admitted to the hospital. Mercury poisoning. Kanellos didn't know dog shit about the new man. Only that he was heavy into the Athens underworld, that his recommendations supposedly came from a couple of Athens bigwigs. On the other hand, the Athens police don't have a thing on him. Interpol, the same."

"Wonderful," Jan Hugo said, wheezing. "Just wonderful."

"We were infiltrated." The Reverend Crous spoke in a voice filled first with awe, then sarcasm. "Our precision machine, infiltrated."

"Very likely," DeBruin agreed.

"All right, then how?" Crous demanded. "How, in the name of God, could this have happened?"

Crous had been eighteen years old when the war broke out. His father organized pro-Nazi youth groups and outfitted them with red and gold arm bands and nightsticks. In 1944 Crous, fellow councilman Van Rooy, and three other comrades set fire to a Jewish safe house outside Pretoria. Sixty-eight people, twenty-five children, died in the blaze. Nineteen others were killed by gunfire trying to escape the house. For months after that, Crous's and Van Rooy's names were whispered in admiration by the legions of Hitler youth in Germany.

"Who, other than the six of us, knew?"

"Only the prime minister," Paul Kilian answered. "You know that."

"The six of us and the prime minister. Fine. Then how could anyone have—" The reverend took in his comrades one by one.

170

"Quite right, Reverend Crous," said Kilian, paving the way for a resonant silence.

The room was cold.

To Paul Kilian's considerable surprise, DeBruin told them about Farrell's visit to the Sea Point house and her untimely discovery of Circular #2452, the council's one written reference to the Missing Sixth.

"This is serious business, Gideon," the chairman said.

"She's read the words. She can't know their meaning."

"We were prepared to pay twenty-five million pounds for that fool painting. She knows that. Somewhere along the line she figured out the twenty-five was meant for something more. Now she has a name for that something."

"She'll confront me. I know her. And that will be the end of it."

"Are we absolutely certain she didn't know about the Sixth before? She is, after all, the one who installed the alarm system out at De Greyling in the first place. Has anyone bothered to consider that?"

Paul Kilian listened. He would not voice the obvious: that the risk was too great, that the words alone were enough, that Farrell must never be allowed to share those words with anyone.

"It would hardly be a grand deduction to put our failed attempt to buy the painting together with the failed theft," the chairman said. "Has she spoken to anyone about this? The American, for example?"

"Confiding in others requires trust, Mr. Chairman," DeBruin argued. "Farrell is not prone to that virtue."

"I wonder," Paul Kilian said. "Would it matter if Meade did know? He already knows the Vermeer is the last of the five. By now he's concluded there is something special about the work. He knows he's on to something. Does it matter if he knows there's an envelope hidden in the back?"

171

The Reverend Crous protested. "Broeder Kilian, his first order of business would be to find out what that envelope contained. And as soon as he knows that, then the whole bloody world will know. And where would that leave us?"

"His first order of business, Reverend, would be to find that painting before anyone else does. Which is exactly why we're using him the way we are. He's a reporter. Reporters don't spread news without their bylines running beside it."

"Let's take the matter of Mr. Meade a step further," the chairman said. "He has a son, does he not?"

"His name is Sean," DeBruin answered.

"Perhaps we should be keeping an eye on Sean."

Meade watched coal-black cloud banks marching like opposing armies from the east and west, bred by the power of two oceans, colliding over the peninsula. The earth quivered with electricity. Lightning stung the horizon. Into the heart of this storm Table Mountain thrust its broad back. Though the mountain was half invisible there seemed, Meade thought, a comfort still to its impenetrability.

He pushed the Toyota hard on his return to Cape Town. It was foolish meeting Sean like this after the incident in Wynberg last night, but, for some reason, Meade urgently needed to see his face, needed to talk to him.

The Clock Tower stood on the south arm of Victoria Basin overlooking Table Bay. As both lighthouse and timepiece, the tower had been a viable idea when it was erected in 1883. Now a neglected maritime museum, the tower rose from a stone base, three graduated stories with a pitched roof and weather vane over a glass-enclosed observation deck. A marble-faced clock read 2:13.

Meade's grandfather had discovered the tower thirty-five years ago, and since their arrival seven months ago, he and Sean had sat through a half-dozen storms here. It was a ritual that kept them mindful of the people and places they'd left behind.

Meade parked in a loading zone along the quay. Inside, Sean stood fixed to the window. A thermos of hot coffee rested on the sill in front of him. A bag of freshly griddled scones sat on the floor. He and his father drank from the same cup.

Storms like this one were therapy, a collision with memory. Their loss, Sean's survival . . . Baja California. Cabo San Lucas. Two weeks in the middle of October. Sand as white and fine as newly fallen snow. Deep-sea fishing, snorkeling, fresh albacore on the grill. No people. Late afternoon of the seventh day. Meade had been working on a short story he'd vowed to rewrite during the vacation. Mom and son had rented the small ketch from a local fisherman. They had joked about the fact that there was only one life jacket, and who would be the one if a hurricane hit. They had gone too far out, stayed too long. The storm roared down on them from the north, completely unexpected. Not a hurricane, but bad. Bad enough.

"I have this picture in my head," Sean said. "We're in the backyard together. It's fall. Always fall; it was her favorite time of year. She's wearing that huge red 49ers jersey you'd bought her one Christmas. Came down to her knees, almost. Her hair's tied up in a purple bandanna. You know how she wore it. Leaves are falling from the huge maple we had. We're playing touch football. Just the two of us. That's how I remember her."

Meade remembered that jersey, too. She'd wear it to bed sometimes. It seemed like he always wanted her when she wore that crazy jersey; it seemed like she always knew that, too. He missed the feel of her next to him, the warmth, the scent. Every bed he had ever slept in since had felt empty.

"She did have a hell of a throwing arm, didn't she?"

Meade stared out the window, his eyes set on the maneuverings of two tugboats and a passenger liner, his thoughts drifting. Time, he realized, had that effect.

At his side, Sean filled the cup and passed it. "I loved her," he said. "I still love her. But I don't miss her as much anymore. I go weeks now without thinking about it. And it's good."

"It is good, Sean."

Sean followed his father's gaze down to his wrists. He turned his arms over, pulled up his sleeves, and looked down at the purple scars exposed there. "We've never really talked about it, have we?" he said. "Don't you wonder?"

"I wonder, Sean. Every day I wonder. But I'll tell you what it's like. It's like holding a transparent bubble in your hands, and inside it is your whole life, staring back at you. And you think, If I make one false move this thing's going to pop. Logically, you know better. And you know it's not right spending your whole life watching every move. But then you think, As long as I've got this bubble, this life here in my hands, here where I can watch it, and tend it, and ignore it all at the same time, then I'm safe. For this moment, here and now, I'm safe. And that's enough. It has to be enough."

"Like if we talk about it, I might pick up that razor blade again," Sean said.

Meade drank. The coffee was hot and medicinal; the warmth settled in his stomach and spread. He looked straight into Sean's eyes and nodded.

Sean leaned against the glass, felt it vibrate, felt the moisture. "When you're eighteen, you can vote, you can drink, you can go off to college. You're a man. You're in control, you have responsibilities. You look in your wallet and it says so right there. Your parents say it's so, and so do your teachers. You can read it in the newspapers. Eventually you start believing it.

"She was my responsibility that day. I was glad, for that reason, that you decided to stay behind. Hell, she could sail rings around me; around you too, for that matter. I knew that. But not that day. That day, I was in charge. In control. Responsible. All that shit. Until that storm hit. When she tossed me that life jacket, I took it, Dad. *I took it.* And then to have the misfortune to survive. It was like this black hole opened up under me. The first time I looked in the mirror I knew surviving was a mistake. I couldn't find those razor blades fast enough. All of a sudden I was swimming in a pool of my own blood, and wondering how I got there. It's not your fault. It's no one's fault. I got lucky. It's over. I'd like it to be over for you, too."

"I'm making progress," Meade said. He took a scone and spread honey over it. "And getting advice from the most unusual sources."

"Mieta." Sean shook his head, but Meade could see the respect in his eyes. "She told me you two had met."

"She speaks her mind. I like that."

"She certainly does."

They both laughed. It wasn't the moment Meade would have chosen to tell Sean about the Wynberg shooting, but he had to be told.

"Is Mieta in any danger?"

"It's possible." Meade drank from the thermos. Then he said, "Your midterm break is only two weeks away. You were thinking of going back home for a few days, anyway. Why don't you do it now and—"

"Are you serious? *You're* staying, aren't you? Mieta's staying, isn't she? And Fazzie? I'm supposed to run for cover because you three are involved in a restricted matter? And then what? Come back when it's over and look Mieta in the eyes? Can't do it, Dad. You did a better job of raising me than that. Sorry." Sean reached for the scones, lifted one from the bag, and took a bite. He grimaced, dunked it into the coffee, and took another bite. He stuck a finger in his mouth, gagging. "You like these things?"

Meade took the scone, spread honey over it, and

devoured it in three bites. "That's the problem with you college kids today. No sense of adventure."

"Adventure! Eating something called a scone . . .?"

Meade dropped Sean in front of the university library. At the outskirts of Rondebosch, in an antique shop called Trinkets and Treasures, he found a pay phone. He called Bartleman, and the call was returned five minutes later. Meade felt like he was walking a tightrope as he asked about the getaway car.

"The closest thing Security's stumbled upon is the report last night of a stolen Ford Taurus station wagon. You couldn't ask for a better wheel dimension fit. Fogwell's got every patrol on the peninsula busting ass trying to find the thing. If it's not down in some ravine out on the Bolands, they probably will, too."

"Aren't you the one who said Security couldn't find a wet diaper on a two-month-old?"

"That's why he's using C.I.B. to do his dirty work, wise guy. Anyway, the Taurus is owned by a dentist. Lives in Clifton, a harbor town along the west side of the mountain. He and the wife were out on their boat for a couple of nights, Thursday and Friday."

"Do you have an address?"

"The dentist doesn't need harassing, Michael." Bartleman gave him the address anyway.

"Any report on the cigar wrapper?" Meade asked carefully.

"Cigar wrapper? What cigar wrapper?" Bartleman's confusion had a ring of truth to it, Meade thought. "Is there a prologue to this? Maybe an epilogue? Anything, just so I can know what the fuck you're talking about?"

"Friday night at the crime scene," Meade explained. "At the clearing, where the killer's car was parked, I discovered a piece of cellophane. It had an iridescent gold tint to it with a red and blue band attached. Very distinctive. I passed it over to a detective in a poorly tailored blue suit. The one thing we agreed on was that it had come from something smokable."

Meade heard the sound of shuffling papers. "You didn't think to get his name?" Bartleman asked. "Your detective in the poorly tailored suit?"

There was a hitch in the machine, Meade thought. Good. He said, "It's not important, Jacob. More than likely a dead end. Thanks for the news on the car."

Meade didn't know what could be gained from a confrontation with Gideon DeBruin. To see the man's face in the light of day? To bring to the surface his own unbalanced emotions? He didn't know. He was willing to use the cigar wrapper as an excuse—the cane impressions, even the fire.

He drove back to the city, left the Toyota in the Argus parking garage, and took the stairs to the first floor. He left the building again with a tour group from Sweden. They climbed aboard a yellow and blue bus. At the first stoplight Meade told the driver there had been a mistake and got out.

Across from the stop, a breadline formed at the entrance to a Catholic church. On the corner, a woman in a frosted sable coat bought seashells from a peddler on crutches.

Meade entered the Foreshore business district on foot. He met Mieta in a deserted office on the second floor of the Opera House, where she was peering through a telephoto lens the size of her forearm. She drank tea straight from a thermos.

"DeBruin leaves the house in Sea Point at 8:30. Clever me, I use a cab and almost miss him. He takes his own car again. He goes straight to St. Stephen's Church on the Loop. Which doesn't surprise me. It's Sunday, and he has an image to uphold. Fine. But he doesn't go inside. He

177

goes around back to the rectory. Goes into a side door. I couldn't tell for sure, but it looked as if it led to a cellar or basement. Something subterranean, at any rate. And he has company. Big-time company." Mieta opened her camera bag and dug out a proof sheet, twenty-four miniature photos on a single page. Of the twenty-four, she had circled six. She pointed to these, one at a time. "I had a friend in the photo library put some names to these. You remember Reverend Crous."

Meade nodded.

"The walking, talking corpse here is Hugo, Jan Fredrick. Chairman of the South African Broadcasting Company." Meade watched as Mieta's hand slid across the sheet. She continued, "Kilian, Paul Andrew. Owns the Central Bank of Cape Town."

One of Sir Greyling's dinner guests, Meade thought.

"This one's Johannes Van Rooy, the Managing Director of Transport Services. The mousy one's H. P. Venter. Harrison Penrod, to his friends. The chancellor of Rand Afrikaans U., in Jo'burg. And of course, the stiff himself." Mieta turned her eyes to Meade. "In case you're wondering, these aren't your run-of-the-mill, quid-spitting Afrikaners. Maybe you already guessed."

"Why the six of them?"

"All I have is newsroom speculation." Mieta shrugged. "You've heard of the *Broederbond?*"

"The name."

Mieta gave Meade ten minutes of background information. Then she mentioned the Executive Council, and then she tapped the proof sheet again. "I'm not saying it means anything, that it has any bearing on what we're working on."

Meade stared across at the building opposite the Opera House. Exposed aggregate and smoked glass. *The Malan Building* was inscribed in gold letters across the front. His vision blurred and a woman's face filled his mind.

Farrell. That there was a connection between their encounter the night before and the unusual activity at the DeBruin house in Sea Point yesterday was, in his mind, a certainty.

"He came straight to the office from the church. Hasn't moved a muscle since," Mieta said. She packed her gear. "I need some sleep. Let me know."

19

GIDEON DEBRUIN'S TEXTILE EMPIRE occupied the seventh
and eighth floors of the building named after the National party's first prime minister. Meade was led to a
conference room on seven with a smoky view of the sea.
The room was dominated by a glistening mahogany table
ringed by a dozen leather upholstered swivel chairs. Clean
ashtrays, air-conditioning, and a framed reproduction of
Pablo Picasso's *Guernica* contributed to its executive atmosphere.

The door opened. Gideon DeBruin limped in. Meade
was surprised by his powerful size. The flat nose and thick
eyebrows accentuated the width of the man's round face;
the close-cropped hair and jagged scar added ferocity.

"We've met." DeBruin made a beeline for the head
of the table but didn't sit. "—So to speak."

"At De Greyling. The night of the fire. I'm—"

"You're Michael Meade. You're a reporter for the San
Francisco *Chronicle*." DeBruin's voice droned with indifference. "Investigative reporter, so-called. Pulitzer Prize
winner. Alcoholic. Fired by the *Los Angeles Times*, put
out to pasture by the *Washington Post*, and tied to a desk
by the *Examiner*. Cape Town's your last chance. In the

last two months you've written articles on the decline of the National party, the growth of the white resistance movement, and the decay of our prison system. Now you're plying your diminished skills on the Greyling incident: for you, virgin territory. Wife deceased. Son studying telecommunications at the university here, a part-time job at the school library, an apartment on Kelsey Road in Rondebosch. He hangs out with a black woman from the *Argus*. Do we have that all about right?"

"Communications." Meade said the word as if he'd picked it out of thin air. "A field you specialized in for some time, was it not? In the Second World War."

Meade saw the contempt on the Afrikaner's face.

"So we know a thing or two about one another." DeBruin drew up a chair. He laid his cane on the table.

"Your limp," Meade said, making a study of the cane. It was finely tooled cherry wood with a narrow rubber tip. Not, he thought, *the* cane. "A war wound?"

"Yes, in fact."

"My father was wounded in the war."

"One of many," DeBruin replied. "Where? In Europe?"

"Here. In Johannesburg. He was a volunteer with military intelligence. Evidently there were people back then more interested in destroying the war effort than in supporting it."

DeBruin stared. "That was a long time ago. Back then, a lot of people perceived the British to be a greater threat than the Germans."

"And some perceived the Jews as the greatest threat. The *Ossewabrandwag*, for example." Meade took up a position at the opposite end of the long table. Then he told DeBruin about his father's discovery of the *Ossewabrandwag* safe house and the radio equipment, about the bomb that destroyed his automobile, and about his death on the operating table hours later. Finally, Meade took a

181

seat. "The story's been in my family for a long time. The bomb was concealed in a suitcase. They knew it was a suitcase because the doctors found a brass buckle embedded in the base of my father's spine. They say the man responsible was called the *Anvil of the Ossewabrandwag*."

"Like I said, that was a long time ago." DeBruin wrapped his fingers around the head of his cane. His eyes played across the table, less anxious now for the duel he had initiated moments ago, but his words no less forceful. "You lose a war, the first thing people do is make you out to be a monster. Suddenly, the enemy has only one face. Yours. But in our eyes, *they* were the enemy. War does that. It breeds enemies. In case you hadn't heard. Oh, sure, I know the enemy eats and sleeps and shits just like we all do, but he's on the other side of the fence and it's war. You think the Jews are any damn different, do you? Try selling that to the Palestinians over on the West Bank, or in some rat hole on the Gaza. In war you sit on the bastards on the other side of the fence before they sit on you. Oh, sure, sometimes women and kids and old men on crutches get caught in the muck, and sometimes it's the women and kids and old men on crutches who slip the grenade in your knapsack. That's the hard and fast of it. It's history."

"History says your side was wrong."

"We saw it differently. Believe what you want. We Afrikaners saw the English running our lives from the high seat of government and the Jews pouring in from Europe with their pockets full and ready to snatch up as much of Johannesburg as they could get their sticky fingers on." For a moment, an emotional glaze colored DeBruin's face, an ancient fury, but it took no more than a shrug and a scoff to wipe it from existence. This, Meade told himself, was not a man to trifle with. "Your father chose sides just like we all did. I assume, because he believed. If he believed as adamantly as we did, then he died well."

"He might have chosen freedom over genocide and equality over genetic superiority, but he didn't die well," Meade said.

"I grow weary of this exchange, Mr. Meade. If this has anything to do with your visit—"

"It has everything to do with my visit." Meade tempered the edge in his voice. "You possess a cane with a broad plastic tip lined with concentric circles. You carried the cane the night Sir Greyling's stables were destroyed. Thirty-six hours earlier, four men broke into Sir Greyling's personal gallery and stole five very valuable paintings. They didn't get very far. Shot to death. The individual responsible was carrying a cane with a broad plastic tip lined with concentric circles. Your cane."

Meade studied the face. Pursed lips, a twitch in one eye, an increasing pallor. The air-conditioning shut down suddenly, and the ensuing silence was complete. DeBruin moved uneasily in his seat. From the inside pocket of his suit coat he withdrew a cigar encased in gold-tinted cellophane with a blue and red band. He removed the wrapper, crumpled it between his fingers, and dropped it into an ashtray.

"Then I should expect a visit from the police," DeBruin said, striking a match. But there was no conviction, only distance, in his tone.

"It's not the police you have to worry about," Meade replied, remembering the company DeBruin had been keeping that morning.

"I spent all day Wednesday in the Eastern Cape," DeBruin said, incorrectly interpreting Meade's statement. "I have acreage and a mill near Klipplaat. Angora goats. Finest wool in the world, you know. I arrived back here in midmorning on Thursday. The airport will confirm—"

"I've already checked with the airport. They confirmed your whereabouts between 6:20 and 9:55 that morning. The trip from Klipplaat takes three hours. The thieves were killed at 2:00. Meaning you could have been there." Meade took his reading glasses from his pocket and laid them on the table. "And you had the other cane with you?"

DeBruin didn't answer, only fondled the handle of the cane that lay before him. He withdrew. His chin fell to his chest and for a moment his eyes nearly closed. He paled. Traceries of deep thought etched his face. And then he rallied. He opened his eyes and took a deep breath. In a single motion he was on his feet. He regarded Meade as one would a household pest and said, "I don't think we'll be discussing this matter any further, Mr. Meade. I hope you've got what you came for. Good day."

Gideon DeBruin returned to his eighth-floor office. A secretary escorted Meade to the elevators. Just as the doors began to close, he reached for the hold button.

"My glasses," he said to the secretary as she turned back. He stepped out. "I left them."

"I'll send someone," she said.

"Please, don't bother. I can find my way."

His glasses still lay on the conference table. The cigar wrapper was still in the ashtray. Meade retrieved both. He slipped the glasses back into his coat. As he laid the wrapper in the fold of his handkerchief, he noted the tiny black letters on the band: *Diego Royale*.

Meade stood on the walk outside St. Stephen's Dutch Reformed Church for a full minute wondering at his motives in coming.

The church was old, adorned with turrets, windows traced with wood and colored glass, and a crenellated roofline. It looked as much like a fort as a church.

He took the stairs two at a time. The doors were handtooled ash, and heavy. The narthex was tiled in marble. Flower baskets graced the entrance. The nave rose to a great vaulted ceiling, on which the war between Lucifer's fallen angels and Gabriel's archangels had been painted.

The tubular sound of a pipe organ heralded Meade's passage. His footsteps rang out in odd harmony.

An odor prevailed, that universal ambrosia which some higher order had reserved exclusively for God's houses. Meade had been brought up to believe that church was a place of worship, only to learn that men did wicked things in God's name. That God's will had been the rationalization for anything from demagoguery to slaughter. Yet the ambrosia of His presence remained; man had yet to exorcise that from His houses.

He stopped at the communion rail. Two women were adorning the altar with yellow carnations. A crucified and unhappy Messiah looked down on them with . . . with what? Meade wondered. Despair? Disappointment? Dismay?

He continued on to the sacristy door and went inside. Communion cruets glistened on a counter next to a jug of wine. An open closet revealed black and white cassocks.

The sacristy exited into a hall that led in one direction to the rectory, in another to a locked door, and lastly to a flight of narrow stone stairs.

The stairs were dark; Meade groped for a handrail.

The door at the bottom of the stairs was the same hand-tooled ash as those at the church entrance. Meade observed the lock and the skeleton key that dangled from it. He turned the key, pushed, and the door swung open.

The table. The seven chairs. The stone altar at the rear. The gold candelabras. The forbidding portrait of John Calvin. The nineteenth-century gas vents.

Meade stood at the threshold and stared. The lingering question of motive gave way—without much resistance, he noticed—to a tremor of excitement.

Allison Roundtree parked in a tow-away zone outside the gallery on Adderley Street. She was furious. As she stepped out of the car a spiked heel submerged in a muddy pool, and a vile litany, aimed directly at her father, poured from her mouth. It was sprinkling again. She opened a rainbow-colored umbrella. She walked briskly to the gallery's private entrance and pressed aggressively at the doorbell to his studio. She waited, pressed the button again, and then again. Age, she fumed, was no excuse for forgetting his own daughter's biannual Sunday brunch. Eccentricity didn't cut it, either. Lousy bastard. Forty-five guests, all expecting an appearance by the famous Miles Roundtree, and he doesn't even bother to call. Allison punched the button a half-dozen more times. There was still no answer.

She gave a restrained kick to the base of the door and then dashed back to the car. He was home, and she damn well knew it. She used her car phone to alert the alarm company of her momentary entrance into the gallery. They exchanged codes.

Two keys gave her access to the entrance. She reset the locks. The equanimity and order of the gallery rushed forward to greet her. Soothing. She stood for a moment absorbing calm from the marble tiles and polished wood. *Her* place. The hottest gallery in the country, and her name graced the entrance.

She hung the umbrella on the door handle. Finger by finger, she pulled suede gloves from her hands.

Then with a clap of high heels, she headed for the heart of the gallery. Casually, she ran a finger across the rough surface of a Siopis canvas, along the silver frame of a Wyeth portrait, and over the glass cabinet that protected a rare Vinland map.

For an instant, Allison thought she heard footfalls drifting down from the studio upstairs, but then the temperature-control system clicked on. A sedative hum filled the room. Suddenly there was no hurry. Her anger abated. She stopped at the front desk and tidied a stack of glossy brochures. She listened to a half-dozen phone messages, nothing urgent. Gloves and coat fell in a heap over the back of a chair.

She strolled toward the stairs, paused at the foot, and struck a pose of mock dismay. "Father of mine. Hey you, partner. You missed one hell of a meal this morning, buster, and I have no plans to forgive you." She waited, bit back a smile, and then said, "All right then, so play hard to get. Just remember, I'm not one of those prissy old maids you can charm with a smile and a swat on the ass. Are you listening?"

When Allison was halfway up the stairs, a blast of cool air swept over her; goose bumps rose on her arms. An overpowering scent of varnish and paint filled her nostrils. She paused again, arms folded now across her chest. "Daddy? Hey—what's going on?"

It took an effort to set her feet in motion again, and the shudder of fear that came over her as she climbed to the head of the staircase stole every ounce of air from her lungs. The studio was a wreck. Broken glass littered the floor. Pigments were splattered over wall and workbenches. Canvas stretchers and brushes lay in disarray, and shelves had been raked clean. Bolts of canvas were half-unraveled. Drawers had been rummaged through and their contents spewed from one end of the room to the other.

Allison teetered on the edge of the landing, gripping the railing, her knuckles white. Her eyes darted from studio to bedroom door, from darkroom to office. Oh, *please*, no. A hand, fingers grossly distorted, protruded from the office entry.

"Daddy?" Allison's voice was childlike in pitch and anguish. At last she moved, legs like rubber. When she turned the corner and saw the colorless form of her father, she froze; turned her head and covered her mouth; gasped. Then her knees buckled and she crumpled at his side, fighting for air. Finally, her hand moved hesitantly to his face, then gently pushed strands of lifeless hair from his forehead. An island of dark brown, dead center on his chest, stained his shirt and apron. A stream of blood ran dry at the corner of his mouth.

"Daddy." Her voice was hushed and nearly inaudible. She took his hands in her hands and pressed them to her lips. Her hands shook. Tears rolled down her cheeks. She lay down beside him, resting her head on his shoulder, and closed her eyes. She drew her legs up to her chest. Finally she opened her eyes again and caressed his face. Her daddy. Her teacher. Her best friend.

"You old fool," she whispered brokenly. "Who did this to you?"

When Meade arrived, the studio seemed shrouded with transparent bat wings, laced with a pattern of purple veins and a scrim of lavender and pink: the fingerprint powder and ninhydrin spray of forensic scientists under the hypnotic glow of ultraviolet floodlights. Voices were hushed: a time-honored gift to the dead. As if, Meade thought, a raised voice might somehow bring the poor devil back to face the day-to-day aggravation of living again. God forbid.

Bartleman was there, but there was no sign of Security. Miles Roundtree, Meade reminded himself, was white, yes, but he was also English. There were three other reporters on the scene. The event, Meade saw, was being treated as a normal big-city atrocity. The first thing he learned was that there was no sign of forced entry; the second was that the coded alarm on the back door had been turned off.

Surveying the corpse, Meade decided the restorer had died at the hands of someone who understood the art of killing. Looking at the random destruction of the studio, he also suspected the killer to be something other than a professional. If, he thought, the intended effect was to convince the onlooker that the killer was searching for something of value, then it made no sense that jars of paint had been indiscriminately smashed. If the intended effect was vandalism subsequent to murder, then why hadn't the killer smashed the Michael Cardew jugs that stood untouched next to the restorer's pottery wheel? If the intended effect was robbery for profit, then why hadn't the killer taken the Tintoretto or the Gainsborough which rested even now against the back wall?

Allison Roundtree had been taken to the hospital in a state of shock, and the gallery's assistant manager had been called in to help assess the damage. Most conspicuous were the defaced canvas stretchers that stood, even now, in vise grips at the edge of a workbench. Working photographs of the restoration in progress had been burned, and the ashes lay on the floor under the bench. Meade had been told that removing the canvas was the most common method in such thefts; and it made sense. Rolled and stored in tubes, canvases could be easily transported. The assistant manager told the police that Miles Roundtree had been working on a painting by the Italian painter Francesco Guardi, but that the title eluded her. To the best of her knowledge, it was the only piece missing.

Meade followed the Forensic team into an undisturbed bedroom. From the doorway, he made note of the untouched wallet and jewelry on the dresser.

The kitchen nook appeared unscathed, as well. A pot of tea had obviously been steeping when the killer was admitted. It was steeping still. Meade left the room shaking his head. A bitter taste invaded his mouth and heat seared the back of his neck. Welling up within him was the manic urge to hit something.

In the restorer's office, he stopped suddenly in front of the broken X-ray lamp on the wall next to Miles Roundtree's desk. There were no X-rays attached to it, but the lamp switch was set in the *on* position. Why?

Outside in the alley, a Forensic man was using ultraviolet light in search of footprints; he was frustrated. Meade stared down the length of the alley. He saw a stray dog on a loading platform, broken glass glistening on the drive, an empty panel truck, and four overflowing trash dumpsters. He toured, hands in his pockets, his mind absorbed in the matter of the damaged X-ray lamp. The switch. Wouldn't the restorer, out of sheer habit, turn the lamp off once he was done using it, or, at the very least, when his visitor arrived? Meade wondered. As a matter of thrift, if not practicality? And Miles Roundtree, if his bedroom and kitchen were any indication, appeared to be a man of both.

Meade was halfway down the alley. He turned back. The object a dozen strides ahead caught his attention only because of its high black gloss. He bent down and held it in his palm. It was the size of his little finger, gracefully tapered toward the center, with a tiny screw protruding from one end. A heel from a woman's dress shoe.

20

PAUL KILIAN, the youngest member of the *Broederbond*'s Executive Council and the least bound by its conventions, had told his people that Gideon DeBruin's daughter, Farrell, dined every Sunday night at a Stellenbosch restaurant called the Broken Bridge. It was located on the outskirts of town where the old Van Wouw Road crossed the Eerste River. The restaurant, Kilian told them, kept the same table reserved for Farrell every Sunday, without fail, at 8:15.

The target should not, he stressed, appear to be arbitrary.

The man was black, broad across the shoulders, with large, lively eyes and a ready smile. He parked his van in the delivery lot out in back of the restaurant. He knocked at the service entrance and waited. The river, a stone's throw away, rumbled hypnotically. Rain scented a quick and fickle breeze. He filled his lungs.

Today, he wore the gray overalls and blue cap of the Pen-West Restaurant Equipment Company. The service notice for booth number fourteen was signed, legitimately, by the restaurant's day manager. The man presented it to a member of the kitchen staff, who passed it on to a flustered maître d'.

"I don't know a blessed thing about this," he told the repairman, returning the order. "A window seal? That's ridiculous."

The repairman's smile was infectious. He pushed his cap down over his eyes. "Just think how I feel. I already put in ten hours, plus change. I know sure as anything dinner's cold and the old lady's probably already called me every name in the book." He chuckled and shook his head. "I can just about say good-bye to a tumble."

Earlier, another man—white, of course, since the Broken Bridge didn't serve people with black skin—out for a late lunch and impressed with the view from a certain booth next to the window, had popped the seal and slipped a simple metal shim along the frame. The fuss he had made over the draft—it had ruined what would have been an excellent lunch, he said—was directed at both waitress and day manager.

The manager's service request had been taken as a rush order by the equipment company. Their service vehicle had been dispatched and rudely sidetracked three hours earlier. Their serviceman, gagged and tied to a tree, had been replaced by one more expert in explosives than in window seals.

The repairman held the order out again. He smiled that same infectious smile. "Hey, *baas*, give a working man a break. Five minutes is all it's gonna take. That's a promise. Promise."

The maître d' sighed. "You'll have to wait until the table is vacant. Nearly done now, if they pass on dessert."

The repairman checked his watch. It was 7:35. At 7:52, he was ushered to booth number fourteen. Privacy walls shielded the table from all eyes except a discreet table for two across the aisle.

The package inside his tool chest was secured to a small square of plasterboard, which was in turn attached to a steel clamp. He didn't remove the package immediately. First he reached inside and attached the detonator wires to the blasting cap in the explosives. Plastic. A measured amount, he called it; his intent was not to level the entire restaurant. The woman was the target. The challenge was not to make a mess of it.

The detonator was controlled by an alarm clock. Simple and efficient. The repairman checked the time again. It was nearly eight. The woman would be ordering her first drink in twenty minutes. He set the clock for 8:45. He gave a studied glance to the underside of the table, then peeked quickly over his shoulder, slipped the bomb from the tool chest, and fastened the clamp to the table support.

It took two minutes to remove the metal shim and replace the window seal. At the kitchen door, the maître d' scribbled his initials across the service order and shooed the repairman out the door. In another two minutes, the man was peering with a satisfied smile into the van's rearview mirror at the rapidly fading restaurant lights.

Cam Fazzie had been watching Farrell DeBruin's Sunday activities since nine that morning. There was but a single development of any significance. At noon, a tan Ford had pulled up along the greenbelt out front. Two men. One, in a striped suit, entered the museum alone. His buddy strolled across the street and bought a candy bar and a newspaper. At 2:25, they traded places. At 4:45, the striped suit used the pay phone on the corner. Ten minutes later, they were gone. Not Security, Fazzie realized, but certainly trouble.

That aside, the gallery had been busy all day, with tourists and Capetonians out for Sunday drives. The lights had just gone off. Fazzie climbed out of the car and stretched his legs. This was not enjoyable work.

In the beginning, Fazzie had put in with Meade simply because the De Greyling estate represented a cornerstone of Afrikaner excess. To see it violated was to see it vulnerable. When it became clear that the government was manipulating the situation, Fazzie circulated the information via underground newspapers in both Europe and Africa. The introduction of the *Broederbond* signaled the government's actual *involvement* in the situation, and this was the most promising weak spot yet.

In the dark, Fazzie circled the museum. The architecture was simple and stout, very Cape Dutch.

The night revived him. The moon emerged as a concave shard amid islands of solitary black clouds. An owl perched on a fence post. Through an opened window he heard a telephone ringing, an impatient voice answering, and the quick dispensing of the museum's weekday hours. A convertible, jam-packed with college kids and spilling out the ragged sound of heavy metal, cruised Dorp Street. They had been at it for the last forty minutes. Now Fazzie saw the driver hold a whiskey bottle to his lips.

A door opened. The curator wore heels. Fazzie followed the sound down seven steps and across the employees' parking lot. A car door opened. The Honda. Fazzie decided he admired the lady's humble taste as much as the strut in her walk. The booze, though, that he couldn't figure; a woman with the world on a string. But that was a lie. Fazzie knew it. Everyone drank. Alcohol, above all else, was the entire country's suit of armor. He would have settled for a short one himself right at the moment.

Then he heard the squeal of the convertible's wheels, the wailing of its horn, and, an instant after, realized the Honda wasn't starting. At the far corner of the museum, Fazzie crouched down against the wall. He saw the convertible cutting tight circles around the Honda. Five guys with arms raised, hooting and jeering. In the driver's hand was a short rubber cord. As they passed next to the Honda's window, the driver slowed, made a display of the cord, and sped off again. The distributor wire. It was an old trick, Fazzie thought. Old and stupid. He stalled for thirty seconds hoping the joke would die of its own shallowness. They might even stop and replace the wire. She would take it all in the spirit of fun, and the bloody thing would be done.

Farrell climbed out of the car. A roar of appreciation told Fazzie it was a bad move. When the convertible slowed, he set off at a run for his own car. It was farther than he thought or he was in lousier condition than he figured, for his lungs were burning by the time he turned the key. Damn cigarettes.

Fazzie hit the parking lot with suitable theatrics, but he was scared; five whites and one lowly black in a town like Stellenbosch was a ready-made invitation for trouble. Two of them had Farrell pinned to the Honda's front fender. Fazzie hit his brakes and turned the wheel sharply, leaving the Ford an arm's length from the convertible's front bumper.

He jumped out with his press card and a notebook held high.

"Hey, boys," he shouted. "Cam Fazzie with the *Cape Argus*. This looks like one hell of a story in the making here. Mind if I take a few notes?"

There was a lull. The two who were holding Farrell loosened their grip and looked up. The driver climbed out from behind the wheel. He was Fazzie's height, stout and indignant. He took a long pull on the bottle. "Maybe you should move on, Kaffir boy. Unless maybe you'd like to be next."

Fazzie moved closer. He put his hands on the opened door and stared at the driver. "What did you call me?"

"Can't you hear, boy? *Kaffir* boy. I think that was the word. Yeah, that was it. Kaffir." He spit on the ground. "Now, by my math, it's five to one. And—"

Fazzie drove the door into the driver's midsection. The bottle fell from his hand, exploding on the pavement.

He doubled over. Fazzie took a fist full of hair and drove him back into the car. Then he slipped the distributor wire from his hand. Before the shock wore off, Fazzie said, "Four to one, boys. Together or separate, it makes no difference to me."

"Four to two," Farrell reminded them.

The boys shot wary glances at one another. "Let's shove this juke down a hole," one of them shouted.

The one on Farrell's right arm let go. "*You* can shove him down a hole if you want. I don't need my picture on the front page of some goddamn newspaper tomorrow morning."

The others hesitated. They watched their friend push the driver over to the passenger side. He climbed behind the wheel and started the engine. That was enough. The others scrambled into the back. A middle finger was thrust Fazzie's way as the car squealed away, accompanied by a fading shout. "Kaffir!"

When the car was gone, they faced each other. "I'm grateful," Farrell said, still shaken.

"Boys will be boys. Isn't that the saying?" Fazzie lifted the Honda's hood. "Some just more than others."

Farrell smoothed her dress. "And I'm sorry."

Fazzie peeked around the hood, eyes narrowed. "Oh, that. I've heard it before."

"Then I should apologize again."

Fazzie tipped his head. When the wire was in place, he slammed the hood and opened the door for her. The engine turned over on the first try. Farrell rolled down the window. "I was on my way to dinner," she said without thinking. "Why don't you join me? It's the least I can—"

And then, looking at Fazzie's face, she realized the implications of what she was saying. *"We won't be able to seat you tonight, Miss DeBruin. Your companion is black."* She saw that Fazzie was putting out his hand, and she took it.

"Stay away from convertibles," he said.

Farrell laughed. "Thanks. I will."

Vineyards, like swells of black water rising and falling in the night, covered the gentle slopes outside of Stellenbosch. Specks of red appeared and reappeared a half kilometer ahead of Fazzie's headlights. The pavement ended, replaced by a meandering oiled road. Columns of oaks signaled the erratic course of the Eerste River. The restaurant was a building of tall timbers and low, broad gables that brought to mind a Swiss chalet. From its several stone chimneys rose plumes of gray smoke.

Fazzie stopped outside the entrance, while Farrell left the Honda with the valet. A flagstone walk and stone steps led her to the door. She disappeared inside. Fazzie eased the car into gear; it was time to go home.

An instant later, a blinding flash turned the trees around the restaurant into filigrees of orange and red. The explosion that seemed a split second behind shook the car. Fazzie's first reaction was to throw himself on the seat. Seconds later he was outside, running against the flow of a panicked crowd. And when, amongst the exodus, he saw Farrell's willowy form, he found himself giving thanks for five drunken, overaggressive college kids and a game that almost went too far.

"Let me tell you a story," Meade said. He looked across the room at Farrell, cradling a drink. Her eyes sparkled with shock and alcohol. Meade could see that the fear had not really set in yet. He tried jarring it loose.

"It begins as far back as 1918. The cast of characters is a small group of well-meaning Afrikaners. The setting is a small town outside Johannesburg. These well-meaning individuals decide to form a club. You know the Afrikaners, they see the English with *their* clubs—the Freemasons, and the Truth Legion, the Sons of England—having a good time and making it stylish to be English.

197

The Afrikaners feel shunned, I suppose. Envious. So they start their own club. They call it the *Broederbond*. Strictly social. Picnics, croquet, Saturday night dances, to begin with. Then someone suggests secrecy. Sure, it's like being kids again. Then someone else suggests the club be more than just a club; that the brothers should do something to preserve the roots of their Afrikaner culture before the English turn it into a footnote of history. Still not such a bad idea.

"But before long, someone suggests dabbling in matters of business and education. Someone says that perhaps the brothers could 'encourage' the common fold to support the Afrikaner baker even if his bread happens to be inferior to the man next door's. They could start their own schools, and any of their neighbors who think their kids might receive something more at the school down the block—well, they'll come around.

"Time passes. Their membership grows. They get selective. They put their mark on the religious community. Sports. Art and music. Eventually, there's only one arena left. Politics. So they form their own party. They build a little confidence. They use the war to make the English look selfish. They adopt a philosophy that makes the blacks look inferior. They stoop to coercion. They win an election today, buy one tomorrow, and by 1948 they find themselves in control. And all the while, the club lurks in the background. They have their own mouthpiece now because the prime minister and his cabinet are all fellow brothers.

"They've discovered something that works. And they like it. The question is how far they'll go to maintain this control. At this point, it's only a matter of how far they *can* go. Blackmail? Financial brow-beating? Bribery? Threats? . . . Murder?"

Meade paced, viewing for the first time the house that Farrell DeBruin called home. A collection of antiques filled the room: a spindled rocker; a mahogany taboret; a Queen Anne bureau; a tall, graceful chiffonier; a damask love seat; a dining table scattered with art supplies.

"The problem with the club, Farrell, is that once the brothers take you into the fold, you're in. The demands along with the rewards. And, unlike you or me, the club allows only one loyalty."

"Good story, Meade." The glass was empty; she pressed it against her cheek. Her eyes, wandering, sought a focal point. "Lousy ending."

"Farrell—" Mead shook his head and turned back to the dining table; he was talking too much, a sign of frustration. He thumbed through a sketch pad filled with hastily drawn still lifes. Broken bottles, an empty china cabinet, a child's playhouse. He pushed that aside and found himself absorbed in a series study of a moored fishing fleet. Ten watercolors. Each different, each the same. All but two were conspicuously defaced by slashes of colored marker: "Too brittle," "No depth," "No feeling." Meade held the unmarked drawings side by side. He moved them into the light. Each depicted a sunset view of four trawlers at anchor on a placid sea. Mainmasts and riggings were delicate veins against a golden horizon. Ducks swam in the shadows cast by the ships' hulls.

Behind him, Meade heard movement: a light step, like one desperate not to disturb, ice cubes dropped individually into a glass, liquor splashed over them.

Then she was beside him.

"They're not signed," he said.

"When they're right," she replied.

"My eye must not be as discerning as yours. I was about to offer a compliment."

"I'm not too good with compliments." Farrell relieved Meade of one of the paintings. She swirled her drink, brought it halfway to her lips, and then set it aside. A lowering of the guard, Meade thought.

She said, "I have this crazy notion that somewhere inside there's a streak of talent. Maybe even some passion."

"I've tried to ignore it myself," Meade said, facing her. "The passion."

Farrell didn't take her eyes off the painting. "It's not that good, Meade."

"Oh, the watercolor. I was thinking more about the artist." He was looking at the side of her face. Finally, she turned. Their eyes met. Meade touched her hair. He sensed the turning of a page, and didn't want it to turn too fast. Didn't want to lose her. He said, "In my dreams, it's a saxophone. Subtle hints that I was meant to make music. One night I'm marching with the Salvation Army Band. Another night I'm playing in a smoky bar waiting to be discovered. Or standing under a blazing sun in the middle of the desert imitating John Coltrane."

She grinned. "Coltrane's dead, Meade."

Meade held her gaze for a moment longer and then touched the painting in his hand to the one in hers. "Is there a title?"

"I call it 'The Resting Place.' "

Meade nodded. "I approve." He gestured to the one in his hand. "And an asking price?"

"You're serious?" Farrell, when she saw that he was, checked the onset of derision and congratulated herself on not screwing it up. "Well, then, the price is in the asking. I'm honored. I think you're crazy, but I'm honored."

She reached out for her drink again, but Meade was quicker. He put his hand over the glass and pushed it away.

"Your father knows that you were at the house in Sea Point yesterday, Farrell," he said. "He was there."

"No."

"Yes." Meade explained.

"You've been having me followed. How dare you."

"We're not the only ones," Meade told her about the men Fazzie had seen at the museum that afternoon.

"That sounds like the police—"

"Not the police. The police don't suspect you. If they did, you'd know."

"The ANC—"

"Farrell. Does the African National Congress know how you spend your Sunday nights? Do they know you're hiding something about the incident at De Greyling? Do they know your father—?"

"Goddamn my father!" Farrell shouted. She wheeled away, covering her face. "And goddamn you, too."

Meade tucked the copy of *The Resting Place* under his arm. He moved toward the door. "They'll be back, Farrell. You'll wait, and you'll hope, but it won't go away. And they'll be back."

The door closed behind him. Farrell hurried to the table, stopped, and stared down at the gin glass. With each passing second she felt the distance between them lengthening. The rumble of his car's engine colored the feeling. She reached out for the glass and then swept it suddenly off the table.

"Meade." Farrell scurried for the door. She opened it to the crackling sound of tires rolling hurriedly over the tiny stones of her drive and the sudden acceleration as the car snaked onto the street. She closed the door again, now leaning heavily against it. "Meade. Oh, Christ."

21

MEADE CAME OFF the pillow in a cold sweat. The image of the smashed X-ray lamp in Miles Roundtree's studio burned in his head. He saw the broken high heel lying on the ground halfway down the alley. He threw off the covers, pulled on jeans, an old wool shirt, and construction boots. A cool breeze filtered through the open windows of the sod house. It smelled of cedar.

Meade's watch read 2:48. He went outside.

The ocean slapped at the beach a quarter of a mile away. He started the Toyota and then jogged back inside. He found one of Fazzie's cigarettes in the breast pocket of his sport coat. It was bent and wrinkled, and he lit it with relish.

Five minutes later he set out. At the top of the hill he opened the gate and pulled the car onto the shoulder of the road. He found a broken tree limb. This he used to smooth away the car's tire tracks. When he was satisfied, he closed the gate again but didn't lock it.

It was twenty-one miles from Muizenberg to the city center. Downtown, the lights of shops and galleries gave an artificial life to the windows lining Adderley Street. Policemen patrolled on horseback. An armored personnel van toured the streets with the patience of a snail. Street sweepers rumbled curb to curb, turning the dust to mud and drinking it in.

Meade parked in front of a stone church.

The alley behind the Roundtree Gallery reeked of decay. With a flashlight held out before him, Meade forged ahead. The gallery was the second establishment from the corner. A shaft of yellow light radiated from the studio's only window. A corridor had been roped off from the street to the back staircase. Meade tried imagining the killer's behavior. The destruction of the studio suggested a reckless confidence, and Meade was counting on this. The Guardi canvas would have been tucked inside a jacket or hidden beneath a wrap. But there would have been something else. Photo negatives, or X-rays, or slides which had drawn the killer to the X-ray lamp in the first place. Disposable items that had already served their function; the killer's aggression toward the lamp, Meade convinced himself, was proof of this. He had found the broken high heel *beyond* the entrance to the studio. He could think of only one reason. The killer was a woman, and she had discarded something in one of the trash receptacles.

Meade scanned the alley. Two of the receptacles were lit by the outside lights of a lady's boutique called Fandango and a department store called the Regal Affair. The other two were hidden in shadows farther on.

Meade drew an empty wooden crate up in front of the first bin, donned an old pair of cotton gloves, and threw back the lid. His search yielded two cartons of packing excelsior, a bag of plastic beads, a pile of crushed boxes, and a bundle of fabric samples. A discarded lunch, a stack of fashion magazines, scraps of carpet, and a broken chair. Bathroom trash, ripe garbage, and a bouquet of wilted roses. When he came to a newspaper dated May 31, he switched his flashlight off and clambered down.

His eyes adjusted. A sudden gust of wind sent an

empty beer can rattling across the pavement. An alley cat hissed; Meade turned and caught the tawny gleam in its eyes. A loose shutter slapped nervously at its frame.

The difference between the first receptacle and the second was a mannequin with a cracked skull, a mangled tricycle, and four empty cases of champagne. A broken teapot, a worn tennis shoe, and a framed photograph with slashes of lipstick across the glass. His hopes diminished.

Office waste spilled over from the third container. Its lid had been thrown back, and its top layer was soaked from the rain. Meade scooped what he could into a couple of empty cardboard boxes. He sorted through a carton filled with accounting materials, through loose files and an empty strongbox. He dug through paper sacks and ripped into plastic trash bags. Meade was about to open a coffee-stained manila envelope when he heard the clomp-clomp-clomp of a horse's hooves. A moment later he was awash in a yellow glow of a flashlight. He recoiled.

"If you're hungry, lad, I'm much afeared you've come to the wrong alley." There was amusement in the policeman's voice. "That is, unless you've a healthy appetite for soggy newspaper."

Meade used the envelope to shield his eyes.

"Good evening, Officer." Knee-deep in trash and completely exposed, Meade was more relieved than anything. "I'm *afeared* that clerk in the lingerie store out front may have thrown my passport in her trash. I'm lost without it."

Meade dug out his wallet. He held up his driver's license and press ID. The policeman urged his mount forward. He pulled up an arm's length away and reached for the wallet. He made a quick inspection of the names and photos and tossed it back, seemingly satisfied. Then he eyed the trash container again. The horse shook his head and backpedaled.

"Better you than me, lad," he said, turning the horse. "Better you than me."

204

Meade gave the envelope a halfhearted toss in the direction of the cardboard box. It dipped and fluttered and dropped to the pavement. He went back to work.

By the time he was finished, Meade was standing inside the receptacle. His pants and gloves were soaked through, his senses numb. He climbed out. He hoisted the cardboard boxes and tossed the lot back into the bin. Yawning, he picked up the stray envelope. Dutifully, he undid the tie and thrust his flashlight inside. His breath caught when he saw the shredded X-rays.

One by one he held the narrow strips against the lens of the flashlight. He saw the dour profile of a woman's face. He saw what was surely a section of a stringed instrument. And when he saw the last two letters in the I. V. Meer signature, he switched off the light. Don't think, he ordered himself. Don't theorize and don't fantasize. Just walk.

As he reached the car, the hiss of hydraulic brakes caused Meade to look back again. The trash truck was a dirty blue. The driver eased it into the alley and stopped at the first receptacle.

In Muizenberg, Meade parked the Toyota a quarter of a mile away from the croquet club entrance. He kept to the trees. When he got to the gate he saw a fresh set of tire tracks where two hours ago he had brushed the road smooth. He saw footprints where the driver had gotten out and shut the gate. They were small and narrow, almost certainly a woman's.

Meade tucked the manila envelope inside his shirt and followed the tracks down the hill. He was a hundred yards from the house when he saw Farrell's Honda. Farrell sat on the stoop with her back pressed against the door. Meade walked in silence up the path. He paused. Her eyes were pools of liquid bronze, clearer than he had ever seen them. Blond hair hung in loose, disheveled curls. She wore jeans and a jean jacket, and her hands were buried in the pockets. Her shoulders were hunched against her neck, the collar of the jacket brushing her cheeks.

There was a hint of laughter in her eyes as she surveyed his attire. "Barhopping, Meade? You?"

Meade looked down at himself forlornly and then glanced at the door. "It's open."

Their eyes met and lingered. "You were expecting someone," she said.

Meade didn't answer. Instead he offered a hand and they went inside. He lit the hut's one gas lantern. Into the center of the room he maneuvered a small, glass-topped coffee table. "Drink?" he asked.

"No," Farrell heard herself answer. A chill turned into a shiver. "Not now."

She moved slowly, stiffly around the tiny room, the jacket wrapped tightly around her. The room was different. There was a new work of art. She actually used those words, and it surprised her. On the mantel next to Sean Meade's ostrich painting was her own watercolor, *The Resting Place*.

"So?" Meade said.

"It looks—all right. Doesn't it? Maybe it's the light." She looked aside and laughed. "I don't know whether to be proud or embarrassed."

"Take off your jacket. I'll show you what I found while I was barhopping."

Meade set the gas lantern on the floor under the table. He emptied the contents of the manila envelope onto the glass top. The negatives had been sliced into strips fifteen to eighteen inches long, none wider than a half inch.

Meade fanned the strips out over the glass. "The Vermeer is hidden in here somewhere," he said.

"Restoration X-rays!" Farrell knelt down. "Miles Roundtree did the work on the Vermeer. Where did you get these?"

"Miles Roundtree is dead, Farrell. You didn't know? It was in the papers."

Farrell shook her head. "I didn't see it."

Meade told her the story without sentiment. Farrell had sought him out a second time. She was here because she was frightened. The question remained: was she frightened enough?

As he talked, the table became a collage of transparent photographic film. Farrell sorted inner layer shots from surface shots. The corner of the virginal appeared, the back of a woman's head, the hem of a yellow dress, the fringe of an orange shawl, the neck of a mandolin, a ray of sunlight.

Meade changed clothes. Within a half hour, a replica of *Two Women and Their Music* stared back at them through a transparent canvas woven of a modern-day cellulose material unheard of in Jan Vermeer's time.

The inner negatives, the X-rays that took the restorer into the pigment layers, the ground layer, and eventually down to the canvas and beyond, were more difficult.

They drank instant coffee. Meade offered her a drink a second time, but she resisted. He watched her. Her eyes were still clear, but the glow he had seen outside was a waxiness in the artificial light of the room. They talked. About living with death, hate, and fear. Meade told her about the boating accident in which Sally had died and about Sean's suicide attempt.

"I can still hear the sound of the phone ringing that summer afternoon. This voice saying, 'It's about your wife. There's been an accident.' And two nights later, that sickening wail of the ambulance taking Sean to the hospital, blood pouring from the cuts on his wrists."

By the time the four inner-layer negatives were assembled and made whole again with clear plastic tape, a purple dawn had crept over the peninsula and the birds were singing their morning song. From the front stoop

Meade watched the bay rise and fall in long shadows. He watched a blade of sunlight cut across the jagged western shore; as the earth turned and the light fell across the tide, it glistened like newly forged steel.

When he went inside again, Farrell was holding out the sheet of gold writing stationery she had taken from her father's study in Sea Point. On her face, Meade could see that resistance had abdicated to a newfound resolve, or perhaps to simple survival. He took the paper and read.

> *Executive Circular #2452. January 12th. "It has come to the attention of trusted friends that the receptacle within which the Missing Sixth is contained has been reported found. . . . Though the receptacle's presence on foreign soil will make its procurement through any but proper channels hazardous, its procurement is essential. . . . We are informed that it will be sold at auction at Christie's of London on January 21st. . . ."*

"I suppose I half suspected something even then," she said, explaining her father's sudden interest in the Vermeer. "I should never have told him about it in the first place."

"His plan was to acquire the painting by funding your museum. Brilliant."

Farrell nodded. "The son of a bitch was never interested in anything concerning art. But a Vermeer hanging in *my* museum: it was an intoxicating prospect, Meade. And when it was stolen— Oh, God, when you told me it was the only one of the five to survive that fire—"

"This expression—the Missing Sixth. Does it mean anything to you?"

Farrell shook her head.

"Within which the Missing Sixth is contained," Meade said. "Contained *within* the Vermeer. Not the Vermeer itself, then. How? How could something be contained within a painting?"

Farrell spread the X-ray negatives out again. She bit down hard on her lower lip. "The question, really, is more *what* than *where.* A microchip could be hidden beneath a layer of paint. A jewel, in a bore hole in the frame. A letter, between the original painting and the relining canvas." She raised her shoulders, shrugging. "But the thing is, it doesn't matter. If we're talking about something tangible, it would have shown up in the X-rays, in any case."

"Would a thorough restoration require more than just the X-rays?"

"Of course. Pigment samples, lab samples, canvas fragments, stretcher tests." Farrell straightened suddenly. "Miles would have stored the X-ray negatives in a desk or filing cabinet—"

"There's a filing cabinet in his office. Next to the X-ray lamps."

"But lab samples and test results require more, a controlled atmosphere of some kind. A walk-in vault or storage room. If Miles didn't . . . If his killer . . ."

"It's possible," Meade said. "It's possible."

A Closed Until Further Notice sign haunted the entrance to the Roundtree Gallery. Barricades surrounded it. It was Monday morning.

Lines of buses arrived from the townships, and the city's proletarian work force filed out. Soldiers patrolled the streets; baking bread scented the air.

Meade and Farrell slipped under the barricade. A uniformed policeman responded to their knock, and Bartleman's name secured their entrance. They were ordered to wait.

The gallery shimmered under the glow of white spotlights and purple floodlights. There was a tremor of hushed voices as fingerprint teams dusted counters and railings, picture frames and sculptures.

Meade went in search of a telephone. Farrell browsed,

the X-ray negatives in an envelope under her arm. Her face was chalky and withdrawn. She felt sick from a night and morning without alcohol. A young man in a white smock sprayed ninhydrin on the frame of a black-and-white photograph. Farrell watched him from a distance. She took a step closer and craned her neck for a better look.

A moment later Meade returned, saying, "There are actually people who consider a fingerprint search, properly conducted, an art form in its own right."

He stood behind her, gazing over her shoulder. Farrell's response surprised him. "I can understand it. The patience and concentration. The discipline. He seems to be enjoying himself, doesn't he?"

Then she gestured at the photo itself, of a woman lying naked in the midst of a tall forest, curled in the fetal position. Her body was caked with dirt. Shadowy overlays, like transparencies of skin, served to obscure the woman in part, but not the fragility or torment of the image.

"It's moving," Meade said. He didn't recognize the artist's name. The word *Rebirth* was scratched on a title card.

"Did you know, Meade, that our fingerprints—those silly loops and whorls and arches that everyone around here finds so revealing—did you know they take their form in the third fetal month? And never change. Never. Not for a lifetime. Imagine, our uniqueness demonstrating itself at such an early stage."

"You know that? How?"

"Experience. Fifteen years ago. Back then I didn't want to be pregnant. One decision led to another, all bad. But they seemed right at the time. I wasn't married. I was working on a career. I shook like a leaf every time I thought about being a mother." Her voice was calm, but it wasn't hard for Meade to detect the underlying battle, one fought

210

many times over. "It wasn't until later, after the numbness and relief faded away. . . . It was an obsession for a while . . . the eyes, the ears, the toes . . . and the fingers. Anyway, that's how I know."

In his search for some right word, for some adequate expression of understanding, Meade came up empty. So he put his hands on her shoulders instead. Farrell gave one of the hands a pat and then held on.

The policeman returned. "You can go on up," he said.

The stairs were roped off, leaving only a tiny corridor opposite the railing. The studio was like a newly discovered mine field, off-limit areas conspicuously marked. Bartleman was in a fury. A state of mind directly correlated, Meade imagined, to a lack of evidence. He asked Bartleman if they had come across a walk-in vault or a storage room.

"You're onto something" was the sum total of his response. Like a windup toy, he led them through the kitchen, past a two-burner stove, a tub sink, and a near-empty refrigerator, to a set of louvered doors. "What?"

Farrell explained the X-rays. While Bartleman held each reconstructed negative up to the light, Meade searched for a reaction. What he got in return, or thought he got in return, was a look of genuine surprise. Bartleman tweaked his mustache. "Are these what I think they are?"

"The man who murdered Miles Roundtree didn't come here for the Guardi," Meade said. He wondered why he had chosen the word *man*. Why hadn't he shared his discovery of the broken high heel? "He came about the restoration Miles performed on the Vermeer from Cas Greyling's gallery."

"Why?"

"That's why we're here. To find out why." Another lie of omission.

"And in the process, dropping another murder investigation right in Fogwell's lap. That's beautiful" was

Bartleman's reply. He shook his head. With a hooked finger he tapped the envelope and passed it back to Farrell. He tossed Meade an inscrutable glance. He was still shaking his head as he reached out and tapped the envelope again. "The problem is, I never could make much sense out of these bloody things."

The louvered doors opened onto a second door, the vault entrance. This one was constructed with high-tensile hardened steel and faced with a three-wheel combination. Miles Roundtree had plastered a bumper sticker across the front. *SHOOT THE MOON.*

Now Bartleman dug a slip of paper from his breast pocket. The combination. He turned the wheel, and the sound reminded Meade of his boyhood days in Maine, of clipping playing cards between the spokes of his two-wheeler, of the attic fan that ran endlessly during the summer. He heard a muted click and the door parted. A breath of cool air filtered out.

Surprisingly, Bartleman started away, saying only, "I'll expect a share in the harvest."

Meade watched him go. He watched him until he was out of sight, and then followed Farrell inside. She groped for a lamp cord. Once illuminated, the narrow cubicle resembled a bank vault of sorts. Against the back wall were shelves heavy with canisters and bottles and jars of chemicals and paints. The side walls, on the other hand, were filled floor to ceiling with stainless steel boxes, all a dark green, a foot long and the width and height of a business envelope. Taped across the face of each was a hand-written note card bearing three letters and a date.

Farrell studied the cards at random, her fingers gliding from box to box. COR–Dec. 12, 1975. KIB–July 9, 1987. BOY–May 1, 1988. POU–Aug. 30, 1981. TIN–Dec. 2, 1985.

Then she theorized. "You have to have known Miles; he would give every restored work its own box purely as a matter of principle. The letters stand for the artist's surname; that's easy enough. Camille Corot, Wolf Kibel, George Boys, Poussin, Tintoretto. And the dates more than likely refer to the day the restoration was completed. But they're arranged according to the year each work was actually painted." She smiled. "There's something dignified in that, I think."

Her hand stopped. She drew the box from the rack. VER—Feb. 18, 1988.

Nico Mustapha's temperature-regulated safe, in contrast to Miles Roundtree's vault, was an old walk-in food locker. Silver-lined, with metal shelves and a cement floor, it seemed cooler.

"Imagine my delight on discovering such a treasure," he said. "A food locker, on the second floor, no less. That was thirty-two years ago. I knew I'd found my studio the moment I laid eyes on it."

Nico was holding the steel box from Miles's safe in two hands, as if some demon lurking within might suddenly cause it to disappear. He placed it on a metal cart. Farrell passed him the envelope containing the restored X-ray negatives.

The cart creaked as Nico rolled it into the locker. Meade carried a small stool, on which the hunched little man settled himself. Farrell closed the door and shivered.

"Miles died without revealing the existence of this box," Nico said, fondling the steel container. Rue and wonder tugged at the corners of his mouth. "Praise be, was it courage, do you think, or—?"

Nico didn't finish the thought. As he cracked the seal, a musty odor escaped. Meade thought of the stale chocolates his grandmother used to force on him; and of his mother's pottery studio after a summer under lock and key.

Nico set the contents, one at a time, on the cart.

Fragments of canvas were sealed in a transparent plastic bag. A pillbox contained tiny slivers of plaster that could have been mistaken for fingernail clippings. Cylinders of molded plastic were stored in a soft paper bag. Minute shavings of wood from the stretchers and frame were tucked into a stiff paper folder. Capped vials protected liquids tinted pink and blue. And lastly, a series of microscopic slides held dried swabs of color. Nico peeked at the restored X-rays and his head bobbed.

"Ah, yes. Like a stocking on Christmas morning." He hopped off the stool. He rubbed his hands together and smiled up at them. "Most revealing, my American friend. Most revealing."

"When, Nico?" Meade asked. "How long will it take?"

Nico chuckled. He held the locker door open for Farrell and flipped off the light. "A man of action, this reporter of ours, my dear. Always in a hurry. Often a step ahead of himself, however."

"I've noticed," Farrell replied. She glanced over her shoulder and showered Meade with feigned disapproval. "Nearly hopeless. Or, in other words, typically American." Then she touched his arm and said more gently, "These things take time."

Nico chuckled again. He led them through the studio into an office that was really no more than a wooden desk and two folding chairs. A pull chain illuminated two fluorescent tubes, which in turn illuminated a high shelf laden with thick, worn books. Nico climbed to the top step of a small ladder. Mumbling to himself and breathing like a winded sprinter, he balanced a volume in each hand. One, Benezit's *Dictionary of Painters and Sculptors*. The other, *The Masters and Their Palettes*. He climbed down.

"Research, Mr. Meade." Nico dropped the books dramatically on his desk. "A tool well used by one under pressure from the impatient."

Suitably chastised, Meade tempered the question this time. "When?"

A smile spread from Nico's mouth to his eyes and finally to his brow. He shared it with Farrell and then said, "Return this evening at, say, 5:00, and we'll see."

A solid wooden door at the back of Nico's studio led to a set of stone stairs. Nico carried a gas lantern much like the one from the sod hut in Muizenberg. He offered a similar one to Meade. The stairs led to an ancient passage beneath the mosque next door. It was damp, and the air was heavy. The stone wept. Eventually, the passage emerged in a wine cellar thick with dust. Nico used a skeleton key on the cellar door, and Meade put the key in his pocket.

The door opened onto a stairwell that led to a neighboring alley. Alone, Meade and Farrell hurried down the alley to the street. They caught the first bus into the heart of Foreshore. The streets were crowded; a restaurant across from their stop was packed despite the early hour.

They found an empty table near the window. Their waitress was a Cape Malay who spoke with an educated English accent. Meade ordered coffee with cream and sugar. Farrell, tea with lemon.

Meade watched her. He could feel the moisture on her brow and taste the cotton in her mouth and could see the fluctuating color of her skin. He said, "The hardest part about quitting is that there's no right time, never that quick step from the shadow into the bright and shining light of sobriety. You have to trip and hurt yourself. Eventually you find out that what you're actually doing is hurting yourself a little less."

"Who said anything about quitting?"

"When was the last time you had lunch out without a martini?"

"When was the last time I had lunch *in* without a

215

martini?" Farrell replied. "My ears are still ringing from last night. It's unnerving expecting the table to explode out from under you. I don't want the papers to say she was drunk at the time."

Meade let the rationalization soak in. Coffee and tea were served with a tray of *verkoek*, a flat bread fried in oil. Then he said, "Farrell, there was a dinner party out at De Greyling the night of the fire. Your father was there."

Farrell didn't look up. Her fingers curled around the teacup. She brought it to her lips and drank. The heat seemed to revive her. "So."

"Sir Greyling called the meeting *business*. Something about a foundation established by his wife and your mother. The funding of a new hospital."

Farrell set the cup down. She pushed a finger around the rim. "It's called the Heart League. Sir Greyling is still pretty involved. Father calls it a write-off he can't afford to give up."

"Does your father consider Sir Greyling a friend?"

"I don't know if the son of a bitch has any friends. If he does, Cas isn't one of them." The finger stopped; her eyes wandered. "Mom told me once he considered the Greylings bad blood."

"Translated?"

"That means they don't bleed pure, unadulterated Afrikaner red, Meade."

"They were outcasts, then."

"The Greylings were too prominent to be outcasts. And too damned likable."

"How would a man who doesn't bleed pure, unadulterated Afrikaner red fit into the *Broederbond*, Farrell?"

She stared. "He doesn't."

"You sound certain."

"I am. I know almost nothing about the Brotherhood, Meade, but I do know that diehard Calvinists are all they take. The Greylings never fit that mold, believe me."

Meade studied the street, the faces, the parked cars, the shadows. "How well do you know the Greylings?"

"Very. I'm the big sister Terrence never had. Terrence tells me everything and then swears me to secrecy."

"Has Terrence ever discussed with you his father's commitment to Judaism or the Zionist movement?"

Farrell's eyes widened. "What exactly does this have to do with the Vermeer?"

"Your father and his friends made a concerted effort to place your museum in a position to compete for a painting he had no artistic interest in. His plans were thwarted by a fellow Afrikaner with diametrically opposed beliefs. Greyling admits to a distinct lack of interest in seventeenth-century art. He admits further that he had almost no knowledge of Jan Vermeer until this work became available. Is it so inconceivable that his underlying motive was the same as your father's?"

22

THE TOBACCONIST in the pipe shop on the corner across from the railroad station searched Meade's face with an appraising look. A silver tooth flashed in his smile. "An American looking for a fire-cured Dominican tobacco at the southernmost tip of darkest Africa. Good luck to you."

"A friend here smokes them," Meade said. "Unless you can think of another brand that comes in a gold cellophane wrapper with a blue and red band?"

"A friend who smokes Diego Royales." The shop owner sniffed. "I call that a friend worth keeping."

"They'd have to be special-ordered, then?"

"Very special-ordered, unless I'm losing my grip on the business."

Inside the glass counter on which the owner leaned, Meade saw a familiar yellow box with the words "Mills— England's Luxury Cigarette" on it. Fazzie's brand. He also saw the shop owner's eyes light up when he asked for two packs.

"Well, no one in their right mind's gonna fault your taste in tobacco. That much I can tell you."

The money was halfway out of Meade's wallet when he paused. "Would anybody in town do that? Special-order something as uncommon as the Diegos?"

The owner glanced at the money in Meade's hand. A moment later Meade had the names of two competitors and change for the phone in back. He left Farrell at the counter and placed his calls. He used Gideon DeBruin's name as a lead; it bore fruit on the second call.

"Mr. DeBruin, certainly. A fine gent."

"Gideon said I might be able to buy a box of Diego Royales from you."

"Did he? I'm surprised. And sorry. We don't stock the Royales, as such. Can't think of a soul in town who does. That, I'm afraid, is the problem with a three-dollar cigar; that is about what you'd pay back in the States, I suppose you know."

"Gideon did say he might be your only customer."

"Indeed he is, but —"

"Thank you."

Rita Hess sat on a stool at the end of the tavern's long wooden bar. The lounge was located a block from Foreshore and across the street from a government high rise. It was called the Quiver Tree. There was a bartender with a beer belly and a cigar, a waitress with a harelip, and a shot-and-a-beer special that ran twenty-four hours a day. Smoke and the slow melody of a baby grand piano filled the place despite the early hour. The patrons were working-class Afrikaners. For them the lights and the music insured a quick escape from the drudgery of work during the day and their matchbox houses at night. For Rita, the lights and the music insured anonymity. She had stopped concerning herself with the bartender and patrons and the occasional passes. At 11:00 on a Monday morning, nobody cared.

The Quiver Tree was not Rita's idea. She had been given a name and an address the day she arrived in Cape Town. Every week she sat at the bar and drank cups of thick black coffee, and every week the call came. She knew the voice, like fine sandpaper working the surface of a snare drum. She had even conjured up a face to match — elongated and bony, bloodshot eyes that drooped above dark circles, a warped nose, and the blue-black of a heavy beard — but in truth he could have been the drunk sitting on the stool across from her. They had never met. Rita hoped they never would. She wasn't afraid of many things, but in this voice she had detected something raptorial.

Rita had always treated him flippantly, but then she had always been successful. Up to now. Yet whose fault was it? She had gained possession of the painting and the document wasn't there. She had done her part; it was their information that had been mistaken. So why this feeling of impending doom?

As always, Rita tried anticipating their conversation. They would discuss the results of her visit to Miles Roundtree's studio. Of course, he would want every gruesome detail. Unfortunately, what Rita had to offer, beyond the gruesome details, was mostly speculation. Facts, he would demand. What are the *facts?* The fact was, Rita fancied herself saying, you and your cronies laid a big goose egg.

They would also discuss the tape, the one Rita had copied yesterday at the motel, of Friday's Executive Council meeting. He would be childishly pleased with the alarmed tone of the session. More importantly, he would be curious about the new voice appearing at the end of the tape. "Our policeman," they had called him. Could their policeman be identified? Could he be useful?

A telephone rang, in a wooden booth near the restrooms. Coffee spilled over the rim into the saucer of her cup, burning her fingers. She listened to a second and third ring. A fourth. The bartender was raising his palms to her as if to say, "Well, what are you gonna do, let it ring all day?"

Finally, she climbed down from the stool.

———

220

Meade stood on a promontory overlooking Clifton Bay. An hour earlier he had called the Argus motor pool, and a gray Subaru station wagon had been left for them in a loading zone at the train station, three blocks from the restaurant where they had eaten lunch.

Meade kept an eye on the road even as he watched the breakers battle the impervious, lifeless rocks below. He empathized with what he imagined to be the ocean's pain, its frustration over an endless confrontation with the inflexible and uncooperative. Yet in the pitted and worn surface of granitic rock, in a ravine yielding pebble by pebble, in a sand dune broken down and reshaped with every incoming wave, he could see an inevitable victory.

Behind him lay the town of Clifton. Houses built on stilts straddled four narrow beaches; split-levels clung to the walls of steep cliffs; and houses built of brick and stone hid among the pines, yellowwoods, and assegai on the mountaintop.

The dentist — the dentist whose Ford Taurus had presumably been used by the killer — lived in one of those houses. The killer, Meade reasoned, had known before stealing the car that the dentist and his wife would be away from their house on the night of the theft, and the next night, as well. He reasoned further that a neighbor would be in the perfect position to know this. Not a full-time resident; this person would be a short-term renter, taking advantage of off-season rates. There would be many such rentals in a town like Clifton.

Across the coast road Meade saw Farrell emerging from the real estate agent's office. She wore blue jeans, tennis shoes, and a turtleneck with the same ease, Meade thought, as she wore a silk dress, shoulder scarf, and heels. In the gray mist she seemed fragile. Her stride, in contrast, was long and purposeful. She kicked a stone as she crossed the road and jogged the last steps to the car. Meade held the door open.

"They showed fifteen rentals on the books. All with long-term leases, and none closer than six blocks to the dentist." She wrung her hands together and shivered. "He gave me a couple of other options."

The first of these options was another real estate agent, an English-speaking firm on the third floor of Clifton's only high rise. A secretary confessed to the firm's recent departure from the rental market, but also mentioned the second name on Farrell's list.

This, an apartment finder's service, was located on the coast road at the edge of town. The building was low and flat with a parking lot out front. It looked like a converted gas station. Back home, Meade thought, they made such places into Mexican restaurants or take-out Chinese. Places to be avoided at all cost.

Inside were two women in their early twenties and four computers. The walls were covered with travel posters and maps. Meade and Farrell went in together.

"Some friends live at 64 Alpine Way," Farrell said, giving one of the women the dentist's address. "We're looking for something within walking distance. Something we can get for a month or two."

The woman talked as she typed. "And what do we consider walking distance? Are we the energetic type?"

"The closer the better," Farrell answered.

"I'm like you," she said, giggling. "Furnished or unfurnished?"

"Either."

"Price range?"

"We're flexible."

"You guys are easy. Kids or pets — I hope not?"

Farrell shook her head.

The woman stopped typing and thumbed through the card catalog on her desk. She looked dejected; she bunched her hands beneath her chin. "I'm afraid the closest thing we have available right this minute is a three-bedroom on Glentana Avenue. But it's a good four or five blocks

222

from the Alpine address. Everything closer is booked solid. I'm really sorry."

"We're actually thinking of something later in the season," Meade told her. "July or August. And closer, much closer."

Now the woman's hands opened like a rejuvenated flower. "Well then, OK. In that case, I have a four-bedroom on Napier, about three blocks from your friends. Three thousand a month. A steal. Wonderful view. Cleaning service included. No pets. Available in mid-August. I also have a lovely little cottage on Prince Alfred Circle. It's a month-to-month, but we haven't heard anything about July. Eighteen hundred a month. Kinda high, to be honest. But you'd look right down on Alpine Way. It's small, but — "

"It sounds perfect." Meade camouflaged his impatience with an ingratiating smile. "Who would the current renter be?"

"Well, her name's Lisa Henderson, but I can't — "

"Would it be possible to have a look? You didn't mention the address."

"If I could just get a little information first," the woman said, her voice apologetic. "Company policy. You know how it is."

Flames danced on the hearth of the Clifton cottage on Prince Alfred Circle. Rita Hess, disheveled and tired, curled up in a ball in the overstuffed chair that was the room's only piece of furniture. Her feet were bare, and she tucked them under her. The fire crackled and popped. The warmth of it soothed even as it fed her fatigue.

In this light, with the clouds closing in outside and the mist fogging the window, she was reminded of home. Spring in the Southern hemisphere was like fall in the North.

In Germany, even in this day and age, her mother

cooked over an open fire. A copper pot always boiling. The tinge of soot on her cheeks and the sheen of sweat on her brow were comforting sights to a child. Every mother in the village was bent over by the time she was forty. It was an expectation, a given, a life cycle. Rita was seventeen, on her first visit to Berlin, before she knew any different. Where she grew up every mother spent her youth finding a man to marry and then the rest of her life wondering why.

It was odd. Rita had loved her mother, had pitied her and wanted desperately to protect her from the evil in their house. But even so, she could hardly recall her face. She could remember the soft yellow of her apron, the gentle touch of her abraded hands, the warmth and comfort of her swollen breasts. She could remember the smell of her vegetable stew and the taste of her maple syrup. But her face was a blur. It was frightening.

What frightened Rita even more was that, though she had loathed and feared him, her father's face still lurked, indelibly imprinted on her brain. She saw him slobbering drunk, face unshaven and teeth stained, his tool exposed between the slit in filthy long johns. And she remembered his smell: alcohol tinged with the grit of manual labor and the nervous sweat of self-loathing. Rita had asked her mother a hundred times what had drawn her to the man in the first place. Was there ever an answer that made any sense?

Rita looked around her. Everything about the cottage reminded her of *his* failure, as a farmer, as a father, as a husband. A man who would allow a stranger to lay his hands on his only daughter, do the things that he did, allow him to scar her with a whip: a man like that was more dog than man.

Rita reached down for the painting curled at the foot of the chair. The scrawl at the bottom of the canvas read *Guardi*. Francesco Guardi. Why she had taken it from the restorer's studio she honestly didn't know. The question had plagued her to the point of looking the name up in an encyclopedia at Sea Point Public Library. A forerunner of the impressionists, it said. A master of pure rococo caprice.

"Caprice," Rita said. "To disguise life's shit in a gown of silk and satin. What a wonderful gift."

She ran her fingers over the deep cracks that age had brought to the painting, and the incrustations of soot and dust that shrouded the Venetian lagoon like fog.

And then she laughed, mockingly. At herself, at the painting, at the whole stinking world. She was still laughing as she unfolded from the chair and knelt before the fire. She stoked it to a roaring blaze. Closed her eyes and felt the heat soaking into her skin. Arched her back and breathed. Then she rolled the canvas into a loose cylinder and placed it in the flames.

She turned her attention next to the Vermeer. For three days it had rested on the mantel. Now she laid it faceup on the floor. She took the mat knife from her purse, exposed the blade, and then, with four quick strokes, liberated the canvas from its stretchers. Even as the painting sagged and curled, Rita, try as she might, could detect no change in the pensive expression on the first woman's face. She held firmly to her mandolin, her dress unruffled, as if there were no other world but her own. The other woman, the one standing so unaffected at the virginal, refused to face her, even in death. Rita had become obsessed with the woman's unseen face, with the gentle slope of her shoulders, and with each strand of hair turned a golden brown by the sun's rays. It was an obsession seeded by the duality of the love she felt for her mother and the loathing she felt for her father. Rita told herself it wasn't real. That none of it was real. But even as the words passed from her lips she doubted them.

She added wood to the fire. She stoked it again. In

the rush of new flames the remnants of the Guardi disappeared. And then, like a sacrificial lamb, the Vermeer, as well, was laid on the fire. The canvas ignited at its heart, and the flames spread outward. The paint melted, bubbled, and evaporated.

With glassy eyes, Rita tended the fire, now in a businesslike fashion. She scolded herself for such sentimentality. She broke the stretcher strips across her knee, tossed the pieces one at a time into the fire, and watched the flames consume them. She closed the hearth screen.

Then she toured the cottage, methodically wiping clean any surface she might have contacted over the last three months. The lease on the house ran until the end of the month, but Rita had no intention of returning. The cottage had served its purpose.

Smoke rose from the chimney of the cottage on Prince Alfred Street. A singular sign of life.

Inside, the curtains were drawn tight. Outside, the drive at the side of the house was empty. Paint peeled from the eaves. Ferrous stains grew beneath the gutters. A tall pine overwhelmed the front yard, and dead needles formed a cushion over the walk. Protea bloomed wild at the foot of a redwood deck.

"Eighteen hundred a month." Farrell grimaced.

The house perched on the side of a steep hill. At a knee-high picket fence, Meade paused. He glanced over his shoulder; with a halfhearted toss he could have landed a stone in the backyard of the dentist on 64 Alpine Way.

"What now?" Farrell asked.

The woman at the apartment finder's service had promised them a tour later in the day. But time, Meade thought, was not a commodity they could afford. "We knock," he said.

He pushed in the gate and followed Farrell to the front door. He rang the bell, and the sound resounded throughout the cottage. There was no answer. It made no sense to knock, but he did. Still there was no answer. They circled the house. A peek through kitchen shutters and a slit in front-room curtains revealed a house devoid of all furnishings, with the exception of a single overstuffed chair.

"I'm not renting anything without a bed and full bath, Meade. Sorry," Farrell joked nervously.

She tried the knob on the back door, and it opened. The sound, as it swung outward, resembled the yowl of an alley cat. Startled, Farrell stepped back. She felt Meade's hand on her arm. He moved past her. The floorboards groaned as he slipped from the porch into the kitchen. Stove and refrigerator doors stood open. Water dripped from the faucet. A chill of disuse infected the air.

In the front room a palpable gloom supplanted the chill: the dank and dark of drawn curtains, with the eeriness of a fire dying unattended in a lifeless room. Still they neither spoke nor reached for a light switch. Meade searched the bedroom and bathroom. He opened every closet and every cupboard and found them all empty. Not a towel, not a sheet, not a single clothes hanger. Bathroom fixtures were glazed with a thin layer of grit.

"Someone calling herself Lisa Henderson may have rented this place," he said, "but she never stayed long enough to unpack."

Farrell stooped before the fire. A last log crumbled. A bed of coals glowed a fierce red-orange, then crackled and spit and faded.

"We just missed her," she said, standing and feeling the draft from the kitchen. "Whoever she was."

From the backrest of the overstuffed chair Meade plucked a long, lustrous black hair. He stared at it, and the answer stared back.

Paul Kilian and Executive Council chairman H. J. Venter drank espresso and nibbled *melk* tarts in the sitting room of the Mount Nelson Hotel. They were discussing the nominations for the upcoming election of the new Executive Council chairman. Venter, as yet, had been hesitant to throw his support into any one camp, and the pressure was mounting. He was not surprised when Kilian broached the subject.

"And you think you're ready to challenge Gideon DeBruin for the top spot?" Venter settled their bill and proposed a stroll down Government Avenue. "Mustering a majority is one thing, Paul. Mustering the respect of the whole is another."

"With your support I'll muster both, Broeder Venter." They stepped outside. "We both recognize that, I think."

"You exude confidence, young man."

"Our goals have always been similar."

"It's our methods that often clash; is that what you're implying?"

The Avenue, as it was better known, was a pedestrian thoroughfare lined with magisterial oaks. A city worker, as wrinkled as a bushman, speared trash with a poker. Pensioners played backgammon on a picnic table.

Kilian said, "You and I have a vision of the future. Gideon doesn't."

"Majority rule?"

"We can't exist for much longer in this vacuum we've created for ourselves. If we let the world think we're taking a conciliatory step or two — let an old Kaffir or two out of prison, invite the ANC and Desmond Tutu over for tea — they'll fall all over themselves clapping us on the back. We could use a little of that. This 'fuck you' attitude of Gideon's isn't reality anymore."

"True," Venter said. He cupped a match over his pipe and skillfully changed the subject. "And what's more, he's creating problems for himself."

Kilian guessed at the chairman's meaning. "The bug in Gideon's office."

"Very revealing."

"Yes?"

"The American paid him a visit."

"Meade."

"It seems Mr. Meade's not giving up on the matter of the cane impressions," Venter said. "He painted a pretty grim picture for Gideon's sake."

"Then Gideon will know we suspect him. Good." Now Kilian told the chairman about the cigar wrapper found near the killer's car outside De Greyling.

"My God, could Gideon be that stupid? Or just that brazen?" Venter chewed vigorously on the end of his pipe. "Which makes the discovery of the killer's car that much more interesting."

"The Ford Taurus."

"The car was abandoned in an underground parking garage in Sea Point. Forensic found a ticket stub on the floor in the front seat. A ticket stub to a May 24th performance of the opera *Nabucco* by the Royal Academy. At the Nico Malan Theater, orchestra seating. The dentist and his wife don't think much of opera."

"But Gideon does."

"Yes, he does, actually."

"What about the ticket stub?"

"We'll know more this afternoon."

Tourists strolled among exotic birds in a glass-enclosed aviary. Beside a pond full of water lilies, Kilian said, "I suggest we have the information about the cigar wrapper leaked to Gideon this afternoon."

"Risky, Paul. Very risky, don't you think? If Gideon does by chance have the Sixth in his — "

"Then he'll use the document to sway the council election his way and secure the chairmanship for himself. But the election is still a month away. No, Gideon should know the walls are closing in on him." In silence they passed a bronze statue of Cecil Rhodes. "We're making progress, Broeder Venter."

"I'm not so sure we agree on that assessment, to be candid," the chairman said. "But even if we are, it's not without complications."

"Now what?"

"Our thieves left behind a remarkably accurate diagram of the gallery and its security system. You recall, of course."

"I recall that it wasn't the diagram we originally provided them with, if that's what you're asking," Kilian responded.

"No. The one provided for them by — whomever — was drawn on a piece of particularly fine stationery. Also a particularly traceable stationery. German made. Imported by Opperman and Nagel in Jo'burg and distributed exclusively through their catalog. Terrence Greyling is on their mailing list, and a regular patron. The stationery, I've been informed, is his."

"Terrence? Are you certain? In league with Gideon DeBruin?" Kilian sounded incredulous. "We need a piece of that stationery, right away. Can we get it?"

"We should be able to arrange something," Venter said.

"Good." They walked past the Garden Tearoom, across a tree-lined promenade, and paused again in the shadows of the Houses of Parliament. "I think it would be wise to tell Colonel Fogwell that we'll attend to young Terrence ourselves."

23

THEY MET FAZZIE in the Argus cafeteria. Like a potter, he was busy kneading an empty Coke can. Eventually, he reduced it to a distorted disk.

"You all right?" Meade asked.

"Let's just say it's been an interesting twenty-four hours." Fazzie arched the can toward the trash, hitting it dead center. Then he stood two cigarettes on end in the center of the table. He balanced a book of matches on top. "And since I'm still in one piece, I won't complain."

Meade traded the cigarettes and matches for the two packs he had purchased earlier.

"What's this?" Fazzie asked.

"That's the good news."

"Two boxes of cigarettes? I'm dying for the bad."

Meade told him about the tobacco shop and De-Bruin's specially ordered cigars, also about the cottage and the long black hair on the back of the chair. "We had a word with the dentist's wife. Her description of Rita Hess was most complimentary. She even called her 'charming.' "

"Whoever said vipers couldn't be charming?" Fazzie said.

"Rita knew about their boat. They'd talked about it

231

a couple of times. The dentist's pride and joy. They spend most of their weekends sailing, the wife said. Rita told them she'd make a point of keeping an eye on their house. They kept the Taurus in the garage, but never locked it."

"Probably made her a set of keys, too." Fazzie slid off the bench and stretched. He circled the table. "The painting was there, then. At the cottage. It makes sense."

"I called De Greyling," Meade said. "They haven't seen Rita since Saturday."

"She won't be back," Farrell said.

"Then we're assuming she found what she was looking for in Miles Roundtree's studio," Fazzie said. "What?"

He didn't wait for an answer. Instead, he dug a sealed telex from a jacket pocket and passed it to Meade. "The international desk dropped this by your desk twenty minutes ago."

The telex was postmarked Tel Aviv. The sender's name was Sterling McCabe, foreign correspondent, Reuters International Wire Service, one of the seven journalists Meade had contacted two days before concerning the identity of the fourth thief.

He read it aloud. "A certain organization in the Israeli government offered this about your unknown thief. He is known under several names: Nessel, Bugerin, but, most recently, Hulster. He first caught their attention in Afghanistan, making waves during the Soviet pullout. Later in Poland, doing his best to make a mess of their elections. My Israeli friends made mention of a group called the Red Wheel, the cloak-and-dagger arm of a political organization that just happens to be gaining some serious support on the Soviet front. The group is at the forefront of the movement to overthrow Moscow's current savior. Nothing wrong with that, I don't imagine, except these people are supposedly carrying around pictures of Stalin in their wallets. I was told to draw my own conclusions. And if *I* have to, old boy, then sorry to say, so do you. Anyway, hope it helps. Over and out, Mac."

"Someone's keeping some interesting company, Yank."

"Could my father be that desperate?" Farrell said.

"No. Hulster was Rita's man." Meade shook his head. "It's Rita who's been pulling your father's strings all along, not the other way around."

Fazzie agreed. "DeBruin presides over this near masterpiece of a theft and then gets blamed when the wall comes tumbling down. And then what? How does he explain to the Brothers that he's been talking in his sleep to a woman with ties to some right-wing political group? Simple. He doesn't." Fazzie nodded enthusiastically. "It's good, Yank. It's very good."

"But it doesn't explain why Rita Hess isn't five thousand miles away from Cape Town."

"Or why," Farrell said, "a restorer who wore bow ties and wouldn't harm a flea isn't still alive."

Meade punched the down button on the lobby elevator, and when the doors parted, Jacob Bartleman was standing there. Farrell gasped.

"What are you doing here?" Meade asked.

"Get in. I've been waiting for ten minutes. Doesn't your friend there, Mr. Fazzie, have a regular job?"

"Only sixty hours a week," Meade replied. "The rest of the time he's practically worthless."

Bartleman grinned. "So I admit it. I've read him. A tad preachy, mind you, but otherwise, a pretty decent pen."

"I'll pass the compliment along. What are you doing here?"

The elevator doors closed them in, and Bartleman pressed the emergency stop. "I was hoping I wouldn't have to come, to be truthful. You remember the cold-storage vault at Miles Roundtree's studio. We were going to share the harvest, remember? And being as I'd be called foolhardy by some for letting you two in there without a babysitter, I was hoping I wouldn't have to ask."

233

Meade explained about the canvas fragments and color samples Miles had extracted from the Vermeer, but he had no intention of mentioning Nico Mustapha. Instead, he held out the telex from Tel Aviv. "This arrived an hour ago."

Bartleman read the telex without batting an eye. "Great. Fuck. Just great. So we're back to politics again. This really makes a mess of it. Just great. The X-ray negatives I didn't think Fogwell needed to see. But this — no way can I keep this one from him."

"The restorer," Nico Mustapha said after escorting Meade and Farrell from the alley wine cellar, through the corridors beneath the mosque next door, to his studio, "begins his task like an auto mechanic."

Nico settled wire-rimmed glasses on the bridge of his nose and ambled over to a cluttered workbench. "Before he fixes, he determines the extent of the damage. He looks, he touches, he tests. We don't have the Vermeer staring back at us from an easel, but we do have Miles's photos and, of course, your remarkable re-creation of the X-rays. The painting, if you're willing to trust an old man's bloodshot eyes, was, shall we say, in need of a tune-up. More than a minor adjustment, less than a major overhaul."

Farrell interpreted. "Meaning a thorough cleaning and selective touch-ups. And Miles took both very seriously."

"Anytime paint is reapplied to the surface of a work that doesn't belong to you, it is a matter of some seriousness," Nico agreed. He dabbed watery eyes with the corner of his apron. Then he looked up. "So, I will show you the road Miles traveled. Then I will show you the path I myself charted and what I discovered along the journey. And in the process, you'll both have the pleasure and dismay of exploring the work of one of art history's master craftsmen."

With that, Nico proceeded to lay two cylinders of plastic — both layered with different colors — under the lens of a microscope. At his invitation, Meade settled over the eyepiece.

"Without question, Miles's first step would have been the testing of pigments. Miles was a perfectionist. He never restored a painting with anything but the original pigment. If that meant concocting recipes long since discarded, then so be it. You're looking at minute samples extracted from the painting itself. Ultramarine is made from powdered lapis lazuli, very expensive. Gamboge, from the resinous gum of a tropical Asian tree. Yellow ocher from native earth, ground and washed. Vermilion from cinnabar, an ore laced with mercury. All staples with the Dutch masters of Jan Vermeer's time.

"To confirm this — this — color chart, if you will, Miles would have run X-ray diffractions on each sample. This requires only a single grain of pigment, you understand, so there's no risk to the work itself."

Nico offered the printouts from his own tests. Then he flipped open a badly worn textbook to a premarked page, citing comparison charts and pigment compositions.

"Yes, yes. Here we are. A curious example." Nico was excited; Meade was reminded of the test patterns on a broken television. "The cinnabar in his vermilion. Take a look."

Meade held the cinnabar test next to the comparisons: samples from Holland, China, and the United States. "Chinese."

"Most observant. You see, during the latter part of the seventeenth century, the Dutch source of cinnabar began to peter out. It was gradually replaced by imports from China. Vermeer painted his *Two Women* toward the end of his life — 1673."

"He was experimenting with Chinese cinnabar,"

Farrell said. "Though it would have made no difference whatever in his work."

"No, my dear, not an iota." Nico hooked his thumbs in the straps of his apron. "I myself became fascinated with the coincidence of Chinese cinnabar being available in a place like Dreft, Holland, a good thirty years before this newer source was cultivated with any vigor.

"Nonetheless, with his color chart in order, Miles would have turned his attention to the stretchers, a simple test of durability and wear. According to his samples, he did the same with the frame, as well."

"Testing the frame isn't exactly standard procedure," Farrell told Meade. "Sir Greyling must have requested that himself."

"Why?" Meade asked.

Farrell shrugged. "An art collector's eccentricity." Which Meade didn't take as explanation; which he knew, searching Farrell's face, wasn't meant to be taken as explanation.

Nico said, "Miles would have relied on something called carbon dating for both the stretchers and the frame, Mr. Meade."

"And?" Meade asked.

"The frame is eighteenth-century. Insignificant. A new owner, a new frame. The stretchers, not so. They're oak, practically new. By my estimate, forty-five years, plus or minus."

"Suggesting the painting was completely restored sometime in the 1940s," Farrell said.

"Suggesting Miles saw no reason to tamper with the stretchers." Finally, using stainless steel tweezers, Nico set about arranging two samples of canvas under the narrow lenses of a comparison microscope. Each sample measured less than a centimeter square. "The one on the left," he said, "is from my sample file. The other is from the painting. Note the pattern, the tightly woven chevrons."

236

Meade peered into the microscope. "A match."

"Venetian. Typical seventeenth century. Vermeer never used anything but. Very well, then. We know the pigments. We know the stretchers and frame and the segment of the story they tell. We know the canvas and its contribution. So far, so good."

Nico rolled off his stool. Gathering steam, he cleared a space for himself. From a metal file box much like those in Miles Roundtree's storage unit, he produced a glass container. From the container he removed a tiny heap of grayish white powder.

"My own research began with the grounding material, an area Miles didn't broach. Why? Because we're dealing with a painting in need of a tune-up, not a major overhaul. Waste not the client's money nor the restorer's time, and Miles Roundtree had plenty to keep him busy." Nico stirred the powder into a soft paste, smeared it across a glass slide, and placed it beneath the microscope. "Remember, Mr. Meade, that in centuries past, canvas surfaces were treated with basically two materials. Chalk and gypsum, both from natural sources and thus laced with microorganisms. Much like our sample here."

"And the Van Dyck you showed me two days ago."

"Ah, a splendid memory, indeed. The Dutch, however, were fond of a denser, smoother surface. They found that adding lead white to their grounding achieved this look. Jan Vermeer was no exception."

Nico rested his hands on his rounded stomach.

"In those days," he continued, "the making of lead white was a labor of love. The sulfide ore was first roasted and then smelted down to the raw metal. This metal was then stretched across huge clay pots containing acetic acid, and the whole works was piled high in a bed of fermenting dung. Which, of course, produced carbon dioxide, which, along with the acid vapors, produced the desired carbonate. Crude, but effective.

"So what happened? In the latter days of the

eighteenth century, the machines took over. Someone had the bright idea of squeezing the raw metal through brass rollers."

"Making it easier to free the pigment flakes from the fermenting metal," Farrell said, the restorer's words drawing her away from the microscope.

"To be sure," Nico replied. "The lead white Jan Vermeer used was nearly pure. The trade-off with mechanization was contamination. Zinc contamination."

"The particles of brass picked up from the milling equipment." Meade nodded. And then the gesture came to a sudden and complete halt. "Nico — "

"Yes, Mr. Meade. The grounding material from the painting Miles Roundtree restored five months ago contained a zinc level of 18,000 parts per million. An impossibility for the year 1673."

"My God, Nico." Farrell's voice came from the depths of her throat, a whisper. "You're — ?"

"Not without confirmation, my child." Nico's raised hand subdued them both. He pushed two photographs across the table, one from the X-ray of the surface, the other from the grounding layer. "Go to the museum sometime, Mr. Meade. Look at any oil painting over fifty years old. Look close and you'll see that nearly every one suffers from what is called *crackling*. Those little tiny cracks that look like splintered glass? It's almost inevitable. As the pigments dry, the oil evaporates. The canvas and stretchers contract and expand. The paint cracks. Yes? But understand this. The crackle starts at the surface, penetrates each paint layer, and *may*, may eventually, even attack the ground layer itself."

"Therefore," Farrell said, "crackle that appears on the surface might not appear in the ground layer, but the *reverse* is impossible."

Nico offered Farrell a magnifying glass. She studied each photo in turn — but only for a moment — dismay shrouding her face. "A forgery."

"Yes," Nico said simply. "The practiced forger will take an insignificant painting from the period in which he intends to work. He'll remove as much of the paint as possible, as close to the ground layer as possible. That done, he sets to work on his own masterpiece."

"Drawing the crackle up through each layer of paint to the surface." Farrell pressed the magnifying glass into Meade's hand. "Nature's way indecently perverted."

"The problem is drawing *all* the grounding crackle to the surface," Nico said. "I've never seen it."

Meade set the glass aside. "A twenty-five million-dollar forgery."

"Not your everyday forgery, however," Nico said, padding across the studio to a table with a hot plate and a teakettle with steam rising from the spout. He poured water over three tea bags. "Not one in a hundred paintings is tested for zinc contamination, Mr. Meade. And a routine examination of X-ray layers would never have revealed the crackle discrepancy. The pigments and the canvas were authentic. As for the quality of the actual painting — " The restorer toddled back to the workbench and looked empathetically at Farrell. "If a curator of Miss DeBruin's skill was taken in, well . . . ."

"And you're convinced Miles didn't know about the forgery?"

"His samples suggest he didn't."

"Unless that's exactly what his samples were meant to suggest," Meade said. "Nico, if Sir Greyling requested Miles's silence on a matter as delicate as a forgery, would Miles have complied?"

Nico expelled a deep and irrevocable sigh. "Yes, it's possible."

"The X-rays that Miles took of the Vermeer would've been done before he worked on the painting."

Nico blinked. "Yes."

"Is there any indication of previous restoration?"

"None."

"Then the oak stretchers — you said they were approximately forty-five years old — would date the forgery."

"I would say, yes." Nico took the magnifying glass in one hand, his tea in the other, and led them into his office. "My last discovery. I must show you."

From the envelope Meade had salvaged from the trash receptacle in back of Miles Roundtree's studio, Nico drew out a single negative. He clamped it to an X-ray lamp. He flipped the switch, and the surface photo of *Two Women and Their Music* came to life. Drawing Meade and Farrell near, he held the magnifying glass up to the negative's upper right corner. "There," he said.

Meade steadied the glass. "Fingerprints."

"Indeed." Nico mustered a halfhearted smile. "It's a common enough technique, really. The artist works the still-moist paint with his thumb or finger, sometimes with his palm."

"The effect is called a soft-focus," Farrell added.

"Once the paint dries, the prints are inaccessible to the naked eye. But they're also an indelible part of the painting, and nothing on an oil painting's surface can hide from the eye of the X-ray." Nico popped the negative from the lamp and passed it to Meade, who slipped it into his inside coat pocket. "We should have one secret between us, I would think. Keep it well."

Hardly a moment later, a sharp knock rattled the studio door. The man responsible was as thin as a razor blade in every feature except his ears, which drooped. He cradled a wide-brimmed hat across his chest. Against the screen, he displayed a silver badge.

24

GIDEON DEBRUIN'S OFFICE on the seventh floor of the Malan Building buzzed with activity. The general manager of his East Province knitting mills argued shipping tactics with a general partner from a cotton mill in Cradock. The thorns in both of their sides were the German-speaking brothers who sat across from them and chewed silently on the stems of identical pipes. The brothers ran De-Bruin's most prodigious Angora goat ranch, four thousand acres outside the town of Klipplaat. Male secretaries sat on either side of a glass-topped table. Alabaster elephants held a huge land map at the corners.

Gideon DeBruin stood at the window sipping iced coffee and leaning heavily on his cane. He wasn't listening. A call from the Reverend Pieter Crous, twenty minutes before, had left him strangely immobilized; feeling, he thought, like a self-incriminating witness to some terrible crime.

But then the *Broederbond* did have a distorted, if not warped, perception of "crime" within its ranks. A matter as mundane as public drunkenness drew a full year's suspension. Philandering called for a halfhearted reprimand. Discussing the organization in public was tantamount to a declaration of war. And there were harsher punishments, DeBruin knew that. The first words a Broeder ever spoke as a Broeder, at the induction ceremony they all went through, reinforced this. *He who betrays the Bond will be destroyed by the Bond. The Bond never forgets. Its vengeance is swift and sure. Never yet has a traitor escaped his just punishment.* Betrayal. A crime worthy of the harshest punishment: death. A crime —

And then the red light on the phone behind him illuminated. A melodic hum filled the room, saving him from his own thoughts. DeBruin spoke without turning. "Gentlemen, my private line. If you'll excuse me."

"Certainly," the general partner replied.

When DeBruin heard the door close behind him, he returned to his desk. He lifted the receiver. "Yes."

"Things aren't getting any better."

DeBruin recognized the voice. In reply he said, "Crous just told me about the cigar wrapper."

"I only found out about it myself an hour ago. Forensic's playing cat and mouse, and I can't find out who's pulling the strings. . . . Your brand, then?"

"It's my brand."

"No prints, which takes the department out of it, but it's too bad you don't smoke something a bit less conspicuous."

"That's helpful."

"That's not the worst of it. You're an opera buff, right? Are you ready for what they found in the front seat of the car used by our killer?" DeBruin listened to the news of the theater ticket stub like a man outside himself. A man who could read the words before they were spoken. "There were three identifiable sets of prints. A receptionist at the Opera House. A reservationist at the theater annex. And a thumb and forefinger . . ."

"Mine."

"Yours."

DeBruin's head reeled. "I need your trust on this one," he managed to say. "We can still come out of this thing."

"We can still come out of it, all right. In fact, this might just be the beginning. Get this. The Vermeer we stole from De Greyling? The Vermeer that was stolen from us? A forgery."

"Good God, what?" Gideon DeBruin couldn't remember the last time he had laughed, but he laughed now. Out of sheer deliverance, he laughed. And the laughter fueled a return of ferocity, and with that, the return of anger. "Who knows about this forgery?"

"The American, Meade. Your daughter. Some restorer named Mustapha. A couple of *friends*. That's it. No one else."

"A couple of friends? Friends, as in allies? Our allies?"

"Friends, as in allies."

"Let's keep it that way. And wait for my call." DeBruin hung up without waiting for a reply. He reached for his cane, the cedar one with the rounded brass head. He gripped the tip until his body shook and his hands hurt. Finally, he faced what he had been hiding from for the last forty-eight hours. He voiced it in a single word. "Rita."

At age thirty-five, Terrence Greyling didn't see himself as having made much of his life. His anticipated worth was three hundred thirty million rand; an active trust fund was valued at ten million. Oddly, he didn't flaunt it. He did own three cars — a Maserati, an old XKE convertible, and a Ferrari he rarely drove — but he insisted upon doing all the maintenance on them himself, wax jobs included. He did own a thirty-two-foot sailboat, but sailing was something he generally did alone. In his early twenties, he had tried on the playboy hat, but the come-ons had always left him feeling like a salesman and, once women found out who he was, like a carnival prize. Drugs had left him wondering what all the fuss was about. Gambling had one irremediable drawback: losing.

He had graduated from the University of Natal law school, but had done so without much enthusiasm. His lack of enthusiasm did not reflect a lack of intelligence, only boredom with the legal profession. Boredom was one thing Terrence acquired with considerable gusto. He had endured in school only because "A Greyling never quits" was a family credo thrust on him at an early age. Graduating sixth in a law school class of 212 normally would have guaranteed writing his own ticket, but Terrence had not applied to a single firm. He had spurned advances of recruiters from three countries.

He turned his attention to wine and horses instead. His 350-acre vineyard on the southern slopes of Paarl Mountain produced a wood-matured sauvignon blanc that, for the last two years, had earned gold medals. His stable of Arabian horses outside the Franschhoek Valley had attracted buyers from as far away as Norway.

But the woman with whom Terrence emerged from the Rondebosch restaurant was neither wine connoisseur nor prospective horse buyer. Her name was Connie, a dancer Terrence "entertained" whenever he was in need of entertainment himself.

Terrence didn't see the black limousine parked across the street. Its one-way windows reflected a gray, somber day and protected Paul Kilian from the eyes of the curious.

Kilian watched as the restaurant door swung shut behind the young couple, arm in arm and several drinks giddy. They were an attractive pair; the dancer wore faded blue jeans, Terrence carried a sport coat over his shoulder. There were a couple of drops of rain, so they huddled beneath his umbrella. His Maserati was parked in a lot two blocks away.

"That's him," Kilian announced, and the limo inched

away from the curb. The driver worked the car into the far lane and set its pace in tandem with that of the couple. At the first corner, two men jumped out.

Ten seconds later Terrence Greyling was trapped in the middle of the front seat, a stunned dancer was left standing at the curb, and the limousine was sweeping back into the traffic. There was no time for Terrence to protest, hardly time for him to catch his breath. From the backseat a leather cord was slipped around his neck. A callused hand covered his mouth and nose.

"Talk only when an answer is required," the man holding the cord directed. A thin-bladed knife dropped from the sleeve sheath of the man at Terrence's side. He pressed its blade against the young Greyling's jugular. "Nod if you understand."

Terrence's head jerked spasmodically. Sweat rolled from his brow.

Kilian nodded, and the leather cord was loosened. The man in back continued, "Four nights ago your father's gallery was broken into. The thieves, as it turned out, were extremely well prepared, to the point of having in their possession a diagram of the gallery and its alarm system drawn on a sheet of expensive stationery. Show him," the man said to his confederate up front.

A full-size piece of hard-surfaced bond stationery, tan in color with a raised border and gold-dusted margin, drifted down into Terrence Greyling's lap. The embossed monogram at the top read, "TAG." A hand, gathering a fistful of hair, thrust Terrence's head forward. "You recognize it, of course."

The knife blade subdued Terrence's attempt to turn his head. "You chicken-shit bastard. Where's your face? Show me your — "

The hand wrenched his head back, and the cord bit into his neck. "If he is insolent again," the man in back said, "cut him. Now, the stationery was ordered three months ago through the firm of Opperman and Nagel in Johannesburg, by *you* . . ."

"Are you mad? I don't own personalized stationery, and if I did, it wouldn't look like that shit" was the breathless reply.

"Show him," the man snapped. Now a copy of the original Opperman and Nagel order form was thrust into Terrence's face. "Read it."

The return address at the top did indeed show Terrence Greyling's name and the Malmesbury mailing address at De Greyling, and the order description clearly detailed the identical stationery used for the gallery diagram. The handwriting also seemed to be his. Even in his distressed state, or maybe because of it, Terrence recognized that.

Kilian tipped his head to the man in the front seat, and he dug out the wallet from Terrence's breast coat pocket. The driver's license and identity card were held out for his inspection. The signatures on both were a perfect match for the one at the bottom of the order form.

"The stationery was found in a desk drawer in the sitting room off your bedroom at De Greyling," the man continued.

"It was put there without my knowledge. I'm being set up, for God's sake. Can't you see that? Why would I steal from my own father?"

"We're not convinced," was the answer. "Convince us. You have thirty seconds."

It was the man in the front seat who saw the flaw; one of those unconscious errors made, no doubt, in the pursuit of matters more pressing. In the information section of the order form, in the tiny boxes labeled Mr., Mrs., or Ms.: a response so automatic that . . .

He pressed the order form into Paul Kilian's hand, punching a finger at the discrepancy. The paralysis of sudden understanding brought a crooked grin to Kilian's face. "Oh, my."

Then he touched his driver on the shoulder. The limousine came to an abrupt halt. The passenger door flew open; the leather cord fell away from Terrence Greyling's neck. Seconds later he found himself, stunned and visibly trembling, in the middle of an early evening traffic jam. A horn blared, and he dodged an oncoming car. Turning, he caught a fleeting glimpse of the limousine as it sped into an alley and was gone.

If there was information to be gained about a lost or forged work of art, London was the logical place to begin; this was common knowledge in the art world.

As it turned out, at 4:55 there was a direct flight from Cape Town to Heathrow Airport in London. Farrell used a pay phone in the Malay Quarter to secure her reservation.

From the city, Meade used the two-lane coast highway to circle the peninsula back to False Bay. The bay road intersected the N2 freeway, and the freeway took them east to the airport. He pulled off the road twice and backtracked once. If they were being followed, he couldn't detect it.

Ten minutes later he was dropping Farrell at the main entrance to the D. F. Malan International Airport, and saying good-bye was not coming easily. They talked about Meade joining her in a day or two if nothing more developed in Cape Town. They talked about being careful, and meant it. Meade was afraid for her. He was afraid for himself.

There were two messages from the home office in San Francisco awaiting Meade when he returned to his desk at the *Argus* an hour and ten minutes later. He ignored them.

Instead, he called Sean's apartment. Sean's roommate, Jeremy, was another American. They both worked at the library. Jeremy told Meade he had gone over to the library earlier in the afternoon, but Sean hadn't checked in for work. He wasn't at the coffeehouse on Bendix, and he wasn't at either of the listening rooms at the Student Center. Jeremy concluded with the adage, "He'll show up eventually. He always does," and Meade hung up.

Then he called the Cape Town Public Library, the university library, and the university's World History Department. No one had ever heard of the Missing Sixth.

Meade punched into the paper's own back-dated files, but the computer interrupted the process, signaling instead an incoming message. Meade hoped for some word from Sean. Instead, the sender heading read, "G. De-Bruin." His message: "I suggest another visit. My office, this evening, your convenience."

25

ONE DIDN'T DEAL with the *Broederbond*. The slogan "Our strength lies in secrecy" permeated every aspect of the club. There were other factors which allowed thirteen thousand men to dominate the lives of twenty-five million others. A Broeder would quote "hard work" or "commitment." An outsider might think of fear or manipulation. But the devotion to secrecy had in many ways transcended itself, and Meade was beginning to understand it. Publicity, public outrage, liberal condemnation, all bent on unmasking or undermining the club, had unwittingly lent an aura of invincibility and invisibility to it. A mystique.

As he took the stairs to the basement and climbed a loading ramp to the street, Meade realized that he, unwittingly or not, had added his own splash of color to the mystique. Who was he dealing with now? Was it De-Bruin, or was it the Bond? Had the message on his computer been personal, or was the Executive Council looking over DeBruin's shoulder when he sent it? Meade imagined the former, though as he walked out into the rain, he admitted he wasn't sure. He was, however, certain of one thing. That the meeting that lay ahead of him would deal directly with the Missing Sixth; that with a simple message on a computer screen, Gideon DeBruin had confirmed his involvement.

Meade jogged down Albertus and made a left on Buitenkant. He ducked into a doorway and waited. Two cars passed. A man on a bicycle pedaled by. Meade followed him. He turned his face up to the cool mist which, like fairy dust, revived an old memory, one sweet and painful. The rain, Sally used to say when he would complain too loudly, was the perfect excuse for poetry and lovemaking. She liked to tease, "You read Yeats and I'll undress." Then she would open the book to something particularly dramatic, like "A Dialogue of Self and Soul," and slowly, to the rhythm of his words and the faltering of his concentration, remove each article of clothing. She did it leisurely — she tossed her shoes irreverently across the room; she carefully rolled down her knee socks; she undid her blouse, button by button; she folded her jeans neatly across the back of a chair — and would scold him unmercifully for taking his eyes off the page. She unfastened her hair; she unhooked her bra; she painstakingly peeled off silk panties. And finally, when he could take no more, and because "A Dialogue of Self and Soul" can be a very long poem, he would ignore her scolding and the book would close. And . . .

The wail of a taxi's horn wrenched Meade back into the present. Jogging again, he crossed in front of the laughing lions that flanked the gateway to the Castle of Good Hope, where troop trucks were parked end to end. Street lamps threw yellow glitter in his path. The city hummed and creaked.

Seven stories up in the Malan Building they met face-to-face in an office dominated by floor-to-ceiling windows, a three-dimensional relief of Africa, and a solid zebrawood desk. Photographs, dated and spanning three decades, cluttered the walls. All, Meade noticed, were of DeBruin himself with an assortment of high-powered hunting rifles and the trophies of big-game safaris. A limp and lifeless cheetah, a once proud lion, a bloodied impala. Meade was pleased; it made his disdain for the man that much more complete.

"What have you learned?" DeBruin asked.

"I've learned that your foray into the world of petty larceny has failed." Meade continued his inspection, photograph by photograph. "And you? What have you learned? How to put a bullet between the eyes of an impala from six hundred yards away? You're a true sportsman. What else? How to carve goats into dollar bills? How to use thumbscrews and nose rings? How to hide behind a boys' club? How to toy with your own daughter's life?"

"Farrell has nothing to do with this."

"And the bomb that ripped apart her table at the Broken Bridge restaurant?"

"That was not my doing. It was a mistake."

"It was a mistake because it failed."

"I'll tell you what I've learned, Mr. Meade," DeBruin retaliated. "I've learned that a plan, no matter how petty, isn't a failure until the game is up. And this game isn't up."

Meade paused at the window, feeling his way. Outside, a splash of white danced on ocean swells the color of steel. The running lights of a tanker celebrated the coming of night.

"Then you possess the painting," Meade said finally. He turned. "But if that's the case, then why am I here?"

"If I possessed the painting, Mr. Meade, your stay in South Africa would have ended days ago."

"But they think you have it," Meade replied. "Your own people. The Brothers. They think you have it."

"What *they* think shouldn't concern you."

"Then Rita has it. The painting. And the Missing Sixth. But if that were true, wouldn't she be back in East Germany by now? *Is* she?"

Meade waited. There existed two possibilities. Either

251

the man who had appeared at Nico Mustapha's studio door belonged to DeBruin, or he belonged to DeBruin's opponents. The one knew of the forgery; the other remained convinced that the original had been taken from De Greyling.

"I wonder at this fondness you Americans demonstrate for game playing, Mr. Meade. One day you'll have to explain it to me." The reply was delivered without haste, almost casually — in a tone that suggested a reestablishment of authority, had there been any question in Meade's mind. Now DeBruin crossed the office to his desk. He dropped easily into his chair and said, "Rita Hess has many things, Mr. Meade, but the Sixth is not one of them. And the same might be said for you and me. However, there is one thing that separates us. And that is your son."

A pall of absolute silence seemed to rob the office of breathable air. A moment later, the drone of a tugboat's low whistle pierced the silence, and Meade straightened; the hairs on the back of his neck bristled.

"Make yourself clear," he said.

"Your son. Sean." DeBruin pressed his lips to the handle of his cane. And then, as if acquiescing to the sorry needs of a child, he withdrew the cane and dug a small box from his suit coat pocket. He opened it, placed it on the desk, and used the head of his cane to propel it in Meade's direction. "We have him."

Meade stepped cautiously up to the desk. Inside the box, nestled in a bed of cotton, lay Sean's high school ring. He had worked a half-dozen weekends at the paper sorting mail and shagging coffee to pay for it, Meade remembered. He plucked it from the box. It dropped onto his little finger. "Where?"

"In a most select place, I assure you. The most select place on the Cape."

Meade looked deep into Gideon DeBruin's eyes, held them until they dropped, and then pushed away from the desk. He told himself to harness the anger, turn it in-

252

ward, use it. Anger was nothing new to him. The sheer terror, however, he had no answer for. He circled back to the window.

"The Missing Sixth must be extraordinarily valuable for you to risk your own life over it." Meade spoke to DeBruin's back. "I should know more about it."

"The Missing Sixth is a document. Beyond that it is not your concern. Your task is to find the Vermeer, or to confirm that it no longer exists. Do so and you'll have your son back. That is our deal. We have no interest in the painting; do with it as you please. The document is sealed in a manila envelope. Wax-sealed. I tell you this, Mr. Meade, because if the seal is broken, or has in any way been tampered with, our contract is broken. Irrevocably broken." Now DeBruin rose. He turned and drew himself to his full height. He positioned a business card against the ring box. "For your information, the police will be putting the Greyling incident aside for the time being. It will remain, however, a highly restricted matter as far as the press is concerned. The numbers on that card are my private lines, both at home and here in the office. I'll expect to hear from you daily. You have seventy-two hours. And, Mr. Meade, let me remind you that your son's life depends on it."

"It was taken this morning," Fazzie said; *it* being a re-markably clear photograph of Jacob Bartleman emerging from the basement of St. Stephen's Church, a step ahead of Gideon DeBruin. "Mieta followed DeBruin there at seven this morning. Same world-beaters as on Sunday. Bartleman showed up fifteen minutes later. He used the main entrance, stayed maybe five or ten minutes. He made his exit through the rectory with DeBruin and the Rev-erend Crous on each arm. The three of them walked through the church courtyard, shook hands, and went their separate ways."

Meade let the photo slip from his fingers. It came to

rest facedown on the ground at their feet. "He's in De-Bruin's corner, then."

"Which means, realistically, that the egg suck at Nico's studio wasn't Security, despite his ID. He belonged to Bartleman, not Fogwell."

"Which would also mean, assuming you're right, that DeBruin knows about the forgery."

They were sitting on cane chairs in front of the sod house Meade had been using for the past two nights. It was a moonless evening. The ocean was a restless shadow stretching beyond their sight. Meade wrapped his hands around a mug of black coffee. He was bombarded by San Francisco memories. A pit barbecue on the beach, building a sand castle at sunset, curling up in a blanket and watching the sanderlings race along the water line.

"Since we're in an assuming mood," Fazzie said, "let's assume that Miles Roundtree knew about the forgery, but for some reason refused to divulge the information the night he died. Where does that leave Rita Hess?"

"Guessing."

"And Greyling?"

"If Miles Roundtree knew about the forgery, then Greyling knows about the forgery."

Out of the corner of his eye, Meade saw Fazzie tense. His face screwed into a knot and his back straightened. Meade saw the reflection of headlights curling down the hill, then heard the protest of an engine.

"Egg sucker," Fazzie hissed.

"He's here," Meade said. The anemic wail deepened. "Cam, why don't you have a look at my art collection."

Fazzie snatched up a full ashtray and two pop cans and disappeared inside the house. The Toyota was the color of a hearse, no markings. The driver switched off the headlights, turned off the engine, and had his door open, all before the car came to a halt. It was Bartleman. His stride was short and purposeful.

He stopped a half-dozen steps away and said, "I was wondering when you'd call."

"I was wondering how long it would take you to get here." Mieta's photograph lay on the ground between the chairs, and Meade swept it up. He studied it, but only for a moment, and then held it out. "The *Broederbond*'s Executive Council. That's fast company for a cop."

Bartleman took the photo and held it at arm's length. His hand coursed pensively across his jaw. He tugged on his mustache, shrugging. "Your logic eludes me, pal."

"They have my son, Bartleman."

Bartleman was still gazing at the photograph, or through it; he turned it over and back, like a shopper gauging the price of an item he wants but doesn't really need. "Sean's a student at the university, isn't he? What do you mean, 'have him'?"

"In 'a most select place.' The 'most select place on the Cape.' They're willing to make a trade."

"Fuck. I told you that first day to keep out of it. I told you it was bad news. But you couldn't, could you? Couldn't resist the urge to play detective again. 'Big-time American Reporter Makes His Big-time Comeback at the Expense of Evil Empire.' Great headlines. Or how about, 'Big-time American reporter condemns only son to the short fucking end of the stick because he just couldn't keep his nose out of where it didn't belong.' How does that sound to you?"

"Not good," Meade admitted. He watched the man he had called a friend turn his back to the house. "How does it sound to *you*, Jacob?"

The breeze had picked up and now charged through the hut, rattling the screen and stirring a dust devil from the sand out front.

Bartleman talked with an eye on the beach and the ocean beyond. "When the Nats first arrested Mandela back in — "

255

"Jacob —"

Hearing his name, Bartleman gave Meade the benefit of his attention once more. "Back in 1963, it was my old man who put the cuffs on his hands. It should have been the highlight of his career. But it wasn't. It took about six whiskeys to get him talking about it, but he'd talk. Like a priest in his own confessional.

"This one, he'd say, *he* didn't have the feel of your run-of-the-mill punk. This Mandela, he didn't hate you with his eyes. He didn't crawl and kick the dirt like your ordinary Kaffir. He didn't *smell* the part of your fist-waving comrade. He was spookier than that. He gave you this 'you can trust me' look. And you did. A natural-born leader, my old man called him.

"Now understand, this is a Nat-sweating, flag-waving Afrikaner spouting this heresy. And a black man with the ability to inspire such heresy made a dangerous combination, and the Nats knew it. You know how they knew, Michael? They were bewildered; which caused them to be scared. They could see people giving a damn about this man. So they made an example of him. Treason, sabotage, conspiracy — impressive. But they didn't just lock him away. Not at all. They told the whole bloody world, 'We've made ourselves safe from this incorrigible asshole by locking him up for good.' You know where? 'In a most select place. The most select place in South Africa.' "

Bartleman's story seemed to have reached an inconclusive end. At that moment, the front screen opened, and Fazzie stepped out. He looked from Meade to Bartleman, and the words rolled thickly off his tongue. "Robben Island."

The shock of seeing Fazzie caused Bartleman to falter momentarily. But then, as if the damage had been done, he plunged on. "The political cartoonists picked up on it. *A most select place.* They ran it into the ground until it became yesterday's joke. But my old man, believe it or not, still uses it every once in a while. A most select place."

"Robben Island is full of political prisoners," Fazzie protested. "Not white Americans. Risk that kind of attention on the Nat's favorite house of horrors? I don't think so."

"I don't think so, either," Bartleman replied. He replaced his hat. "So DeBruin won't be using the prison's facilities. And he won't involve Security."

Bartleman started for his car. He glanced back at Fazzie. "I've said too much."

Fazzie shrugged. "I wasn't taking notes."

Bartleman nodded. A minute later, he was gone.

They were both staring back at the hill when Fazzie articulated what both were thinking. "Generous, wasn't he?"

"Extremely."

"You don't believe him."

"I didn't say that." A cold tremor started at the base of Meade's spine and galloped across his back. He hoped for a gust of wind to blame it on, but there was none.

"He wasn't lying," Fazzie said. "About Sean, that is. About the island."

"No, he wasn't lying. But a sudden case of conscience is one thing. Betraying the club is another. I wonder if he's that strong?"

"There's a third alternative, you know."

"That he's playing the same game he's been playing all week."

"These degenerates won't think twice about killing Sean, Yank. Not if they think we're screwing with them. They may kill him anyway."

"I should've sent him home."

"You tried. Which was more than I did," Fazzie said. He crushed a cigarette out under his heel. "Sean's stronger than you think, Yank. Believe me."

The gust of wind came at last; it tugged at the loose flaps of Meade's jacket and sent strands of hair flying.

"Vodka straight up," he said. "It cuts through the cold better than anything I know, Cam. Two shots side by side, one after another."

"Yeah, I know. You came to this African paradise to escape the cold. Now here you are freezing your ass off, and a drink sounds pretty good." Fazzie knew Meade's problem. Everyone in the newsroom did; it wasn't even gossip anymore. He passed Meade a smoke and cupped the lighter for him. Then he said, "I'll make you a deal, Yank. Skip the drink. Find the painting instead. I'll take care of Sean. When it's all over, we'll have dinner. On me."

Meade looked beyond Fazzie to the sea. "Tomorrow we'll see just how impenetrable the famous Robben Island really is."

For a moment, Fazzie just stared. Then he sucked air into his lungs and began pacing in a circle. "Want to know, do you? I'll tell you. The waters surrounding the place are off-limits for a stretch of two miles. They use gunboats and helicopters as insurance. And there are only a half-dozen places to land a boat, even if you could get through. The airspace over the prison is similarly off-limits and monitored by radar twenty-four hours a day. There's a very specific law that says they can blast away at anything that intrudes into those areas, and ask questions later. Am I getting through to you?"

"We'll see," Meade said again.

The helicopter rose from the roof of the Argus Building as it did every morning at 6:00 A.M. It was at once a traffic watch vehicle and an emergency transport for fast-breaking stories. This morning the pilot had taken on two additional passengers. Fazzie strapped himself into the seat next to the pilot. Meade crouched in the back.

258

The pilot was accustomed to unusual requests; his reputation among reporters in the field was that he rarely asked questions. He was also well aware of the airspace restrictions governing the area around Robben Island.

"The trick, obviously, is not to be obvious," he told Meade as the helicopter pitched forward. The lofty towers of Foreshore looked momentarily like canyons of glass and exposed aggregate. Then they crossed the border between land and sea, and a sweep of brilliant blue opened up before them. "I'll use the fishing fleet as a guise. We'll make radio contact, see what they're going after today, and then shoot a report over to the feature editor's desk back home. Make it very legitimate. Which means you'll only get about two minutes of decent viewing."

The island lay in a northwesterly direction ten kilometers from the mainland. Meade had equipped himself with binoculars and Fazzie with a borrowed 35-mm camera and telephoto lens; he opened a side window and leaned out.

The island, as they approached, was shaped like an elongated heart, south to north. "Lengthwise, it measures about five and half kilometers," the pilot announced. He set the helicopter on a parallel course with the eastern coast. "Maybe two kilometers at its widest."

The prison occupied the northern third of the island. A series of chain-link fences, all capped with rolls of barbed wire, formed a cincture around eight or ten flat-roofed buildings. Guard towers rose around the perimeter. Revolving radar screens perched on concrete pillars. Three helicopters rested on a circular pad. Despite the early hour, men strolled in the runways surrounding clapboard barracks. Meade spotted goalposts on either side of a dirt field.

Beyond the fences was a complex of more modern structures, these of red brick. There were tennis and basketball courts. "The warden and his men," the pilot said, as the helicopter banked. "That's their housing."

259

At the center of the island, a barren and desolate stretch had been given over to a series of small adobe huts. What looked like a tall barbed wire fence surrounded them, and men patrolled on horseback.

"Isolation," Meade ventured.

The pilot glanced over his shoulder and nodded. Again he adjusted course. Below them a host of fishing boats traversed the glassy blue waters of the South Atlantic. The pilot made radio contact.

The farther south they flew, the more rugged the island's terrain became. Cliffs jutted out over the ocean. The ground was pitted with huge holes. They saw canvas-covered trucks winding along a narrow, tarred road.

"The quarries," Fazzie said. He was shooting pictures at a furious rate. "Granite. I've talked to several people who have had the pleasure of working in those hellholes. They tell me the western quarry is still active. Not so, the one to the east. It's been abandoned for maybe two years now." Fazzie glanced briefly at Meade. "They say that if your friend Bartleman is giving us anything close to the straight stuff, and if Security Branch is really *not* involved in this, then that's where they'll have Sean."

Now they saw light reflected off the watery surface of the flooded eastern quarry. Upon its rim three huts perched. From the chimney of one a wisp of smoke rose. There was an off-road vehicle of some type parked behind the hut. Signs of life, Meade thought, as Fazzie ran off the last pictures of the roll, and the island disappeared behind them.

26

MEADE CALLED Sean's apartment from a pay phone in town. By now Sean's roommate, Jeremy, was at least annoyed if not concerned. They had planned on attending a lecture by Jesse Jackson the night before, and Jeremy had been forced to "eat" a twenty-dollar ticket. Meade told him Sean's pickup had broken down in the mountains. He mentioned the Cedarberg Mountains and the Olifants River. Sean had been forced to walk to the nearest town. He had just called, Meade told Jeremy.

"Don't worry about the ticket. I'll take care of it," Meade managed to say. "Don't worry."

After he hung up, Meade said the last two words again, out loud, and felt sick.

He called the Cape Town University Criminology Department. Peter Hawthorne, the ex-forensic scientist, shared an office with a full-time professor. Meade posed his questions about the X-ray negative and the fingerprints in purely hypothetical terms, and, as he had hoped, it was Hawthorne who suggested the rendezvous.

Thirty minutes later, they met in the Argus underground parking garage.

"You look terrible, mate," Hawthorne said. He used

a droplight to expose the fingerprints on the surface negative Miles Roundtree had taken of the Vermeer. He used
a 35-mm camera with a special lens to photograph the
prints. "I'm the one working nights these days. What's
your excuse?"

Meade perked up. "You're working? Where?"

"The County Coroner's office had a couple of things
they couldn't handle. A friend gave me a call."

"I'm glad to hear it." Meade borrowed a cigarette.

Hawthorne talked as he worked. "There was a time
when this forensic business was all seat-of-the-pants.
Shoot, nowadays an infrared spectrometer can tell you the
type of material a bullet passed through or identify a hit-
and-run automobile from a paint tracing found on the
victim's belt buckle." Hawthorne smiled to himself and
fiddled with his light meter. "We use this thing called
neutron activation to detect gunpowder on the back of a
killer's firing hand. Remarkable. The Arson Squad uses
gas chromatography to figure out what started an
insurance-fraud fire when there's nothing left but damp
ashes and smoldering coals."

Meade wasn't listening. He paced and smoked and
replayed in his mind everything he had seen from the helicopter.

"Then again, fingerprinting" — Hawthorne continued his dissertation unabetted — "is as old as the hills. It
was the brainstorm of this British anthropologist. Sir
something or other. The English started printing the local
populace almost eighty years ago. Some people say the
Pass Laws grew out of that practice, that the Afrikaners
weren't that creative and they only refined the practice
when they came to power in the forties. Who am I to
argue?

"It was all done by hand then. Printing, cataloging,
searching. Influx control was an Afrikaner obsession.
You've heard it all. The passbooks, the work permits, all
that rot.

"Now the Pass Laws are history, but the obsession? Oh, no, it hangs on like a nagging cough." Hawthorne took the lens off his camera. He rewound the film. "Now it's computers. Now a print search, which in yesteryear might have taken four techs two weeks, can be processed in two hours by an optical recognition station and a mass memory system. You're impressed, I can tell."

"Sorry," Meade said absently. He slipped the X-ray negative back into his coat pocket.

"I teach a class in criminology at the university," Hawthorne said. Meade nodded. "Oh, you know that already. Anyway, I'll use their lab and one of their computers. I still have my access code to the banks in Pretoria, if they haven't voided it. I should have an answer in a couple of hours."

"Are the print banks in Pretoria tapped into Interpol or any of the other European centers?" Meade asked.

Hawthorne shook his head. "You'd have to go through the Crime Research Bureau for that, and without Security clearance you can kiss that idea good-bye."

"I'll call you," Meade said. "Thanks for the help."

While Farrell took a taxi from the Hotel Jerome to the Witt Library, the man following her drove an old Fiat convertible.

The Witt Library was affiliated with the Courtauld Institute of Fine Arts. Both were tiny parts of the vast and esteemed London University. The Witt was located within viewing distance of the Marble Arch in a less-than-inspiring building on Portman Square. Beyond lay the weather-beaten fields of Hyde Park.

Farrell had spent four years at the university, and a good part of that time at the Witt. The document archives on the second floor were dedicated to the proposition that nothing was too insignificant to save. Here, the serious researcher could find a handwritten letter from Rembrandt, a government study on the negative effects of Italian art on children, and a photostat of a Scotland Yard inquiry into the theft of a Renoir from the London Gallery sixty years ago.

At the reference desk, Farrell filled out an information request on Jan Vermeer van Delft's *Two Women and Their Music*. "The complete file," she told the clerk. "I'll be upstairs."

The singular chamber that was the third floor represented the most complete portfolio of painters and paintings assembled anywhere in the world. Farrell still rarely ventured to an auction or showing without first paying a visit to this floor. The room itself was divided by dozens of lengthy wooden filing cabinets, each fronted by attached workbenches and mounted swivel chairs. Within each cabinet were row after row of green file boxes, each kept under lock and key. Each was devoted to a different artist; within each box lay reproductions, details, and descriptions of most if not all of the works produced by that artist, along with annotations, biographies, and fact sheets. Pablo Picasso filled fifteen boxes; Jan Vermeer and his forty works, only one.

Farrell signed the daily log and showed her passport. Next to the information desk was a coffee urn that was always full, and Farrell filled a tall Styrofoam cup for herself. Then she allowed a matronly clerk to lead her through the chamber. The files were categorized by country and century. Holland, seventeenth century. Row fourteen.

After the clerk released the lock and removed the file, she scrawled the date and her initials on the time registry affixed to the lid. "Twice in two days. Well, now, aren't we popular?" She was talking to Jan Vermeer's box. Then she smiled down at Farrell. "Well, maybe I shouldn't be so surprised, should I? After all, Vermeer is Vermeer, and he'll never be too old for discovery as far as I'm concerned."

"No one else like him," Farrell said. She stared at the

woman's back as she sauntered off. Then she stared at the registry. Yesterday? There were no restrictions on the use of the Witt's facilities, and no fee. Identification was required, but only as a means of keeping track of materials in circulation. The Witt was a casual place, but it wasn't a hangout. Art dealers and collectors used it extensively, but there hadn't been a Vermeer on the market since Cas Greyling's purchase of the *Two Women and Their Music* forgery six months before, and not for six years prior to that. A student, then, Farrell thought. Or a historian. The logic was sound enough, but not sound enough to mollify the queer feeling tiptoeing around inside her head.

She produced a notebook from her purse. She drew her coat tight around her and sipped coffee. This was her element. And today, she reminded herself, she was sober — a thought that caused her to shudder despite the coat.

Farrell worked quickly, thumbing through the reproductions and standing three master prints against the cabinet.

The research material from downstairs arrived.

Jan Vermeer, a biographical sketch noted, was born in Delft, in the Netherlands. *Two Women and Their Music* was his penultimate work. In ill health at the time of its completion, he offered the painting to the pastor of St. Cecilia's Catholic Church, where it was hung in a place of honor in the choir loft. There it remained until water damage forced the closing of the church ninety-two years later. The year was 1765.

A deed of sale, a statement of transfer, and a handwritten note to a Father Lars Saslow — all copies — verified that the painting was then sold to a Dutch shipbuilder and explorer, Jacobus Tasmas Dubois.

Nineteen years later, after the English successfully retaliated against the Dutch for their intervention in the American Revolution, a debt-ridden Dubois sold the greater part of his collection, including the Vermeer, to the royal family of King William III. A scant eleven years later, in 1795 following the French invasion of the Netherlands, the monarch's vast art holdings were distributed among a handful of loyal Dutch families. Neither the families nor the affected works were listed in any document Farrell could find.

Then, following an unexplained interval of nearly a century, came an 1891 auction release from Sotheby's of London. The release was yellowed with age and painfully brittle. It noted the purchase of *Two Women and Their Music* by a Sir Marshall Blunt, an industrialist from Dublin, Ireland, for forty-seven thousand pounds. The seller had requested anonymity.

There were four other clippings. Three were reviews of the Blunt family collection on tour during the late twenties. The fourth, in the *Londonderry Sentinel* dated June 2, 1932, announced the sale of the Vermeer to the family collection of Joseph Shapiro, a German Jew and noted investment banker. An excerpt from a book written in 1953 by the banker's son, Dr. Emery Shapiro, took the history through the war years. It was called *The Pillage of Europe's Great Art Treasures*.

An outspoken opponent of Hitler, Joseph Shapiro spent much of his fortune in support of the anti-Nazi cause. His bank raised millions in marks and guilders for the same purpose. Forced into exile in the late thirties, the Shapiros took refuge in Amsterdam, where the father's anti-Hitler campaigns escalated. Hitler's revenge came a year later when the Netherlands fell to the German army and the entire Shapiro collection was confiscated. Joseph Shapiro's assets and those of his bank were frozen. Five weeks later, the elder Shapiro was dead, the victim of an apparent heart attack. Emery Shapiro and two sisters fled Europe for the African continent and settled in Johannesburg, South Africa.

All but three pieces of the Shapiro collection were later unearthed in the salt mines of Alt Aussee, in Austria. A Rembrandt and a Botticelli were discovered in Munich, on the walls of an air raid shelter. The recovered pieces served to pay off the huge debt run up by Joseph Shapiro during the war. The Vermeer was presumed destroyed in the Allied bombings of Munich in 1945.

For forty-three years the only suggestion to the contrary, Farrell discovered, was offered in a two-column article from the *Global Art Review*, a monthly periodical published in Tel Aviv. The article was less than a year old. An English translation had been attached, and Farrell was immediately struck by Dr. Emery Shapiro's byline. The article reported that police in Amsterdam had discovered a trove of valuable art in an apartment rented by an unnamed University of Amsterdam professor. Counted as part of the find, purportedly, were a Terborch, a de Hooch, and a Vermeer. The article went so far as to hypothesize that this Vermeer must be the only one unaccounted for, his *Two Women and Their Music*.

Not so.

In its next issue the *Review* called the affair "an elaborate hoax perpetrated by disgruntled students at the local university." There were, apparently, no charges filed. The byline in this instance was not, as Farrell had expected, that of Dr. Shapiro; the second piece was a wire-service story from United Press International.

Farrell read both articles a second time and then, for the first time in her nineteen years of utilizing the Witt Library facilities, committed the cardinal sin of the professional researcher. She folded the articles and slipped them into her purse.

The rest of the file was dedicated to the clippings and announcements surrounding the resurfacing and sale of the ostensible Vermeer six months ago. Farrell read through these twice, seeking some form of revelation. When it didn't come, she closed her notebook.

She was setting the file aside when she heard her name.

"Miss DeBruin, isn't it? Farrell DeBruin?"

Farrell turned, half expecting a security guard or one of the clerks. It was neither. The man approaching her looked older than he had in his police uniform. Farrell remembered the angular cut of his face, but not the smile.

"It's Jacob Bartleman," he said, holding out a hand. "Sorry to intrude, but, a friendly face this far from home, I just had to speak up."

"A Cape Town policeman is not the first person one expects to encounter on the third floor of the Witt Library, Captain," Farrell said, still grappling with her surprise. "You must be an exceptional lover of art."

Bartleman laughed. "Would it impress the hell out of you if I said that on the wall of my very own study back home there hangs an original Irma Stern?"

Irma Stern was South Africa's answer to European expressionism—highly collected. "I might even go so far as to ask which one."

"It's called *The Ghost Rider*." Bartleman watched as Farrell replaced the contents of the document file. "One of her earlier works; 1918, to be exact. It's a family heirloom. What can I say? My grandmother. I have to give her the credit."

Farrell appraised him. Bartleman's hand had wandered to his mustache. Below it, he fashioned a modest grin.

"You were working on Miles Roundtree's murder," she said. "Has it been resolved?"

"My counterparts in Security managed to connect the case with the Greyling business. I didn't have much choice but to tell them about the X-ray negatives you and Michael Meade pasted together. That's life. It's their case now." He glanced briefly at the Vermeer reproductions and then added, "I had some time coming to me."

Farrell followed his eyes. "So you're in London looking for just the right piece to hang next to your Stern."

"I'm sorry? Oh, my being here." Bartleman bowed his head, grinned, and tugged at his mustache. "I hope you'll accept a small confession. You see, I was in a cab driving toward my hotel—I'd just had breakfast in a little place along Park Lane—when I saw you walk in here. By the time I reached the lobby I'd convinced myself you might be interested in having dinner with a fellow Capetonian. I walked back thinking that by the time I got here I might have come to my senses. Well, I didn't."

Farrell tried recalling the last time she had eaten dinner out alone, other than her customary Sundays at the Broken Bridge in Stellenbosch. She couldn't. The only other option was room service, which made no sense on a summer's night in London. "How does Italian sound?" she said.

"My mother was Italian," Bartleman responded. He gave her a conspiratorial glance. "But you won't mention that around Cape Town, I hope."

Farrell smiled. "I'm staying at the Hotel Jerome. Shall we say 7:00, in the lobby?"

Bartleman clambered to his feet. He offered his hand again.

On his way out of the building, he stopped at the reference desk on the second floor. He opened his wallet long enough for the elderly clerk to get a glimpse of his badge.

"Yes, sir?"

"There's a woman upstairs. Her name is Farrell DeBruin. She checked out a document file some time earlier. When she returns it, very quietly put it on hold, in my name. Bartleman." He spelled it. "I'll be back before 5:00."

269

Twenty minutes later, Farrell returned the Vermeer box to the third-floor counter. "All through?" the librarian asked.

"Yes, thank you," Farrell replied. The sign-in log was on the woman's desk behind the counter. A pen lay across its open face.

"Tomorrow?"

"No. No, thank you."

The librarian patted the pockets of her apron, and the keys inside jangled. She smiled. "Well, in that case, I'll just put our friend Vermeer to bed."

She started down the aisle, humming, the clomping of her shoes a lazy accompaniment. Farrell watched until the woman was out of sight. Then she circled the counter to the desk and flipped open the sign-in log. To her dismay, the previous day's entries were gone.

Meade was ushered into the Greyling mansion by a butler dressed in tails. He was escorted to the second floor. Sir Greyling was waiting in the gallery. He wore a dark blue suit and drank tea scented with ginseng.

Meade was drawn wordlessly to the far corner of the room where the empty spaces still lent an air of vulnerability to the entire gallery. The brass nameplates were like dog tags of the missing, the dead, and the presumed dead. Meade found himself staring at the former place of honor of the masterful forgery of Jan Vermeer's *Two Women and Their Music.*

He ran a finger around the edge of the plate and over the pressed lettering, and spoke without turning. "A certain South African art collector, one with a penchant for the impressionist era and a taste for the modern, an art collector who freely admits to a distinct lack of interest in the 'near photographic realism' of the seventeenth and eighteenth centuries, is informed, ostensibly through an old friend back home"—now Meade glanced over his shoulder—"that a certain seventeenth-century master-piece has without explanation surfaced in the European art community. The artist's name is Jan Vermeer. The work is entitled *Two Women and Their Music*. This is a major event because the art world had written off the painting as a casualty of the war. The collector admits, at least to the naive, that he can appreciate Vermeer's work for its uniqueness, but deep down finds it a bit bland for his taste. Still, he pursues it. He says the investment value alone is worth the risk. He credits the hunt, the competition, with the rejuvenation of an old man's diminishing spirit."

Meade turned away from the blank spaces. His eyes fell on a bronze statue of three angels and a sketch bearing the signature of Pablo Picasso.

He said, "The painting's owner has chosen to remain anonymous, but this is not particularly unusual. Certainly not enough to discourage the collector, now that his blood is pumping. The painting is scheduled for auction. Which means competition. A risk the collector sees as unacceptable. He offers the seller's intermediary such an inordinate amount of money that only a fool would take the chance of selling through normal channels. The art world is stunned. The collector is chastised for his deliberate breach of protocol. Frustrated museums and envious dealers are disturbed to the point of threatening legal action. But this deal is only unsavory, not illegal. The collector is unmoved; his coup has succeeded."

Meade worked his way back to the center of the gallery. Sir Greyling stood, thin-lipped, with the cup and saucer balanced in one hand, awaiting him.

"Your painting was a forgery," Meade said. "It was stolen from your walls with the help of your own house-guest, whether you know it or not, and now five people are dead, including Miles Roundtree. The Missing Sixth is still at large. And my son, Sean, is being held prisoner

271

by members of the *Broederbond*. I'm sick of your game, Sir Greyling. I have sixty hours to find a painting that may, in fact, no longer exist. You have ten minutes to tell me about the Missing Sixth."

Greyling stared, and then conceded, "I didn't know about your son. I'm sorry." He circled to the gallery's sitting area and chose the nearest of two armchairs.

"Very well." Sir traded his teacup for a briar pipe. "The Missing Sixth, Mr. Meade, is one of six documents created by the German General Erwin Rommel. This was in 1944." Greyling seemed to Meade to be searching for the right words. "Rommel was in the hospital when it all began. He'd been driving back from a conference in Normandy when a couple of Spitfires opened fire on his car. He sustained a head injury which left him bedridden."

"I've heard the story," Meade said.

Sir Greyling tipped his head. "Rommel was a man possessed by two things, Mr. Meade. War and country. So much so that he refused to see what was going on right in his own backyard. But things changed while he was in the hospital. Or perhaps the change had begun earlier, and he came to a decision while he was there . . ."

"That being your interpretation."

"A logical interpretation." Sir Greyling held Meade's gaze. "Rommel had fought and survived two wars by this time. He'd been shunned by the German nobility and disregarded by the military caste that dominated the *Wehrmacht*, and he'd seen firsthand the mess they'd made of things in the First World War. And then there was Hitler. Rommel was never comfortable with the doctrine of Teutonic superiority; hell, he'd been a victim of it himself. The man was basically apolitical. The allies found a letter after the war, a letter he'd written to his wife from the hospital. The Holocaust, in his words, had become an unbearable cross. By then he was also realizing, or at least admitting, that the atrocities and the looting and plun-

272

dering weren't confined to the Germans, that they were happening all over the world."

"You're referring to Africa now," Meade said, at last taking a seat. "The *Ossewabrandwag* and the Grey Shirts."

"Then came whispers of the assassination plot against Hitler. Rommel was part of it, a big part of it. It was one of the most intricately conceived plots in all history, and it should have worked. It would have saved the world a year of war and so many lives that it makes me sick to think of it."

"The plot was betrayed, wasn't it?"

"Yes, Mr. Meade."

"By whom?"

Greyling held up a hand. "Hitler had conceived an escape route out of Germany, were things ever to fall apart, via Italy and Algeria to South Africa. He relied on Rommel to arrange the matter of the escape in Africa. The assassination was to take place on a practice run of the escape route. In an apparent plane crash."

"What happened?"

"It was betrayed, as you said. Supposedly by someone here in this country. Maybe Rommel knew who, maybe not. Later, he was linked to the plot and formally arrested. So much for that." Greyling waved the subject off. "Back to our story. After a month in the hospital he was sent home. Put out to pasture. His command had passed into other hands.

"It all added up. The aborted assassination attempt. The accusations. The atrocities. The talk of a Fourth Reich. Rommel began documenting the whos and the whats. Talking to people who saw what he saw and felt as he did about it; by that point in the war, there were plenty. With his wife's help—her name was Lucie Maria, by the way—he began putting his lists together. Names, places, deeds, witnesses to the deeds. By location; that's important.

273

Germany, Western Europe, Eastern Europe, the U.S., South America, and Africa."

Meade watched as Greyling tamped tobacco into his pipe. He still didn't light it. "Does this make any sense to you, Mr. Meade?" he asked.

"So the African list is hidden in the back of the Vermeer."

Greyling merely tipped his head. "Rommel was a lover of art. Or at least a collector. Paintings mostly, and that's what he used to hide his documents in. Six paintings."

"Between the original works and their relining canvases."

"Apparently so." Greyling pursed his lips. "Lucie Maria admitted later that it was her husband's intent to see the paintings delivered into Allied hands via Switzerland. It almost happened. The paintings were crated and packed in the back of a truck at Rommel's house when the Germans showed up. The documents were extracted on the spot by no less than Hermann Göring. What Hitler did with them once they were in his hands, no one knows. Destroyed them, if he had any sense left by then. The paintings Göring took care of. He made a bonfire of them, in Rommel's front yard."

"All except the Vermeer. Is that what you're suggesting?"

"Never found. And evidently Hitler searched, too. But by that time, Rommel had committed suicide and Hitler had lost his trump card." At last, Greyling struck a match over his pipe. "But it's fairly certain the painting never made it into Allied territory."

"I'm curious," Meade said. "You tell that story as if it's documented in every history book in the world. How come it isn't?"

"In fact, the war was Hitler's ally. By then, things had gone to hell and a half in Germany. Six pieces of paper no one had ever laid eyes on weren't exactly news. I can only guess, but no doubt Hitler alerted a friend or two in this country—and he had an armload—just in case the Sixth came to light."

"Whose names are on the list? DeBruin's? Venter's? The Reverend Crous? Van Rooy? Kilian?"

"Certainly not Kilian. Too young. But he'd like to be the next Executive Council Chairman, and you can believe the Sixth would help him get it." Greyling sucked hard on his pipe. "There were three hundred thousand members in the *Ossewabrandwag*. Fifty thousand Grey Shirts. DeBruin, Venter, Hugo, the Reverend Crous? They were more than just members, I know that much."

"And they were behind the theft."

"Indeed."

Meade stood up. His fitful gaze settled on the portable bar against the near wall. The vodka was Russian, the gin English. His chest ached. He tossed out his next question like a lifeline. "Yet you knew about the Sixth. How? Hitler had an armload of friends here, you said. But not in the West Alliance."

Greyling pushed a hand through his shaggy mane. "Göring tried to use the information to make things easier on himself when he was captured at the end of the war. Nobody believed him. Well, almost nobody. There was a man on the Allied interrogation team; he passed the story on. It caused a tremor in the Jewish underground, and the tremor reached the Alliance. You don't forget a thing like that."

"No," Meade agreed. "And the forgery?"

In response, Greyling actually managed an ironic chortle. "In the beginning, I never thought of questioning the work's authenticity. The painting had already passed muster with people who should have known. Well, it wasn't the painting I'd bought anyway, was it? When I found out what an unfortunate buy I'd made, I assumed the document had been destroyed, or never existed, or that

275

the stories were just stories. Certainly there was no point in leaking the news of the forgery to the *Broederbond* and letting their search continue." Greyling tapped his pipe against the edge of an ashtray, tapped it against the palm of his hand, and quickly latched on to a new topic.

"I heard about Miles Roundtree's death. He was a good friend."

"Had you sent Rita Hess back home four months ago after she tripped the alarm in your gallery, Miles might still be alive. And you deliberately lied to the police about the incident."

"Yes, I did let her back into my house, Mr. Meade." There was a new energy in Greyling's step as he rose from the chair, a renewed vigor in his voice. "My reasons were sound. You'll have to take my word on that. I knew she was setting herself up with Gideon DeBruin, or someone on the Executive Council—but it got away from us . . . from me."

"From *us*? From you and the Essenes Society? Is that what you mean?" Meade looked down at the pencil in his hand. He didn't wait for a response. "And you have no idea where Rita is now."

Greyling shook his head. "It's been—since Saturday." He stowed the pipe in his pants pocket and led Meade to the door. "I do know that if Rita has any idea the Vermeer is a phony, then she won't give up. It's her special gift, you see. Her relentlessness."

They walked down the stairs and outside in silence.

"And you, Mr. Meade, will you give up?" Greyling put a hand on Meade's elbow as they reached his car. "By now you know it would be a disaster if the Missing Sixth ended up in the hands of Rita Hess's cohorts. They'd simply use it as a tool of extortion or sell it to the highest bidder. And I think you know it would be a tragedy if it ended up in the hands of Gideon DeBruin and the *Broederbond*."

Meade followed the course of a gull as it hastened for the coast; the sun was a white disk drowning in a pool of pastel blue. Then he opened the car door and climbed in. He started the engine. Finally, he leaned out the window. "I'm curious, Sir Greyling. Whose hands would you have the Missing Sixth end up in?"

27

HISTORY, from what Meade discovered in the Argus library, had painted its own bleak picture of Robben Island.

Centuries past, the entrepreneurs of the Dutch trading empire, a law unto themselves, had banished and interned onto Robben Island hundreds of princes and lords from the Far East, leaders who had dared revolt against the mass plundering of those European marauders.

Later, when captured slaves from the islands of Sumatra and Java dared mutiny against their sellers, their mangled and fettered bodies were cast into the freezing waters offshore.

When the exiled Makanda, the first black ruler to lead an armed resistance against British colonial rule over a century ago, tried swimming the channel back to the mainland, all that survived was the hand-tooled quiver he had carried over his shoulder and a single arrow.

Later still, the island proved a remarkably successful quarantine for lepers.

And finally—and Meade knew this without the help of the newspaper's back files—when antigovernment politics became the country's most incendiary crime, the barren rock became Africa's version of Alcatraz.

Meade made two wrong turns in his search for Langa, Cam Fazzie's home township. There were no road signs, and the map he was relying on lost its continuity when it came to the residential areas of the Flats. Certainly an unintentional flaw, Meade tried to assure the cynical part of himself, but he was feeling particularly cynical after his visit with Sir Cas Greyling.

And then he saw the sign. It was outsized, with large black letters on a dirty white background.

WARNING

THIS ROAD PASSES THROUGH PROCLAIMED BANTU LOCATIONS. ANY PERSON WHO ENTERS THESE LOCATIONS WITHOUT THE PROPER PERMIT RENDERS HIMSELF LIABLE FOR PROSECUTION FOR CONTRAVENING THE BANTU URBAN AREAS CONSOLIDATION ACT OF 1945 AND THE LOCATION REGULATION ACT OF THE CITY OF CAPE TOWN.

Meade decided against the permit. On the one hand, he wasn't certain the law still applied. On the other, he reminded himself that the only whites he had ever seen in the townships anyway were policemen and soldiers.

Beyond the entrance a rundown shopping center touted five or six shops—a liquor store, a grocery, a discount department store, a video arcade, and a donut shop—and twice as many vacancies. The bulk of the activity, which was considerable now that it was evening, centered upon the open market in the parking lot outside the shops.

Meade stopped. The air was tinged with the scent of coal smoke. A man sold secondhand furniture from a flatbed truck. A woman sold wrought-iron candlesticks from a station wagon's tailgate. There were flats of dried peaches, tables filled with handwoven wicker, tubs loaded with fresh fish, and racks stuffed with used books. A blind man in a rocking chair played the accordion; the music inspired a cluster of people into hand clapping and swaying. Emaciated chickens pecked at the pavement and a pig sulked in a makeshift pen. A massive, boisterous woman brewed sorghum beer in discarded oil drums.

Meade watched the township entrance for several minutes. Cars rattled in and out. There were men and women on bicycles and many more on foot. The faces were all black. Meade looked beyond the entrance and saw a yellow Honda pull into the police station parking lot a half block away. When no one got out, he turned away.

A table heavy with bloody sheep's heads and bundles of florid tripe caught his eye only because there were no customers. Meade asked the woman behind the table for directions to number 79 Sixteenth Street. She gestured with a dripping finger and said, "In the corridor. Just look for the Catholic church and keep going."

The "corridor" proved to be a shallow valley formed by neat rows of tiny brick houses and outhouses in back. The church was granite with a square bell tower and plywood windows. Sixteenth was the first street beyond the church.

Fazzie lived in four rooms with a tin roof. A baby oak took up most of the yard. "I was beginning to wonder," he said from the doorway. "Everything OK?"

Meade told him about the yellow Honda. "But I couldn't be sure."

Fazzie nodded. He led Meade inside. The living room doubled as a dining room, dominated by a sofa, a dining table, bookshelves, a wall filled with stereo equipment, and hundreds of record albums.

The kitchen was the size of a walk-in closet. The stench of sulfur permeated the room. On a tiny counter to the left of the sink Meade saw a bottle of ammonia, a square of paraffin wax, a bag of charcoal briquettes, what looked like the casing for a low-caliber bullet, a small yellow box imprinted with the words "Rice Starch," and a tin of sulfur crystals. On a two-burner stove sat a Pyrex saucepan. Ice filled the sink.

"What's this?" Meade asked.

Fazzie wore rubber gloves. He nestled a glass beaker deep in the ice. "That was a good story you told me about your old man, Yank. Sad story. Now the story's got its hands on your son and my friend. A story like that needs an ending."

Fazzie didn't leave room for elaboration. "You talked to Greyling," he said. "Find out anything?"

Describing his visit to De Greyling from beginning to end, Meade talked and paced. *A story like that needs an ending:* the words stung. On the table in the living room a typewriter had been pushed aside to make room for a map of the Cape Province. Robben Island was circled in black. On the kitchen table was a suitcase, exactly like the one Grandma Meade had taken on a visit to New York City when Meade was ten. It was made of a stiff cardboard, water-stained on the inside and covered with an indistinguishable floral pattern. The handle was a blackened brass with a key lock underneath. On either side of the handle were brass buckles. Beside the case lay an elbow section of plastic conduit pipe. It was capped on either end, and tiny holes had been drilled in both caps. In one corner lay a roll of duct tape, a plastic stopwatch, a dry cell battery, and two lengths of heavy-duty electric wire.

By the time Meade finished his description of the Missing Sixth, he and Fazzie were facing each other across the table.

Fazzie turned away long enough to light a fire under one burner and place the paraffin over a low flame. "This thing? This Missing Sixth? It exists?"

"Enough people are covering themselves in case it does."

"Big stakes, Yank. Big stakes. A person could make

the Brotherhood look like Humpty-Dumpty with that thing." Fazzie's voice hung in a vacuum. "Turn the Nats inside out."

Fazzie went back to his work. He weighed out the ammonia and lit a flame under the Pyrex pan. He watched the mercury in his thermometer rise, gradually cut back the heat, and clapped his hands in appreciation. "Ammonia. Potent stuff, Yank. And you can buy it in any grocery store in town."

"What's going on, Cam?" But by now Meade knew, of course. He took stock of the scene, from the concoction on the stove to the cardboard suitcase, and found a hollow spot growing in his stomach, a film of moisture spreading beneath his coat, and a tremor of excitement opening like a flower.

"This is my Uncle Mac's formula," Fazzie said. "Sulfur flour. Two percent. Always, always use in flour form only. And just a touch." Fazzie measured the sulfur flour out on a triple-beam gram scale. Then he used a mortar and pestle to grind a dozen charcoal briquettes into a pool of fine black powder. "For a little pyrotechnic display," he said.

"Why starch?" Meade asked, watching Fazzie manipulate the scale again.

"It's the perfect absorbent. But never *ever* corn or potato starch. Unh-unh. Rice. Always rice." Fazzie studied the thermometer again. He stirred meticulously, once, twice, and then shut the flame down. He plunged an eyedropper into the paraffin, which, by now, was the consistency of buttermilk. "Careful, careful. Work, don't talk. Three percent. No more, no less. For textural purposes. And finally, a drop of water. Why, I don't know. Then we ice it for a while."

"Dynamite."

"Not dynamite. Close. Better, safer." Fazzie looked up and smiled. Then the smile faded. "Mieta's half out of her head with worry. She knew Sean was a potential tar-

282

get. I didn't tell you this, but she asked Sean to leave even before you did; I could have added my two cents' worth and didn't."

"It's not your fault."

"Twenty-two-year-old college kids aren't meant to be used like pawns on a chessboard, Michael."

"It's not your fault," Meade said again, and waved his hand at the stove. "I don't know what this is all about, but it isn't necessary."

The living room was only ten feet away, but it felt to Meade like a haven from some type of contagious disease. He looked at his watch; he had already squandered sixteen hours. At the table, he pored over the map of Robben Island. Next to it, Fazzie had laid out the photographs he had taken from the helicopter. The quality was only fair, but the sequence took Meade from the prison complex and the jailers' housing south to the isolation huts and finally to the quarries.

Fazzie carried the paraphernalia from the kitchen counter out into the living room. He opened the suitcase and laid it on the floor.

"Take a look at the last two photos," he said. The photos he referred to, taken as the helicopter drew away from the island, confirmed the sheer cliffs that encompassed the island's southern end. Yet there was also evidence of a shallow cove and a narrow strip of sand. "There's our way onto the island. And according to my sources, there's a way up that cliff, too. A path, or steps carved into the side years ago."

Fazzie shrugged. "It's the only logical place, Yank."

Fazzie used duct tape to secure the dry cell battery and stopwatch to the inside wall of the suitcase, at the base of either buckle. For the first time now, Meade noticed the tiny metal tab attached to the stop button of the watch. A second such tab had also been fused to one end of the longest length of wire.

Despite himself, Meade watched. The throbbing in

his head had given way to a dull ache in his stomach and the relentless bombardment of guilt. Eight months ago Sean had been a telecommunications major at Berkeley, the kind of kid who marveled at the Golden Gate Bridge every time they drove across it. Just before moving to Cape Town they took in a 49ers game. Sean's big concern that day had been adjusting to rugby; he wanted to know what a *scrum* was. Now Meade was sitting under a vibrating tin roof while Sean was on a prison island halfway around the world from the Golden Gate Bridge. At his feet a man was assembling a bomb in a suitcase and using the word *logical* to describe it all.

Fazzie took the plastic conduit pipe and one length of the wire back into the kitchen. Meade thumbed absently through the jazz side of Fazzie's record collection. When Fazzie reappeared, Meade realized that the concoction from the stove had been packed inside the pipe. The length of electrical wire now ran through the pipe and out from the tiny holes in each cap. Fazzie lashed the pipe into one corner of the suitcase.

"You'd better see this," he said, a directive which had Meade kneeling over the suitcase like an eager schoolboy. "Easiest thing in the world, Yank. Start with your stopwatch. Fuse one wire to the metal tab on the stop button. That's contact point one. OK, done. Contact point two is the metal tab at the other end of this wire. Very carefully attach the tab to the side of the suitcase, directly above the stop button. Done. Our longest length of wire runs through the pipe, to the blasting cap, through the explosive, out the other end of the pipe, and back around to the dry cell. Done. You run your shorter wire straight from contact point one to the dry cell. What we haven't done yet is connect the wires to the poles of the battery. Not now. When the time comes. Now set your watch; we'll say, thirty seconds. When the buckle on the left side of the suitcase is raised, like this, it presses down on the watch's starting button. Go. When the counter hits zero, the stop button on the watch pops up, which causes your two contact points to connect, which completes your electrical circuit. Pow."

"You're crazy."

"I like the stopwatch because it's loud. Loud enough to give the poor slob holding this thing a thirty-second heart attack. And if Sean or I die on that island, Yank, I want to know that Gideon DeBruin had his thirty-second heart attack, hear?"

Meade didn't answer. He had failed somewhere along the line to muster the conviction to protest. Fazzie, for his part, closed the suitcase and threw himself across the sofa. He said, "The waters around the island are heavily patrolled. You saw that. Pleasure boating is strictly prohibited. But they look the other way for the fishing fleets. Business, you know. And I guess there are fish that actually like water that cold."

"So?"

"So—" Fazzie consulted his watch. "In exactly thirty minutes, give or take, the Hout Bay coloreds will be returning with their catch of the day. A good friend is one of their fleet captains. With a little persuasion, and a bottle or two of rum, I think maybe I can catch a ride out in the morning."

"Good. Let's go."

"This is a solo effort, Yank," Fazzie replied. "They'll talk to me only because I'm a friend. You, on the other hand, look like every egg sucker that's ever waved a nightstick in their face."

Meade looked at him. "I don't like it."

"Hey, Yank. I don't care for it much myself. But I'm either going after Sean or I'm going after the painting. I'm sure as hell not going to sit here and listen to music." Fazzie swung his feet back off the couch. "We've got two alternatives. The painting and the island. Let's not argue over who's best suited for which alternative. We've got what? Sixty hours? Let's just do it and get it over with."

The suitcase fit snugly on the floor of the Toyota's backseat. Fazzie had given him a key ring with eight tiny keys on it. Meade hadn't protested. He would find a back alley in town and dump it, and they would laugh the whole thing off later. He followed Fazzie out of the township on a dirt road that paralleled the railroad track.

In a residential area in Pinelands, the alleys were bathed in darkness. Meade carried the suitcase from one trash bin to the next. Lifting one lid and then another, he found himself constructing a fantasy about a couple of adventurous boys, out exploring, who happen upon this unopened case that in the wink of an eye becomes a hidden treasure chest. That in the wink of another eye becomes. . . . Meade carried the suitcase back to the car.

In Observatory, he tailed a trash truck through a four-block-long business district; he could toss the suitcase in the back at any one of fifteen or twenty stops—just an absentminded homeowner who had missed getting his trash out in time. But by now, some other force compelled his inaction. *Twenty-two-year-old college kids aren't meant to be used like pawns on a chessboard*, he heard Fazzie say.

Still, he played it out.

Among the bulldozers and road graders of the Zonnebloem redevelopment area, Meade stopped again. He drove along the wharf. He toured Foreshore. He crept through the back streets of the Malay Quarter. The excuses were limited solely by the limits of his imagination. But it was only when he was parked at the rear of St. Stephen's Dutch Reformed Church, reconstructing in vivid detail the chapel in the basement and picturing the havoc a simple homemade explosive could wreak there, that he realized the game had changed, that the game was playing him now.

He drove back to the Argus Building and parked in the underground lot. He locked the suitcase in the back of his own Land Rover. Inside, he used the pay phone in the cafeteria to call Peter Hawthorne about the fingerprints on the Vermeer X-ray.

"Forget South Africa, mate," the forensic scientist said. "I took those prints back to 1927. The computer spat back a big zero."

"Telling us?"

"Telling us that the owner of those fingerprints wasn't born in this country, was never a citizen of this country, and never entered this country in a legal manner. Period."

Hout Bay, to the south of Table Mountain, was both village and harbor; and both village and harbor lived and died by the generosity of the sea.

The fleet that called Hout Bay home consisted almost entirely of colored men and their low-lying trawlers. By dawn every morning they could be seen slipping past the last harbor buoy out to sea. An hour later, trawl or seine nets were in the water and stayed in the water until sunset when the fishermen returned to unload, weigh, and distribute what the sea had yielded. Under the arc lights of the quay they repaired their precious nets and scrubbed their tackle, then returned to their homes in Grassy Park or Lavender Hill or Lotus River thirty miles away.

The fleet captain was named Tobias. He was eight years Fazzie's senior. Their friendship had begun on a soccer field fifteen years before. Tobias was the finest goalie Fazzie had ever faced. Fazzie was the only player ever to have scored two goals on the fisherman in one game.

Mostly, the Hout Bay fleet fished for snoek and crayfish. But as Tobias said, "We're not particular. We can't afford to be particular. Most times, the steenbras and the red roman, they'll run year-round. But for what? Most times, when all's said and done, the men with the money toss us a few cents per kilo, and all we have to show for it's an aching back. *Sies.*" He spat, disgusted. He took a short pull on the white rum Fazzie had passed among them. Then he threw up his hands and chuckled. "True, we do better with musselcracker and elfish, and the restaurants fall all over themselves when the kabeljou run. Problem is, every year the season grows a day shorter, and every year there's fifty more boats. But who can complain? For now, we work eight days a week. Lobster season ends in two weeks. Open season on snoek runs till August. We survive. We own our own boats. So who can complain. *Sies.*"

Thirteen men. They sat among the folds of their olive-green nets like veteran tailors. Backs bent, stiff fingers working needles and nylon to repair the rips and snags that were a perpetual part of the trade. They were dressed in rubber dungarees, their heads covered with hats or scarves against a light drizzle. Three women joined them. Their laughter was strong, a barometer of the day's harvest.

When Fazzie asked about the waters off Robben Island, the raillery came to a complete and sudden halt. The needles stopped. And then started again. Only Tobias glanced up. His eyes were lit with curiosity and amusement. He pulled on the rum, swished it over his gums, and swallowed. His laughter was thick with irony.

"Robben Island. I see. Fazzie, my old nemesis, you're wondering about the waters. The lobster harvest or the steenbras? Do we bottom fish for cod or trawl for snoek? I think, perhaps, no. I think we are talking about anything but the waters or the fish or the hows and how nots. Yes? The question is what? If not fish, then what? There is the prison. There is the danger the prison brings. There is the trouble that comes with flirting with the danger. There is nothing else."

"There is something else," Fazzie answered.

He told them. He told them as much as he could, without the names, and without the faces. But he could see by their expressions that the names weren't necessary and they were peopling the story with their own faces. For a quarter of an hour their needles were still, their bantering put on hold.

In the end, it was Tobias who put it into words. "You're going to waltz your black ass right up to Robben Island, do a little after-hours detective work, and then waltz back out again with this friend of yours. This is your plan? Yes? *Sies.* And you'd like us to risk our boats to get you there?"

"And back," Fazzie replied. He lit a cigarette and passed the pack. "The fleets have free rein in those waters. No one else does."

"Tomorrow night is the new moon," one of the women said. "What better omen? And the weather smells like the first day of spring."

"Say we get in close," the weather-beaten man on Tobias's right said, "say, a half click from the cliffs, south side: the current, shit, the thing'd hand deliver a small raft straight into the cove."

"We dock the night in Table Bay," a man with a pocked face and bright gray eyes said. "We've sold there before. The prices, they're not a rand worse than here at home. Why not?"

"And the tides—for once, the accursed things are in our favor." Enthusiasm mounted.

"Another good omen."

"We'd be back to the island before dawn."

"And back home by dark, fat with fish. No problem."

Tobias eyed them each in turn. He ran the back of his hand over his mouth and spat. "No problem, you say? Good omens? Fat with fish? *Sies.* But just one mistake, just one helicopter that happens to be in the wrong spot at the right time or one patrol boat making an unexpected turn, and we lose our boats."

"He's right," Fazzie agreed.

"We've been standing still for too long, old man," the woman said. Her head was bent over her needle, but Tobias knew the words were meant for him. They all did.

In the silence, he grabbed for the rum bottle. He looked from one man to the next. Then at the women. "Risk our boats and our livelihood on a white man. Is that it? You tell me, what has any white man ever done for us? Answer me that."

Now the woman stood up. She folded her arms across her chest and held Tobias's gaze. "You are right," she said. "We risk our boats and our livelihood if we do this thing. You are right also that the Boers have done everything in their power to make us feel powerless. They tell us where to live and where to die, where to buy our groceries and where to sit on the bus. Are they also telling us now which principles we can stand for? Which battles we can fight? Have they done such a good job of seeding our hate that we see every man who is not one of us as the enemy? If so, then the Boers have won, and we should give no more thought to this boy or Robben Island or taking a risk that says to the Boers that we still have the courage to judge each man for himself."

Tobias acknowledged the woman with a simple nod. He drank. He took a second pull, deeper, and winced. Night had set deeply over the harbor now, and the arc lights hovered above them like a halo of yellow fire.

"You speak well, woman. You shame me, and I thank you for the reminder. . . . If only it were that simple." Tobias turned his whole body in Fazzie's direction. After a moment, he expelled a deep sigh and said, "Which of us is crazier, I don't know, my friend. I do know we weigh anchor at 4:30, and we won't be waiting on the tardy."

28

IN THE BEGINNING, Jacob Bartleman had been an easy man to be with. He spoke of his friendship with Michael Meade as if they had known each other forever.

The restaurant was Farrell's choice, an Italian place with tuck-and-roll upholstery, two blocks from the university. Pomponio's. A fixture in the neighborhood for as long as Farrell could remember.

The wine had been a mistake. Farrell had called for their third bottle ten minutes ago, and she was doing most of the drinking. Was the panic she felt good or bad? She didn't know.

Bartleman, in turn, was doing most of the talking, and Farrell wasn't certain when the conversation had turned to the Vermeer.

"I always had the suspicion Michael knew more than he was telling me." Bartleman used an admonishing finger in jest. Farrell didn't know what Meade had told him. She looked at her watch. It was 7:50. Meade was expecting a call in ten minutes. "Well, we can be sure of one thing, I suppose. He doesn't know where the damn painting is. If he did, it'd be hanging on Cas Greyling's wall again, and Michael would be on his way to another Pulitzer."

Bartleman lit a cigarette and replenished their wine. He said, "What about you, Farrell? I noticed you were doing some work on the Vermeer at the library this afternoon. Think it's still around? The genuine article, that is?"

The wineglass came to a sudden halt at Farrell's lips. She hadn't expected Bartleman to know about the forgery. Hadn't the man at Nico Mustapha's studio identified himself with a Security Branch ID? She withdrew the glass, deliberately touched the wine with a fingertip, and then pushed it aside.

"It's more a matter of perception at this point, Captain." Evasion was Farrell's specialty; even half drunk she could employ it with skill. "I'll give you an example. The bombing at the Broken Bridge restaurant in Stellenbosch."

"Yeah, I know. I know. One table, in a restaurant filled with snits and Boers, eight kilometers from the nearest telephone. In most people's eyes, not much of a statement."

"Yet who do the police blame?"

"When Security doesn't have a clue, Farrell, they blame terrorists," Bartleman lamented. "It's believable, and it keeps a half-spooked public half-spooked."

"Exactly. In your business, a mistake is just a mistake. No offense intended."

"None taken."

Farrell formed a steeple with her hands. "On the other hand, I put my name behind a very expensive piece of merchandise. It turned out to be a very expensive fake. That's not the kind of mistake I can afford."

"I get the picture." Bartleman toyed with his mustache. "Any progress?"

Farrell looked at her watch again. "I'm sorry, but I have to make a call," she said. "It may take a few minutes."

"Home?" he asked.

"The museum," Farrell heard herself say, and she put a smile behind it. "It's like my baby. And it's bedtime. It would be rude of me to ask you to wait. I'll get a cab—"

"Don't be silly." Bartleman waved the suggestion off with both hands. "I can't think of anything more boring than my hotel room. I saw two call boxes in the back. Put your baby to bed, and I'll order dessert."

It was 8:00; Farrell didn't argue. She closed herself inside the phone booth and gave the operator the number in the Argus cafeteria. Two minutes later, Meade answered.

"I did it," she said.

"Did what?"

"Wine with dinner."

"You all right?"

"I don't know."

"Take a hot shower and don't get out until the water runs cold."

"I'm in a call box in the back of an Italian restaurant, Meade. And anyway, who wants to take a hot shower alone? I'd rather have another drink. I can blame it on London, or Jan Vermeer, or you, for that matter, for leaving me here alone."

"For me it's Paris," Meade said. "It's like a lover you can't quite let go of. I always come away from there with the same nagging ache deep down inside. It never fails. I keep hearing this voice say, 'If only you had done something a little different, or tried a little harder, things might have turned out better.' "

"I know," she whispered. "For me, it's the fog. I keep thinking, here is the perfect place to hide. Though I'm not even sure from what. Until I look in the mirror."

"It's work, isn't it? Hiding."

"Yes, Michael, it is."

Meade waited a moment and then said, "How's London otherwise?"

"Does that mean we're back to work?"

293

"This doesn't feel like work."

"I liked it when you touched my hair."

"You're drunk."

"I liked it before I was drunk."

"I liked it, too."

"Maybe we could do it again sometime, do you think? Without the son of a bitch who happens to be my father getting in the way?"

"I'm more worried about Sean than I am about your father," Meade said. He told Farrell about his last meeting with her father, about Sean's abduction.

"Oh, God, no," Farrell said. "It can't be true . . ." Her words trailed off.

When the silence gained too much momentum, and Meade could sense Farrell slipping away, he told her about the Missing Sixth. When he was done the silence returned, but this time she used it as a stepping-stone, saying, "I went to the Witt Library today, like we planned, but unfortunately I wasn't the only person researching Jan Vermeer. Someone else checked out his file box yesterday. And it makes sense that whoever it was saw the same research material I did and probably sat in the same bloody chair. Coincidentally, yesterday's sign-in sheet was missing. I talked to the clerk, but she wasn't on duty yesterday."

"We're a day behind," Meade said. His voice rose. "Could whoever it was have drawn the same conclusions as you?"

"Do you believe in intuition, Meade?"

"Devoutly."

"Well, a familiar name crept into the picture again, in the document file at the Witt. Shapiro. Do you remember? Dr. Emery Shapiro?"

"I remember. How?"

In reply, Farrell gave a quick sketch of the Shapiro family's wartime history. She began with the father's personal crusade against Hitler and ended with his son's exodus to Johannesburg. Then she reiterated the contents of the two articles from the *Global Art Review:* the first, written by Emery Shapiro himself, detailing the discovery of the paintings in the Amsterdam apartment and containing the author's personal speculation about *Two Women and Their Music;* and the second, calling the incident an apparent hoax perpetrated by disgruntled art students at the expense of one of their professors.

"Does it strike you as odd," Farrell said, "that Shapiro wrote the first piece but not the follow-up? It did me."

"That's what wire services are for, Farrell."

"His family once owned the painting," Farrell argued. "Wouldn't you hang around to find out if you were in his place?"

Meade nudged the conversation in a different direction. "The individual who sold Cas Greyling the Vermeer insisted on anonymity. Greyling accepted the condition. A condition Christie's was also prepared to live with, had the painting gone to auction. In effect, everyone involved had accepted possession of the work as the equivalent of title."

"In most of Europe, the title on a movable piece of property, like a painting, converts from bad to good within three years. Possession is the only requirement."

"And proof of provenance?"

"As crazy as it sounds, no one really gives a damn where a painting's been, once it's deemed authentic. In this case, the painting was kept at the Courtauld Institute, in a vault, under lock and key. Christie's handled the validation. I was there. So were the insurance people. Christie's followed normal procedures. And once it was done, everyone was happy."

"We need the seller's name, Farrell. Can you find it?"

"I don't know, Meade. It's a matter of ethics," Farrell

295

replied. Meade heard a deep sigh. "All right. I'll try. There's an auction tomorrow. It's a starting place, anyway. Maybe I can arrange an invitation."

"We'll talk again tomorrow night," Meade said. "And the next time you have the urge to go out and dine alone, call me."

"My God, Meade, I almost forgot—I'm not alone. I'm with a friend of yours."

Meade drew a blank on acquaintances in London. "Who?"

"Jacob Bartleman." The response Farrell had expected didn't materialize. "The policeman. From Cape Town. Remember?"

"The policeman from Cape Town is a member of the *Broederbond*, Farrell. He's working with your father. It's no accident that he's—"

Farrell didn't hear the rest. A tapping at the phone booth door preceded its opening; it was Bartleman. "I thought you'd deserted me," he said. "The ice cream is melting."

"I'm sorry," Farrell said, her hand over the phone. And then into the phone she said, "Polly. Sweetheart, you'll have to deal with that matter yourself."

"Is he there?" Meade asked.

"That's why I hired you."

"Eight o'clock, tomorrow night."

"I have to get off now. And don't forget to water my lilies. Be good." Farrell hung up.

"We were talking about the auction," she said, gathering up her purse. It was the first thing that came to mind, and it was a mistake; Farrell realized it almost at once.

Bartleman stroked his mustache. "That sounds exciting. When?"

"Tomorrow, at Christie's. I . . . . I'm staying over."

At his desk, Meade used the computer to call up the paper's back-dated library files. He typed in a name and time frame: Dr. Emery Shapiro, 1940 to the present.

Meade waited. His empty stomach talked back like a spoiled kid. He poured coffee and borrowed a cigarette from the janitor.

Five minutes later, the library produced two articles. The first was dated September 16, 1948: only a matter of months, Meade surmised, after the National party had officially taken control of the country. Dr. Emery Shapiro, a German Jew, art historian, and professor at the University of the Witwatersrand in Johannesburg, had been arrested, along with fifteen others, on charges of subversion and disrupting the electoral process. Shapiro's permanent visa had been withdrawn pending further review.

A month later, over the protests of university officials, Shapiro's visa was canceled and his stay in the country, after eight years, was terminated. All titles in his controversial collection of books, essays, and pamphlets were placed on the country's objectionable literature list and banned from publication and distribution. It was reported that Shapiro intended to join the emigration to the newly founded state of Israel to be reunited with his sister.

Meade flipped off the computer.

He called the airport.

Then he called Cam Fazzie, and the most difficult forty-eight hours of his life unfolded before him.

29

THE OCEAN CHURNED at Cam Fazzie's feet and lapped at the rotting pillars of a dock twice his age. A lining of silver gray seeped into the black of the western horizon. It was the one time of day, he thought, when you could almost feel the earth's perpetual motion.

Fazzie hunched his shoulders. He stomped his feet. Shafts of steam escaped through his clenched teeth. He chain-smoked, paced, and stomped his feet again. He heard an answering thump in the distance; another, then many. Footsteps without bodies. Closer. Voices.

"We'll catch no fish standing around with our hands in our pockets, old chum." A ghost materialized, of mist and shadow, a ghost gathering momentum and form, dragging behind it a band of other shadowy forms. It was Tobias. He wore green rubberized dungarees over a thick tan sweater. A blue stocking cap covered his head.

"In an hour," he said, lumbering toward the pier, "the tide will be our enemy. For now, it extends a helping hand. I suggest we take it."

Fazzie followed Tobias and two crew members aboard a trawler with the Latin words *Deo Volente* stenciled across the stern. A sliver of gold scored the horizon. The cormorants stirred. Soon they would be shrieking. A stream of dogged fisherman trudged through the fog. As dawn carved out its place in the sky, Fazzie heard a bellow of laughter, followed by a litany of well-meaning profanity. The laughter and profanity evoked a memory. He was thirteen. His father spent the summer teaching him to swim—in the *vleis*, the unrestricted marshes of the Cape Flats—and Fazzie took to it like a fish. A year later, he went to the beach off Mossel Bay, full of bravado, and was cursed and pelted with stones. He never went back. And oddly enough, it still hurt. Sixteen years later and it still hurt. Why?

He let it go, giving himself over instead to a study of the boat that would see him to Robben Island. It rode low in the water. The cabin and bridge deck were lumped together well up near the bow. Astern of the main deck, trawler nets were rolled and positioned beneath a simple winch. On top of the nets lay a row of plastic floats. Lengths of steel cable were coiled in each corner of the deck, attached to thick slabs of timber, the otter doors.

"Picture a bag being pulled through the water by those cables," Tobias said, crawling up from the engine compartment. "The water forces the doors away from the boat, and the pressure keeps the net open."

"And the floats hold the mouth of the net open at the top," Fazzie ventured.

One of the deckhands slapped his side. "The man's a genius, boss."

"A natural," Tobias deadpanned. "A once-in-a-lifetime natural."

The problem, Tobias thought as he bounded up the ladder to the bridge, was that he liked this once-in-a-lifetime natural. He started the engine. They cast off and he eased into the harbor. Mist and bay glimmered a milky pink.

On the one hand, Tobias told himself, there wasn't a

thing he could do about the man in a blue suit with a cane who had knocked on the door of his Lavender Hill home late last night. Or about his "request." Get the reporter to the island just like he wants, the man had said, and make sure everything is under control the next morning. Simple as that.

On the other hand, Tobias had never seen a thousand rand before.

And he knew the rules by now. The man wasn't *asking* at all. Tobias could take the money; he could think about the new roof they had needed for two years; he could think about a new dress for his lady; he could even think about a bicycle for the kids. Or, he could come down to the harbor one day and find his boat on fire or the hull punctured with holes.

Tobias looked over his shoulder at Fazzie, settling himself in a deck chair. Fazzie was a friend; it was true. But he had put himself in jeopardy. Tobias had no intention of doing the same to his own family. In the end, the fisherman told himself, it wasn't even a choice.

The miracle was not that a long-distance telephone allowed Meade to place his call from Cape Town to Paris in only a matter of minutes. The miracle was the power of his imagination and its ability to transport him, even as he waited for the call to be completed, if not bodily, then certainly in spirit to the very streets of that city.

Paris. Sally and he had planned two weeks in the city following their wedding. Two weeks had turned into six. Paris was a love affair in its own right. They had returned twice over the years. A single phone call brought it all back, and Meade didn't want the memories. Not now, maybe never.

What he wanted was the hand he had once held there, the scarf blowing in the wind next to him, the melody of sensual and provocative laughter that only Sally could provide. What he wanted was the last four years back again. A second chance. Her, and only her.

He closed his eyes. His hand clutched the receiver of the phone as if it alone might draw him back to the present. But it didn't. The memories pounded him like a sledgehammer.

Meade had fallen in love with the noise of the city. The hissing tires, the blaring horns, the boisterous voices. He had fallen in love with the sound of violins and rushing water and cathedral bells. Sally had fallen in love with the trees. The chestnuts and the poplars and the planes. She had called them the perfect grace note to the ancient buildings with their grand and moldering facades, their ornate cornices, their outlandish dormers. She had fallen in love with the lights and the rain and the fog. And the most poignant memory of all was that they had fallen in love with each other all over again.

Meade stood in a phone booth in an airport four thousand miles away and could just as easily have been sitting at any one of a dozen cafes along the Boulevard du Raspail, the memory of them was so strong. He remembered a simple picnic at the Luxembourg Gardens. He remembered a river cruise with six courses and a dark purple sky the likes of which he had never again experienced. He remembered the wine and the intoxication that had nothing at all to do with wine.

And then there was the river, the Seine. It had drawn them daily like a magnet. The willows cascading like botanical waterfalls from the street to the walks along the banks. The boats and the barges and the bellow of their horns. And there, at the heart of the Ile de la Cite, the Cathedral of Notre Dame. Meade could picture their first ferry crossing to the island, hands clutching and hearts pounding, as clearly as if it had been yesterday.

He remembered the hours they had spent in bed, the

301

passion and the fire he had since relived in fantasies a thousand times over.

When the phone connection was finally made and Meade heard the voice of André Saint-Claire, he was both grateful and mortified. How dare André intrude on such intimate memories.

Saint-Claire was the *Chronicle*'s French correspondent in Paris. By overnight courier, Meade had sent Saint-Claire copies of the X-ray negative Miles Roundtree had taken of the forgery and the enlargement Peter Hawthorne had made of the fingerprints.

"Safe and sound," the Frenchman said of the information's arrival. "Your explanation was a trifle vague, but I assume that was by intent."

"I need to know who those prints belong to, André. You may have to take it back a few years."

"Shouldn't be a problem. I've a contact at Interpol who owes me a favor or two. It's sure to be an eighteen- to twenty-four-hour job, though."

"Thanks."

"Thanks! Is that all you can say? You haven't paid me and my fair city a visit in five years and all you can say is, thanks. That's terrific."

"I don't know if I ever really left completely. I think that's the problem."

Saint-Claire chuckled. "No one ever does once they've seen it the way you have."

An appropriate response eluded Meade. He reverted to business instead, saying, "I'm en route to Israel. I'll call from there tomorrow night."

The heat would have been unbearable in Tel Aviv had it not been for the wind blowing in off the Mediterranean. The plane was twenty minutes early. Meade bought a day-old *New York Times* and fell asleep in a taxi four-deep in passengers. He awoke, from what gratefully turned out to be a dreamless sleep, fully refreshed.

The *Global Art Review,* the periodical that published the articles Farrell had mentioned, was now called the *Weekly Recorder: A Journal of Fine Art.* The magazine kept its offices in a shabby brick building on Rehov Hanna. The Two Lions of Judah had been carved above the stone entrance.

The signs inside and out were written in Hebrew, Arabic, and English. Dr. Shapiro's name didn't carry much weight with the office staff, and after twenty minutes, Meade was ushered to the desk of the Executive Editor. His name was Elon Kolleck. He wore a black pinstripe suit and red vest bulging over a voluminous girth, and waddled like a goose. His pencil-thin mustache traced an upper lip damp with perspiration.

Meade introduced himself, flashing his press card.

"We don't get many Americans," Kolleck said with mild enthusiasm. He toyed with a silver pocket watch and drank sparkling water from a crystal goblet. "You were asking about Emery Shapiro. Not exactly a newsmaker, Emery."

"Your office staff would agree."

"That's why they sent you to me. I was Emery's editor. But that was before the buyout. Most of the old staff moved on or was moved out." Kolleck smiled. Was it a memory sweet or wistful? Meade couldn't tell. "Hardly more than a year ago. Is that a long time? I don't know."

"Then Dr. Shapiro was a casualty of the buyout, too."

"That didn't sound like a question. No, it didn't, but I'll assume it was and ask, Why? Why do you ask?" Kolleck formed a moving steeple with his fingers. He was still smiling.

"I'm doing a feature on the Dutch painter, Jan Vermeer. Of a historical nature. Unfortunately, the history behind one of his last works, *Two Women and Their Music,* has proved to be a problem."

"The painting was sold last year, was it not?"

Meade explained the loss of the painting during the

war and its rediscovery years later, but didn't mention the theft. "I'm concerned about the years in between."

"And you think the readers of the San Francisco *Chronicle* will be interested. Huh." Kolleck's eyes flickered. "Would I have assigned such a story? I must confess to some doubt."

The editor reached for the phone anyway, asked for the research department, and gave them the dates of the articles. He also requested Dr. Shapiro's employee record. Photostats of all three were on his desk almost immediately. He read in silence.

"You're of the opinion that Emery might know something about the Vermeer's undocumented period. Am I reading you at all correctly?"

"Yes." Meade looked down at the pencil in his hand. Except for his less than enthusiastic conclusion to his prison exposé, he hadn't taken a note or written a word since the theft. He wondered if he ever would. He said, "Dr. Shapiro is, or was, somewhat of an authority on the art situation during the war."

"Ah. His book, of course." Again his eyes danced. "I found it a tad emotional."

"He wrote the first article for your magazine under his own byline. I'm assuming he went to Amsterdam himself."

"A valid assumption—" Kolleck exhaled on the face of his watch and used his sleeve as a polishing cloth, "if I recall."

"The second piece was a standard wire-service piece. I'm curious."

Kolleck turned over Shapiro's employee information again, but didn't really look at it. "The explanation is twofold. On the one hand, the follow-up wasn't too exciting. You'd agree, I imagine. Wire-service stuff, as you said. We ran it, no doubt, as a reader courtesy. On the other hand—" He tapped the employee record with his finger—"Emery terminated with the magazine a week after the first story appeared."

Meade stroked his chin, soaking in the words. "And you remember. Why?"

"I remember because we were friends." There wasn't much to his smile now. "At any rate, we liked the same wine. Is that friendship? I've come to wonder."

"I'm sorry. I meant why he terminated with the magazine. Was it unexpected?"

"From the magazine's point of view, you're asking. If I recall, he was working on several other things at the time, stories at various stages of completion. So I would say yes, it was unexpected."

"But you said you were friends. Did he give a reason?"

A weariness settled over Kolleck's face; his shoulders drooped, then raised in a defensive shrug. "Emery considered Jerusalem home. I think he was eager to return. I recall some mention of a teaching position at the university there."

Meade waited, hoping for more, but when Kolleck opened his pocket watch and stared conspicuously at its face, he asked, "Is Dr. Shapiro still in Jerusalem?"

"I can only assume. We haven't spoken since the day he left Tel Aviv." Meade saw now that the weariness was hurt. Kolleck pushed the employee record across the table. "He left a forwarding address. I wrote once or twice, but never did get a response. You may have better luck."

Meade took a phone number and address from the employee file and then gathered up the two articles. He gazed at the first. He read to himself the part about the treasure trove and the apparent identification of works by Gerard Terborch, Pieter de Hooch, and Jan Vermeer. Then he scanned the second. The police called it "A hoax perpetrated by disgruntled art students from the local university."

He read the line out loud. "A hoax perpetrated by disgruntled art students." Slowly his eyes came away from the page and settled on the hands of the circular wall clock at the back of Kolleck's office. Its ticking was amplified in the lull. Feeling the quickening of his own heart, Meade said, "Art students talented enough to create the illusion, if only for a time, of the works of three seventeenth-century Dutch masters. Some hoax."

Twenty-two miles southeast of Tel Aviv lay the ancient city of Jerusalem. Meade opted for a cab. And while his driver rambled on about his Sephardic heritage, Meade, with the expressed intent of keeping his eyes off his watch, absently studied the stout-hearted pines that meagerly endowed the surrounding hills.

Meade realized that by now Fazzie was on board the fishing boat and, in four or five hours, if all went well, would be setting foot on the shore of Robben Island. Sean had been a prisoner now for twenty-four hours. Meade pictured a bruised and battered body; Sean, he knew, would not have been taken easily.

Was it mere coincidence that Dr. Emery Shapiro had suddenly resigned from the *Global Art Review* only days after the apparent discovery of his family's long-lost Vermeer? Was the disappointment of the hoax too great? And why hadn't the paper gone into more detail about the hoax? Or was it only Meade's own involvement that made it seem like a compelling story? He reminded himself that *involvement* was not supposed to be part of the newspaperman's repertoire. Objectivity: that was the ticket. Did his involvement explain the empty notebook in his jacket pocket? The messages from the head office in San Francisco he had so conveniently put off answering?

In the bibliographic notes that had accompanied the announcement of his Pulitzer eight years ago, one of

Meade's contemporaries had described him as "possessing the natural instincts of a hunting dog and the cool detachment of a cat burglar."

Sally's death had changed all that. Now all he remembered of those years were the flowers she would leave on his desk in the morning. The walks they had taken on the beach, and her silly jokes. The scent of her hair as they made love. The strength and pride she had exuded during childbirth.

On impulse, Meade took out his wallet. He opened it to an old snapshot. There was Sean, a high school graduate in his cap and gown, an arm draped around his mother's shoulder. But the voice Meade heard was neither Sean's nor Sally's. It was Farrell's. *I liked it when you touched my hair.*

His driver talked on. He was explaining the British mandate. Meade caught the part about the Ottoman Turks having made only one mistake in their four-hundred-year rule over the city. "Four centuries of kicking butt from here to Algeria, and who do the crazy mongrels side with in the First World War? The Germans."

"Bad choice," Meade agreed.

On the side of a conspicuously dry hill, a greeting had been cut out of thick, olive-green shrubbery. *Bruchim Haba'im.* "Blessed is your arrival."

Beyond the next rise, built atop a well-worn nub of a mountain, stood the city itself; within it, the Old City— towers and buildings and domes hewed from stone the color of a noon sun, shades of yellow and gold and ocher, surrounded by a towering stone wall. Beyond and to the west rose the concrete and glass towers of a more modern Jerusalem, the Jewish side. And to the east, the Arab version, a muted reflection.

Meade mentioned the Hotel Kidron.

As it turned out, the hotel was located at the foot of Mount Zion on Rehov St. Stephen, within walking distance of the Wall. The cabdriver used his thumb to indicate the Zion and Jaffa gates.

"Two of the eight," he said. "You want in or out of the Old City, you use one of the eight gates. That, or sprout wings."

He pulled into the half-moon drive that serviced the hotel's main entrance, and Meade climbed out. Departing South Africa had not quelled his paranoia; he surveyed the street. He saw a woman in high heels with a briefcase and an umbrella walking next to an Orthodox Jew in a wide-brimmed beaver hat and white knee socks. He saw a trio of teenage girls in halter tops and cutoffs, crossing the street in front of an Armenian with a pointed black headdress and flowing black robe. He saw two soldiers with automatic weapons slung over their shoulders, lumbering past a young man who was waiting at a bus stop and chomping on sunflower seeds like it was his last meal. A double-decker bus rumbled up to the stop. The man boarded. The woman who took his place at the stop wore a maroon beret and carried a basket under her arm.

At the hotel entrance, Meade looked back again. The people moved in waves. He checked in and took the stairs to the sixth floor, Room 609. He laid his bag on the bed and dug out the piece of paper on which he had written Dr. Emery Shapiro's last-known telephone number and address.

Meade tried the phone number, but it was no longer in service. He wasn't surprised. In the bottom drawer of the nightstand he found a city directory. There was an abundance of Shapiros—but no Emery. Four listings under E. Shapiro, but no reference in any of the four to a doctoral status. The numbers yielded an Ephraim, an Eleazar, and two Elijahs. Meade called the Liberal Arts Department at the university. He lied. A family emergency, he told the secretary at the other end of the line, but didn't elaborate. To embellish a lie, Meade had learned, was to expose it. The secretary responded with an address and phone number that bore no resemblance to the ones in the employee file. The new address was in Rehavia, in West Jerusalem.

Meade dialed the number. A woman answered. In Hebrew. Meade's query about English was positively met, but his introduction and query about the doctor was less so. After a moment's hesitation, the woman excused herself.

When she returned she said, "Dr. Em isn't feeling very well at the moment. I'm his nurse. I do believe it might be better if I took your number and had the doctor return your call at his convenience."

"Nothing serious, I hope?" Meade replied.

"The doctor is not a well man, I'm afraid," the woman stammered. A voice echoed in the background. "He has been ill for some time, actually."

"I'm sorry," Meade said, and then asked, "Could I impose on you for one last favor? Tell the doctor it's about Jan Vermeer. Tell him it's about *Two Women and Their Music*. About a forgery."

It was nearly two minutes before Meade heard the nurse's voice again. She said, "The doctor will meet you in the Old City. At the Western Wall. The Wailing Wall. In one hour. How will he know you, please?"

Meade described himself and then hung up.

30

THE AUCTION AT CHRISTIE'S that day focused on the sale of *Fine Old Masters*. Not quite the *Important Old Masters* in stature or price, but a step above the *Old Masters*, and several steps above the *Old Masters Drawings and Prints*. The auction house was located on King Street, and Jacob Bartleman was waiting for Farrell when she arrived.

The building was a pale granite. A huge gray awning stretched from the arched entryway to the curb. Valets wore vests and matching ties. Doormen wore top hats. The lobby, tall columns and a painted ceiling, was quiet. The auction was well under way: an usher offered them a glossy pink and green catalog of the day's featured works.

A sweeping staircase, rising below broad skylights, was flooded with an ecclesiastical light. The hall was octagonal in shape, with a cathedral ceiling. Like something out of Camelot, Bartleman whispered. On the walls hung some of the more notable works available. And while the auctioneer set the bidding in motion, potential buyers browsed, examined, and made last-minute calculations. Televison cameras recorded the event. Resting on an easel next to the podium was a small oil Farrell recognized, by Gaspar Verbrugghen the Younger.

When they were seated, she explained the bidding process to Bartleman. An opening bid, she told him, was predetermined by the house. From there the bidding proceeded in increments of a hundred (in pounds) up to five thousand, in increments of five hundred up to ten thousand, and by thousands from there on up. Overhead, an electronic monitor tracked each bid; yellow lights translated changing prices into dollars, francs, marks, lira, and yen. The Verbrugghen was bought—"knocked down," in the vernacular—by a New York gallery for sixty-five hundred pounds.

With each lot, the auction grew more rambunctious, while Farrell grew more anxious. She participated half-heartedly in the bidding for a boring work by an eighteenth-century English painter named George Romney, and bid aggressively for a haunting oil by José Clemente Orozco of Mexico. She would have loved the Orozco, and the price wasn't out of line at twenty-seven thousand, but there wasn't much call for Mexican mural art in stately old Stellenbosch, Farrell realized. She dropped out at twenty-one thousand.

The man she had come to the auction to see was John Laudermilk, Christie's youthful General Manager. He and Farrell had been steady companions for two years. They had shared an apartment for six months, invested in stereo equipment, and opened a joint savings account. Serious business, for graduate students. News of Farrell's pregnancy had brought out the paternal instinct in John Laudermilk, but had only left her frightened and out of her head with guilt. The abortion sent Laudermilk into exile for eight months in Jamaica. By the time he returned, Farrell had gone back to the Cape, had won the assistant curatorship at the National Gallery in Cape Town, and had fallen victim to despair and remorse. They had exchanged two letters, hers trying in vain to make amends, his stating an adamant refusal ever to see her

311

again. Of course they had, over the years, broken that vow. Not often. Lunch two or three times at the Catch; dinner, perhaps six years before, with his new wife at the Pure Harvest. That was the last time. The new wife had insisted, and Farrell understood; John still looked at her with the eyes of a forlorn lover.

Laudermilk's slight form could be seen every couple of minutes peering out from behind the stage curtain or conferring with the auctioneer between lots. Calm, but intent. Immaculately attired.

Lot number 21, a fifteenth-century van der Weyden, was placed on the easel next. As the bidding proceeded, Farrell turned her attention to a sketch by Gustave Courbet, an early work from the artist's days in Paris. It was called *The River Crossing*.

"That's one I'd hang," she said in Bartleman's ear, gesturing to the catalog, and spicing the lie with a bit of Courbet history. "But I'm only willing to go as high as ninety-five hundred pounds. I don't think we'll make it."

Then she closed the catalog suddenly and stared beyond the podium.

"That bastard," Farrell whispered, her voice vehement. She handed Bartleman her fountain pen. "Did you see him? That bastard."

"What is it?" he asked.

"Clive Kenney." Real name, real enemy; though Farrell didn't know if Clive Kenney had ever really been to London or not. "A debtor. A cheat. A slimy weasel."

"I didn't know weasels could be slimy."

"Take my word for it." Farrell was on her feet. "I'll be back. Push the Courbet to the limit if I don't make it in time. Not a pound higher, though."

"Fine," Bartleman said, but Farrell was already striding down the aisle.

John Laudermilk stopped cold when he saw Farrell. He looked older, hair thinning, pale. His voice, however, was as buoyant as the day they had met. "You! You magnificent creature. Six interminable years," he said. "Let me take a gander at you. God almighty, how the bloody hell are you? You look—God, you look wonderful."

Farrell smiled. They hugged, deeply, and then face to face, swaying, hand in hand. "Look at you. You're losing your hair and you still look great," she said.

"Keep it up, kiddo."

The bidding on the Courbet had begun. Farrell held his hands. "I've missed you."

"I've missed you, too." He bowed his head, embarrassed. "I have three kids."

Was it possible, Farrell wondered, that four simple words could wield such a heartrending blow? For an instant, she couldn't breathe. Then felt old, remorseful, and resigned, in fleeting, consecutive intervals. And ended by saying, in a tender voice, "John, I know I'm off-limits, but I have to talk."

Laudermilk's shrug, Farrell saw, was not as off-handed as he would have liked. "Great. I'll have a bottle of vino brought up to my dressing room."

"Now, John. It's important. Please."

He led her into a vacant office. She told him about the Greyling theft, and then she told him about the forgery. Laudermilk's expression hardened. His voice, as well. "Source?"

"The samples were from Miles Roundtree. Nico Mustapha turned it up. I was there."

Laudermilk nodded; he knew the names, and the reputations. Still he said, "We ran that painting through the mill, kiddo. You know that. You were there for that, too."

"Miles Roundtree was murdered for his trouble, John. I need to know the seller's name. Off the record. Absolutely confidential, you have my word."

John Laudermilk pushed away from the desk. He toured the room, slapping at the furniture. "Even if I knew I couldn't tell you, Farrell. You know the rules."

"This one isn't being played by the rules."

"The Institute handled the sale. They snapped it right out from under our noses—"

"Christie's got their commission, John. I know. Cas Greyling told me." Now it was Farrell's turn to read the expression on her old lover's face. Her voice, low and tender, bridged the many years of their separation. "This has nothing to do with the commission or the Institute. None of that matters. It doesn't. You know that. That's not what this is about. I understand that you might not know the actual seller. But there had to be an intermediary, other than the Institute. A dealer or a collector handling the negotiations. Someone you approved of. You wouldn't have done it any other way. I know you. That's why you're so damn good at what you do. Please, John. One name."

Laudermilk ran his hands vigorously through his hair. "There's something going on, Farrell."

Farrell moved closer. She took his face in her hands, stroked his hair. "Yes, there is something going on, my sweet and dear friend. And, yes, as serious as your imagination is painting it. I need this one favor."

"And we'll laugh the whole thing away over dinner some night, right?" He lifted his gaze from the floor, peered with intent into her eyes, and said brusquely, "All right, a name from the past. Ready? Viktor Mannheimer."

"Viktor? The million-dollar junk dealer?" From behind a facade of eclectic antiques, Viktor Mannheimer bartered rare coins with royalty, traded gold bullion with the Japanese, and hoarded paintings worth millions. "He's still alive?"

"He'll outlive us all. And he'll be dead and in his grave before he'll reveal a client's name, kiddo. Even to you." Farrell wouldn't release Laudermilk from her gaze. He shook his head. "Remember his shop?"

As graduate students, a visit with Viktor Mannheimer was more or less required. A return invitation was considered meritorious; and Farrell and John had both received their share. "On Crown Passage. How could I forget?"

"Nothing's changed. What we didn't know in the old days was that he has an office in the back. With a loo attached. OK, so it sounds crazy, but that's where he keeps his records—in the loo, in the linen closet."

"Not crazy," Farrell said, grinning. "Typical."

"And you can bet it's wired, kiddo. And you can bet it was done very neatly."

Both Farrell's and John's introductions to the world of security systems and electronic gimmickry had come at the hands of Viktor Mannheimer, tinkerer *extraordinaire*. She said, "Meaning, the old man did the job himself."

"Naturally."

Farrell didn't return to the auction floor. Instead, she left the house, in the fervent hope of never seeing Jacob Bartleman again, by an employees' exit off the alley.

Viktor Mannheimer was not like most art dealers. He didn't wear double-breasted Savile Row suits or Turnbull and Asser shirts; he favored gabardines and tweeds, and the only tailor he knew on a first-name basis was an arthritic uncle in Tel Aviv. You wouldn't find a Tiffany pen in his vest or a Dunhill writing pad in his briefcase; he carried a pencil over his ear and took notes on paper napkins. He didn't drink malted whiskey or twelve-year-old Scotch because, in his words, a drunken Jew was more appalling than a drunken Irishman. Mannheimer didn't belong to the Friends of Covent Garden or the Freemasons, but he did contribute regularly to the Institute of Contemporary Arts in the hope that someday man might learn to paint again. He didn't eat at Frank's or the Savoy; he owned the deli on the next block. His shop wasn't on Bond Street, or on Jermyn or Duke or Bury either; he had been in the same building on Crown Passage for thirty-one years and lived on the second floor with seven cats, a bulldog, and a hoard of art worth five million pounds.

Located off Pall Mall in St. James, Crown Passage was more alleyway than thoroughfare, but over the years it had become a London fixture. A bookshop sold bound editions of Rilke and used copies of Lardner. A confectionery made chocolates from scratch. A café sold meat pies and mustard-seed cakes. An awning with the word *Antiques* painted across its face hung over a great wooden door flanked by spotless fifteen-foot windows.

Farrell had been a graduate student the first time she gazed through those windows. That day it was an eighteenth-century book-and-desk set staring back at her; today it was a honey-colored harpsichord and a Louis XIV parlor set. That day it was a hungry scholar researching a thesis; today, well . . .

She went inside. The box under her arm contained jars of wine jellies, the only vice she ever remembered Viktor Mannheimer admitting to.

Chimes sounded as the door closed behind her, and scents of musk and linseed and beeswax rose up to greet her. The sounds of a Bach concerto filtered from hidden speakers. Brass and wood ceiling fans churned in unison. There were cameras, and there were guards—a system Farrell had been introduced to—but they were never seen.

The shop was busy but not crowded. A man and woman pored over a neoclassic table and chair set. A clerk told a white-haired lady the story behind an eighteenth-century filing cabinet. Farrell ran a hand over the counterpane covering a four-poster bed. A woman with a store name tag pinned to her sweater offered her coffee or tea and slices of banana bread from a tray on wheels.

"Coffee would be wonderful," Farrell said. The woman poured from a silver pot into a paper cup, apologized for the disparity, and then offered cream and sugar.

"The shop looks great. Just terrific," Farrell told her, meaning it. "It's been so long."

"You've been in before?"

"Many times. Viktor was a tutor, of sorts. Of course, that was fifteen or sixteen years ago." Farrell dug a business card from her purse. She told the woman about the museum in Stellenbosch and used a wistful smile to cement her connection with Viktor Mannheimer's past. "So, is the million-dollar junk dealer around today, or is he loafing?"

"That nickname! Oh, dear Lord, I haven't heard it in years." The woman reached out and touched Farrell's arm. She stifled a laugh with a finger over her lips. "Viktor just hates that name. It's so American."

"I know. I'm responsible, I'm afraid. I gave him the name myself after he came back from New England with a boatload of Sylvan cookstoves." They both laughed. "Is he here?"

"Oh, I'm so disappointed. He's in New York."

"The auctions, of course." As Farrell had suspected, and hoped. The summer "season" in auctions extended from June through July, and New York was generally a month ahead of London; their Important Old Masters sale began the following week, and the buyers were already congregating. Farrell held out the box. The ribbon was bright red. "Does our junk dealer still like his wine jellies?"

"Oh, you sweet thing. You know Viktor, they won't last a week. Oh, he'll be so disappointed he missed you."

"Is his office still in the back?" Farrell ventured. And when the woman nodded, she asked, "May I? I thought I'd leave a note."

The woman said, "Absolutely. He'd love it."

"If you don't mind, I'll powder my nose while I'm back there," Farrell added.

"Take your time." The woman beamed. "It's a pleasure having you back after so long."

The office, as it turned out, was large enough for a partially stripped mahogany desk, a barber's chair, and in one corner a full suit of armor, proud as a centurion.

Farrell left the jellies on a backless stool. She tucked a note under the ribbon. The bathroom had a Do Not Disturb sign taped to the door. Farrell pushed it open and stood for a moment on the threshold. A stool, a clawfooted bathtub, a wall cabinet, a freestanding sink, and a counter were illuminated by a yellow night-light. A portable typewriter perched on a metal stand in front of the stool. A vase full of wilted chrysanthemums littered the counter. Water dripped in the sink. It smelled of potpourri. The linen closet John Laudermilk had told her about was next to the bathtub. A lamp chain dangled from the ceiling. Farrell pulled it and closed the door behind her.

For nearly a minute she stood, her back against the counter, staring at the closet. She knew two things about Viktor Mannheimer. She knew that, though he saved every scrap, the records didn't mean a lot to him. The saving, on the one hand, was a lifelong scruple duly imposed on him by his mother. On the other, if the record was that important, he kept it in his head, anyway. She also knew that Viktor Mannheimer was basically lazy, and therefore not likely to install a security system that was more trouble than it was worth. Farrell pushed away from the counter. She turned in a slow circle, took in the floor, baseboard, walls, and ceiling. She hand-searched the counter, top to bottom, yanked on the plug chain in the sink, and lifted the typewriter from its stand. She flushed the toilet and played with the faucets.

Finally, her attention settled on the night-light. It was the kind that plugged into a wall socket with an opaque shield over the bulb. Farrell ran her finger behind the shield, felt the heat of the bulb, the tip of a wire, and then a slight shock. Her grin was pure respect. She switched the light off.

The linen closet opened without a sound, but a hearty voice nearly put a stop to Farrell's heart. "A good day to you, Viktor. Shalom." It was Viktor Mannheimer's own voice. "Have you thanked God yet for all the suckers in the world? If not—"

Farrell found the tape player and pushed the off button on the automatic message. "Very funny, Viktor. Very funny."

Her hands shook as she worked. Blue files filled cardboard boxes which filled four shelves. A black marking pen labeled the boxes by year. The "Current—Active" box was front and center, waist high. The files were tagged with a day and a month. January 17th, 1988. A copy of a two-page contract with Cas Greyling, a copy of the Vermeer title, and a handwritten note addressed to Viktor Mannheimer were stapled together. The contract copy listed V. Mannheimer as the selling agent, but the lines next to "Seller" and "Seller's Signature" were conspicuously blank. The word *Anonymous* had been scribbled across the title. But the scrawl at the bottom of the note read "Em Shapiro."

31

MEADE ENTERED the Old City of Jerusalem on foot. He used the Jaffa gate and was immediately consumed by the Armenian Quarter, a walled enclave within a walled city. He stumbled into a maze of dark corridors and narrow, winding paths, all cut of yellow stone and dulled by age. He slipped into a tenement house entryway and pressed up against the door. He waited and watched for two minutes. His ears tuned into a foreign silence; whether the drone of decay or the hum of privacy, Meade couldn't tell. Merchants whispered in an unintelligible language. Veils covered the faces of humble churchgoers. A wooden clapper resounded from a cathedral courtyard, while Meade's own footsteps echoed like taps on a hardwood floor. The streets were alleys; the alleys were funnels of gloom. Shadows, everywhere, and shadowy glances. He smelled incense and cooking meat. Candlelight flickered from behind the windows of cramped tenements. Then stone steps, a low archway, a forged iron gate—and it was all behind him. No greeting, no farewell, yet Meade felt strangely relieved.

He followed a band of noisy tourists down Rehov Habad. Like good tourists, most of then donned hats and scarves and made the mandatory stop at the Habad Synagogue.

Meade took a winding staircase down into the Jewish Quarter.

The lanes on this side of the city were still hauntingly narrow, the roads broken and twisted, the courtyards filled with shouting and laughter.

Why, Meade wondered, had Emery Shapiro chosen the Western Wall for their meeting? Because there were people? Because his own house might reveal answers he had no intention of sharing? Or because he went to the Wall every Thursday and had no intention of changing his schedule for a reporter with grand illusions?

A narrow stone path wound eventually to the Stairs of Rabbi Judah Halevi. Down the stairs and across a wide plaza stood the Wall. Just beyond, Meade's eyes were drawn to the glistening Dome of the Rock, and then past the city walls to the bent trees on the Mount of Olives, across the Kidron Valley to a cluster of low huts, and finally, to the remote shimmer of the Dead Sea.

The plaza was a vast floor of rock and tile. It was mostly empty. The Wall's huge cuts of Herodian stone were, in this light, more white than gold. Only the ululations of swaying women intruded upon the silence. They cried, like wounded animals, and droned, like bagpipes. The sun bore down with a vengeance.

Meade stopped before a low fence that bisected the plaza's farthest quadrant. Beyond the fence, worshipers were deep in prayer, men and women purposely segregated.

"A mere painting takes on a distinct insignificance in the face of the Wall, wouldn't you agree, sir?"

Meade turned. The man behind this vigorous, schoolmasterly proclamation was slight of build, dressed in a neat brown suit. He held a flat-topped hat in two hands behind his back. His beard was gray and meticulously kept.

Wire-rimmed glasses perched on a hawkish nose. His voice had given no clue as to his age, but his eyes were milky with cataracts.

"Dr. Shapiro."

"The Wall has survived since the Second Temple Period—did you know?—five hundred years before Christ. A Vermeer? A Vermeer is a mere trinket in comparison."

"Others refer to such trinkets as expressions of the soul, Doctor. Gateways to the unconscious."

"You don't believe it." His smile was that of a tired fatalist.

"We all have our gateways. For me—" Meade shrugged, even as his concentration magnified—"van Gogh's landscapes, Blake's poetry, Singer's fiction. And you, Doctor? As an art historian. As a professor of art history."

Shapiro scoffed. "Art has become a commodity, sir. If it sells, it has value. Van Gogh sold one painting in his lifetime. And to whom? A pitying brother. An Australian holding company, for God's sake, makes a mockery of his life by paying fifty million dollars for a couple of irises. And all in the name of prestige and image. As for Blake? Much too deep. Singer? Too ethnic. No, we admire the computer whiz in this day and age, not the creator of art. We shower accolades on the Wall Street manipulator, not the craftsman and his tools. And with every tribute to technology and financial trivia, mankind slips a little further into the muck of his own self-glorification."

Meade turned the conversation then to the *Global Art Review* articles, and on the doctor's face he saw the fatalistic smile erode into a scowl of mistrust, only to be replaced by an inoffensive smirk of irony.

"Were you there?" Meade asked. "In Amsterdam, when the story broke, or—?"

"Does it matter?" Shapiro brushed the question aside and gazed in the direction of the Wall. "You mentioned a forgery. That sounds frightfully more important than my whereabouts when a particularly worthless story broke."

"The paintings were found in an apartment house." Meade persevered. "Were you allowed—?"

"Inside? Not on your life. The apartment house was sealed like some sacred tomb, and the police fed us crumbs of information as if we were annoying beggars. Perhaps that's how they do business in Amsterdam; I didn't wait around to find out."

Meade wouldn't let go. "Which led to your speculation about *Two Women and Their Music*. You must have insisted on seeing it. The painting once belonged to your family, after all. Curiosity, if nothing else."

Shapiro dabbed his forehead with a freshly pressed handkerchief. Meade noticed the monogram. He also noticed the unobtrusive diamond on his middle finger. "I was shown a photo," Shapiro explained. "It was . . . shall we say, an emulation of Vermeer's style, nothing more."

"And the subject?"

"The subject? If I recall, the subject was Christ, not women, and not music."

"You must have been disappointed."

"I was inaccurate, sir, not disappointed. I projected fantasy onto fact for my own benefit. It's called unprofessional behavior. I looked in the mirror and didn't care for what I saw. That's why I quit," he said, as if anticipating the question.

"Ironically, six months later, the object of your inaccuracy surfaces anyway and is sold for an exorbitant amount of money. It seems unfair."

"To some South African, wasn't it?" Shapiro used his hat like a fan; he glanced from the Wall to Meade and then momentarily at the white-hot sun.

"Sir Cas Greyling. Does the name mean anything to you?"

Shapiro shook his head. "I can't say that it does."

"The painting was stolen from his private gallery five days ago. Three days later the stolen work proved to be a forgery."

Meade watched as islands of concentration and wonder tracked across the doctor's pale face. From the Wall, a *shofar*, a ram's horn, resounded, echoed, and gave way to a low chant. Bodies swayed. Meade said, "You were a German Jew. You sought exile from the war in South Africa. Did you find it—saner?"

The cloak of fatalism returned. "The disease had long arms, if that's what you're asking."

"The disease but not the retribution."

As Meade told the story of the Missing Sixth, the lines on Emery Shapiro's face deepened. He seemed to shrink. But when the story was over, his eyes flashed. "You, sir, are a—" His mouth twisted. Heart and soul tried squeezing truth from a paradox his head refused to consider. "Then this document, this Missing Sixth, it wasn't— You're saying it wasn't found? You're saying it still exists? That it's somehow contained in the original—?"

In that moment, they were interrupted by a young woman dressed in a gauze blouse and blue jeans. She wore a maroon beret on her head. Dark, tangled hair framed a masculine face. In her arms she bore a basket filled with loaves of bread. She bowed her head and spoke directly to Meade.

"Excuse me, sir. I'm intruding, I know. Please forgive me." She raised her eyes slightly. "This is the anniversary of my father's death. He died two years ago in the fighting on the West Bank. I wish to honor him. He stood often at the Western Wall."

It was understood: women did not venture onto the men's side of the Wall. The opposite was equally true. Meade was about to plead his ignorance of Jewish tradition when Dr. Shapiro stepped between them. He smiled, touched the girl's hand, and then took hold of her basket.

324

"You serve your father well, my child. What was his name?"

"Josef Yehudai, and I am Hara, but—" She held fast to the basket, dipping her head in Meade's direction. "But *he* reminds me so of my father. I wanted—"

"I will pray for Josef Yehudai," Shapiro said gently, relieving her of the basket. "Come."

"But truly. He—" The woman accompanied Shapiro to the end of the fence, wringing her hands. Meade waited and watched. Ritual, his grandfather once warned him, has a cunning way of reaching the soul and an even more cunning way of closing the mind. The doctor wrapped a dark gray *tallith* around his shoulders. Then he began his trek. Hat on head, eyes forward, the basket held with reverence before him. When he reached the Wall, he pressed an opened palm to the stone, and Meade turned to observe the woman's reaction.

She was no longer by the fence. Meade searched the crowd to the Wall, and then backtracked. He located her standing under a stone arch at the mouth of an excavation site. Which seemed odd, since the view from where she was standing wasn't . . . wasn't nearly as . . .

Meade looked back at Shapiro, who was now embracing the basket of bread, now placing it at the foot of the wall. The flood of panic was instantaneous, instinctual—and too late.

"Doctor!" Meade leapt the fence. "Doctor Shapiro. The basket—"

Running, he saw the woman dip beneath the arch. He shouted again. An instant later, an explosion rocked the plaza. Meade saw a flash of orange where seconds before Dr. Emery Shapiro had been praying.

Meade's search for the woman proved futile. The excavation site gave access to a half-dozen corridors that led eventually to the Dung Gate, and at least as many that didn't.

The police detained him for questioning; three men in a cluttered office with a photograph of Golda Meir staring down on them. Meade smoked cigarettes like he had in the old days, one after another. His hands shook when he realized that the basket of bread, and the bomb within, had been intended for him. He was straight with the police about everything except the Missing Sixth.

He spent an hour and forty minutes poring over the photos and sketches of the Israelis' Known Criminal and Terrorist File. Broken down by age and sex, it was the most complete "Rogues Gallery" Meade had ever seen. He recognized the woman in a newspaper photo taken the moment after an explosion in the Rome airport. She was not Israeli, but East German. Two names were given: Mina Grizel, and Hara, a member of a political organization known as the Red Wheel.

Meade clenched his teeth and swore. Rita Hess, Hulster, the fourth thief at De Greyling, and now a masculine woman named Hara in a maroon beret.

Ten minutes later, he was given permission by the police to accompany them to Emery Shapiro's house in a neighborhood called Rehavia.

"Expensive," the driver said in response to Meade's queries about the neighborhood.

"How expensive?"

"Expensive for a university professor without tenure. For an art professor with a full-time nurse, damn expensive."

Shapiro lived on the fifth floor of the Alfass, an apartment house with security, a lobby chandelier, arrangements of pampas grass, and a swimming pool no one ever used. His nurse of eleven months took the news of his death hard; she went immediately into shock. An ambulance was summoned.

For an ailing professor and his nurse, the apartment was foolishly large. Eight rooms, three without so much as a chair in them. The others were cluttered with icons and potted plants and overstuffed furniture. Shapiro had dedicated an entire library to the study of art—books, periodicals, manuscripts, documents, and copious notes in the professor's own hand. The room smelled like Grandfather Meade's study in the old house in Maine. Cedar and cigar smoke.

It was well after dark when Meade stumbled upon the spiral notebook tucked on top of years of tax records in an old chest of drawers turned file cabinet. A simple rubric at the top read, "Personal File." It began with the words:

> As early as 1938, Hitler had become obsessed with the vision of transforming his hometown of Linz, a sleepy, dour city in Austria, into what he himself called "the artistic Mecca of the New Europe." The idea of the transformation of this provincial capital lived with Hitler for the remainder of his life. He imagined a modern metropolis with three or four times the city's prewar populace. At its shining heart he envisioned a massive array of public buildings, erected to the memory of Adolf Hitler, archdictator, designed by Adolf Hitler, master builder, and filled by Adolf Hitler, marauder extraordinaire, with the artistic treasures he would loot from the four corners of Europe.

The "requisitioning" of these artistic treasures, as Shapiro's account told it, began in earnest with the onset of the war. Not the pillaging of the Huns or the plundering of Alexander the Great, but the German way, meticulously planned and ruthlessly administered. In Poland, Austria, the Netherlands, France, Belgium, and Luxembourg, the systematic rape of art was carried out on the heels of the invading German army, the cooperative effort of generals, art experts, and bookkeepers.

Take from the Jews, confiscate from the museums, "purchase" from dealers and collectors.

As the years passed, though not a single brick was ever laid in Linz, Hitler quietly amassed the greatest personal collection of art ever assembled. But according to the doctor, Hitler didn't hang these paintings or display the sculptures; he stored them in dark rooms in Berlin, in underground air raid shelters beneath the *Fuehrerbau* in Munich, and eventually in the Alt Aussee salt mines in Austria, naturally temperature and climate controlled.

Hitler had no use for modern art, perhaps because of the unbearable weight of his own personal failure as an artist and architect. He accepted the old masters because not even his petty mind, as the doctor put it, could buck the judgment of centuries. The more photographic the painting, the better he liked it; the less prolific the artist, the greater the appeal. Therefore, Watteau and Vermeer and Fragonard became his obsessions.

There was another side to the disease

—Meade read the words in a hushed whisper as a lab man from the police scrounged about; he had insisted Meade wear cotton gloves—

As the number of paintings and sculptures, rare books and manuscripts, tapestries and rare coins soared into the many thousands, Hitler began to use selected items as rewards for his weary war machine. After General Heinz Guderian and his tanks ran roughshod over France, he was presented with an eighteenth-century jasperware vase. After General Gerd von Rundstedt's forces penetrated the rugged Ardennes country north of the Maginot Line and captured Sedan, he was rewarded with a bronze by Auguste Rodin. But Hitler's

favorite almsman was also his most successful commander, General Erwin Rommel.

Rommel was the perfect beneficiary, an art lover
with no money and no standing. After he repulsed an
Allied advance at Vailly, a courier presented him with
a small oil by Alfred Sisley, and the handwritten note:
"Your success, well done. A. H." Following his
triumph at Sidi Rezegh, Rommel found Delacroix's
Moon over the Ruins of Missolonghi hanging on the
wall of his home in Swabia. There were others, as
well, but for his greatest victory, in Tobruk in June of
1942, came his greatest reward—Jan Vermeer's masterful *Two Women and Their Music*. Rommel must have
understood the significance of the victory in light of
the sweetness of the reward. He hung each and every
painting in a small chamber off his bedroom, and
drank many a glass of wine in their honor.

Why was it, I ask myself, that he felt the urge to
have the Vermeer copied? Did he fear, Vermeer being
one of Hitler's favorites, its repossession? Of course,
whatever the reason, it remains a miracle of fate;
Rommel's other paintings having been destroyed as
punishment for his alleged part in the bungled assassination attempt on Hitler.

So it was true, Meade thought, that Shapiro knew nothing of the six documents Rommel had drawn up. This
last line confirmed it.

But he did know something.

At the bottom of the page the account continued. This
in a different pen, the ink blue and nearly depleted. And
a less precise script indicated its renewal at a different
time, perhaps in a different frame of mind.

The painting was, of course, thought lost, or perhaps
destroyed. But it appears that Rommel was alone in his

329

decision to have the Vermeer duplicated. Even his
wife, Lucie Maria, knew nothing of its whereabouts. It
was a stroke of pure genius that Rommel would have
chosen as his forger the only man . . .

Meade turned the page and found, to his astonishment,
that the next two pages had been torn out. The shredded
edges of the paper were still trapped inside the spiral wire
of the notebook. Knowing better, he searched the book
front to back in the faint hope that the pages had been
reinserted someplace. No, Meade thought, the doctor had
removed them, and more than likely destroyed them, after
receiving his call this morning.

But if this were true then why, Meade wondered,
hadn't he destroyed the entire journal?

He went through the account again, page by page. This
time Meade focused particular attention on the margin
notes that had been scrawled in pencil throughout the
journal. Some had been hastily erased, some crossed out.
He deciphered what he thought were two names and a
city. The city, though only a faded "Amsterd . . . ," was
clearly Amsterdam. On the same page there was also a
broken phrase that read, "A look into the . . . ," followed by a black smudge and then, ". . . of H. Gelderblom." And on the last page there were three words
which Meade deciphered as saying, ". . . could Hoogendijk
know . . ."

32

BY EVENING THE FLEET had traveled two hundred miles, and their holds were heavy with *snoek*. Come nightfall, the trawlers had congregated four kilometers west of Robben Island. A direct course back to Table Bay would take them within rowing distance of the island's southern shore. The sobriety of the task at hand settled upon them.

For the first time in hours Tobias relinquished the controls to one of the crew. He pulled up a chair next to Fazzie. Now the island was a ghostly shadow just two kilometers away. He said, "Let me tell you about the waters around here, Superman. Cold, very cold. Rough, and fickle as a woman in pajamas. This isn't like kicking a soccer ball around on a Sunday afternoon. You know that; you're not stupid. But I'll say it anyway, just to make myself feel good. Sharks. Lots of them. Tigers mostly, and very nasty. As for the island itself, I've told you everything I know, which is to say that your best bet would be to forget the whole thing. The kid's most likely dead anyway."

"I'll expect you an hour before dawn," Fazzie replied. He watched Tobias's face and the tension gathering around his eyes. Finally, he filled a canteen from the boat's water barrel. "We'll make it as far south as possible by then."

"*Sies.*" Tobias shook his head even as the raft inflated at his feet. "No dawdling, Cam," he said. "If you're not there, I won't wait. I can't. I won't sacrifice my boat for you or anyone else. Nothing personal. And a two-man raft is sure not about to see you or anyone else through the ten kilometers of hell that separate the island from the coast. It's as if God didn't intend it."

Fazzie slid the raft into the water. He followed the oars in, and Tobias tossed him his haversack, a coil of nylon rope, and the towline.

"Go well, Cam Fazzie," he said.

"Stay well, good friend." Fazzie peered back momentarily, but by then Tobias had already turned away. "Thanks for the lift."

The fleet slipped into darkness. The raft bobbed in swells of black. Fazzie peeked over his shoulder at the island. Then he plunged the oars into the water. He didn't look back again until he felt a halfhearted breaker carry him over the reef line. A rising tide pushed him toward the shore.

Promontories of craggy rock jutting into the water formed the walls of a small bay backed by a cliff fifteen stories high. When the raft touched bottom, Fazzie tumbled out. He dragged the raft onto a narrow beach and stowed it in a bamboo grove at the foot of the cliff.

Shivering, Fazzie burrowed into the sand. He stared up at the sky. The shimmering of innumerable stars was overwhelming, and the thought occurred to him that he was alone. As alone as he had ever been. He spent nearly a minute listening to the pounding of his heart in his ears. A black man found cavorting on the shores of Robben Island, he reminded himself, a bitter taste filling his mouth, could expect to spend the rest of his life there.

This thought propelled him to his feet. For twenty minutes he walked along the base of the cliff wall searching for the stone steps he had been told about. When he found them, he drew away from the cliff face and peered up. It was a daunting sight. The steps were worn from years of wind and rain, and they did little to offset the steepness of the face.

He peered at the rim. A moment later, he saw a beam of light, saw a shadow behind it, and dropped to his stomach. He rolled over. The beam—that of a high-powered flashlight—reflected off a bramble of cliff-dwelling willows, over tentacles of ivy, and across the face of smooth granite. Then it was gone.

Encouraged, Fazzie checked his watch. It was 10:15. He sipped water from the canteen. Then drank thirstily. He looked back at the cliff and grimaced.

Before discovering his current profession, Fazzie had been a thief, and a good one. Before picking the locks on white suburban houses, he had been a high school dropout. Before dropping out of school, he had been a terror on the soccer field. But there was never a before when he had climbed mountains. He told himself that the way down would be easier.

Four hours earlier, Meade's life had been unexpectedly spared by a little man in a brown suit and gray beard; that another attempt would be made was not a matter of debate.

The police dropped Meade at the station house two blocks from the Hotel Kidron. He used the pay phone located at the top of the steps on the wall just outside the station entrance.

The operator dialed the number in Paris and told him to hang on. Meade did so, for upwards of five minutes. He spent the time with his back pressed against the rear of the booth, staring into a lifeless street. The taxi driver from Tel Aviv had warned him about Jerusalem's night life. "Picture a cemetery in New York City, only half the size and twice as dead."

Meade allowed himself a momentary glance at his watch. Jerusalem and Cape Town were in the same time zone. It was 9:45. He fashioned a picture of Robben Island's southern shore, the high cliff walls and the shallow cove as seen from the backseat of a helicopter.

A voice shook him. It was the operator. A second voice followed. This one belonged to André Saint-Claire, the French correspondent to whom he had sent copies of the fingerprints from the forgery.

"Do listen closely," he said. "The year is 1937. The place is Amsterdam. A most extraordinary work of art has just come on the market. The signature in the upper left corner is none other than I. V. Meer, the initials in monogram. Recognize it? Provenance unknown, but no one seems to care where the painting has come from because an eminent art historian named Abraham Bredius certifies it without question as the work of Jan Vermeer of Delft. They call it *Christ at Emmaus*. A hundred eighty thousand pounds later and it becomes the most acclaimed work in the Boymans Museum collection. Some well-thought-of voices call it Vermeer's most important work. Fine.

"Two years later a private collector in Rotterdam, a certain D. G. van Beuningen, puts down two hundred twenty thousand guilders for a small canvas called *Interior with Drinkers* and signed with the initials P. D. H., 1658. Experts enthusiastically ascribe the work to Pieter de Hooch.

"In 1941, the same Van Beuningen drops another half million guilders for an oil painting called the *Head of Christ*, and hardly a month later another I. V. Meer discovery, the *Last Supper*, demands a million six in guilders. Again no provenance is established and no one's minding. Oddly, no one's minding that it's always the same dealer either, a Dutch character named Hoogendijk."

"Hoogendijk?" Meade took his notebook from the inside pocket of his coat and hurriedly opened it to the notes he had taken in Emery Shapiro's study. "Spell it."

Saint-Claire did so. "You've heard it."

"About an hour ago."

"Well, in April of 1942, Mr. Hoogendijk sells to another Rotterdam collector a de Hooch called *Interior with Cardplayers*. And not cheap—roughly a couple hundred thousand in guilders. Within a matter of weeks, the same buyer puts down a million and some change for a rather undistinguished Vermeer called *Isaac Blessing Jacob*.

"Six months later, like a gum ball from a machine on automatic pilot, up pops yet another Vermeer. This one's titled *Christ and the Adulteress*. Some way or another, it ends up in the hands of Reichsmarschall Hermann Göring."

"Göring?"

"The one and only."

"How? Through this guy Hoogendijk?"

"Can't say. I do know that Göring shelled out a million six for the work. Along the way, an unknown Terborch is discovered and a remarkable portrait by Frans Hals. The whole spree ends in 1943 when the Netherlands state government pays a million, three hundred thousand for a thoroughly average canvas with the same I. V. Meer signature. This one's called *The Washing of Christ's Feet*. Fine.

"After the war, the Allied forces discover Göring's *Adulteress* canvas in the salt mines at Alt Aussee, in Austria. They trace it back to Holland. The Dutch Field Security Service gets it in their heads to find out who's been doing business with enemy forces. A four-month search leads them to your friend Hoogendijk. It takes Mr. Hoogendijk about five minutes to point the finger at an aging Dutch artist, extremely well-off and living like a king in Amsterdam. His name is Han van Meegeren. A more successful forger there's never been. The aforementioned ten paintings? All van Meegeren's. Vermeer was his forte. The negative you dropped in my lap this morning? The fingerprints?"

"Van Meegeren's."

"The one and only."

Meade watched an empty taxi as it lumbered down Rehov St. Stephen. A couple strolled arm in arm. A man in a gold caftan and matching cap climbed the stairs to the station entrance. Meade said, "What became of Van Meegeren?"

"Can't say. What you've got is what I managed to pry away from the iron men at Interpol. The whole package."

"You're a prince, André." Meade watched the man's gold caftan billow in the wind; his face was hidden in shadows. "Look for a case of English gin on your doorstep one of these days."

André Saint-Claire was a notorious drinker of Scotch whiskey. He grunted. "Rewards to stagger the imagination. Sarcasm and gin. Call me again, anytime."

"I will," Meade said as the phone went dead.

The man in the caftan had reached the top of the stairs. He looked at Meade through wire-rimmed glasses. A thin smile creased his bearded face. A hand reached beneath the caftan and Meade grabbed hold of the door handle. He was halfway out when the hand emerged from the gold robe again cradling three or four *assimonin*, Israeli telephone tokens.

Meade pushed open the door. His shirt was soaked through. He caught the last streetcar of the night back to the hotel. He jogged from the street to the revolving doors at the entrance. The lobby was quiet; Sabbath was upon them. He stopped at the registration desk and changed rooms.

As he rode the elevator to the fifth floor, the scene from the Wailing Wall swept over him in colors so vivid that he was forced to hold on to the handrail. The Wall's golden stone had been scorched a dirty black. The stench of charred flesh hovered in the air. An old man had covered Shapiro with his own bloody shawl; scraps of bread were trapped in his beard. *Bread.* "A loaf of bread and thou." A communal offering. The body of Christ. Manna from heaven. *"Is nothing sacred?"* Meade said the words out loud, slamming an open palm against the wall as the elevator eased to a halt. The doors parted. A woman with young children on each arm stared back at him, the uncertainty on her face a reflection of the turmoil on his.

"I was just wondering if anything was sacred anymore," Meade said. He stepped past them into the fifth-floor vestibule.

He waited thirty seconds. Rock music echoed from a room near the end of the corridor. Laughter and loud voices drifted from an open door opposite the elevators. A woman in a long nightgown and glazed eyes carried an empty ice bucket to the machine at the end of the hall. Meade caught a waft of marijuana. He didn't hurry. His new room was number 510.

Inside, he toured the room like a man possessed.

Finally, he threw himself on the bed. He grabbed the phone from the nightstand and dialed room service. A woman answered. "May I help you?"

"This is Room 510. Send up a bottle of vodka. Stoli, if you have it. A bucket of ice and a chilled—"

"Sir?"

She repeated the word twice more. Meade threw his head back against the pillow and stared up at the ceiling. His mouth was dry, his hand like glue on the receiver. One drink. One drink? You? Why not ten drinks? That should be enough to bring that old man back to life again.

It might even get Sean on an airplane back to San Francisco. Absolutely.

"Sir? Is everything all right?"

"Everything's fine," Meade said into the phone. "Make it a pot of hot coffee instead, would you? Cream and sugar."

Meade took a hot shower while the operator placed his call to London. He was still wearing a towel around his waist when the coffee was delivered. He dressed and packed and was stirring cream into his second cup when the phone rang. The sound of Farrell's voice was like a visit from the sun on a winter's day back home.

"Are we alone tonight?" he asked.

"Alone and sober," was her answer. "A hotel room is no place to get righteous, Meade."

"I know." Meade tried reaching across the long miles that separated them. "Back home, along the wharf, there's a café. It's called the Dry Dock because of a bad habit the owner once had. They serve fresh fish, fresh bread, and hot coffee. Outside, there's an old black musician who sits in a wheelchair and fills the air with the sweetest saxophone I've ever heard. After my last drink, ten months and two days ago, Sean and I went there every night for six weeks. The Dry Dock was our refuge. I'd like to take you there sometime,"

"Would tonight be too soon?"

Meade smiled. Had she been there at that moment he would have taken her in his arms and kissed her. He would have kissed her and felt the heat and passion of her body against his, and taken her into his bed, and. . . . But instead of telling her that, he hid behind a question, saying, "Is our friend from Cape Town still around?"

In response, Farrell told him about the auction and about the alley exit at Christie's. "But when I got back to the hotel, there was a message at the desk. From Bartleman. A very cordial message. No hard feelings. In fact, he hopes to see me back home sometime, he said. Somehow I don't think it's that simple."

"No." London, Meade thought, had either served Bartleman's purpose, or else he was still very near at hand. "And the auction?"

"The auction led to an old friend," Farrell said. She explained about Viktor Mannheimer's role in the sale of the Vermeer, and then added, "It was Shapiro, Meade. Dr. Emery Shapiro. Have you talked—"

"Shapiro." Meade stared down at his coffee. "We talked. All in all, I think Dr. Shapiro took a rather dim view of this less than perfect world we live in."

"Something's happened," Farrell said.

"Shapiro's dead, Farrell." Meade didn't go into the details of the explosion; he also didn't mention that fate had spared the real target. He told her instead about the incomplete account in the notebook he had found in Emery Shapiro's study. Then about his conversation with André Saint-Claire.

"Oh, Meade. Van Meegeren's story is required reading in every art history department in the world. I should have seen it," Farrell said. Meade heard an exasperated sigh. "The problem is, if you believe the history books, van Meegeren *retired* in 1943. He'd lost his touch. Or his drive. He was a morphine addict and had more money than he knew what to do with. Why would he have done it?"

"Obviously Rommel knew about van Meegeren. Maybe Rommel flattered him, or threatened him with exposure. Wouldn't that be the forger's worst nightmare?"

"The only way van Meegeren could have duplicated the original so authentically would've been with it sitting in front of him the whole time."

"How long would it have taken him?"

"At best, three months."

"All right. Rommel and his wife put his six lists to

339

paper after his release from the hospital in August of 1944. By the first of October he'd been arrested in connection with the assassination attempt. Therefore, the original painting had already been delivered to van Meegeren by then."

"But the copy wouldn't have been completed yet," Farrell said. "And Rommel was dead twenty-four hours after his arrest."

Meade carried the phone to the window. "Leaving van Meegeren in possession of an original Vermeer and a copy that was nearly irrefutable."

"If the paintings they found in that Amsterdam apartment house last year were van Meegeren's . . . ? Vermeer and de Hooch and Terborch. Those were his specialties. And Shapiro saw it. He knew it was a forgery, Meade."

"He saw it, but not until *after* he had written the first article for the *Global Art Review*. Then he put it together. The forgery and the original. Why wouldn't the one lead to the other?"

From the window, Meade could see a taxi, a lone sign of life, idling on the corner near the hotel's side entrance. The driver sat on the hood with a magazine in his hands; he waved off two customers.

"Farrell, in Shapiro's journal he mentions several names. He mentions Amsterdam, which makes sense. He also mentions a Dutch art dealer named Hoogendijk."

"Van Meegeren's dealer. Very second-rate."

"Also the one who put the police onto van Meegeren," Meade said. "But there was also a third name, in the margin notes. Gelderblom. Shapiro says, 'A look into the . . .' and then something illegible, 'of H. Gelderblom.' Does that mean—?"

Meade left the question unfinished. He placed a hand on the window. It was vibrating wildly. Meade listened for a noise strong enough to create such a sensation. The city was quiet. He looked into the street, where city workers lingered over an open manhole. He looked across at the building opposite the hotel. It was the night of the Sabbath; with the exception of a desk lamp burning at the rear of a single office, the building was dark. *But the Sabbath did not permit exceptions.*

"Meade?"

"Farrell, stay on the line, but don't say anything." Meade saw a man standing at the office window. The window was open; in his hand, the man held what looked like a bullhorn. It was pointed directly at Meade's hotel room. In the interior of the office, vaguely illuminated by the desk lamp, Meade saw another man. He was hunched over a computer, his fingers frantically working the keyboard and headphones covering his ears. Meade had only read about such a device, but he knew he was right; the bullhorn was a transmitter, either of lasers or microwaves. Inside the office somewhere there was a receiver. The receiver picked up the laser-enhanced vibrations of Meade's voice and fed the signal into the computer; the computer put words to the vibrations.

It occurred to Meade that perhaps the situation had changed: that now the information he possessed was of more value than his elimination.

Suddenly, the man at the computer looked up. His mouth moved and he waved a hand in Meade's direction. The man with the transmitter responded by stepping quickly away from the window. A moment before the light in the office went out, Meade saw the man at the computer reach for a telephone.

Meade took his own phone into the bathroom. "Farrell."

"Trouble?"

"Yes. Company."

Farrell didn't wait for an explanation. She said, "Gelderblom is a Dutch surname. Which doesn't mean it couldn't be a village or a street, or, for that matter, a brothel or tavern."

"We know Emery Shapiro started in Amsterdam. All we can do is the same."

"There's a hotel downtown. It's called the Herengracht."

"I'll meet you there tomorrow morning."

Ten minutes later, Meade was on the street searching for a taxi. At 11:10, he was walking through the corridors of a deserted airport. He placed his call to Cape Town even as the public address system announced the boarding of his plane from Jerusalem to Rome, where he could catch a second flight later in the night to Amsterdam.

Five thousand miles away, Gideon DeBruin sat at his desk in semidarkness creating a paper airplane out of the yellow telex he had received thirty minutes before.

A circle of diffused light pooled beneath a small desk lamp. Within the pool sat a gold pen and pencil set, a tape recorder, a digital clock which read 11:15, a snifter of brandy, the half-empty bottle, four crumpled pieces of paper, and a photograph. The photo was of particular interest. It was a grainy black-and-white of DeBruin, his wife, and four nattily attired kids, all bows and ribbons, bow ties and suspenders. Farrell was all of ten or eleven, DeBruin imagined. He recognized the setting—the summerhouse on the Tsitsikamma coast. Good times. He said the words out loud because the sound anesthetized his doubts. His hands shuttled in and out of the light, to fold the paper, to replenish his brandy, to fondle the photo. Shell-shocked, every one of them. Not a smile, not a mischievous grin, not a hand held or an arm draped around a single shoulder. Asking why was foolish. He knew why. "A photograph is a mirror of life itself. Serious business. A family portrait is an heirloom in the making, like a marriage license or a death certificate, not a jamboree or a carnival. Backs straight, chins high, scrap those bloody grins." Those were his words; now he was filled with an inexplicable longing for one lousy smile, one meager grin, one hand touching or arm embracing, one bloody sign that Father was only human after all.

The phone rang. DeBruin propelled the photo with a flick of the wrist beyond the reach of the light. He pulled the phone into the darkness. "Where are you?"

"In Jerusalem," Meade said. "I've just stood by and watched another life fall by the wayside in the name of your Missing Sixth."

"I know nothing about that. But I do know that another life hangs in the balance. Your son's. I'm concerned only with the painting," DeBruin said. "What information—"

"I've made a decision," Meade interrupted. "I've seen enough lives destroyed in the last week. Six days ago, the police arrested a man named Ama Siluma, a stable hand at De Greyling. The police, in their infinite wisdom, have come to the conclusion that Siluma was somehow involved in the theft at De Greyling. They have also concluded that he was responsible for the stable fire. You and I both know how ridiculous the police can be, don't we? Therefore, before we talk about the information in my possession, we're going to talk about Ama Siluma's release."

"You'd risk your own son's life on a Kaffir you've never met?"

"I'm more concerned about the look on Sean's face when I tell him I could have and didn't."

DeBruin unfolded his paper airplane and stared at the telex from Jacob Bartleman. It read: *Guess who's been in contact! Your friend, Rita. Yeah, Rita Hess. From Jerusalem. She thinks we can help each other. I'm thinking she might be useful. And maybe it's payback time . . .*

Into the phone DeBruin said, "Your bargaining position must be very strong, Mr. Meade. Very strong, indeed."

"In twenty-four hours, the Sixth will be in my possession. In thirty-six hours, it will be in your possession. That should explain the strength of my bargaining position. I've met my conditions. Have you?"

DeBruin depressed the play button on the tape recorder and laid the telephone receiver next to it.

"Dad. It's me." It was Sean's voice. "I don't know where I am exactly, but the sky is incredibly clear, wherever it is. It's Friday night, I know that. The Gemini stars, Castor and Pollux, are out tonight. On the western horizon. Do you remember?"

Castor and Pollux, of course. For the last two months, he and Sean had been following the local astrodata charts, and tonight was the first night the Gemini stars were to have appeared in the Southern Hemisphere, and for less than an hour. "I'm OK, Dad. I'm alive, anyway, and—"

"Satisfied?" DeBruin asked.

Twenty-two-year-old college kids aren't meant to be used like pawns on a chessboard, Meade thought. Not without retribution. "Play it again," he said.

33

FAZZIE COULD NOT HAVE KNOWN that the broken stone steps he was climbing were a century and a half old. They were the only confirmation of a Khoisan settlement that archaeologists suspect lasted less than five years.

Carved from the island's own granite, the weather-worn steps were covered with ivy and myrtle. Halfway up the face, Fazzie stopped to take stock of himself. His heart was pounding and sweat was coursing down his face. One shoulder had grown numb from the weight of the rope coiled over it. The straps of his handgrip cut into the other. His lodestar was the light he had seen along the rim; that which gave substance to the words of a white policeman. He pushed on. Twice he sent loose stones tumbling.

Ten meters from the rim the stairs ended. Fazzie laughed and swore in the same breath; his sources hadn't told him about this. But logic overcame his frustration. A matter of primitive self-defense, he thought, to thwart an attack from above. The Khoisans would have had a rope ladder and some system of retrieval.

Since turning back was out of the question, Fazzie worked his hands into a crack a meter up. He searched for a foothold. A second crack, caked with moss, led to a tiny ledge. An eroded pocket brought him to a forgoten piton left by a climber more experienced than he and surely, Fazzie thought, more daring. He found a smooth lip and summoned his last reserve of strength. He scrambled up, rolled twice, and collapsed.

Fazzie raised his head. He had climbed to the highest point on the island. An expanse of broken rock fell away through a scattering of gnarled and bent trees. He saw tussocks of wild grass and thickets of scrub oak. Fifty meters inland lay the eastern quarry.

He crawled to an outcropping a dozen paces away and wedged himself into a hollow between two boulders. He threw off the coil of rope and dug into his haversack. The whiskey bottle was wrapped in an old T-shirt, along with a pair of binoculars. He twisted off the bottle cap and took two strong pulls, then a third.

Then he focused the binoculars on the quarry and was drawn almost at once to flecks of light along the far rim. The roofs of the three low-lying structures took shape around them. A fountain of smoke curled skyward even as it had the morning before.

Fazzie saw another light; this one moved, floating along the rim like a firefly. Fazzie followed the light as it dissected first the quarry, then the rim, then the plateau beyond. When the light disappeared, Fazzie scrambled back to the cliff. Around the stump of a dead tree he tied one end of his rope. He left it coiled there.

Then he worked his way back past the outcropping, through slabs of gray granite, to the quarry. He dropped into the pit and settled on a rectangular platform of rotten wood. A rusted iron rail served as a backrest.

Minutes later, from across the quarry, a shaft of light fell from an opened door. The light was more yellow than white, that of a fire or lantern. A figure filled the doorway, a flashlight in his hand. This time the light cut a direct path into the mouth of the quarry pit itself. Near the floor of the pit, it stopped. In a field of rocks, the beam fell across a small, rectangular structure. For a moment, the light was jerky and erratic, as if the flashlight were being used as a hammer. It reflected off of something metallic. Just as quickly, it was over; the beam was ascending the pit again.

Fazzie's watch read 11:35. He jumped off the platform, discovered a protected depression between two rocks, and waited.

He took the island map from his pocket, the pencil-thin flashlight from his jacket, and used his handgrip as a shield. Hardly a moment later, the map disappeared in his closed fist. Jacob Bartleman hadn't lied to them. That wasn't the question. The question was, Why had he been compelled to tell Meade about the island in the first place?

Fazzie arrived at two conclusions. The first he didn't believe: that a member of the *Broederbond* had suddenly been stricken with pangs of conscience. The second had been with him since the previous night, and was backed up by the forlorn expression on Tobias's face today. It came to Fazzie now in the form of an *Argus* news brief. "In an unfortunate case of mistaken identity, two men thought to be Robben Island prisoners, and attempting to leave the island in a two-man raft under cover of darkness, were shot . . .

"We'll see," Fazzie thought. He packed his handgrip.

An hour past midnight, he set out.

There were a dozen footpaths within the quarry. A first led straight to the floor and deep pools of stagnant water. A second led to a den of wildcats, their yellow eyes like sunbeams, their hissing like snakes. A third petered out halfway around the quarry at the foot of a broken-down toolshed. Fazzie checked his watch. Realizing he could not afford another delay, he backtracked and made for the rim.

347

Adapting the low crouch of a military man, he covered a hundred meters in two minutes, then ducked into the rocks again. Below, the black soul of the quarry reflected the brilliance of the sky. A flutter of wings and a darting shadow signaled the passage of a bat. Fazzie used his binoculars.

When he was satisfied that all was clear, he came out of the pit running. Fifty meters on, he paused behind a bedraggled pine. Another short burst and he was peering over a half-used roll of tar paper. The buildings were a soccer field away now. From within the least dilapidated of the three structures a soft yellow light quavered; a lick of smoke rose from the chimney.

Fazzie filled his mouth with whiskey. He wiped sweat from his brow and eased the pounding of his heart with a series of deep breaths. While he was capping the whiskey bottle, the door to the house swung open again.

This time the man made no attempt at surveying either the quarry rim or the surrounding grounds, but proceeded directly to a structure at the bottom of the quarry pit: a toolshed much like the one Fazzie had seen earlier.

When the man reached the shed, he ran the light over the door, gave a quick tug at what Fazzie guessed was a padlock, and made an abrupt about-face. He was back inside the cabin three minutes later. As the door closed Fazzie clambered to his feet and ran, flat out this time, reaching the footpath in twenty seconds. A quick jump and two lateral steps took him out of view of the cabin. He stopped and held his breath. Three minutes passed. The wind played a fluted tune in the stone canyons. A pair of bats performed aerial stunts that made up in energy what they lacked in grace. That was all.

The path was steep and longer, Fazzie discovered, than he had anticipated. The shed rested on a platform two meters above a pool of rank-smelling water. The shed was rough-cut pine, a meter and a half square, and the height of a man. A hinged door, with a padlock dangling from an eye hook, formed the entire front of the shed.

Fazzie tapped on the door. He pressed close to a narrow gap along the door frame.

"Sean? Are you in there?" The whisper seemed amplified in the night. "It's Cam."

From inside came an anxious shuffling, the clang of steel on steel, a rattling of the door as a body fell against it. "Cam! My God, is it you?"

"It's me."

"Get me out of here, man."

"That's the idea, buddy."

From an inside coat pocket, Fazzie produced a thin leather case, and from the case, a slender steel pick. This he worked into the keyhole of the padlock; an instant later, it popped.

When the door opened, a face gaunt, bruised, and caked with dirt stared back at him. Fazzie embraced him quickly, saying, "You look like shit."

Sean's hands had been cuffed behind him and his ankles were fettered in leg irons. The handcuffs took Fazzie thirty seconds, but though he had seen a dozen different kinds of leg irons in his time, he had never encountered anything like these; they seemed from another century.

"Anything broken?" Fazzie said, bending down.

"Ribs." Sean fell back against a wooden shelf. The very act of breathing was a struggle. "Where's Dad? Is he all right?"

"Last I heard he was fine. He's working the other end of this mess."

"The painting. That document."

"He wanted to be here, Sean. You'd better know that."

Fazzie worked two different sets of picks into the irons, but without success. He tried a third and gave up. From another pocket he took a pair of bolt cutters. He snapped the chain off as close to each iron as possible. Then he tied strips of his own shirt around Sean's ribs, but the stabs of pain produced by that simple act were not encouraging. He wrapped Sean in his safari jacket.

"Can you walk?"

"I'll make it."

Sean's knees buckled the moment he stepped out of the shed, and Fazzie caught him under the arms. "Hey, buddy, if you want to live through this night, we've got to make time. Hear me?"

At the quarry rim, Fazzie wasted another minute grappling with the leg irons before starting down the cliff.

By the time they reached the beach, Fazzie was frantic. The sky to the west was already paling. Sean was shock white. His body was covered with a sickly sheen. And though his pants and shoes were soaked in blood, it was the pain in his ribs that worried Fazzie more than anything.

Now, Fazzie half carried, half dragged Sean to the water's edge. He laid him gently in the sand. The tide lapped over his feet. Fazzie held the whiskey bottle to Sean's lips, and a grimace was followed by a hint of revival. Fazzie left him with the bottle and raced back to the bamboo grove for the raft. When he returned, gulls were congregating. Screeching, they circled, dove, and scratched their signatures in the sand. Long-legged sandpipers, impervious to the bloody stain coloring their water, choreographed a ballet around the ritual of dawn feeding.

Fazzie helped Sean aboard the raft, then pushed it into the water. When they hit the first breaker, Sean groaned.

"Hang on, Sean."

They crashed through a second breaker, and his eyes rolled. Crawling aboard then, Fazzie half expected Sean to pass out, half hoped he would.

350

Minutes later, they spotted the *Deo Volente*. Alone. The fleet was nowhere to be seen. "That's our ride," Fazzie shouted, putting his back into the oars.

Sean pulled himself up against the back of the raft. The trawler was slowing, coming about in the direction of the raft.

"He sees us." Sean tried raising his arms.

Fazzie glanced over his shoulder, nodding. When he turned back to his oars, he saw a flash of orange top the rim of the cliff. He heard a gunshot, was thrown suddenly back in the raft, and saw to his horror a stain of red spreading across his jacket.

"I'm hit," he gasped. For a brief moment, there was no pain. "Sean, I'm hit. I've been shot."

"My God, no." Sean struggled to a sitting position. A second shot caught Fazzie in the shoulder, and the oars fell from his hands. A third sent a fountain of water into the air. A fourth ripped into Sean's leg and punctured the raft's canvas floor. Sean grabbed the oars, plunged them into the sea, and grimaced at the pain rippling through his body. Still he rowed. Two more shots rippled the water behind them.

The trawler moved in. The shooting ceased. Fazzie's eyes closed, his nostrils flaring with quick breaths. The trawler rocked slowly, engines idling and smoke spewing from the exhaust ports. Sean drew the raft up on the starboard side.

Tobias was alone. He climbed down from the bridge deck. He stared down at them. The forlorn expression Fazzie had seen before was now a look of total dejection. Fazzie wanted to say that he understood, that the trap was sometimes just too big to escape, but he couldn't talk.

"We have to hurry," Sean shouted, nodding in Fazzie's direction. "He's been shot. I think it's bad."

"It's bad, yes." Tobias gazed down at Fazzie. His head bobbed. "He's dying." Then his eyes took on a metallic

351

glint and focused on Sean. "You'll die too, I'm afraid. You both will. No one has ever escaped from the island."

"But—but we're not prisoners. For God's sake, get us out of here. This man needs a doctor. Can't you see that we're not prisoners? You son of a bitch. Can't—?"

Through glazed eyes, Fazzie saw Tobias turn away. He climbed the ladder back to the bridge. The engine rumbled, and the trawler started away.

With the exception of Gideon DeBruin, the Executive Council of the Afrikaner *Broederbond*, for all its influence, still had no knowledge of the Vermeer forgery. What's more, the apparent betrayal of one of their own continued to blind them to any such possibility.

"Only a complete and total moron could look past the noose you've tied for yourself, Gideon," Chairman Venter was saying. "Evidence? There's enough evidence of your presence at the murder site that night to see you charged and quite likely brought to trial."

"Which is exactly why you don't believe it." De-Bruin looked from man to man. "Because if you did believe it—"

"What we do believe, Gideon, is what we know. That the four men hired by this committee to retrieve for us a most important document, and thus fulfill one of the highest-level directives ever set by our organization, were killed with your gun."

DeBruin's eyes widened. The scar on his cheek darkened.

"Yes. The Walther, from your collection. You were sloppy, Gideon. The cane impressions, the cigar wrapper, the ticket stub. Sloppy and careless. To suggest that you were not the perpetrator of the actual killing and theft is only to infer that your accomplice, Miss Rita Hess, was. . . ."

The chairman waited. DeBruin's reaction to this revelation, one shared with the Council by Paul Kilian less than two hours ago, was to bow his head.

"You don't deny your involvement with the woman, of course."

"No."

"Well?"

"If the woman were my accomplice, would she be littering the crime scene with evidence of my involvement? How much sense does that make?"

Paul Kilian laughed under his breath. "Gideon, I hate to disappoint you with the prospect of a less than loyal accomplice. A possibility you have certainly surmised, however grudgingly, for yourself. Unfortunately, that would not in any case excuse your duplicity, would it?"

"Nor are we necessarily convinced of her disloyalty," the chairman added.

"Gideon—" The Reverend Crous, a troubled ally, arose. "Your association with . . . with this woman, this Rita Hess, is . . . at the very least, damaging . . ."

"At the very *least*, indeed," Kilian said.

"We were involved," DeBruin replied. A shadow fell over his face. "Sexually. Perhaps I was naive enough to think even romantically. I let my guard down. Rita filled a void I've managed to ignore for a long time. If she was acting, then perhaps old age has left me with a blind eye. Yes, we were involved, but not . . . do you honestly think I would give up—"

"With the Missing Sixth in your hands," the chairman interrupted, "exactly what is it you'd be giving up, Broeder DeBruin?"

"Since having the former in my hands is an impossibility, I have not considered getting or giving up anything, Mr. Chairman. I'm sorry to disappoint you."

"At the very least, Gideon," the Reverend Crous reasserted himself, walking the length of the table, "it has to be assumed that Rita Hess found out about the

Vermeer and our plans through her association with you. How?"

"Your conclusion is undeniable, my good friend. In your place I would have concluded the same. As to the question of how, I cannot say." Of course, by now De-Bruin knew the explanation. But how could he reveal to the council that he had been covertly taping their most private sessions, a direct violation of the committee's own bylaws—and doing so at the request of the prime minister himself? Instead, he made a feeble stab at humility. "I was careless. I have put myself in jeopardy with my fellow Brothers, and I apologize."

"That's bloody noble of you," the chairman scoffed. "And what about the jeopardy in which your fellow Brothers have been placed?"

"His name was Hulster," Paul Kilian said, seemingly out of the blue. "Hulster. The late and mysterious addition to our team. Do we recall? An East German. A member of a group known as the Red Wheel. A serious group, gentlemen. A dangerous group, given the information I've gathered."

"The Red Wheel is an underground movement organized in 1986 when Mikhail Gorbachev began to undermine the KGB hierarchy," Jan Hugo said. "They've been after our support ever since."

Paul Kilian allowed his wandering eyes to settle momentarily on the chamber's ancient iron shutters and the gas vents behind them, and then on Gideon DeBruin. "It appears that not everyone is as enamored with Gorbachev as the West is. Unfortunately, this group is more enamored with Stalin."

"This is no militant rabble we're talking about here," Hugo added. "These people are well organized and well connected. They've already funded anti-independence movements in three or four Baltic states, and have actually convinced a good number of the Soviet peasantry that they were better off forty years ago."

"Yes," Kilian agreed. "Rita Hess didn't wheedle her way into Cas Greyling's life by mere chance."

"What are you suggesting?" the Reverend Crous asked.

"Only that it is not beyond the realm of possibility, Reverend, that the Sixth has fallen, even if by pure chance, into the hands of some rather formidable individuals." Paul Kilian shrugged. "Can you imagine, from one point of view, a more powerful tool of manipulation? Tell me, Reverend, what would you do if someone wielding that piece of paper, with your name on it, asked for a favor, or two, or ten?"

"Excuse me, Broeder Kilian," Gideon DeBruin said. "Gentlemen, Rita Hess does not possess the Missing Sixth. Nor do her alleged counterparts in the Red Wheel. You see, there is something you should know about the Vermeer . . ."

34

THE AIRPLANE CARRYING Michael Meade from Rome banked in the morning sun. Amsterdam's miles of man-made canals appeared as ribbons of white light. Towering trees and tiled rooftops followed the wanderings of these waterways. Meade glimpsed fields carpeted with yellows as vibrant as a summer dress and reds as startling as a pomegranate.

A cab ride from the airport pumped life into the aerial image. Like the golden city of Jerusalem, old Amsterdam was a beguiling symphony of wood, brick, and stone. The houses fronting the tree-lined canal were the houses of seventeenth-century merchants, shipping magnates, and sea captains. The apartment buildings were cramped and elegant, with lattice windows and graceful gables like scrolled triangles. The canals were filled with hundreds of dilapidated houseboats, painted with greens, yellows, and reds and alive with flower boxes of tulips, carnations, and daisies. Meade saw a retired windmill. Stone bridges. Bicycles and barges, and always, always the water.

The inner moat was called *Herengracht*, and the taxi nudged along the crowded avenue that paralleled it. Steam rose from the water, and intent faces hunched over chessboards. Women strolled through flower stalls and antique shops; men stood on street corners sampling fresh herring and drinking beer. A red Volkswagen had stalled at a railroad crossing, and a train engine and two boxcars came to a halt. A side door on the first boxcar opened and Jacob Bartleman climbed out. Four men followed. They started down the street.

"Stop the car," Meade ordered the taxi driver. "Quickly."

He passed thirty guilders into the front seat and leapt out. Out of the corner of his eye, Meade saw a woman stand her bicycle next to the door of a local bakery. The moment she was inside, Meade stepped between two parked cars to the sidewalk and jumped onto the bicycle. It was old and rusted. He careened into the street and passed Bartleman easily. As he picked up speed, he peeked over his shoulder. Bartleman had stopped. His hands were on his hips.

The Hotel Herengracht was less than two blocks away. Meade pedaled hard; he didn't look back again. His nostrils were awakened by the smells of baking pastries.

At the hotel there was a room reserved in Farrell's name and a note, but no Farrell. The note read, "I'm at the university's Art Foundation. I have an idea. Meet you here at 11:00? Would it be too bold to say I've missed you? Sorry, can't help myself." Meade read the last two lines again and again. To his surprise, they didn't change; he was learning to believe them. He left his own message in return. Then he paid a bellboy ten guilders to return the bicycle and caught a second cab to the central police station on Kalven Straat.

The station house was four stories of red brick and tiered gables. Marble steps led to heavily barred double doors. Inside, it was crowded. Meade pushed past a uniformed officer guiding a man in handcuffs, and a family of gypsies huddled around the front desk.

Were prostitution and hashish still legal in the Netherlands? Meade wondered. He flashed his credentials and asked to see someone about a case from the resolved files. The duty officer was flustered. He was too young for the job.

"Your name again," he said, shuffling papers and glancing back at Meade. "You said Michael what? Meade? Meade. Holy Christ. Sorry. Meade. From the United States. Brigadier Post, our station commander, said he'd see you personally, said he'd—" The duty officer caught himself in midsentence. His palms flew into the air. He jumped up and came around from behind the desk. He took Meade by the elbow. "I guess it was supposed to be a surprise. You and the commander, you two are friends from way back, isn't that it? I apologize. I wasn't supposed to say. Commander Post will have my head if he finds out. He's very fond of his surprises."

"Is he?" Meade said. Then I'm expected, he thought. I step into the central police station in Holland's biggest city, straight from a bombing at the world's most sacred monument, and the station commander is expecting me. Except he doesn't want me to know it. Meade felt the hair on the back of his neck bristle.

"It's all right," he said to the officer. "We'll pull it off."

"Thanks. Thanks, I appreciate it." They stopped before a glass-enclosed cubicle. The man inside held a telephone between his ear and shoulder while his hands were busy polishing a revolver with a square of muslin. The duty officer tapped at the door and poked his head in. "Would you have time to see an American newspaperman, Brigadier? A Mr. Meade, from San Francisco."

The station commander used the barrel of the gun to wave Meade inside. His phone conversation ended with the words, "It sounds most interesting. I'll look into it."

He pushed away from his desk but didn't stand. His hands continued working the cloth while his eyes appraised Meade. He looked to Meade like a politician with a favorable bargaining position. His flaxen hair was slicked back in a vain attempt to cover a bald spot.

He gestured blandly toward an empty chair opposite the desk. "Sit. Please, sit. I'm Brigadier Adrianne Post. How can I be of assistance?"

Meade reintroduced himself. He talked. About the Vermeer, and about theft. And all the while Cam Fazzie's words played about in his head. *The Broederbond is an international organization, Yank. Their tentacles stretch out as far as your own backyard in California. They've got as many connections in the Middle East as they do unsavory cronies in Argentina. Europe is like a second home. Where do you think the word* Broeder *comes from? Check out a Dutch dictionary sometime if you're interested.*

It occurred to Meade that if Brigadier Post was merely cooperating with Gideon DeBruin, or the Broederbond's Executive Council, then he might not have knowledge of the Vermeer. Certainly, knowledge of the painting would lead in time to information about the Missing Sixth, and Meade could not envision either the Council or DeBruin sharing that kind of information. In which case, Meade thought, he might be able to camouflage his true intent. On the other hand, watching Post drop the revolver's hammer down on the firing pin, all the while smiling insipidly, Meade realized he wasn't up to it. He was cold and hungry and tired, and he wasn't up to it.

"Eleven months ago," he said, "detectives from this office were called to a flat on Flower Street—"

"*Bloem Straat,*" the brigadier corrected without expression.

"Bloem Straat." Meade tipped his head slightly. "To investigate an alleged cache of stolen or lost paintings. The names Vermeer, de Hooch, and Terborch were mentioned."

The brigadier peered with one eye into the end of the

359

barrel and then glanced in Meade's direction with both eyes. "How do you know this?"

"I read the newspaper," Meade answered. "Several days later, the matter was written off as a hoax. I'm interested in the details."

"That's all?" Post asked, shrugging.

There was a hint of disappointment in both the words and the gesture, and when Meade was asked to wait at the desk of a junior detective, he concluded that it was probably genuine. He borrowed a cigarette. When a copy of the police report flashed across a computer screen, the detective called Meade over.

The report was printed in Dutch, German, and English. An anonymous call made at 9:35 P.M. the night of July 3rd of last year had summoned police to an apartment on Bloem Straat where it was suspected that an unknown number of stolen art treasures were being stored. The caller's direct reference to unspecified works by the Dutch masters Pieter de Hooch, Jan Vermeer, and Gerard Terborch provided reasonable cause for further investigation. Inspectors Nicolas and Slegel responded to the call at 11:05 and found the flat locked. The building manager provided access. A large number of paintings were, in fact, discovered. But evidence of a working art studio and the apartment manager's assurance that the tenant was a working artist led the officers to delay procedural investigative steps. The apartment was sealed until the tenant's return the following morning. The tenant's assertion that the paintings were of his own creation led officers to seek the opinion of Colonel Jan Workum of the department's Fine Art Squad. Colonel Workum confirmed that the paintings were, in fact, not the products of the artists in question.

"This doesn't tell me much," Meade said. "Where are the names and addresses?"

The detective punched a finger at an abbreviated

phrase at the bottom of the report. *No char. Del., victim req.*

"No charges were filed. It shouldn't have happened. The tenant requested that all vital information be withheld. That's his right."

However, a follow-up report proved more informative. The report indicated that Alan Schysler of 34 Kerk Straat NW, Frans Kruis of 59 Noorder Straat NW, and Gregorius Jacob of Maurits House, University of Amsterdam, were charged on July 5th, A.M.., with obstructing justice and civil disobedience in connection with the Bloem Straat incident. Detainees were held at Central Headquarters until July 5th, P.M., when charges were dropped.

So the owner of the paintings, Meade thought, considered in the eyes of the law an unsuspecting victim, had maintained his anonymity by insisting his own name and address be withheld from the police report. He had protected himself from further exposure by refusing to press charges against the three art students responsible for the incident.

Meade slid his chair away from the desk. When he stood up, he found himself with an obstructed view of Brigadier Post's office. A step to his left provided him with an unobstructed view of Post himself, huddled in front of his own computer terminal and deep in thought. The smile gave him away; it was the same insipid grin Meade had seen earlier.

The detective had pulled a phone book from his desk drawer. "We'll get you a couple of phone numbers," he said.

An ally, Meade thought. "Thanks."

Meade took note of the numbers and went next door to a coin shop. A clerk directed him to a telephone in back. The operator informed Meade that the phone at 34 Kerk Straat had been disconnected five months ago. The housemother at Maurits House on campus told him that

Gregorius Jacob had left school at the beginning of the spring term. He had, however, provided a forwarding address, in Venlo on the West German border, which Meade memorized.

His third call, to the residence of Frans Kruis, proved more successful. The voice was thick and dour, but unmistakenly that of a young man. "Hullo."

"Mr. Kruis?"

"This is he."

"I have some news for you," Meade said. He lowered his voice. "In a very short time, Mr. Kruis, a man of average height, with very short brown hair and a graying mustache, will be paying you a visit. The man is a South African policeman. He'll have some questions for you." Meade now resorted to pure guesswork; he held his breath. "Questions about Gelderblom. Some very unpleasant questions. I would advise you against answering your door."

"Who is this?"

"I'll answer your whos and whys in one hour at the Nieuwe Kerk. I'll be in the second-to-last pew. I'll be wearing a dark sport coat."

Meade set the receiver back in the cradle. He left the shop via a loading dock out back. A United Parcel truck was parked alongside. Meade asked the driver if he could catch a ride as far as the truck's next stop.

Thirty seconds after Meade's departure from the police station, another phone call was placed. This from the office of Brigadier Adrianne Post, long distance, to the Cape Town residence of Paul Kilian. It took two minutes to complete. The connection was poor.

"The reporter just left," Post said. Kilian insisted on hearing every detail, and Post obliged. He even went so far as to read the police reports verbatim. "But you didn't tell me about the cop," he concluded.

362

"What cop?"

"The cop who showed up on my doorstep an hour and twenty minutes ago. The C.I.B. captain from Cape Town. Bartleman. I was surprised."

"Bartleman? Jacob Bartleman?"

"Mmm. Then we're both a little surprised," Post said. "Bartleman said the Council put him on Meade's trail. Not true?"

"One of our esteemed council members has taken to acting in his own best interests," Kilian replied.

"Ah. It begins to make sense then," Post sniffed. "At any rate, I told Captain Bartleman I hadn't been notified. I suggested the normal checklist, and he agreed whole-heartedly."

"And he passed with flying colors. Naturally."

"Turns out he's a friend, yes. So I put out the wel-come mat."

"*Was* a friend," Kilian replied. "Is that clear? Was."

"Fine. Enough said." There was a pause. "How do you want it done?"

"Bartleman is a pilot. He'll almost certainly have chartered his own plane, no doubt out of a private air-port . . ."

Nieuwe Kerk. The New Church. The first stone had been laid in 1408, making its name a mockery in this day and age. Fire swept aside this Gothic masterpiece twice in the first century of its existence. One hundred thirty-six years after its inception, the north transept, the last obstacle facing a fourth and fifth generation of builders, was com-pleted and christened. It lasted one century. Again fire closed its doors. But, alas, these were the Dutch. They had wrestled with the sea for eight hundred years. The Nieuwe Kerk had only momentarily succumbed to some-thing as ephemeral as fire. They simply built the church again, more grandiose than ever, with stained glass and spires, urns and finials, monuments to generals, a gilded pulpit, and a brass and marble choir screen. Meade was met by the drone of an ancient pipe organ, the musky scent of incense, and, by his estimate, a thousand candles aflame.

Meade was ten minutes early. He slid to the middle of the second-to-last pew and knelt down. He watched a twisted man on crutches drag himself painfully down the aisle. He watched an old couple eulogize the stations of the cross. Above the altar, he watched the Last Supper explode into life as sun and stained glass met in a glorious confrontation of color and light.

For a moment Meade thought he heard angels sing, voices as pure as new snow. He followed the sound to the choir loft. The angels were young boys in red and white cassocks. A gray-haired man exhorted them with a baton and a lilting sway. Their voices soared. Meade saw a young man in blue jeans and a leather jacket enter the church via a side entrance. He wore a billed cap which he failed to take off. Meade eyed him as he walked through the transept into the nave and down a side aisle. He dabbed his fingers into the holy water bowl next to the last pew and genuflected. He held onto the back of the pew.

"I'm Frans Kruis," he said. "What's this horseshit about Gelderblom?"

"He came."

"Somebody came. I didn't wait around for an intro."

Good, Meade thought. Bartleman was showing his predictability. A confrontation was inevitable; that was good, too. Meade gestured for the boy to join him. Kruis hesitated momentarily, then clambered into Meade's pew and sat down. He was tall and slouched, his face pinched and stoic. Blond hair fell in tangles from under his cap. Meade introduced himself and said, "Something's come up, Frans."

"No shit. Are you gonna tell me about it, or should I go light a candle in your honor first?"

"His name is Jacob Bartleman. As I said, he's a South African policeman, and if you know anything at all about that country then you know they don't play by the same rules as policemen everywhere else. You're the last link in this town to a very serious problem Mr. Bartleman and some of his friends have. I'm referring to the prank you and Alan and Gregorius staged eleven months ago. The hoax at the apartment house on Bloem Straat. It may be coming back to haunt you."

"Horseshit. Gelderblom dropped the charges. It's over. No harm was done." Kruis pushed himself to the edge of the pew bench. "Han Gelderblom was an asshole, is an asshole, and will always be an asshole. Not to mention the most pathetic art professor on campus. He thought he was going to impress the hell out of us with some half-ass little tour of his studio. He wanted somebody, anybody to take him seriously. A faggot with no talent. Pitiful. He couldn't even teach art history. He tried telling us he'd painted all those pictures. Horseshit. The police may have believed that line, but I don't. Not then, and not now. I may not be the most talented son of a bitch in the world myself, but I do know a thing or two about seventeenth-century art. And I know Han Gelderblom couldn't paint a still life with crayons, much less an oil that looks like a Vermeer."

"You're right." Meade stood now, drawing himself to his full height. "Gelderblom lives on Bloem Straat. Where, please?"

A curious smile cut across Frans Kruis's face. He stared past Meade to the lines forming in front of the confessionals along the south wall of the nave. The smile spilled over into a laugh, and he said, "You don't know shit, do you?"

"I know Han Gelderblom may well have in his possession a painting by Jan Vermeer of Delft that doesn't belong to him. And I know that Mr. Bartleman and his friends are willing to go to extreme measures to get their hands on it, Frans. I need an address."

The voices in the choir rose, gaining power and virtuosity with each note, and climaxing in a final "Amen." Frans Kruis stood up suddenly. He held out his hand to Meade and said. "All right. I don't know shit about you, but better you than them, I suppose. The Paleis Tuin. Sixty-four West. You're five minutes away."

Meade nodded. "Be careful," he said.

"I'll listen to the music awhile. Maybe go to confession."

A block from the church, Bartleman stepped out from a café entrance. Neither his appearance nor the gun surprised Meade. Meade had counted on his being alone, and he was. Bartleman guided him around the corner between buildings. He put the gun back in his shoulder harness.

"Whose side are we on today?" Meade asked.

"I'm sorry about Sean."

"Sorry? Then you lied. About Robben Island?"

Bartleman shook his head. For a man who had aligned himself with Gideon DeBruin, he exuded a strange confidence, Meade thought. "I meant it. I'm sorry."

"Is he alive?" Meade asked.

"He was twelve hours ago." Their eyes locked; Meade's heart stood still for an instant. Bartleman said, "I can't help Sean, but I can help you."

"Why?"

"The fucking thing's got out of hand, that's why."

"It's been out of hand for years, Jacob. How'd you get involved in the first place?"

"It's a long story."

"Tell me."

"Suffice it to say that change comes from the inside, Michael."

"That's very noble."

"Now I've got a chance at the leverage I need."

"Leverage? How?" Meade said. Bartleman offered him a cigarette. Meade shook his head. "A condemned man's last smoke, Jacob? No, thanks."

"Fuck. Take the bloody thing." Bartleman cupped a match for them both. "I meant what I said, Michael. I can help you."

"How?"

"Rita Hess."

"You and Rita?"

"She's here," Bartleman replied.

"You know that? How, I wonder."

"It doesn't matter."

"And she was in Jerusalem, too." The men in the office across from the hotel, Meade thought. Rita's men. And the taxi idling on the street outside the hotel. Her taxi. "Now she's enticed you into the fold."

"Not exactly." Bartleman blew smoke aggressively from his lungs. "I can get you the Sixth. That's the bottom line. If you'll help me in return."

"How?"

"Work with me. Simple as that."

"Correct me if I'm wrong, but aren't you working with DeBruin? And if I'm not mistaken, he's a rather unpopular man with the Brothers right now. Which makes you a rather unpopular man with them. Work with a dead man?" Meade shook his head again. "You turned your back on the club, Jacob."

Bartleman crushed out his cigarette. His confidence hadn't flagged. "Work with me. Together we can put an end to this madness."

"I can't."

"Can't, or won't?"

"Can't *and* won't." Meade held his gaze a moment longer and then turned away. He could feel Bartleman's indecision. A trolley rumbled down the street and Meade jumped aboard. When he looked back, Jacob Bartleman was gone.

35

THE TROLLEY APPROACHED the Hotel Herengracht from the opposite side of the street. A raised median landscaped with tulips and tall elms separated it from the hotel. Meade stepped off.

He was in the middle of the median when he saw Farrell standing on the walkway in front of the hotel's fountain. She wore blue jeans and a bulky sweater. Her arms were folded across her chest. Her pale face scanned the boulevard. Meade felt the pressure welling inside him even as he watched her. At last, their eyes met.

She raised a hand slightly and smiled.

Meade stepped off the median and into the street. He jogged through the traffic. He slowed as he reached the walk, then stepped forward and took her in his arms. They kissed, and, as she pressed against him, he could feel the urgency running wild in her as well.

They kissed again, deeper, and her taste and her scent enticed Meade to draw her closer still. His hands moved over the length of her back. For a moment he lost all awareness of time and place. He took hold of her hair and kissed her ear. He could feel her heart beat and hear the sharpness of her breath.

She touched his face, and their lips met again, even more urgently because they knew that this moment, with all its power and all its passion, had no future, because even now time and place were again intruding.

Meade took her hand. "We have to hurry."

For an instant, Farrell drew him back. She kissed him gently this time. "There'll be time," she whispered. "As much time as we choose."

Meade looked into her eyes and touched her lips with his fingertip. "I know."

He waved down a taxi. When they were inside, he gave the driver the address on Bloem Straat. Then he asked Farrell about her visit to the University Art Foundation.

"You already know about Han van Meegeren's arrest," she said, "so I won't bore you with that. And you know that by the time he was arrested he was more interested in morphine than art."

"Addicted, you said before."

"Before his trial, and before he was convicted, van Meegeren spent six weeks in the county jail. Six weeks, but no withdrawal. As it turned out, he had a visitor. Twice a week. A woman, a fellow addict. She used the name Maria van Cleve, but I skimmed over the transcripts of van Meegeren's trial. Poor Han was prone, shall we say, to an occasional outburst. And evidently, his ex-wife's testimony set him off. He went into a tirade, shouting that the only person who had ever shown him any decency during his confinement was someone named—are you ready?—Heda Gelderblom."

"Who had an illegitimate son named Han Gelderblom," Meade conjectured, "who inherited his father's last, and truly unknown, forgery: *Two Women and Their Music.*"

"The only one he had ever done as a replica of an original. The timing was perfect. The father was destined to die in a jail cell, and by then Rommel had committed suicide. Leaving the finished forgery *and* the original both in the care of a morphine addict—and her son."

"But the original wasn't in Gelderblom's apartment the night the police were called there. It couldn't have been," Meade said. He told Farrell of his trip to police headquarters earlier, and of his encounters with Kruis and Bartleman. "Shapiro was suspicious enough of the situation to make contact with Gelderblom, and charming enough or threatening enough to convince Gelderblom that there was money to be made from his father's forgery without giving up the original."

The car that followed their taxi was a Renault, yellow, with islands of rust around the wheel wells, and temporary plates. Meade caught sight of it a block from the hotel; he had their taxi driver make an unnecessary stop at a corner mailbox and a U-turn in front of the Royal Palace, just to be sure.

Bloem Straat paralleled a narrow canal called Grizelgracht. Mirrored on its glassy surface were the huge elms that stood along its banks. A vendor in baggy pants and wooden shoes sold fresh herring from a pushcart. A soccer ball rolled between two kids and a bronze statue of King William I. The Renault snuck into an alley a block away.

The Paleis Tuin was a narrow, cramped apartment building of dirty brown brick, with lattice windows trimmed in a dirty white. A woman on the fourth floor shook dust from a small throw rug. The caterwaul of a beginning violin student escaped from an open door two floors below.

The building's main floor had been converted into retail space, a market on the left, a pharmacy on the right. The apartment entrance bisected the two storefronts and led up a flight of stairs to a security door. The intercom register indicated an H. Gelderblom in number 301. Meade pushed the call button, but there was no answer. He rang for the manager, a Hendrik de Witte, in number 202.

The man who pushed open the door sixty seconds later was a giant in faded dungarees with a three-day-old stubble. His greeting was in Dutch, his voice a resounding baritone, and he shook his head as if apologizing.

"We're not looking for an apartment, thank you," Farrell said. "And my Dutch is lousy. How's your English?"

"Lousy," he replied. "But not as lousy as your Dutch."

"We're looking for Professor Gelderblom."

"Me, too. The lout's two months behind on his rent, and I haven't seen him in over three. What's your interest?"

"As much worry as interest. Mr. Gelderblom's name has been associated with a robbery last week in Cape Town, South Africa. Now there's a rumor floating around that the stolen painting might actually have been a forgery." Farrell expounded upon her position with the museum in Stellenbosch and Meade's journalistic interest. "We're not of the same mind as the police there, and we can't seem to get any cooperation from the police here."

"You're surprised?"

"Could he have left a note as to his whereabouts?" Meade said. "With a neighbor perhaps, or in his room?"

"Not with me, for sure. I haven't checked out his room in weeks. And only then to clean out some of the spoiled food, and such. But it couldn't hurt to look," de Witte admitted. He folded his arms across his chest and leaned against the doorjamb. He glanced at Meade and shrugged. "Problem is, he still owes two months on the rent."

Meade didn't argue. He took fifty guilders from his wallet. "Will this help?"

De Witte took the money. "Like I said, it couldn't hurt to look. It's not very damn pleasant, though."

An Out of Order sign on the elevator forced them to use the stairs. An eviction notice from landlord to tenant hang on Han Gelderblom's door.

"I really don't want to," de Witte said, tapping the notice. "He's OK most of the time."

A blast of stale air assaulted them when De Witte released the dead bolt. He walked straight for the balcony, drew aside lace curtains, and threw open the doors with enough force to send them crashing against the outside wall. A waft of fresh air helped some, but the mustiness had eaten into the furniture, and the stench of dried paint and turpentine seemed to have soaked into the walls.

At once it became clear that Han Gelderblom was a collector in earnest. If there was a flat surface to be had, then on it stood a wine bottle. Hundreds of them, all empty. Stacks of newspapers rose to the ceiling. Framed photos cluttered every wall. The patina of dust, a chalky skin over everything in the apartment, had a history far older than the months of Gelderblom's absence. There were cat droppings, lots of them, but no cat.

There was also the stuff of a well-meaning painter who didn't get much done. Stretched canvases, stretchers awaiting canvas, jars filled with brushes, palettes caked with dried paints, untouched tubes of pigments, opened cans of thinner and turpentine, and in the center of it all, a tall easel. On the easel stood an unfinished landscape, and pinned to the corner of the canvas was a picture postcard of the Dutch countryside that was obviously the model for the work in progress. Scattered around the room were four or five such works in progress, postcards pinned to each. If nothing else, Meade thought, it was sad. Sad because the desperation was so palpable. It clung to everything in the room.

"Have you noticed the books?" Farrell said, wiping dust from a thick volume with a portrait of Jan Vermeer of Delft sketched on the cover.

In stacks on the floor, bed, and kitchen counter, the

selection of books was indeed impressive. Meade scanned the titles. Art books and histories, mostly. *The Art of Pigments. Picasso and His Women. The Way of the Baroque.* And then he began to see them. *Vermeer and the Use of Light. Jan Vermeer, the Unknown Dutchman. Vermeer, Lasting Impressions. Through the Eyes of the Dutch Master. Vermeer, the Impersonated.* Vermeer and more Vermeer.

"An obsession passed from one generation to the next," Meade whispered. "The poor bastard."

"The poor bastard owes me two months' rent." De Witte settled himself against the inside of the door and rubbed the face of his watch. "Probably facedown in some filthy canal."

Farrell had turned from the books to the walls, and was gazing at Han Gelderblom's vast collage of black-and-white photos. The closer she looked, the more engrossed she became. Men and boys. Without exception, men and boys posed in scenes as varied as any photo album. Portraits and group shots. Taken on beaches, in the mountains, in the city; in restaurants, homes, and offices. And no repetition. Never the same subject, never the same setting. She used a handkerchief to wipe away the dust and grime. Evident in the styles of clothes was a chronology that leapfrogged from the fifties to the present and back again. Farrell even went so far as to take several frames off the wall, studying the backs of the pictures to confirm what she had suspected all along. They were not photos at all, but glossy clippings from magazines. Mounted, matted, and framed with the care of a loving parent.

And then the pattern broke down. A woman, lean and blowsy in appearance, stood laughing, a bottle of wine dangling from one hand. Oddly, this picture's glass was cleaner than any of the other's. Farrell took it down, and another break from the pattern revealed itself. An actual photo. The woman appeared again, and then again. First, in repose in a lounge chair next to a canal. Next, with an older woman, their arms draped around a lamppost at night. Both photos. She was not a pretty woman, and even an excess of makeup had not managed to conceal the dark circles beneath her eyes or the fatigue in her posture.

"Are you and Han Gelderblom friends?" Farrell glanced over her shoulder at Hendrik de Witte.

"He was all right," de Witte answered. He used the past tense and the words propelled him away from the door. He roamed the room. "We used to have a beer or two down in my place. Talk politics. Play a game or two of chess. He was lonely. Who isn't? We went out once in a while. To a club I like pretty well. But he wasn't too comfortable about the ladies. I didn't mind. I'm not too comfortable around 'em, either. There was a café we both liked. Tweekbak and Wijn, it's called. He drank the wine, and they didn't mind me bringing in some vodka. He liked classical music. Rossini. Opera. Sometimes the neighbors complained. Once, he showed me his office at the school. A tiny thing, but neat. Nothing like this."

Meade scrounged while de Witte talked. He took the lid off a gold-plated jewelry box. He leafed through a folder of ungraded school papers. He wound a music box with a ballerina on top and listened remotely to "Edelweiss." He stared at a placard attached to the wall above the mantel. It read, "Only the Word of God Transcends the Evil of Man." Beneath it, held between onyx bookends, were copies of the Koran, the Talmud, the Bhagavad-Gita, the Tripitaka, and the Old Testament. There was room for a sixth volume as well. Almost certainly, Meade thought, the New Testament.

Meade opened a desk drawer and found a stack of unopened mail. He thumbed from one envelope to the next. When he saw the letter from Dr. Emery Shapiro, his heart skipped. It was dated the first day of February. Like the rest of the mail, the letter hadn't been opened. Unlike the rest of the mail, there was evidence the envelope had been fondled many times, in an overlapping collection of multicolored paint stains and fingerprints. One corner had been slightly ripped, as if the recipient had once succumbed to temptation, only to resist in the end.

Meade glanced over his shoulder. Farrell was using her handkerchief on one of the photographs. De Witte was next to the couch now, bending down and pulling a book from under one of the cushions. Meade slipped the envelope into the breast pocket of his jacket.

When he turned, de Witte was thumbing through the book he had found. Meade glanced at the cover. *Van Meegeren: The Forger's Forger*. A snapshot fell from between the pages and tumbled to the floor. Meade retrieved it. Age was evident in the quality of the paper, the grain of the reproduction, and the hairstyles of the subjects. There were four women in lace gowns, very painted, very inviting. They were standing in front of a stately old building, a frilly shawl draped from shoulder to shoulder uniting the four. The word *Gracht* was stenciled in black along the curb.

"I've seen that one before," de Witte said, looking over Meade's shoulder. "Sure thing. I remember."

Meade flipped it over to the back. The inscription was in Dutch. He held it up so the dungareed manager could get a closer look. De Witte chortled. "Says, 'To Han, A night on the town. *De Gratie Hal zwans*. The Grace Hall swans.' "

Farrell had joined them now, and Meade passed her the photo.

"That's her," she said at once, indicating the tallest of the four. The wide smile and tired eyes were there again, and so was the wine bottle. "Heda Gelderblom. It has to be. The walls are filled with her."

Meade looked from Farrell to the photo and then back

to de Witte again. "What did you mean, 'I've seen that one before'?"

"The photo. The picture." De Witte used the back of his hand to slap at the four women. "Only bigger. In Gelderblom's office at school. In the university."

"*Gracht* means 'canal' in English," Farrell said, staring at the stenciled word on the street-side curb. "Which canal? Can you tell from this?"

"We don't paint the names of the canals on the streets, lady. It might confuse people. That's *Gracht Straat*. Canal Street, in the red-light district. You can't tell?"

"And Grace Hall is a brothel," Meade said.

De Witte slapped himself on the forehead. "You must be a reporter or something, right? Only problem is, I've never heard of Grace Hall."

36

MEADE TRIED BUYING a second favor from Hendrik de Witte, but this time the dungareed giant wouldn't take money. He would settle for the truth instead. So Meade told him the truth, less the Missing Sixth, and when he was finished, de Witte led them down the back stairs to the cellar. The cellar stairs emerged in a shed off the back alley. De Witte's pickup truck was parked in a carport next to the shed. There was a man in a dark suit at the head of the alley, but no sign of the Renault. On de Witte's signal, Meade and Farrell ducked into the pickup's front seat. Ten minutes later they were in the hotel garage climbing into Farrell's rented Peugeot.

When they emerged from the garage, Meade withdrew Dr. Emery Shapiro's letter from his breast coat pocket. He used a nail file from Farrell's purse to open it. Inside was a photostat copy of a certified check for eight hundred thousand pounds. A short note read,

My dear Mr. Gelderblom:

The sale of your father's painting was completed this past week. There will be no problems. The original

378

was examined by the authorities and, of course, verified. I had no difficulty substituting your father's work once authenticity was established. The original is now en route back to you and should be in your possession within the week. As per our arrangements, a numbered bank account has been opened in your name at the Zwingli Bank in Zurich. Your share of money, less the enclosed check, has already been deposited for you. I have disposed of my share in a similar fashion.

I don't expect we'll be meeting again. A full and rich life to us both.

Dr. Emery Shapiro

P.S. Please destroy this letter the moment you have read it.

"Then it was the original you examined, after all," Meade said in time. "There should be some consolation in that."

"I remember standing in the security vault at the Institute in London. Four of us, the painting, and a truckload of Christie's electronic gadgets. In the corner was an enormous wooden shipping crate with reinforced walls and sheets of Styrofoam. We joked that the seller probably shipped himself and the painting in the same box." At a stoplight, Farrell looked over at Meade and grimaced. "The forgery was in the crate all the while. All Shapiro needed to make the switch was five minutes alone. Who could deny him that; it was his painting. He'd demanded anonymity and gotten it. When the sale was finalized he simply had the crate, with original now sealed inside again, sent back home or to Amsterdam. What could be easier? And van Meegeren was *that good*, Meade. Down to the last brush stroke. Down to the burnish on the frame. Down to the fray on the canvas."

Canal Street was no different from the rest of old

Amsterdam: a narrow, meandering street flanked by cobblestone walks and rambling apartment buildings of brick and stone. Maybe it was a touch shabbier than other parts of the city; maybe the graffiti was a trifle more vulgar; maybe the planter boxes suffered some from neglect. But it wasn't, Meade thought, despair you felt; it was resignation, drift, defeat.

There were store fronts, several blocks' worth. Here a man or woman could purchase the use of a woman's body for any purpose desired. The competition was fierce, as manifested in the window displays where nearly naked women strutted and fawned and spread their legs in blatant invitation.

In the doorways they stood in lace and satin, chiffon and silk, thighs exposed to the crotch and breasts exposed to the nipples, tongues slavishly working circles around their lips, and every salacious gesture was verbally reinforced. Wary customers hid beneath umbrellas and behind turned-up collars. Tourists gawked and fantasized and blushed; some became customers themselves.

Farrell and Meade cruised this human market block by block, looking for some sign of Grace Hall. Meade propped up the photo from Han Gelderblom's flat on the dashboard. It was a corner lot; they knew that by the location of the curbside street sign, but things had changed after nearly half a century.

"They're so young," Farrell whispered, startled by the girls calling out their prices and specialties. She added sarcastically, "Doesn't experience count for anything in this business?" And then jocularly, "Which one would you pick?"

"Her," Meade answered without hesitation. "Stop the car."

The woman in the doorway made a mockery of Farrell's assertions about youth: wrinkles and makeup and a smile augmented by a gold tooth and a wide gap. She exposed a shriveled breast as Meade approached. "You can have it all for ten guilders, sweetheart, and what you don't see will make you cream in your pants for months. I got some things for your woman, too. She don't have to be shy with Greta."

"You're a goddess," Meade agreed. He handed her twenty guilders. "After I find my sister. She's at Grace Hall. It's important. Do you know where it is?"

"Now you listen to Greta, darlin'. She's just using the tools God gave her, that's all. Don't blame her for that."

"I don't," Meade replied. "But Dad just died and he left her some money. Which one's Grace Hall? For her sake."

The woman shoved the money into her corset. "It's not Grace Hall anymore, darlin', not for fifteen years now. It's the Wild Rose. I always did like Grace Hall better; you'll call it that for Greta's sake, won't you? Sure you will. Far corner of the next block and across the street. But you won't find anything like me there."

"I'm sure," Meade said as he sprinted back to the car.

Inside, he passed on the woman's directions.

Grace Hall, as it turned out, was a six-story brick building with fire escapes across the front. The four half-naked women holding court in the front window urged them inside. Meade dropped the brass knocker on the door.

The woman who answered was a hefty figure in her early fifties. She wore a low-cut gown and lipstick that was nearly purple.

"Come in, come in, come in. Welcome." She called herself Mrs. Bellington, and she guided them inside with an open palm. Once the door was closed, the perfumed air of Grace Hall assaulted them; it emanated from walls covered with pink and lavender paper, from full-length drapes and silk linens, disguising the decay. "My, what a handsome couple. I can see we're in for a memorable time.

Now the first drink is on the Wild Rose, if that appeals, or we can get right to the business at hand."

"You're very kind," Meade said. He showed the woman his passport and press credentials, then introduced Farrell. "To be truthful, we'd like to talk about one of your regular guests. It's very important. He's in extreme danger. You all are, in fact."

This last statement caught the woman's attention. "We have many regulars."

"Han Gelderblom."

"Han?"

"He's been living here for three months. We know that." This was an educated guess, but the woman's startled expression confirmed it. Meade said, "We're not the only ones trying to find him."

"Six people have died over a painting Mr. Gelderblom owns," Farrell said softly. "We're trying to prevent any more deaths. Please."

With this, Mrs. Bellington's hesitation evaporated. "I knew he was in some kind of trouble." She alerted two of her off-duty girls, and they scurried in different directions. Then she touched Farrell's shoulder. "We'll find him."

Mrs. Bellington showed them through the house to a broad staircase. They followed the soft glow of red bulbs all the way to the sixth floor. From there a narrow drop-down staircase led to the attic and what Meade realized was a church. Not as old as the *Nieuwe Kerk*, but nearly. A holdover, the woman told them, from the sixteenth century and the days of the Reformation when Catholics were forced into hiding and built churches, real churches, in basements, in crawl spaces, in underground sewers, or in attics just like this one.

"I have one other idea," Mrs. Bellington said before they climbed the stairs. "You peek up there, and I'll see if he's not down in the basement with his cat."

Meade followed Farrell up.

There was water in the finger bowl at the entrance. The nave, hardly bigger than a bedroom, was dominated by ten wooden pews. Statues of the twelve apostles stood in tiny wall alcoves. Gilded sconces held layers of candle wax. Thick wooden beams and a low ceiling forced Meade to duck his head.

In the back was a church organ, its ivory keys and knobs now stained yellow and chipped and laced with cracks. It had been converted into a table, supporting an electric hot plate, a saucepan, and a coffeepot. An opened can of beef stew sat on the hot plate. Jam had been spread over two pieces of bread, but Han Gelderblom was not there. A mattress strewn with books lay on the floor in a nook beyond the organ.

The chancel was large enough for a priest, a pulpit, and a tiny altar. Above the altar was a bejeweled crucifix. On either side of the cross hung framed paintings: a Dutch landscape which reminded Meade of the work they had seen in Han Gelderblom's apartment, and Jan Vermeer's *Two Women and Their Music*.

"It's the original," Farrell said at once. "My God, it's magnificent!"

"Yes," Meade said. In an attic church above a house full of busy whores. Since when? Since 1945? While a handful of panicked Germans scoured the European continent, and the rest of the world lamented its alleged destruction.

Farrell stepped up to the altar and carefully lifted the painting from its hanger. A faded rectangle was left in its place. She set it facedown on the chancel floor.

"Not here," Meade said. Oddly, though, it was he who hesitated, hoisting the painting and running a hand over the back of the canvas. He turned it slowly, while his thoughts returned momentarily to the apartment house on Bloem Straat.

"What is it?" Farrell asked.

"Nothing." Meade shook his head. He led her to the staircase, carrying the painting. They were halfway down when Rita Hess stepped from the shadows at the foot of the steps. In her hand was a pistol, and she was pressing its barrel against Han Gelderblom's head. He was a small, baleful man with thinning hair and thick, tortoiseshell glasses. In his arms he cradled a Siamese cat.

"Rita."

"You should never have trusted the boy at the New Church, Mr. Meade. Frans Kruis? Certainly you must have known he would talk to me. After all, he's just a boy. And the apartment manager? You can imagine how eager he was to please me."

"That was foolish."

"Put the painting down, please," Rita said. When Meade hesitated, she leveled the gun at Farrell. "I've killed before, Mr. Meade. And I will gladly kill again. Put the painting down. Now, please."

"It has to end somewhere, Rita," Meade said. He lowered the painting into Farrell's hands and she balanced it against the wall. "You don't owe Gideon De-Bruin or the Red Wheel anything."

"True," Rita said. She thrust the barrel end of the gun beneath Han Gelderblom's jaw again, and he gasped. "But it's no longer the Red Wheel I'm concerned with. Or Gideon."

Meade tried again. "Sir Greyling will pay a fortune for that painting and what's inside it. You know that."

Rita nodded toward the top of the stairs. "Now I'll ask you to return to the church. Please. And draw the staircase up behind you." She turned the gun on Farrell again, saying, "Before I lose patience, Mr. Meade."

Meade took Farrell's hand and they retreated up the stairs. He raised the staircase. A minute of silence passed. Then they heard a dull thud, a groan, and a body crumpling to the floor; and finally, the hasty diminuendo of footsteps. Meade dropped the stairs. Han Gelderblom lay bleeding on the landing. The Vermeer's frame and stretchers had been tossed at his feet. The painting itself was gone. Meade heard screams and a door slamming.

"Farrell, find a telephone. Call an ambulance." Meade took the stairs two at a time. On the landing, he paused and turned. "And look for a New Testament."

"A what?"

"The Bible, but just the New Testament." He raised his eyes toward the attic. "Somewhere up there."

Three women, gowns flying, had followed Rita Hess into the street. One had run halfway down the block shouting. Another had collapsed at the curb. She was crying. The third was Mrs. Bellington, the house madame.

"What kind of car?" Meade shouted. "What kind of car was she driving?"

"It was dark blue. It was—small. A compact, I think. The windows were dark, too. Tinted, you know. It was—"

"A Honda," the woman in the street called back. "A dark blue Honda."

As Meade leaped behind the wheel of the Peugeot, he heard the wail of a siren.

At a stoplight on an overpass he caught sight of a blue Honda. It was headed for the harbor. He was a half kilometer behind. There was traffic, but rush hour was still an hour away. He was blessed with a green light as he reached the overpass, but as the road dropped back toward the water, it forked. East to the harbor, north toward the railroad yards. Instinct told him east, and as he swerved around the cloverleaf, he caught a distinct glint of dark blue. A busy frontage road led to the Prince Hendrik Quay, the pungent scent of diesel, and the trumpet of harbor tugs. Meade jockeyed from one lane to the next and back again. A car horn blared; in the rearview mirror he saw an angry fist shaking.

The quay road first rose onto another overpass and then dropped down into a confluence of streets that seemed to lead irrevocably toward the water. Meade glimpsed a sign marking the Ij Tunnel, but no blue Honda. He plunged on. Suddenly he was aware of the sweat beneath his jacket and the moisture on the steering wheel. He resurfaced on the other side of the tunnel doing 125 kilometers per hour.

Fate smiled on him. The Nieuwe Leeuwrder Road, the highway beyond the tunnel, rose up after a kilometer onto the back of a high dike. Meade was just sixty seconds from the dike. The blue Honda looked black against the clouds massing on the horizon.

Five minutes later, the road dropped off the back side of the dike, and the city gave way to a flat, green expanse of farms and dairies. The shallow, murky waters of the Zuider Zee lay like an oil slick off to the right. A windmill churned beside a field of yellow tulips. A single-wing prop plane drifted toward earth.

It wasn't until the plane was on the ground that Meade realized he had seen the airport turnoff but hadn't made the connection. He slammed on the brakes, cut a U-turn from dirt shoulder to dirt shoulder, and headed back.

It was less than a kilometer to the airport road turnoff. The gravel surface was unexpected; the car fishtailed as Meade plunged into the turn.

The Netherlands was a country built so close to the ground that you could see everything in the distance but little close up. In the mist, the airport control tower reminded Meade of a huge buoy adrift at sea. As he approached, a low, flat structure materialized at the tower's feet, and then a fleet of airplanes loomed, moored in rows adjacent to the runway.

On the tarmac at the head of the runway sat a light

blue twin-seater. The Honda was parked alongside. The door on the driver's side stood open.

The blur of the plane's duel propellers told Meade he was too late. The plane lurched forward and taxied onto the runway.

At the airport entrance, Meade used his horn to alert the security guard. "The plane moving onto the runway. The light blue one. It has to be stopped. It's an emergency."

"Are you—?" The guard must have seen the urgency in Meade's eyes, or heard it in his voice. "All right. I'll try," he said, jogging back to his guardhouse.

Meade eased the car over the median separating the road from the runway and sped through an open gate in a tall chain-link fence. He swept past a luggage wagon, a fuel truck, and the moored fleet onto the tarmac. An airport employee made a vain attempt at flagging him down.

By now the plane was on the runway and picking up speed. There was an instant, when he was twenty meters behind and gaining, when Meade asked himself what he would do if he did, in fact, overtake the plane. It was a moot question; a moment later the plane was airborne. At the end of the runway, Meade pulled up. He climbed out, his role now relegated to that of frustrated spectator.

The plane forged skyward. Like a bird riding an updraft, it lifted painlessly into the air. It banked. The wheels withdrew into the undercarriage. It gained altitude.

Then, quite suddenly, the plane stalled. A trail of gray smoke seeped from the engine. The nose dipped, straightened, and dipped again.

An explosion filled Meade's ears the instant before an orange ball of flames engulfed the plane. Bits and pieces of debris flew in every direction. Beneath a fountain of black smoke, the remains of the fuselage arced languidly toward earth.

Only the brazen, hysterical cacophony of sirens disengaged Meade from his absorption with the burning wreckage in the field less than half a mile away. How long had he been staring? He honestly didn't know.

A fire truck plunged down the runway, a yellow rescue vehicle close on its tail. Together they rumbled off the end of the tarmac and into a field of bright yellow tulips.

Patrol cars with red and blue globes flashing converged on the crash from opposite directions. A low-flying helicopter hovered nearby, causing the tulips to bend in self-defense. A loudspeaker crackled with instructions. Meade climbed back into the car. In reverse, he cut a half circle, stopped, and then followed his tracks back down the runway. He pulled up next to the blue Honda. He left the engine running and got out.

The Honda's front door was wide open. The keys hung from the ignition. Inside, there lingered a subtle hint of perfume. The Vermeer lay draped irreverently over the front seat. The secondary canvas lay in a heap on the floor. There was no manila envelope.

In the glove compartment Meade found the car rental papers. The name on the form read Lisa Henderson, the same name Rita had used in renting the cottage in Clifton. Meade tossed the papers back into the compartment and shut the door. He rolled the Vermeer into a cylinder and tucked it under his arm.

He was halfway out of the car again when he saw a cigarette lighter lying in the middle of the passenger seat. It was silver with inlays of abalone shell—the same lighter, Meade realized, he had admired during his interview with Rita in the courtyard at De Greyling, the day of the theft. He remembered her fondling it like a keepsake of some importance. Now she had left it behind. By design or accident? A sign of victory or an admission of defeat?

Meade left the lighter on the seat. He opened the Peugeot's trunk and slipped the painting down behind the spare tire. Then he drove back to the terminal. He found the flight information desk next to the control tower. The man behind the counter smoked a black cigarette and wore sunglasses tinted a rose color.

Meade introduced himself. The man was impressed; he had been to San Francisco once himself, he said. Meade played the part of the proud native pleased to hear a visitor's impressions of his homeland. The man recalled the girls on Broadway, and the tart he had picked up at Coit Tower. Meade encouraged him. They talked about the action in Golden Gate Park on the weekends, about the sophisticated wags, as the man called them, in Sausalito, and about the campus strays at Berkeley.

Meade accepted a cigarette.

"Where the hell was that plane going in such a hurry?" he asked, as if the bastard deserved what he'd got.

The flight report was already on the counter. "All hell's going to break loose any time now," the man told Meade, flipping the report open with authority. "Back to London. One stop—Norwich. An American plane, as it turns out. A Cessna 208 Caravan. Not much plane for a trip like that."

"Crazy. How do you figure it?" Meade joked. "London? Obviously not a local guy, then?"

"Naw." The man jabbed at the registration with his cigarette and carelessly swept a fallen ash from the page, staining it. "But get this. Asshole's a South African. Cop, no less."

Meade stared. "Jacob Bartleman."

"Yeah—" the man stared back—"as it turns out. I guess it's Jacob. Could be. J. Bartleman."

"Jacob." The name came out a low hiss. Meade was already turning away.

The police were waiting at his car. The security guard from the gate paced with his hat in hand, and Meade suggested a drive to Canal Street.

Three patrol cars and a police van were parked at odd angles in front of Grace Hall. An ambulance was backed up against the curb, its rear door open. Canal Street spectators loitered behind sawhorse barricades; they smelled blood, which had a way of diminishing the sexual appetite. The women wore shawls or plastic raincoats over their lace gowns now. The tears and hysteria, Meade noticed as he climbed out of the car, had been replaced by signs of boredom and wide yawns. He saw a bottle making the rounds and smelled hashish.

The door to the hall opened. Four white-clad men carried Han Gelderblom out on a gurney.

Meade and his police escorts went inside.

On the sixth-floor landing, two detectives and a man with a camera were huddled together. Farrell was not there. One of Meade's escorts and the chief inspector exchanged stories. Meade hadn't told them about the original painting in Rita's car, only the relining canvas.

"No painting and no woman. Both, we're assuming, victims of this mysterious plane crash." The detective showed his displeasure by clicking his tongue off the roof of his mouth. He looked Meade over. "And you saw this woman—you say her name was Hess?—you saw her board the airplane?"

"I missed the turnoff. By the time I got there, the plane was on the runway. Her car was there. She left her lighter." Meade shook his head slowly. "But no, I didn't actually see her board."

The detective exchanged a glance with his partner. "Stranger things have happened," he said. "We'd better talk to someone at the airport. Maybe they've got a body count from that crash by now."

It cost Meade thirty guilders, but Mrs. Bellington, Grace Hall's well-endowed madame, allowed him the use of her private office. The walls were covered with travel posters.

Even a direct line to Cape Town took several minutes, and Meade stared nervously at the hands of his watch. When the connection was made, the switchboard at the *Argus* rang the number in the cafeteria. Meade let the phone ring for a full minute before the operator suggested he try another time. Then he had her dial Gideon De-Bruin's office. Mr. DeBruin, he was informed, was in a meeting and could not be disturbed. Meade left his name.

Finally, he called the Hotel Herengracht. Farrell had not returned.

Meade was on the sidewalk out in front of the brothel and climbing into the Peugeot when Mrs. Bellington caught up with him again. "Well, I nearly forgot," she said. "You are Michael Meade, aren't you?"

She held out an envelope. "This is for you, dear."

Meade's name was printed in stilted letters across the front. He didn't recognize the handwriting. "What is this?"

Mrs. Bellington raised her shoulders. "All I know for sure is that I'm a hundred guilders richer than I was two hours ago." Then she opened her palms. "There were two of them. The one, the older gentleman, said the envelope would explain itself. I took his word for it."

"Can you describe him?"

"He was tall and distinguished. Oh, and he wore a hat."

"And a cane? Did he carry a cane?"

"That I can't say." Mrs. Bellington backed away. "He said he'd come around sometime when he wasn't in such a hurry. Oh, and your pretty friend, the young lady, she went with them. Though I must say, she didn't seem too happy about it."

Meade tore open the envelope. On a half sheet of flimsy white paper were printed the words, "You'll want to meet me at the Amstel Locks at 6:30. It's not over yet."

37

IRONY. The prison on Robben Island being a black hole for the National party's most outspoken enemies, it is in the same breath a black hole for the *Broederbond*'s most outspoken enemies. The hand that wears the glove, as it were. The irony of the matter was that neither the Bond nor the party had been informed of Sean Meade's incarceration there. They had knowledge neither of his confinement nor of his escape. It was a case of independent thinking within an organization that functioned on the premise that the whole is more important than the one. It was a case of self-preservation in which the lines of allegiance became hazy. It was a mistake.

The pilot of the prison ship spotted the bobbing life raft despite the rain and mist and the onset of evening. A litany of foul language, essentially adding up to, "What now and why me?" spewed from his mouth.

It was 6:25. He was due back in Cape Town by 8:00. He was an hour ahead of schedule. There had been only forty-two transfers, a slow day. A lot so mangy, the pilot thought, that the greatest surprise was that they were all still alive when the hold was opened. Not that it mattered; corpse or half-corpse, the money was the same. Still, some days were worse than others. This load had come in from Leeuwkop, a maximum security hellhole outside of Pretoria, and they were bald and bruised, half-naked, skin and bones. Two of the poor devils had been reamed so many times that they couldn't have stood if they tried.

"Kaffirs and coolies." The pilot spat out the words and then he spat on the deck. The strong ones, he thought, turn coat and become prisoner guards with foul mouths and *kieriekops* to beat their brothers into submission, and the weak ones get rifle butts and hard-ons rammed up their asses. And here I am hauling the garbage.

In the distance, the raft appeared empty, oars dangling from the cleats, inflated sides half in, half out of the water. Probably a cast-off from a careless fishing charter, the pilot figured. So get your sagging ass home. Then he saw a head lolling against the side and arms dangling in the water.

"Ah, shit in December." He hesitated, thought of radioing back to the island. The bloody thing was off-limits as it was. "And all you'd need is to have your bleedin' license revoked."

But he couldn't do it. The man in the raft didn't show much in the way of life, but the pilot couldn't leave a man, half-dead or not, in waters like these. His conscience wouldn't allow it. He called down the pipe to his first mate. A minute later they were alongside. A rope ladder was dropped over the port side. The first mate leaned over the rail and watched one of the crew climb down. He nodded, then shook his head, and then raced back to the pipe.

"Two men, Captain. The one white as flour, the other black as sheep dung." His voice was pitched with excitement. "Angus says he thinks maybe they're dead."

"So we'll just leave 'em, huh? You simp," the pilot growled. "Haul their asses aboard and do it quick."

The Amstel River was the inner city's oldest waterway. The Amstel Locks provided the only access upriver. They were busy and noisy with a tumult of crashing steel, blaring horns, and curious tourists.

Meade parked the Peugeot three blocks away. The Renault—the tail they had avoided earlier—had picked him up again outside of Grace Hall. Two men climbed out. One wore a high pompadour and a semigloss suit. The other was tall and dark and, from a block away, looked like a well-behaved drunk. Now, however, their tactics changed. There was nothing surreptitious in their approach: make eye contact, send a message. Meade was content with this. Bartleman's death had convinced him that these two would be reporting to the Executive Council, not to DeBruin; as Meade had predicted, Bartleman's association with DeBruin had finally caught up with him. Assuming the explosion was the work of the Council— and Meade could see it no other way.

The Vermeer was now in a cardboard tube Mrs. Bellington had found for Meade; he carried it beneath his coat.

To the west, the setting sun threw its blood-red fire halfway across the sky, and geese converged on the city in formation. A cargo ship followed the opening and closing of lock gates upriver. A black limousine occupied a narrow drive designated for "Emergencies Only," and the vehicle's driver followed Meade's progress through mirrored sunglasses.

The lock platform was separated from the riverbank by a chain-link fence and concrete steps. The noise reminded Meade of the railroad yard back home; an image he couldn't shake, any more than he could the image of Jacob Bartleman's Cessna exploding in midair. To ask how Bartleman had gotten involved with Rita Hess was like asking why he would ever have trusted her. And what, after all, had they planned together? To betray both the

Red Wheel and Gideon DeBruin? To sell the Sixth to the highest bidder?

Meade saw the trio standing with their backs to the guardrail at the farthermost corner of the platform. He was genuinely startled. He had surely expected Gideon DeBruin. Instead he found himself staring at Sir Cas Greyling. With him was a lean, swarthy man Meade didn't recognize. Between them, defiant and erect, stood Farrell. Greyling's hand was raised. He stepped forward as Meade approached, and reached out to shake his hand, but Meade had turned his attention to Farrell. Her nod was nearly indiscernible.

"You all right?"

"I'm not sure," she said, stepping away from the rail. "I've never been abducted at gunpoint before."

"That was rude, wasn't it?" Greyling said. "But we did have to insure your presence here, didn't we, Mr. Meade?" Now Greyling turned his hand in the direction of his unknown companion. "This is Major Uri Vegan. The major is an official in the . . . Israeli intelligence community."

Meade looked back at a face that could have been hewed from petrified wood, at eyes as dark as black water. He held Vegan's gaze for only a moment; the Israeli's presence here was no surprise.

"I owe you an explanation, I suppose, Mr. Meade," Sir Greyling said, "and I might as well start at the beginning. Which in this case is 1938, when I emigrated to South Africa from Berlin. At the time there was, I can tell you, sufficient reason for concern."

"Your mother was Jewish," Meade said. "Her maiden name was Kramer."

"Eighteen months later, I enlisted in the West Alliance."

"And spent the next forty-five years in the company of the very men the Alliance stood against."

"The war hurt, Mr. Meade. And confused. A German Jew? Germans killing Jews? Jews seemingly lying down like sheep, playing the part of the persecuted rabble? The more I fought back, the more angry I became, and the more I saw myself as German first. Which led to being an Afrikaner first. I don't expect you to understand. But I never lost touch with my heritage, or my feelings, or my people. The Essenes Society showed me that a good number of my people didn't like the persecuted-rabble image any more than I did. I joined them in 1979. Eventually my involvement in the movement began compromising my work in Parliament.

"And then, of course, there was this unknown entity called the Missing Sixth. The resurrection of *Two Women and Their Music* provided us with a remote possibility. A rumor. But our movement takes even remote possibilities seriously. Yes, I thought I was buying the genuine article when I engineered the purchase of the Vermeer. When the Sixth wasn't there, it was a disappointment, to be sure, but then we were prepared for that. When Miles Roundtree discovered the forgery, it was actually a rekindling of hope.

"When Rita and the Red Wheel became involved, we decided to wait and watch. Unfortunately, waiting and watching cost me four rather special pieces of art. But in another sense, it also thrust you into the picture. I believe in fate. And when you walked into my gallery that first morning, I saw an opportunity. A remote one, perhaps, but as I said, we don't discount the remote."

"And like the men you claim to be opposing," Meade said, "you accepted manipulation as a justifiable means to an end. Admirable."

Greyling acknowledged this neither by a change of expression nor verbally. Instead, his voice took on the air of a man accustomed to demanding and ultimately receiving.

"Rita Hess is dead now. So is Captain Bartleman. If anyone has the Sixth, then you do."

"And you'd like it."

"Some people think the deeds represented in that document are better forgotten," Major Vegan interjected. "As if Nazi atrocities were an aberration and will cease to exist if we just leave it alone."

A lock gate closed with a vicious crash behind them; water tumbled, flooded, and pooled. Meade wondered momentarily if Vegan's statement represented a threat, or merely a warning. Or could the statement simply have been the major's way of pleading his case? In the end, Meade wondered if he was being completely candid himself when he answered, "I don't happen to be one of those people, Major."

"The Missing Sixth does not belong in the hands of an American newspaperman. You know that. To ask the uninvolved or unconcerned to act on the information in that document is to doom its creator's purpose to the whims of fence sitters."

"Your comments suggest an insight into exactly what its creator's purpose was, Major," Meade replied. "Which suggests an awareness of the Sixth's contents. Could this be true?"

"The Essenes Society is the only organized group capable of bringing justice to bear on the deeds that may be represented in the Missing Sixth; let me put it that way. To say, or even imply, that reparation has already been made would be a mockery."

"I followed Rita to the airport. She boarded Jacob Bartleman's plane before I could stop her. She left this behind. This, and only this."

Meade revealed the tube containing the canvas of the original *Two Women and Their Music*. "This is the painting you actually purchased six months ago, Sir Greyling. The remnants of the frame and stretchers are in the hands of the police. There was no document, no envelope. I assume it went up in flames with the occupants of the plane."

"This is true?" Greyling asked.

"To the best of my knowledge."

"Most unfortunate." Greyling studied him. "Most unfortunate."

"You know what I find most unfortunate, Cas?" Farrell interjected. "I find it most unfortunate that Miles Roundtree became a victim of your game of international intrigue. Most unfortunate that you didn't have the insight to see the danger your game was putting him in. Or perhaps you did, but didn't have the guts to warn him?"

"Miles was only one man, Farrell."

"A particularly kind and gentle man."

"Yes." Greyling tucked the Vermeer under his arm. He gave Meade a last, piercing look. "If you're lying—" Then he paused, as if changing his mind. "If you do, in fact, have the document, you'll not get back into South Africa easily. That was your plan, wasn't it? They'll be waiting. And, of course, you'll have to bring it in yourself. To entrust it to—" Greyling broke off; Meade's expression hadn't changed. "No, I rather think you're telling the truth, aren't you. Well . . ."

Then, without so much as a nod, Greyling and the major turned and trudged away. Meade followed their progress across the lock platform, up the stairs, and into the deepening night.

38

WHEN THEY WERE BACK in Farrell's Peugeot again, she presented Meade with a worn copy of the New Testament from the church above Grace Hall. It had been in her handbag all along.

"It was under Gelderblom's pillow," she said. "How did you know?"

Meade told her about the placard above the mantel at the apartment on Bloem Straat: *Only the Word of God Transcends the Evil of Man*—and on the mantel itself, the five books from what was surely a six-book set.

"At least some of man's interpretations of the Word of God," he said. "The Talmud, the Koran, the Hindu Bhagavad-Gita, the Buddhist Tripitaka, and the Old Testament—"

"But no New Testament. Very good. And if Han Gelderblom had some way or another become aware of the Missing Sixth, he would no doubt have thought of it as representing the evil of man." Farrell smiled appreciatively. "Open it."

The book fell open to the first chapter of Luke's Acts of the Apostles. With unintended ceremony, Meade withdrew an envelope the color of freshly cut hay.

He ran his finger over the surface. He stared at the handwriting on the front—German, he guessed—and the signature at the bottom. He was impressed by its condition after all those years and struck by its unexpected weight, as if that alone gave substance to what was inside.

Then he turned the envelope over and gazed for a moment at the unblemished seal of General Erwin Rommel, his initials intertwined and flanked by a sickle and plow. *If the seal is broken*, he heard Gideon DeBruin say, *our contract is broken*. How many deaths? Meade thought. Eight alone in the last week, assuming Rita Hess had perished along with Jacob Bartleman in that plane. Six million a half century ago. Could anything revealed in this envelope restore six million lives, or eight, or even one? His own father's? Perhaps his own son's? Thinking about Sean now was like stepping into a void; the more he tried to avoid the thoughts, the wider the void became.

It had also occurred to Meade that his most potent weapon might well lie beyond the seal. That knowing the contents of the Sixth would be a source of considerable leverage—a thought that had often spurred him on over the last two days. Nonetheless, he passed Farrell the envelope, saying, "My German's not too good. Would you mind?"

"It says,

I, Field Marshal Erwin Rommel, son of Erwin Rommel of Heidenheim, swear under forfeit of my good name and that of my father that the information herein contained is factual and true and that I myself have borne witness to those facts or have verified those facts through sworn witnesses of character. I undertake this challenge for the health and well-being of my country and that of all nations. I ask forgiveness of those who will see my actions as traitorous, and grant my forgiveness in return.

400

She handed the envelope back and added, "The signature is his."

"Yes."

Then she said, "Greyling was right. It won't be easy getting it back in. The Brothers will think you have it—" She tipped her head toward the envelope, "whether they know for certain or not."

"Then they should know," Meade said. "Two days ago Cas Greyling told me that Paul Kilian was mounting a drive for the chairmanship of the Brothers' Executive Council."

Farrell was impressed. She said, "Kilian is the one council member we know for certain can't be affected by the contents of the Sixth. Not directly, anyway."

"Because of his age. Exactly. Which makes him the one council member who would actually profit from the exposure of the others. Unfortunately, contacting him privately won't be easy."

"But it will," Farrell replied. "He's on the museum's mailing list. And phone numbers are mandatory."

The shop was called the Purveyor. The sign in the window said, Open Until 10:00 P.M. Before stepping through the doorway, Meade peeked back over his shoulder. The men from the Renault were still close. The one in the glossy suit was crossing the street a half block away. His partner was a ghostly shadow in the Renault's front seat.

Inside, the shop accommodated merchandise the way Han Gelderblom's apartment accommodated wine bottles and newspapers. Office supplies were stacked on floor-to-ceiling metal shelves. Office furniture was arranged warehouse style beneath samples of track lighting. There was a section of used and out-of-print books.

In the stationery department, Farrell showed a bearded clerk the manila envelope in which the Missing Sixth was preserved. She requested a half-dozen exactly like it. The clerk, as it turned out, was embarrassed to explain just how infrequently the hemp envelope was requested. Yes, he could certainly provide her with something close—but, well, who knows how long they've been on the shelf? Farrell assured him that age was not a deterrent. They found a reasonable match for the deep ocher sealing wax on the envelope's flap, but reproducing Erwin Rommel's family crest, the intertwining initials flanked by a sickle and plow, was not to be. Farrell settled for a blank circular stamp and two letter stamps, an *E* and *R* in a Gothic typeface. Meade met her at the checkout counter with a packet of writing paper and a selection of four black ink pens.

At a pharmacy in the next block, they bought postage stamps and a butane lighter. For ten minutes they pored over the store's photocopy machine.

At a café overlooking the harbor, Meade chose a table on the patio. On the face of each of the half-dozen envelopes they had bought, Farrell used one of the four black pens to reproduce the preface Rommel had introduced his historical document with. Meade, in turn, filled the envelopes.

Then, across the flap of each he applied a generous dollop of the ocher sealing wax. This he pressed flat with the circular stamp. Within the circle, he inlaid and intertwined the *E* and *R* initials. A low flame, Farrell explained, would cause the wax to expand unnaturally and, in cooling, to simulate the cracks of aging; for this Meade used the butane lighter.

He then addressed one of the envelopes to the *Argus* in Cape Town, and a second to his rental house in Muizenburg. These he smothered in stamps and deposited in different mailboxes. They deposited one of the remaining four envelopes in the Hotel Herengracht's strongbox in Farrell's name. Their last stop, with the Renault still in pursuit, was at the United Air Freight night counter two blocks from the airport. Their two-day service to Cape

402

Town, for the envelope addressed to the museum in Stellenbosch, cost Meade twenty-eight guilders.

Finally, they left the rental car in an overnight parking lot and were walking down the airport concourse by 9:55 with the remaining three parcels in a leather briefcase tucked securely under Meade's arm. Their Pan American flight for Cape Town, with stops in Tripoli and Kinshasa, boarded before Meade could complete his call to the *Argus*. The two men in the Renault were replaced by a pipe-smoking man with no carry-on luggage and a hastily knotted tie.

39

"MY MOTHER TOLD ME a story two days before she died,"
Farrell said, as the airplane burst through the clouds over
the North Sea and the night lights of Amsterdam threw
out sparks of farewell. "She was sure I'd hear about it
someday, and I suppose she wanted me to be prepared.
But you know, Meade, I can still see the look on her face.
From the unloading of this . . . festering burden, and the
guilt she must have felt not letting it just die with her. It
was about my father . . ."

"About the war," Meade said.

"Yes. This was in 1944. It seems that a certain element of the German high command—even they must have
known the war was lost by then—planned to have Hitler
assassinated. It was meant to look like an accident. A plane
crash due to engine failure."

Meade's eyes widened. He picked up the story and
continued it for her: "During a practice run of his escape
route out of Germany. To South Africa by way of Algeria
and Italy."

Farrell was equally surprised. "You've heard this."

"Rommel had been charged by Hitler with securing
the route through Africa."

"Which he did. Everything from the refueling sites in Tangier and Lagos to the men pumping the gas. Everything. But since Rommel was also part of the assassination plan, he made certain the men watching over the last leg of the trip, through southern Africa where the accident was to occur, were men who had supposedly turned against the *Ossewabrandwag* and the Grey Shirts. Well, one of them evidently hadn't."

"The man who betrayed the plot."

"Yes. And to make things worse, later betrayed Rommel's part in the whole matter."

"Your father."

Farrell tipped her head. "A despicable rumor, my mother called it. But she didn't really believe that." Now Farrell hung her head in dismay. "And after all that, the war dragged on for another whole year. Senseless. Even my father must have seen that."

A stewardess rolled a refreshment cart down the aisle, and the tiny liquor bottles rattled in harmony with the wheels. Farrell watched and shivered. Every muscle in her body constricted.

Meade knew what she was going through; he took two pillows and a blanket from the overhead compartment, raised the armrest between their seats, and doused the reading lamps. He took her in his arms. He stroked her hair. And talked.

He told her about the wine country north of San Francisco and about his property along the coast there. He had bought the land eight years ago. Twelve acres. There was a narrow patch of white, sandy beach, protected by promontories of black rock. He told her about the house he had started building, more of a shell than a house, really, and on hold for the last four years. It was set in a small forest of birch and alders and redwoods. He had seen bear and deer and red fox.

He started to tell her that San Francisco was only an

hour and twenty minutes away when he realized she was asleep. This was good, because it gave him the courage to suggest out loud that perhaps she would consider spending some time there. Give them a chance to see what they were like together away from . . . away from all this.

By the time they reached Tripoli, two of the three envelopes had been removed from the leather briefcase in which Meade had been keeping them. One had been zipped into the lining of Farrell's raincoat. Another was concealed within the pages of Han Gelderblom's New Testament. The third remained in the briefcase, which remained on the seat between them.

There was an air of decay about the airport in Tripoli. The smell of damp wood, Meade thought.

Farrell befriended the two black kids in the sitting room of the ladies' lounge. The boy was huddled on a vinyl-covered couch awaiting the return of his sister. He very politely asked if Farrell would check on her while she was in *there*—just to make sure she hadn't flushed herself down. He had said all this with a near-empty box of candy on his lap and a caramel stuck to his teeth, and knew enough about bribery to hold out the box as incentive.

Farrell chose a peanut cluster. "What's your sister's name?" she asked.

"Thandi. Thandi Moshele. She's seven. Mine's Lucas. I'm thirteen. Dad calls me Luke."

"I have a cousin named Luke," Farrell said. "Where are you from?"

"Cape Town, in South Africa. In Mitchell's Plain. We're on our way home. Dad works on a freight ship in Cyprus. This is the first time we've seen him in two years, because we're just now old enough to fly on the plane alone. See, Mom can't leave home. She did something to make the police mad and now she can't teach anymore.

Not for three years." He said all this as if discussing a trip to the grocery store. Then he licked his fingers. "So she does laundry at home now. Banned, it's called."

"Yes, I know about that," Farrell said. "I'm sorry."

At that moment, the door to the bathroom swung open. A round-faced, pigtailed girl with a stuffed rabbit in her arms bounded out. She saw the woman talking to her brother and froze. A thumb popped into her mouth.

"That's her," Lucas said. He waved her over. Then he studied the last two pieces of candy and made his selection. In one long sentence he told his sister all about the woman and their conversation, and that everything was all right because she was a friend even if she was white.

Farrell held out her hand. "Hello. I'm Farrell. I didn't expect you to be so pretty. We're on the same plane for home."

The girl named Thandi gave her hand to Farrell, but so quickly that they hardly touched. Then she breathlessly snatched up the last piece of candy. Her brother watched, swallowed, and then, as if a lost train of thought had suddenly returned, shot Farrell a wide-eyed glance. "You said you know. Know about that. About Cape Town, did you mean? Or about being banned?"

In a low voice, Farrell said, "What I meant was that I know about making the police mad. I know because I've done something to make the police mad, too."

"Are you banned, too?" Thandi whispered. "Like Mommy? Can't you have friends over? Can't you go out when it's dark? I didn't know white folks could be banned—can they?"

"Sure they can, dummy," her brother answered; he was still staring at Farrell with wide eyes.

"But you're not, are you?" Thandi said.

"No, sweetheart, I'm not banned," Farrell answered. "I guess I could be. I think any of us could be. See, I have something the police want. Something they'd do almost anything to get their hands on, I'm afraid."

"What?" Thandi said. "What do you have?"

"Why are you going back, then?" her brother interrupted, in a voice melding insistence and disbelief. "Dad says he'll never go back. Not in a thousand years. And as soon as Mom's done with her time, he'll get her out, too. Why would you?"

"Because—" At that moment, Farrell's attention settled on the empty candy box. "Well, I think your mom would understand. Dad, too."

It took eight minutes to complete the call to the *Argus* in Cape Town; Meade counted them off on the electronic ticker tape that ran along the wall. His chest ached. He saw Lucas and Thandi Moshele emerge from the ladies' lounge. Two minutes later, Farrell appeared. She walked straight for the telephone booth and grabbed his hand. She pressed against him, whispering in his ear. A lover's greeting, Meade thought. Except her eyes and her words told a different story, one that caused him to look conspicuously away from the brother and sister he had observed moments before. Then a telephone three thousand miles away was ringing, and there was no time for debate.

It was after midnight in Cape Town. The switchboard operator at the *Argus* connected Meade with the pay phone in the cafeteria. It rang once. Mieta answered; she sounded as if she were in the next room.

"It's Michael. Have you heard anything?"

"They're alive," she answered. "And safe, we hope. Pure luck. We got a call from a man in the shipyards. He used Fazzie's press card because Sean didn't have a lick of ID on him. For a while we had them in a clinic in Nyanga, but the Boers are on the hunt. One of the doctors offered his house, so we had to chance the move. Sean's got four broken ribs, a punctured lung, and some internal

408

bleeding. Also a bullet hole in the leg. He's patched up like a mummy, but he'll make it."

After a moment, Meade began to breathe again. "Can he travel?"

There was a pronounced pause. "If he has to. Does he?"

"Mieta—"

"I love your son. Did you know that?"

"I asked him to leave once, Mieta. I won't again. Those are the kinds of choices he has to make himself. But I need to see him." There was a second pause, less formidable than the first. In a gentle voice, Meade asked, "And what about Fazzie?"

"Not good," she answered. "A goddamn gunshot wound in the chest. Another one in the shoulder. He's bled himself nearly white. One minute the doctor's tossing around the word *critical*, the next minute he's calling his condition 'guarded.'"

Meade tugged at the back of his hair. "I found it," he said at last.

"My God. You have it? Now? With you?"

"Yes."

"And you're coming back? Why? Are you mad? Fazzie knew you would. You are mad, and I'm just as mad for sticking my neck out."

Her sigh was so conclusively resigned that the only reply Meade could muster was "I know."

"So what can I do? Tell me quick, before I change my mind."

First Meade told her about the cardboard suitcase in the backseat of his Land Rover, and about the hidden key under the hood. Then he told her about Paul Kilian, and about Lucas and Thandi Moshele, the brother and sister Farrell had just befriended. And finally, about the rendezvous he hoped to have in a matter of hours at a certain Dutch Reformed church in downtown Cape Town.

For ten minutes they talked and debated and schemed.

Then Meade waited. Eventually, a second sigh filtered over the phone line; this one was the product of sheer fatalism. "All right," Mieta said. "I'll work on it."

"Thanks. Their names are Luke and Thandi. Look for a red candy box." Meade wondered if his own lack of confidence showed. He paused again, looking not for a reply, he realized, but for a reason to prolong the security of their conversation. In the end, however, in a voice thick with emotion, he said, "You tell Fazzie we made a deal, OK? Tell him he owes me dinner, and I won't have him copping out over something as halfhearted as a bullet in the chest."

He heard a short laugh and a voice as thick as his own. "You got it."

"OK." Meade leaned heavily against the side of the booth. "Love to the kid."

With the line to Cape Town still open, Meade gave the operator Paul Kilian's private number. The phone rang twice; the answering voice was sharp and alert.

"It's Meade, isn't it? I knew it. You're a smart man."

"A predictable one, anyway," Meade answered.

"You're in Tripoli by now."

"Yes."

"And you have the document in your possession?" Kilian didn't wait for an answer. "Yes, of course you do. You wouldn't have called otherwise," he said, and again didn't wait for a reply. "This number, it's very private. How did you come by it?"

"You're a patron of a certain Stellenbosch museum, are you not?"

"Farrell. Of course. A smart lady." Now Kilian paused, but only for a moment. "I need proof, you realize. That you have the document. An example of the contents would be sufficient."

"Rommel grants his forgiveness to those prodigal types

410

who might find his efforts traitorous. He also puts up the good name of his father as collateral. A little out-of-date, I thought, but oddly enough, you believe him right from the start."

"By contents I meant an example of the goods," Kilian said.

"Yes, I know what you meant. But that would require breaking the general's seal. Therefore, in gaining your trust I bring the document's authenticity into question. That seems to me the act of a desperate man."

"Hardly. There are a half-dozen court-worthy methods of proving the document's authenticity, with or without the seal. A seasoned reporter like you would know them all." Kilian paused. Then chuckled. "And I most certainly have never thought of you as a desperate man. What's more, it occurs to me you wouldn't have called unless you knew for certain that your son was out of danger."

Meade didn't respond, but his grip tightened on the receiver. As if Kilian sensed this, he said, "Yes, I know about Sean's stay on Robben Island. Don't be surprised. It was Gideon's secret for a time, but I don't like secrets much, unless they're my own. Let's not mince words, Meade. We both want something. You, on the one hand, want Gideon DeBruin. After all, he killed your father and kidnapped your son. Who could blame you? And you think I can help you get him. Which I can, of course. I, on the other hand, want the chairmanship of the Executive Council; surely you've heard that, somewhere along the line, no doubt from Cas Greyling."

Meade scanned the concourse. He spotted the kids near the loading gate. They were sitting on the floor. Lucas Moshele held a book on his lap with one hand and a baseball mitt on the other. His sister clutched the candy box and groomed the fur of her purple rabbit. Farrell was seated a few feet away, her eyes fast upon him.

Meade said, "Sir Greyling also mentioned the competition you face in your quest for the chairmanship. I can take care of the competition for you. I'm also in a position to provide you with the necessary ammunition to control any remaining opposition. Am I making sense?"

"Perfect sense. A straight trade. You get your shot at Gideon DeBruin; I get mine at the Missing Sixth."

"Exactly. Are we in agreement?"

"Oh yes, Mr. Meade, we are. Though I wonder just how far we can trust one another."

"I called and you were waiting. We need one another. Trust has nothing to do with it."

"A premise I approve of wholeheartedly. Very well." It took less than five minutes to cement the terms of their arrangement. Then Kilian said, "You realize, of course, that all this puts me at odds with the Council. That the Council will have its own plans for you when you return. Which means all of Security Branch and the army, too."

"The Council won't know about our arrangement until it's too late," Meade said.

"True." Kilian chuckled. "Now, about Gideon De-Bruin. Tell me where and when?"

"He is to be in the basement chapel of St. Stephen's Dutch Reformed Church at nine o'clock this morning," Meade answered. "He is to believe that I am still acting under the terms of our contract concerning my son. I will deliver the Missing Sixth to him personally. He is to look for a cardboard suitcase. Most importantly, he is to be alone."

"I'll see that he gets the message."

They didn't deplane in Kinshasa, in Zaire, but Meade saw the four newcomers board. Not together, but it didn't matter. Their identities were broadcast by the shapeless suits and colorless ties they wore. Meade looked for briefcases or carry-on luggage, but glancing from one to another found, instead, a rolled-up newspaper; a toothpick wedged into the side of a mouth chewing gum; sunglasses and a porkpie hat; and a raincoat tucked like a football under an arm.

The plane was over South Africa when two of the four cornered Meade near the rest rooms. The one with the raincoat positioned himself indiscreetly in the aisle. A piece of paper unfolded from the suit coat pocket of the one with the toothpick. Wiry and nervous, he displayed the paper along with a badge against his chest.

"Know what this is?" he said, smoothing the creases, chewing his gum.

Meade stared at the man's face. It was as smooth as a peach, featureless. A high forehead glistened. He reeked of cinnamon and lime. Halfway down the aisle, Farrell sat with a teacup in her hand and Han Gelderblom's New Testament on her lap. The man with the sunglasses and porkpie hat peeked over a seat back farther along.

"I don't," Meade answered finally. He focused on the face again. Concentrate. "What is it?"

"You haven't looked." A grin spread around the toothpick. He rocked from foot to foot. "He hasn't looked," he said to the one with the raincoat.

"He's shy. Can't you tell? He's the shy type. The women, bet they just mother the son of a bitch to death."

"Well, fine. Then we'll just have to mother the son of a bitch to death too, won't we?" He took the toothpick out of his mouth and jabbed at the paper. "This. It's an arrest order for your friend. Yes, indeed, *that* friend. The one and only Miss Farrell DeBruin. It appears some new evidence has come to light in that explosion several days ago. At the restaurant in Stellenbosch? The Broken Bridge? Know the one?"

"That's very amusing."

"No, no, no." The man had a childlike way of protesting. "You're supposed to say—are you ready for this?—

413

you're supposed to say, What kind of evidence? And then I'm supposed to say, I can't say."

Now Meade's eyes dropped to the man's chest. But not at the arrest order, at the badge. "Oh, please, please. Be my guest," he said, handing the wallet over. "You're familiar with the Security Branch of South Africa's police department. Sure you are."

Even as Meade returned the wallet and Security badge, a bead of moisture traveled down his spine. Now his gaze took him beyond Farrell and beyond the porkpie hat to the front of the plane, to the seats occupied by Lucas and Thandi Moshele. Meade saw a tiny hand dangling in the aisle. He saw a baseball mitt pop above the seat back. To involve them, Meade thought, had been sheer folly. Finally, he asked the question. "What kind of evidence?"

"I can't say." Delighted, the man orchestrated his next thought with a wagging forefinger. "I do happen to recall something about, let's see, about activities bent on the furthering of or calculating to further a state of terrorism. Yes, indeed. Furthering or calculating to further. That's it. Pretty close. Pretty darn close, don't you think?" he said to his partner.

"Your memory's a bloody national treasure, big fellow."

"Know anything about South African law?" The man thrust his jaw in Meade's direction. "I'll tell you a thing or two about South African law. Even if she isn't *charged*— and this is serious business, these charges—she'll spend six months in jail, no questions asked. And a woman like your Miss DeBruin, look at her—have you ever set foot in a South African jail?—she'll never survive it."

Now Meade scanned the arrest order. He saw the word *terrorism* and two references to *objects of communism*. Had the plane been over California or New York, he might have laughed. As things were, he hadn't the air in his lungs for it.

414

"Lies," he said.

"Of course they're lies." The man snatched the order back. "Hey. Truth isn't the point; it's where the lies lead. We're willing to deal. That's the whole idea, after all, isn't it? Isn't it? This very official assemblage of lies is our bargaining chip."

"I'm listening."

"You have the document."

"Yes."

"May I see it?"

"In the briefcase at my seat."

The man didn't budge; his tongue moved the toothpick from side to side; he blew a small bubble with his gum. "We're talking about the original, of course?"

Meade stared, at the badge first, then at the arrest order. Then he allowed his eyes to drift a moment, nervously; when he looked back, the man was grinning. Meade's voice exuded resignation. "In the Bible. The New Testament."

"That's better. Why don't you talk shop with my friend for a bit. I'll take a quick peek."

When the Bible was in the hands of his partner, the one with the raincoat took hold of Meade's elbow. "Paul Kilian sent me," he said, talking out of the side of his mouth. "My friend with the toothpick there thinks he's looking at the original envelope. Is he?"

"No."

"Fine. Then we can talk," he said. "Your arrangement with Mr. Kilian has been altered. Considerably. Are you listening?"

Meade didn't answer at once. A sudden emptiness laid siege to his stomach. Finally, he said. "Go ahead."

"Now, my toothpick-chewing friend, and everyone else on board, thinks this airplane is going to land at D. F. Malan International in about two hours. It won't."

"Which means?"

"Which means that problems will force an emergency landing some miles from Cape Town."

Meade turned, his face colored with disbelief. Still, it made no sense to protest, and he forced his attention back to the aisle. He said, "What kind of problems?"

"Suffice it to say that our pilot will have only one possible alternative for landing. That being the Kuils River farming district due east of the Cape Flats. Vineyards. Miles of them. A very nice cushion."

"Assuming he clears the mountains of the Papegaai-berge."

"If he doesn't, none of it makes any difference, anyway." The intonation of the man's voice suggested that the outcome was of no interest to him, one way or the other. "Let's hope our pilot is talented enough to overcome those problems. You have, very much by our design, been given seats next to the emergency exit. Assuming a plane of this size can manage the landing we have planned, you will be the first out of the plane. In exchange for the original envelope, our people will have a car waiting for you. The road will almost certainly be to the south. I suggest you make haste in that direction."

"This is your plan?" Incredulity wrapped itself around Meade's words.

The man shrugged. "If this plane lands at D. F. Malan International, there will be two hundred Security policemen converging on it before it has taxied a quarter of a mile. And they'll use those charges against Miss De-Bruin, and by then they'll have trumped up some against you, as well. And all your efforts will have been in vain. Take your choice."

"You're giving me a choice?"

The man chortled. "When my friend returns, he'll mention some scheme relating to the airport. Nod your head duly. Are we clear?"

"Crystal," Meade said, as the man with the toothpick returned. He carried Han Gelderblom's New Testament under his arm.

"You're not to be alarmed by the police at the airport," were his first words. . . .

Sunrise colored the southern hemisphere in brush strokes of pink and purple. Converging oceans bled indigo.

At some point directly above the city of Stellenbosch, seemingly within shouting distance of the mountains of the Papegaaiberge, two things happened. The first could easily have been mistaken for a minor encounter with turbulence. Meade felt the plane shake momentarily, dip, and then shudder. In truth, the plane had lost considerable power. Moments later, a minor explosion rendered one hundred nineteen passengers breathless with fright.

"It's happening," Meade said. He slid his hand under Farrell's. Their fingers intertwined.

"I know almost nothing about you," Farrell said. "I've never even met your son."

"I've thought about that. What you would say to each other. Especially since he says exactly what's on his mind, and so do you." Meade tried to smile. "I think you two would . . . would do well together."

"And we've never made love," she whispered.

"When we do—" He kissed her forehead and then her lips, gently at first, and then deeply, fiercely.

The plane shuddered, the fuselage groaning. They lost altitude with heart-stopping speed. Outside Meade's window were the snow-laden peaks of the Papegaaiberge. Moments later, clouds blinded them to everything but the sensation of free-falling.

The flight attendants scurried through the aisles exhorting passengers to fasten their seat belts. A copilot's voice came over the intercom. He was only slightly calmer than the attendants. "For reasons unknown to us, we have lost power in our number one and four engines. We are making preparations for an emergency landing. Please follow the instructions of your flight attendants. We have control of the plane, but are losing altitude quickly. Please don't panic. We are doing everything we can."

Meade glanced toward the front of the plane. The man with the chewing gum in his mouth was peering back. Beads of sweat were evident on his brow. He bit through his toothpick. A flight attendant grasped his shoulder and guided him back down into his seat.

A wave of actual turbulence grabbed hold of the plane, and it was as if they were being dragged down a flight of stairs. At last, they broke below the clouds. The astonishment of seeing open space before them gave the passengers momentary relief.

But the moment soon passed, and the flight attendants began shouting instructions of a more desperate nature. Crash position. Fire controls. Exit priorities. Moments later, the copilot was informing them that a certain amount of good fortune had come their way in the form of unpopulated vineyards below; from the plane they could see the vines moving in the wind like ocean swells.

Through the window Meade saw a farmhouse, very Dutch in design with whitewashed barn and stables. Roads the color of red clay ran in three directions. South to the highway—the road Meade had been instructed to look for. East, back toward the mountains. And north through the vineyards and eventually to the Kuils River. At a thousand feet the pilot released his fuel; it left a murky film on the plane's fuselage.

Even when the passengers were instructed to put their heads between their knees, Meade continued to gaze out the window. Two semitrailers moved in unison down the highway. A road grader hugged the shoulder. There were other cars, but three had pulled off to the side and stopped. A man stood with a foot on the bumper of one of these and watched their descent through binoculars.

The last thing Meade saw before huddling down next to Farrell was a pickup truck parked alongside the northbound road, perhaps a half mile from the house.

He wrapped his arm around Farrell's shoulders. She was shaking. "Don't let go," she said.

Over the intercom, the copilot counted down their rapid approach, his voice becoming increasingly strident. Then there was the sound of the undercarriage scraping over the vines, as grating as the screech of metal against metal. Screams echoed through the cabin. The plane groaned and shuddered violently. The left wing tore free, and the plane collapsed on its side. The acrid scent of smoke filled the air. People flooded the aisle.

Meade threw his full weight against the emergency exit, and the door gave way. A rubber slide automatically released from the undercarriage, flopped open, and expanded even as it curled forward to the ground. Meade grabbed the briefcase. He tumbled, more than slid, down the emergency ramp. Farrell followed. Vineyards consumed them.

In an effort to escape the line of vision of the four Security men still on the plane, they crawled under the wing and made for the nose.

Directly ahead lay the farmhouse.

Behind stretched a blackened swath of mangled grapevines. The plane smoked but miraculously didn't burn. Three or four field hands, bags over their shoulders, stood in awe of the spectacle. The pilot, Meade realized, had surely sent out distress signals to Stellenbosch and Cape Town, and fire and ambulance crews would be on their way by now.

Using the farmhouse as their compass, he and Farrell set out in search of the pickup truck he had spotted earlier on the northbound road. Footpaths cut diagonally through the fields, and crossing them was like moving through a jungle; in order to stay out of view of the three cars and the plane, they burrowed on all fours.

A hundred yards from the wreckage, they stopped. They could see heads and shoulders bobbing above the vines as the plane's passengers scattered in all directions. A helicopter arrived from the west. They heard a siren. Three women emerged from the farmhouse. A man on horseback darted from the stables and moved with amazing speed through the fields toward the wreckage. Farrell and Meade traveled back along his path to the northbound road.

The pickup truck was parked on the shoulder a quarter of a mile along. By a stroke of remarkable good fortune, the keys dangled from the ignition.

Meade started the engine. The gas tank was almost full. He drove three miles and then pulled over again. Farrell discovered a map in the glove compartment. She laid it across her lap.

"I know we're going back to the city," she said. "I'm just not sure why."

"There's a gas station outside the airport. We'll stop there first."

The map gave no indication what road they were on, but the M23 secondary road lay less than a mile to the north; it, in turn, led eventually to the Kuils River township and the confluence of highways that bled into the city.

"You're not going to explain, are you?" Farrell said, hardly a question in her voice.

"It'll explain itself," Meade replied.

The gas station was situated at the crossroads of the airport road and the N2 freeway. Meade parked the pickup out back. He left the engine running and climbed out.

Mieta had called the station attendant a "cousin." He was weather-beaten and severely erect. Meade asked him for the key to the men's rest room. He held out his hand and said, "Fifty rand, *baas*."

About eighteen dollars, Meade thought, pulling out a

420

wallet filled with shekels, guilders, and rands. It was a bargain at any price. He peeled off five ten-rand notes, and the attendant slapped the key into his palm. Meade went back outside and around to the back. An Out of Service sign had been taped to the bathroom door. Inside, the room smelled of disinfectant. The cardboard suitcase was stashed on the floor in the one and only stall, exactly as Mieta said it would be.

The newspapers would call it a miracle.

One hundred nineteen passengers escaped the wreckage of Flight 698 with only an assortment of cuts and bruises. Half would be treated for shock and later released. A man with a history of coronary problems suffered a minor heart attack; he was taken by ambulance to a clinic in Bellville.

The buses that shepherded the rest of the passengers and their luggage to the airport were gray and green army vehicles. The papers failed to mention that an unusual number of Security Branch policemen acted as escorts to the transfer.

The airport, a forty-minute drive from the crash site, was an ultramodern complex on the dwindling sands at the edge of the Cape Flats. The fog here was black from township coal smoke and diesel exhaust.

The buses congregated in front of an empty hangar normally used for storing surplus military cargo planes. Beyond the hangar doors, the transport police had gathered.

Immigration officials stood behind empty tables preparing to search all carry-on luggage. The parents and spouses, children, lovers, and friends who an hour ago had been awaiting the plane's arrival at its assigned gate had been ushered here in airport shuttles. Among them, had anyone taken special notice, was a *Cape Argus* photographer named Mieta Angeni, and with her, a fellow reporter from the Ghetto. They blended in perfectly; in the reporter's hands were a bunch of white roses and a camera case. Mieta held an oversize canvas bag and a red candy box.

Following the plane crash, the man with the toothpick had ignored his previous orders and opened the envelope from Han Gelderblom's New Testament; it was a good decision. By now, the Executive Council of the *Broederbond* had been informed that the document was a fake, and they were taking every precaution. Under the strict gaze of the transport police, the passengers were ushered one busload at a time across a fenced walk to the hangar. One by one they were searched, shown photographs of Farrell and Meade, and questioned.

For Farrell and Meade were now suspected terrorists, accused of planting a bomb that had caused a near-disastrous plane crash—and it was at them that the passengers directed their anger and fear. There was, however, no explanation for the thoroughness of the search now taking place. Garment bags and camera cases tumbled open on a makeshift examination table. Immigration officials went through duffels and diaper bags, briefcases and cosmetic kits. They hand-searched a baby stroller, rummaged through a golf bag, and emptied a backpack.

Lucas and Thandi Moshele emerged from the second bus in a group that included a tennis player, a priest, a mother and her daughter, and a quartet of Japanese businessmen. As they entered the hangar, Lucas held fast to the burlap bag containing their jackets, their coloring books, and his baseball mitt. In her arms, Thandi clutched her stuffed rabbit and the red candy box. Farrell had given them a description of the photographer. She was tall, almost a head taller than Farrell. Her hair was close-cropped, as short as Luke's, perhaps shorter. She would be carrying a red candy box just like theirs, only full.

The boy nudged his sister, using a thumb in her side

to draw attention to the slender, rangy woman working her way through the crowd. They saw her oversized canvas bag. The candy box was red, like theirs, but bigger.

"That must be her," Luke whispered. He tugged at his sister's arm. "She's taller than Dad, even. And look at her hair. It's shorter than mine, and I just had a haircut. Come on."

Thandi hesitated. She shuffled her feet, chewed on the well-gnarled ear of her rabbit, and felt the tears pooling in her eyes. She was still shaking from the ordeal of the crash. She wanted her mother.

The hand she felt on her shoulder was large and rough, like when her dad wrestled with them and forgot his own strength; there was no intention to hurt, but Thandi gave a sharp gasp, more from surprise than from pain. She looked up and saw not the man but the uniform. The silver badge, the black tie, the shoulder strap, the epaulets, the billed cap. He neither spoke nor looked at her—his eyes were on the rest of the crowd—but his firm grip propelled the kids back into line. Now the tears spilled over Thandi's cheeks. Sobs were muffled in the fur of her rabbit.

"Look," Lucas said. "She sees us."

Mieta was at the head of the crowd now; her companion with the camera case and roses stood close behind her. Thandi glanced up and their eyes met. Mieta's smile was as warm as a mother's lap, her nod confident and reassuring. She crouched down and pressed a finger to her lips. Then she tapped lightly at the candy box under her arm, nodding again.

The momentum of harried travelers and the persistence of the police carried Lucas and Thandi to the head of the line. Now Mieta turned a sterner gaze in the older brother's direction. Her desperation expressed itself in an equally desperate act of charades: she placed the bulky canvas bag on the floor between her legs, mimicked the bag opening, the candy box dropping inside, the bag closing again. Then she gave a nod that said they had to do it now because they were next in line, and in thirty seconds it would be too late. Luke whispered in his sister's ear. The photographer saw Thandi's little head bobbing in response, her pigtails bouncing in counterpoint. Please, God.

The mother and daughter ahead of them dumped the contents of a purse and backpack on the table before the customs officials. Now the policeman called out to them, and a fresh stream of tears flowed down Thandi's face.

Suddenly, she broke away from the line, calling out, "Mommy, Mommy, Mommy," and running with outstretched arms toward the photographer. Mieta dropped down on her knees and caught her in her arms. For the briefest moment, the crowd absorbed them. The red candy box disappeared inside the canvas bag, which passed quickly into the hands of Mieta's companion. Her own candy box tumbled intentionally to the floor. With the child in her arms, Mieta rose. She stepped over the barricade and started back toward the line.

She soothed, "I'm sorry, child. I'm not your mommy. I'll bet she'll be here soon, though."

"Hey, her candy." Mieta's companion had followed them over the barricade. He was rushing forward with Mieta's candy box. "The kid dropped her candy. You don't want to go home without this, do you?" he said, smiling up at Thandi.

Mieta took the candy and pressed it into Thandi's hands, winking. They were walking between two policemen now, and Mieta sensed the officers' relief. "These nice men won't hurt you, I promise," she said, glancing from one policeman to the next and settling her gaze on the stocky, black one.

"We wouldn't do that," he replied. "But I can ask you and your brother a question or two, can't I? Just for a minute?" He held up a black-and-white passport photo of Meade and a driver's license reprint of Farrell, both enlarged to the grainy state of Wanted posters. "These people were on the plane with you. Did they try to talk to you?"

The little girl buried her face against Mieta's chest and shook her head. She came away sucking her thumb and mumbled, "Can I go home now?"

"Sure, you can," Mieta answered, rocking her. She glanced with wide eyes at the officer. "Is it OK?"

Exasperated, the policeman looked from the candy box in Thandi's arms to the stuffed rabbit and back again. He made a quick inspection of Luke's burlap bag, checking the coloring books, the baseball mitt, the sleeves of their jackets. And then he waved them away.

Mieta watched him go. Then she whispered into Thandi Moshele's ear, "God bless you, child. You're very brave." She set the girl back down. A man was jogging through the hangar in their direction. "It's Uncle John," her brother cried, and they raced toward him.

Mieta's companion took her by the arm. He passed her the canvas bag and the flowers he was carrying. "You're beautiful, lady. A veritable Athena. Now let's get out of here."

Back in the truck, Meade laid the suitcase on the front seat between Farrell and himself. They pulled back onto the highway and headed south toward the city.

On the airplane the night before, fatigue had been Farrell's ally, her escape; now, it was her bane. She would sleep, if she could, and never wake up. Instead, she stared out the window. The sun was a crown of yellow fire anointing the horizon. The truck joined a growing line of buses and bicycles. Finally, Farrell mustered the nerve to face the suitcase. "You haven't told me about this, Meade. Why not?"

"It's a long-overdue gift," Meade replied.

Farrell filled her lungs. She arched her back and used her fingers like a comb, stretching blonde hair off her forehead. "You know what I need, Meade? I need a very long, very stiff drink. That's what. You've got a bloody wreck on your hands, mister, and she needs a drink."

"Forget the drink," he said. He turned now and peered at her profile. "Come home with me instead. To the States. To San Francisco."

For an instant Farrell neither spoke nor moved. Then she faced him, her hands dropping slowly from her head and folding across her chest. Her voice was hardly more than a whisper when she said, "Don't fool around."

"There's the place up north. The house. It needs work, but . . ." Meade reached across the suitcase and touched her arm. "You could paint. And I've always got my typewriter."

Farrell's hands formed a steeple touching her lips. She searched his face. Then she looked away, her eyes apparently finding some peace in the cracked vinyl of the dashboard before her. "What's in the suitcase, Meade?"

Meade had wanted to save her from this somehow, but only now did he realize what a foolish notion that was. In a business district along Jason Avenue, he pulled over to the curb. He left the engine running. Then he flipped the buckles and keyed the lock. He raised the lid. The bomb was held fast in the one corner by duct tape. The plastic stopwatch and the dry cell battery were lashed to the side wall at the base of either buckle. The wires were neatly coiled, awaiting a last connection to the battery terminal and the watch.

Meade wanted to say something about the primitive construction. About the timing device—how the simple maneuvering of the left buckle set the stopwatch in motion. Or about the triggering mechanism—how once the watch stopped, the contacting of the two metal tabs completed the circuit. But he didn't. Instead he opened the briefcase he had been carrying since Amsterdam, removed the manila envelope from inside, and carefully laid it at the bottom of the suitcase. Then he closed the case and rekeyed the lock. He set out once more.

Farrell stared at him. "This has to do with my father, doesn't it? A long-overdue gift. A fucking bomb?" Her voice rose in pitch. "Have you lost your mind?

"Meade, what are you planning?" she demanded, as they pulled up at the entrance to St. Stephen's Dutch Reformed Church. *"Tell* me."

"I'll go in alone," he said, hoisting the suitcase and climbing out. "I'll only be a minute."

"Only a minute. Is that all it takes?" Farrell followed him up the stairs. The doors were hand tooled and heavier than Meade remembered. "He'll assume the Missing Sixth is inside the case, of course. How is it triggered? By the lock? By raising the lid? Is it instantaneous, or is the victim rewarded with a few moments of good old-fashioned terror?"

Meade's footsteps slapped against the marble of the narthex. The nave rose to a great vaulted ceiling. The church smelled of freshly cut irises.

"My father didn't last long enough to have memories of the terror," he said deliberately. "His only piece of memorabilia was the brass buckle they dug out of his spine on the operating table."

"So it is the terror that interests you." Farrell grasped his arm with two hands. "No. No. You won't do it. I've said it before: I know almost nothing about you, Michael Meade, but I've been in your arms and I've looked into your eyes, and I know enough. For all the hate I've felt for my father and for all the hurt the son of a bitch may have caused you and a thousand others, his death is not the answer. Not to the Meade I know. Not to the man who half an hour ago offered me a second chance at life. It isn't the answer. Tell me it's true. Please. Tell me."

Meade paused. Her expression was tormented. Her eyes were like magnets. "It's true," he said, touching her cheek.

Meade set the suitcase in a pew halfway up to the altar. He motioned Farrell into the row ahead. Then he again maneuvered the buckles and lock and raised the lid. He stared down at the bomb, hesitating. Finally he turned his attention to the stopwatch. Thirty seconds, Fazzie had said. When the watch was set, Meade closed the lid. He felt liberated.

At the altar, a man dressed in a clergyman's robe genuflected, turned, and stepped past the altar rail. Hands clasped, face hidden by his hood, he proceeded down the aisle. As Meade watched his approach, the muscles in his arms and shoulders tightened. The robe billowed; now his stride was long and purposeful. But his step slowed as he drew even with the newcomers. Then he stopped. He was young and dark skinned. He made the sign of the cross and offered Farrell his blessing.

Then he bowed his head in Meade's direction and crossed himself again. "Mieta sent me," he said. "Mr. DeBruin is not alone. Be careful."

Meade also bowed. "Thank you, Reverend."

"I have a car parked at the east entrance to the rectory," he whispered. "Your son, Sean, is with me. There is also a plane waiting that will see you out of the country, if that's what you desire. But do not be long."

He bowed again, turned, and proceeded down the aisle to the narthex. Meade saw the church doors close behind him.

Then he picked up the suitcase. Farrell followed him through the nave to the altar. Meade made no attempt to stop her. A side door took them to the west sacristy.

The sacristy led to a narrow hall that led to the rectory; the same route Meade had followed just four days before. Here he stopped. He held Farrell back by the arm. "I have to do this alone," he said. "And you have to trust me. Please."

Meade didn't wait for a response. He silently bypassed the rectory entrance in favor of the steps at the rear. The staircase was lit by a single bulb.

It was steep and narrow, and Meade found himself treading lightly. The stairs ended at the solid wooden door of the basement chapel. A skeleton key dangled from the lock.

Meade glanced down the hall. There were two open doors, one leading to a well-stocked wine cellar, the other to the janitor's closet and the antiquated controls of the old gas chamber.

He turned the key, and the chapel door opened. Gideon DeBruin sat at the head of the table, his cane in hand. At his back, standing beneath the portrait of John Calvin, was Paul Kilian. The gun in his hand was a low-caliber revolver.

"You eluded my escorts," he said, "which doesn't surprise me. However, I'm glad you found the truck I had left for you instead. Either way, you had to come."

"A man of his word," Meade said. "I'm impressed."

"A man cannot always be a man of his word, Mr. Meade," Kilian replied. "It was necessary for me to alter our arrangements somewhat."

"I'm not particularly surprised." Meade viewed either man as he would an obstacle in the road; they had ceased to have the attributes of men.

"I had to consider the man I was dealing with," Kilian replied. "You would want Gideon here to see the actual document before he died. It occurred to me that only *that* would complete the circle. Only that would satisfy the depth of your need for revenge. Wasn't it Poe who said, 'Injury's revenge is only rightly served with a smile of satisfaction'?"

"It wasn't injury that concerned Poe as much as it was insult," Meade answered.

"Fools," DeBruin said. "Let us expose General Rommel's Missing Sixth and see whether we are dealing with insult or injury or pure nonsense."

"He's right, of course," Kilian said. "The table seems an appropriate place for the unveiling."

Meade stood the suitcase on the table and laid the ring of eight keys beside it. Then he retreated. "You'll understand if I've had enough of your Missing Sixth."

"If the document isn't in the case, Mr. Meade, you know, of course, that you won't get out of this church." Kilian delivered his warning even as DeBruin placed the suitcase on its side.

From the doorway, Meade saw DeBruin flip the right buckle, then the all-important left one. As he was pulling the massive door closed behind him, he heard the ominous ticking of the stopwatch.

The door closed, locking automatically. But when Meade reached for the skeleton key in the lock, it was gone. Who could have taken it? The question remained unanswered; from behind the door, Meade heard Gideon DeBruin scream his name. For after all those years of homemade explosives, DeBruin would know.

Beyond the door Meade could picture DeBruin tugging at the lid, tearing frantically at the handle, and struggling madly with the key ring. Eight keys, thirty seconds. He heard someone pulling at the door handle, then pounding at the door, and he knew that it was Kilian.

When the pounding stopped, Meade knew that the ticking had stopped.

Finally, he turned to go. Farrell was standing at the bottom of the stairs. "Michael?"

"It's over," he said to her. "There's nothing more. I didn't complete the circuit, Farrell. You were right. His death isn't the answer."

430

As they climbed the steep stairs back to the rectory, he felt the intertwining of her hand with his own. It felt different somehow, lighter.

Meade knew that when DeBruin did get the suitcase opened, he would see the bomb inside, recognize its construction, and know the damage it would surely have inflicted had the wires been properly connected to the battery terminals. Then he would see the envelope. With a last reserve of adrenalin, and with a last, dying spark of hope, the hope that Rommel never mentioned his name, he would open it. And seventeen blank pages would stare back at him.

What Meade didn't know was that, while Gideon DeBruin and Paul Kilian were struggling with the suitcase, other hands, less than thirty feet away, were busy manipulating the controls of another executioner's device. That moments later, the iron shutters on the gas vents in the chapel wall began to open. What Meade couldn't hear were the groans of those rusted gates after a half century of neglect. And what he couldn't see was the panic on DeBruin's and Kilian's faces when the stench of sulfuric acid and coal gas invaded the room seconds later.

Meade and Farrell were at the rectory door when they heard footfalls behind them. They turned. At the landing above the basement stairs they saw Sean. He was smiling. In his right hand he cradled a metal object which he now slipped into his pocket.

He started forward, but weak as he was, he stumbled and nearly fell. Pain distorted his face.

Meade met him halfway and took him in his arms. "I thought I'd lost you," he said.

Sean shook his head; color retreated from his cheeks even as they spoke. Meade supported him as they walked through the sacristy and onto the altar.

"How's Fazzie?" Meade asked.

"Better."

Meade felt Sean's weight against him. He said, "It's over now."

A wan smile returned to Sean's face. He nodded. "I know it is."

As his father led him across the altar toward the exit and the car waiting for them outside, Sean withdrew the metal object from his pocket again and carefully laid it on the communion rail. As they walked out the door, flames from a dozen eucharistic candles reflected upon it: the skeleton key to the chapel door.

Mieta's car was parked on the second level of an hourly parking garage. It was a twenty-minute walk from the hangar. When the doors of the car were locked around them, Mieta extracted from her bag the candy box she had exchanged with Thandi Moshele. She slipped off the lid, and the car filled with the aroma of chocolate. She removed a thin layer of bubble wrap. Beneath it, she discovered a manila envelope. She examined the prologue and signature of Reichmarshal Erwin Rommel. Then she turned it over. The flap was sealed by a dollop of ocher wax, with the intertwined initials, *E* and *R*, flanked on either side by a sickle and plow.

A separate note was addressed to Cam Fazzie.

Someone once said that a person could make the
Brotherhood look like Humpty-Dumpty with this.
That it could turn the Nats inside out. Well, it's all
yours, my friend. Use it well. However, there's still the
matter of the dinner you owe me. It so happens I know
a restaurant in San Francisco. It's called the Dry Dock.
I think you'd like it: You can sit down and eat at the
same time.

The note was signed "Yank."